THE SWORD

THE SWORD

by

Daniel Easterman

Magna Large Print Books
Long Preston, North Yorkshire,
BD23 4ND, England.

British Library Cataloguing in Publication Data.

Easterman, Daniel
    The sword.

    A catalogue record of this book is
    available from the British Library

    ISBN   978-0-7505-2827-6

First published in Great Britain in 2007 by Allison & Busby Limited

Copyright © 2007 by Daniel Easterman

Cover illustration © Brighton Studios.com

The moral right of the author has been asserted

Published in Large Print 2008 by arrangement with
Allison & Busby Limited

Magna Large Print is an imprint of Library Magna Books Ltd.

Printed and bound in Great Britain by
T.J. (International) Ltd., Cornwall, PL28 8RW

Dedication

To Beth. Who else? Who better?
To put it differently: Here's another one, Dido.

Quem for beijado por ti
Até se esquece de Deus

Natália dos Anjos

Acknowledgements

Many, many thanks to those who helped get this right, in particular, my dear wife Beth, for her shrewd comments on the text and for keeping everything running smoothly despite her own busy schedule, my agent Vanessa Holt, for her skilful management and advice, and my astute publisher Susie Dunlop. Thanks too to Sebastian Gutteridge, who carried out so well some calculations that seemed impossible to me.

Al-janna tahta zilal al-suyuf

'Paradise lies beneath the shadows of swords.'

*From the sayings of the Prophet
collected by al-Bukhari, vol. 4:73*

PART ONE

Chapter One

IN THE LIGHT GARDEN
OF THE ANGEL KING

The Gardez-Zarghun Shahr Road
10 miles south of Zareh Sharan
Eastern Afghanistan
Monday, 27th November

High up in the hills, where ospreys danced with amur falcons, and white-tailed eagles swooped on what little prey could be found in the arid landscape, a man with powerful binoculars was watching events unfold beneath him. The binoculars were fixed on a small tripod. They could magnify objects one hundred and fifty times. That was enough to let the unseen watcher in his eyrie keep track of everything that took place on the valley floor.

A long wooden stake, about six inches in diameter and just taller than a man, had been fixed in the dried riverbed the previous day. This morning a jeep had arrived with seven Taleban soldiers on board. They had offloaded a single man who was clearly their prisoner. He seemed to have been badly treated: what the watcher could see of his flesh was covered in cuts and bruises, and he walked painfully, like a man who has been whipped on the legs or bastinadoed.

15

They had fastened the prisoner to the stake, with his arms tied behind it. Even though it was clear that the prisoner could never work his way free, one of the Taleban was told to stay behind to act as an armed guard. The others drove off in the jeep, followed by a cloud of ochre dust until it was out of sight. When the roar of its badly tuned engine finally faded, an absolute silence descended on the valley.

The watcher adjusted a tiny receiver in his ear. It had a wireless connection to a state-of-the-art parabolic microphone that allowed him to hear a normal conversation at almost one thousand feet away. The parabolic dish was turned directly toward the stake below, near which the microphone had been placed during the night. All morning there'd been silence. Now there was music from the guard's radio.

Not very far away, the mountain peaks were white with snow. A bitter cold lay on everything. It was as though the air was ice.

Some yards set back from the road, the prisoner heard the same music. Somewhere behind him, a Dari song crackled on a small radio. It was an upbeat little number, a party song, *Az yad-e rokhat mastam...* 'I am drunk remembering your face'. He strained for the words, as though eager to snatch some meaning from these last minutes of his life. It was being broadcast by Radio Free Afghanistan. Local stations no longer dared play music, not even hit songs by pop idol Farhad Darya. More and more of the country was gradually falling back into the hands of the Taleban, and music was being banned again. Except for this one thing, the prisoner thought: he was in the hands of the Taleban, and his guard was tuning in to the latest hits.

He sighed, trying to size up the area to which he'd been brought. Juniper, tamarisk, and wild pistachio trees dotted the scrub-covered hillsides, but there was nothing down below but rocks. They'd brought him to this spot several hours ago, when the sun was starting to rise out of India and Pakistan, lifting itself over the Toba Kakar range, just in front of him. To the north, the Hindu Kush straddled the world, its white-topped peaks emblems of impossibility.

Just across the border, where the Toba Kakar mountains get into full swing, lay the vast tribal region of Waziristan, where Muslim missionaries preached to the pagan inhabitants. Up there in the mountains, Pakistan had been developing its nuclear weapons programme, and a little further east, had carried out its infamous test explosions. What was worse, Waziristan was now Taleban country again, with Islamic rule imposed across its towns and villages. Khost, not many miles from where he now stood, had been the original recruitment base for al-Qaeda, under the leadership of Ayman al-Zawahiri, Bin Laden's doctor and right-hand man.

Western analysts thought al-Qaeda and the Taleban had been defanged. The prisoner knew better. Militants were still crossing the border openly into Afghanistan. Some came in cars provided by Pakistan's intelligence service, others made their way more slowly and more securely on foot by night, using local woodsmen as guides.

His current mission concerned something else entirely, something he thought – with a gnawing in the pit of his stomach – could prove more dangerous than the other two put together.

His captors had taken him several yards off the narrow road – it was more a track than a road – to a flat spot in which a tall post had been planted. They had tied his hands behind the post and left him with a single guard, a powerfully built Durrani tribesman who wore a striped turban, both ends of which hung down tress-like past his shoulders.

The guard sat on a rock, catching what little heat he could from the sun, still far from its midday position. His foot tapped to the forbidden music.

The prisoner, a short-haired man in his late twenties called John Navai, looked round for the hundredth time. This was one of the most desolate places in the world, he thought, not a region where the cavalry would come sweeping down from the hills. He was not surprised that no one had come to rescue him, by road or by helicopter: from the beginning he'd known that he would go in alone and, if captured, die alone. His identity had to remain a dark secret, even if it cost him his life. John was an MI6 agent, and his mission to Afghanistan was, he had been told, of supreme importance to British national security.

They'd already interrogated him higher up in the hills, at a secret base accessible only by mule and nimble foot. It had been a place of steep precipices, of crumbling rock on twisting paths, of deep gullies, and the snow-tipped needles of unnumbered mountain peaks. A world familiar to him, yet at heart as alien as the empty craters of Mars, a secret, inviolable realm that no one entered or left without permission.

They'd kept him in a smoke-filled cave, among a stinking collection of sheep and goats, and shackled him to a ring set deep in the wall. The floor had been covered in bat droppings, and in the day, further down from where he'd been held, the ceiling was black with their velvet hanging bodies.

His cave, he began to realise, was part of a complex, linked by underground passages. It was perhaps fifty feet below the surface, and accessed by a steep sloping tunnel whose entrance was heavily concealed behind undergrowth. A ventilation shaft set in the ceiling was the only source of air from the outside.

Each day they'd fed him a breakfast of boiled curd and stale bread. As he ate, a turbaned cleric called Hajj Ahmad had preached to him gently in English, asking him to convert to Islam and thereby save himself pain and death. Each day he'd remained quiet, and the *akhund* had smiled in respect for his decision. He was a Christian, they said, so they would not put him to death for his refusal to convert. If they killed him, it would not be for spiritual obstinacy but for his other offences.

What these were was soon explained. Hajj Ahmad said that the prisoner was a British spy, that he worked for MI6, or that he was a UK military intelligence officer attached to the Allied Rapid Reaction Corps HQ in Kabul. The prisoner was dressed in a flat-topped Afghan hat, and wore a woollen cloak over his body; he could have passed for a native. He did not admit to speaking either Dari or Pashtu, but his interrogator had only to look at his face to see he might have Iranian parentage, even if he did speak English with a strong English accent. Hajj Ahmad had a PhD in engineering from Newcastle University, and he had a fine grasp of English dialects. His prisoner was middle class, from somewhere in the south of the country. A lot of Iranians had fled to places like Brighton after the revolution, and Hajj Ahmad was sure this man was the child of exiled parents. Guesswork, of course; but Hajj Ahmad was good at making guesses.

The torture started every day after the call to convert. It was carried out by a succession of Afghan fighters under the direction of their soft-spoken leader, Hajj Ahmad. The prisoner knew exactly who his captor was. Hajj Ahmad was an Egyptian Arab, like his close friend al-Zawahiri. Originally a member of Egypt's notorious Islamic Jihad, he'd been recruited in 1981 by a group set up by Bin Laden to fight the Russians in Afghan-istan.

He'd stayed on as a member of al-Qaeda, one of several hundred 'Afghan Arabs' who'd realised the impossibility of safely returning to their home countries, where warrants were out for their arrest. In 1998 he'd helped set up Bin Laden's umbrella organisation, the Islamic Front for the Fight against the Jews and Crusaders. A medieval name, perhaps, but the Jews were citizens of modern countries, and the Crusaders were Americans,

Europeans, Australians and anyone who supported them.

He had studied torture under the Russians; in exchange, he'd passed on raw intelligence, enough to convince them he was their man, when all along he was God's and no one else's. His given name was Ahmad and his next was Ibn Abdullah, the son of God's servant. In his heart, whatever his actions, he tried to serve his Creator.

They'd tortured their prisoner by every means available. They possessed almost no technology – no electric prods, no high-speed drills, no headphones through which to deliver high-pitched sound – but long centuries of warfare – and Hajj Ahmad's tutors – had taught them how to hurt a man.

They knew when to start and when to stop, when to cut and when to staunch, when to use harsh words and when a display of affection. They'd used flame – a little here, a little there – and near-suffocation, pressure from heavy rocks that nearly broke his spine and took whatever breath he had away, sharp knives that flayed him, and bandages and ointment to help him heal, ready for another session in three or four days' time. The hours passed slowly, as though their one and only purpose was to bring pain, and then intensify it.

None of what they did was sadistic. They wanted information from him, and he made a point of giving them none, not even his name. He could have stopped the pain at any moment, just by telling them what they wanted to know. But he

21

knew that, if he did that, they'd kill him anyway.

He'd spoken with them in English, since the slightest hint that he knew either Dari or Pashtu would have blown his cover. In an attempt to draw him out, Hajj Ahmad asked one of his fighters to recite Persian poems to him. In between torture sessions, the man would chant softly to himself, mystical verses by Rumi which he knew by heart, and his prisoner would listen and remember his father's voice reciting the same poetry. But he never gave himself away, not by so much as a flicker of an eyelid.

A damp chill would creep into the cave, where it was cold in all seasons. It hurt at times to remember the light. When the sun shone, Afghanistan was more beautiful than any place he'd known.

There had been a day when he'd visited the tomb of the emperor Babur in Kabul. Though badly damaged by the recent wars, it had retained its character, a low roof and pillars over a simple sarcophagus, swallowed by light and air. The inscription on the tomb said that Babur lived eternally in the light garden of the angel King, where he was both king and angel.

Sometimes, they would let him sit by the entrance, looking out on a night sky that blazed with millions of stars. They told him the stars were lamps held by the hands of angels in the first firmament. He did not believe them. They told him God was watching. And he still did not believe them.

Chapter Two

A JINNI OF THE JINN

His legs were starting to give way, and his back hurt as though a thousand demons of hell were attacking it. Slowly, he allowed himself to slide down the pillar, fearing all the time he might never get back up again. Perhaps they'd just shoot him in the back of the neck while he crouched there. He hoped he wouldn't piss himself when the time came. He hadn't emptied his bladder since just after waking, and his initial discomfort was rapidly turning to pain.

He looked up and down the road. There had been no traffic for hours now. His captors must have sealed off this stretch of track. He wondered if they'd leave him exposed to the elements once they'd finished with him.

He'd told Hajj Ahmad that he was a Christian, that his mother had brought him up in the Anglican Church, and that, as a Christian, he was entitled to the protection of Islam. Christians and Jews, he said, were guaranteed their safety, even if they did not convert.

'You are deluding yourself,' the mulla had replied. 'We are at war with the Christians and the Jews. The sheikhs have declared jihad, and they have made holy war a duty for all true believers. You are a spy in a time of war, and your

23

life is forfeit a thousand times over.'

He had told Hajj Ahmad that he had a wife and child at home, that his wife was innocent of any wrongdoing on his part, but that if they killed him, they would kill her as well, and ruin a little child's life. His wife was called June and his little girl was Mary. He told that to Hajj Ahmad, as though their names would make him soften.

'Do you want to make June a widow and Mary an orphan? She's five years old.'

'How many widows and orphans have the Americans and British made in Afghanistan?' Hajj Ahmad rebuked him. 'In Iraq? Innocent women, innocent children, who died because they were Muslims. My wife was Iraqi. She was in Baghdad when your war started, visiting her family. They all died in an American attack. You are nothing special. Your heart is nothing special. Your wife and child are nothing special. Your love for them and their love for you are nothing special. If you do not tell me what I want to know, then I will make this torture seem as nothing. If you think you have suffered before this, think again. I can inflict more pain than you can imagine. You will tell me what I want to know, and then I will reward you with a speedy death.'

The sound of a motor truck came from further up the valley. As it drew nearer, the guard switched off his little radio and concealed it in his turban. John watched him stand and come towards him.

'You can't squat down there! Hajj Ahmad is coming. You can't let him see you like this. He'll think you've been resting.'

They came back in a battered Ford pick-up

24

that showed traces of blue paint but was an overall rust colour, dented and holed, but very fast. It came down from the hills, trailing clouds of ochre-coloured dust, like a winged demon or a jinni of the jinn.

There were three men in all: two guards sporting old Russian AK47s and bandoliers stuffed full of magazines, both seated in the rear of the truck next to some large planks. At the wheel was Hajj Ahmad. They parked the truck about twenty yards behind the pole. Hearing the tailgate go down, John wanted to see what they were up to, but he'd barely managed to get himself back to a standing position when the cleric entered his field of vision.

'You have been very brave,' his tormentor said. 'But we are in the endgame now, and your courage will soon be tested beyond breaking point. You will break, I assure you of that. But the sooner you tell me what I want to know, the sooner I will give you a quick and painless death.'

Out of sight behind them, the mulla's companions, joined by the guard, had started to assemble something from their wood, hammering away with easy, sharp strokes that rang out among the steep hills like the notes of an imperfect bell.

He spoke to the mulla quickly.

'Don't you realise that anything I tell you in the heat of pain will be deliberately misleading? I'm not a spy. I've told you this a thousand times, and still you won't listen to me. I'm a journalist. I work for the *Guardian*. Have you heard of it?'

'I used to read it,' said Hajj Ahmad, smiling. 'A fine newspaper.'

'Then why won't you believe me? My papers are in my bag, but you refuse to treat them as genuine. All you have to do is make a telephone call to my editor, and he'll confirm my story.'

'I would like to do that. But if I made a phone call to London, don't you think I'd soon be tracked down? You must know that if you know nothing else. That's your job, isn't it? Tracking people down.'

'Then send a telegram, something.'

Hajj Ahmad smiled.

'I have done that. One of our people sent it from Kabul. A man calling himself Ronald Anderson answered. He confirmed that a journalist called Mike Smith is indeed on the staff of the *Guardian*. Unfortunately, that did not get you out of the woods. Someone called Clement, or perhaps a secretary acting on his behalf, made a bad mistake. They sent the return telegram from a post office situated inside MI6 Headquarters. Vauxhall Cross, if my memory serves me. No doubt you know the post office in question.

'Now, if you'll forgive me, I think my friends have made things ready. Let me unfasten the cord round your wrists.'

He felt himself freed, but was frozen to the spot, afraid to look round, for he knew that, when he did so, he'd see his fate and that the mulla and his guards would permit of no escape. The heart had gone out of him. How could his cover have been blown so stupidly?

'Mr Smith, or whatever your real name is, I have brought you here to be executed. I now intend to carry that out. Let me warn you, however, that you will not die quickly. The death I intend to inflict will be excessively painful, probably more painful than you can imagine. I will explain it all in a moment. Now, please turn round.'

Behind him stood a cross, seven feet or more high and five feet wide, a blasphemous intrusion on the Afghan countryside, a symbol of an alien religion and an alien deity.

John's first reaction was horror, not so much that they were planning to crucify him and to subject him to God knows what while they did so, as that the cross itself had no right to be in this place.

'This is blasphemy,' he said. 'The Koran clearly states that Jesus was never killed nor crucified.'

'But it goes on to say that someone else was substituted for him. There was a cross, the Koran has never denied it. But the Prophet Jesus never died on it. And you must know yourself that crucifixion was a common form of execution in the Roman empire.

'Let me explain to you what will happen. It's important you not be in the slightest doubt about what you will suffer as long as you are on the cross.

'You will be lifted onto the crossbar and your arms will be tied to it. Your ankles will be nailed to the outsides of the vertical column. When that is done, we will put long nails through your wrists, between these bones...' He pointed to his wrist, unsure of his terminology. John closed his eyes tightly, struggling to take it all in.

'The radius and the ulna,' he said, as though helping a student through a translation exercise.

'Thank you. Yes, the nails will go in between

your radius and your ulna. Not through the hand, as your Christian painters would show it. The bones of the hand are too weak, they would not hold your weight. Your ankles will be the same, between two bones.

'You will also find a small seat on the vertical strut. It is there to give some relief. It will keep you alive longer, it will prolong your agony. Death may come in hours, if you are lucky. But luck is never the issue among believers. It is God's will that counts. And today, God wills you to suffer.

'You will die from one or more causes. There will be the shock of being nailed: if you have a weak heart, that will kill you. You could become dehydrated, but we will take steps to prevent that. Over the hours, your chest muscles will grow weaker and weaker, until you suffocate.

'Once you have been suspended, the weight of your body will pull you down until your shoulders and elbows are dislocated. They will pop out of your joints, tearing ligaments in the process, making it much more difficult for you to raise your chest and breathe. Because your arms are stretched out, your chest cavity will be expanded, making it even harder to drag air in.

'But you will come to all that in time. Or you can be spared. Tell me who you came here to see, and what it was you brought for him. Or, if not a thing, information about a thing. Where it is, who has it, how it got there. Do you understand? Did you bring a sword, or news of a sword? You know what sword I mean, don't you? Did you see a document, a letter? An Arabic letter? A very ancient letter. Do you know where the sword is?

Has it left Cairo? Have your people taken it, or is it still with Goodrich?'

John did know what the mulla meant: he knew nothing about a document, but he had heard about a sword, and someone had told him about Goodrich. Goodrich didn't have the sword, they were pretty sure of that. His people were sure al-Masri had stolen it, and they were almost as sure it had been sent to Afghanistan, to Bin Laden. That was why he had been sent to Afghanistan, to find out. But if only he could hold out long enough, he swore he would pass nothing on to Hajj Ahmad. Everything depended on the sword, on whether it was genuine or not, on whether they could stop it falling into the wrong hands. Beside it, his life was of no greater importance than the life of the yellow snail crawling at his feet.

He said nothing, so they stripped him and nailed him, first his right foot, then his left, and the pain was more terrible than anything he'd ever known before. And when they pinned him to the crossbar by nails through his wrists, he screamed for mercy and wet himself, and prayed for a quick death.

He hung like that for hours, and every moment it felt as though his entire body was about to fall apart. There was no part of him that did not ache ten thousand times, no inch of his flesh that did not burn, no scrap of muscle that was not torn or in the process of tearing. The effort of lifting himself up onto the little seat brought a few moments' relief to his overstrained chest and lungs, at the price of pain beyond all measure in his ankles and feet. But the second he took the weight off his ankles, he would slump and suffer the double agony of pain in his ankles and a sensation in his chest as though he was drowning in lard.

He tried to think of anything that might distract from the mounting agony – his home in Cambridge, his parents, who had fled from men like Mulla Ahmad all those years ago and made a new life for themselves in England, June, Mary, old friends, colleagues; but none of these thoughts lasted more than a second or two. He tried to remember pieces of music, songs that had moved him, singing 'Jerusalem' at morning assembly in the Leys School, poetry that had lifted his spirits, his father's voice rising and falling as he chanted odes by Hafiz in the early morning, June's face that had bewitched him all those years ago; but the memories merely flickered like meteorites passing through a dark sky, and vanished.

Moments passed, hours passed, for all he knew days went by, and still he hung, thinking that every moment he would die. From time to time he managed to open his eyes, and on every occasion he would catch momentary sight of Hajj Ahmad, standing still and silent, watching him. There was blood in his eyes, mixed with tears, and blood ran in streams from his nose and ears.

He thought he would have screamed out loud from the pain, but he did not. His lungs could scarcely draw air into his chest, much less provide the strength to shout or scream. At most he moaned, and did so until his moans were the only sound in the universe, and his body became the universe, and the universe was in freefall, spinning out of control.

'Just speak to me, Mike. Just a word. A name. A hint. Tell me where the sword is kept, tell me who has it, and I will end this for you in an instant.'

He struggled to open his eyes, and through a blood-red haze saw his persecutor facing him, lifted up to his level by some sort of stepladder or other elevation.

'How ... long have ... I been ... up here?' he asked, his voice rasping, dry as sandpaper, each word choking him.

'Half an hour,' the mulla said. 'I'll come back.'

Half an hour? It had seemed like half an eternity. What would an hour be like? How could he get through a day? How could he face a long night when bitter cold would replace the sunshine?

All semblance of thought vanished. He was just a machine struggling for a moment's comfort or an end. Like an automaton, he would push up and fall back down, tearing fragments of muscle, ripping ligaments, severing nerves, shredding tissue.

Several times he collapsed into unconsciousness, only to be brought round by a rapidly acting drug Hajj Ahmad injected into his thigh. The stimulant kept him awake for long, unendurable minutes, until it wore off and he sank back into a deep well of darkness again. He lost all track of time. His seconds and minutes were measured now in pain.

'How long?' he asked, his voice croaking with thirst. It was as if his throat had been filled with hot sand.

'Ten minutes,' came the sheikh's placid voice.

'Tha ... that's ... impossible.'

31

'Just one word. Just one name.'

He tried to shake his head, but it would not move. His heart was beating faster and faster, as though about to burst. Hajj Ahmad's drug was racing about his system; he could feel it weakening his heart.

More blissful blackness, more agony pulling out of it. His buttocks were raw from the slipping and sliding of the rough wooden seat beneath them. He could feel his ankle- and wrist-bones grating against the thick nails that held him in place, and the pain in those places was transmitted across his body into all his joints. His mouth and nose were full of blood and mucus. Fear cut through him like a rusty sword.

Up in the hills, a lammergeier circled on long wings, drawn to the spot by the smell of blood and the sight of naked flesh. The watcher put down his binoculars, balancing them so that the lenses would not catch the slanting sun. From a pocket he took out a mobile and dialled a number half-way across the world. The call was transmitted to England by one of several US telecommunications satellites constantly orbiting the earth.

'Malcolm? Listen, I think he's about to break. They're going to kill him anyway. If he talks, they'll know we can't find the bloody sword. In the next few minutes. Do I have your permission to go ahead? Yes? I'll do it now. Give my love to Christina. Ciao.'

Shutting off the phone, he reached behind him for a rifle that was already attached to a short tripod, and made it fast in front of him. It was a Barrett.50, the best sniper's rifle in existence. With its long barrel, it could deliver almost 13,000 foot/pounds of energy, enough to kill a man half a mile and more away. It had already been zeroed earlier that morning, and all he needed to do was aim and fire. To be sure of the wind and how it might affect his shot, he used a whizz wheel, calculating the correct angle for the shot.

Down on the valley floor, Hajj Ahmad watched his victim writhe, and knew he had to make up his mind quickly. If he left his prisoner much longer, the man's heart would give out or he would suffocate without giving the information the sheikh wanted. Or he might go on for several more hours. Despite what Hajj Ahmad had said, Smith had not been on the cross for minutes, but for over three hours now. He had held out well, but now it was time to bring things to an end.

He went up the stepladder again and spoke loudly to his victim, promising him rest at last.

At that same moment, from out of the clear sky, from the habitation of eagles and hawks, from the distant hills, came a sharp report. The bullet took the dying man in the chin, passing through his lower skull and destroying his cerebellum, killing him instantly. He did not choke or cry out, but simply slumped, blood pouring from the wound in his head.

Hajj Ahmad leapt from the ladder and threw himself flat on the ground. His colleagues followed suit. But there were no more shots. With eyes accustomed to the harsh terrain, they scoured the hills ahead of them, but they saw and

33

heard no one.

Hajj Ahmad swore beneath his breath, then got to his feet, dusting himself down. The marksmanship, he thought, had been worthy of an Afghan, but no Afghan possessed the sort of rifle that could cover such a distance with such accuracy. He didn't even think it worth sending men out to hunt down the gunman: whoever had carried this out would have backup built in all the way to London.

Chapter Three

IN THE CITY VICTORIOUS

**Two months earlier
Cairo, Egypt
Monday, 18th September
2.05 p.m.**

Cairo was hot and stuffy, the air thick with sand from the desert, the Nile swollen and turgid, its water ochre-coloured. From north to south, from east to west, the great city was stuffed with people, clogged with cars, raucous with donkeys, motorbikes, and the crackling loudspeakers of fifteen thousand mosques. This was the largest city in the whole of Africa, the thirteenth most populous in the world. Fifteen million people scrabbled for space along the narrow margins on either side of the Nile.

Jack Goodrich was English, nominally C of E, and a member of King's College, Cambridge, where he'd been an undergraduate and post-graduate; but for several years now, he'd counted himself one of the fifteen million, a citizen of this great metropolis. Cairo was raucous, dirty, smelly, hot, dusty, and unkempt, but he loved the place with almost religious devotion.

He had barely sat down in the battered leather barber's chair when the first bomb went off. The barber, an astute man of middle years called Ali Hamid, swore softly in Irish, *pog ma hon*. It was an old swearword, taught him years before by an Irish professor, with the assurance that it would be meaningless to ninety-nine point nine per cent of the human race.

Jack, being English and famously impertur-bable, ignored the imprecation. He knew what it meant, of course, everybody at the university did, but he'd never let on to Ali.

'Where the fuck was that?' he exclaimed.

Ali, who owned the little barber's shop near the American University, preferred not to think of the bombings that had been terrorising the city in recent months. They were bad for business.

'Nowhere near here,' he reassured his client. But they both knew that the bomb might have been anywhere: a small bomb close at hand, a large one far away, and any number of combinations in between. It might have been a suicide bomber at work, or a car bomb detonated by a timer.

Imperturbable or not, Goodrich was anxious. His greatest worry was that the explosion had been at either the American or the British em-

35

bassy, which were both fairly near at hand, just a step across the river. His wife worked at the British embassy as a secretary. Ever since they'd been in Cairo the Goodriches had shared a single ongoing fear – that one or the other might be caught up in a terrorist attack, either at the embassy or the university.

'Stay for now, Professor,' Ali said. 'The bomb could have been anywhere. It's too early for news, but I'll leave the radio on for the first bulletin.'

He spoke in Arabic, in the dialect form peculiar to Egypt, in which Goodrich was as fluent as any foreigner had a right to be. Over the years, the professor had learnt more Cairene Arabic from his shaving and hair-cutting sessions with Au than from the formal classes he'd once paid for in the department.

Ali stood poised, shaving brush in hand. He was a prima donna among barbers, if such a thing exists. If he'd been on a stage, he would have strutted. The lather glistened on the bristles, rich as cream. Goodrich shook his head, telling him to wait.

'I'll try ringing. If she answers, there'll be no need to worry.'

There had been several terrorist attacks in the past week, most of them on foreign targets.

He took out his mobile and dialled. Nothing. He looked at the signal bars.

'Ali, what's wrong with this place? I can get a signal across the road anywhere in the university. I can get one next door, in the Café Faruq...'

Ali shrugged.

'We've been through this before,' he said. 'You

have to be patient.'

He bent forward and switched off the radio.

'Try now,' he said.

This time it rang, and Emilia answered.

'Go away, Jack. We're perfectly all right. The bomb was right on the other side of the river, at the Anglo-American Hospital. We're still waiting for a report on the casualties.'

'Doesn't Dr Fathi work there?'

'Yes, and his wife is a nurse there too. Jack, you've got to stop calling me like this. Every time a bomb goes off somewhere in Cairo, the phones in here all start ringing like mad. You should know by now that this is one of the safest places in the Middle East. We learnt our lessons from the Yanks in Mogadishu and Lebanon and Baghdad.'

'I get worried, that's all. And I don't buy your story about how safe the embassy is, or how much the Americans learnt in Beirut. There's nowhere a suicide bomber can't get to if he really tries.'

'Someday you should try getting past security here. You'll see. Now, shouldn't you be working?'

'I'm in Ali's. Having a shave.'

Emilia had never met Ali. The little barber's shop was strictly male territory.

'Tell him to go easy on the aftershave, please.'

'Why?'

'If you're lucky you'll find out tonight. Now, my boss wants me to take some dictation.'

The connection went dead. Jack put the phone back in his pocket.

Ali straightened the striped sheet over Jack and freshened the shaving cream in his old, cracked mug. No one lathered like Ali. Goodrich had

37

once suggested he get a badger-hair brush, but the barber had gently explained that badgers were religiously unclean, which meant they could neither be eaten nor touched.

In his way, Ali was devout. He prayed five times a day, fasted every Ramadan, attended his local mosque at noon on Fridays and dozed through the sermon. Best of all, he went on a pilgrimage every three or four years – not to Mecca (which he was saving for his retirement), but to the annual *moulid* celebrations at the tomb of the great Egyptian saint, Sidi Ahmad al-Badawi.

He started to strop his straight razor lazily against the leather strap reserved for his own use. He never shaved until the edge was perfect. This was what he liked best about his job: the fact that his regular customers trusted him. Bearing in mind that most of them were teachers from the AU, Americans and British for the most part, their trust said a great deal. In Algeria, the hardline religious had made throat cutting their trademark. The trust went both ways: in Baghdad, extremists had cut the throats of barbers who shaved the cheeks of non-believers.

As Ali began to scrape the bristles from Goodrich's cheeks, radio news stated that there had been a second explosion at the Carrefour supermarket in the Maadi Mall to the south. No more information was available. In the stillness that followed, they could hear sirens drift through the city streets. This was the largest city in Africa, but every time the sirens sang, it seemed to shrink to a handful of streets and alleyways.

Chapter Four

BROKEN ENGLISH

Cairo
2.30 p.m.

Back on the street, he experienced that momentary panic all outsiders feel in Cairo: too much
traffic, too many people, too much noise and
dust, too many smells. He was standing on a
pavement in Tahrir Square, the city's largest public space. Big Mercedes saloons ('chicken's arses'
in local slang) snarled at buses, the buses roared
at anything that threatened to get in their way,
mopeds charged bravely (and often fatally)
between everything else, and everywhere Goodrich looked he saw young men in jeans and
children in baggy sweaters, old women in shabby
galabiyyas, young women in headscarves all
risking their necks just to cross the road.

He looked at his surroundings: traffic signs that
had gathered dirt and rust long ago, posters for
the latest products of the Egyptian film studios,
shop signs in Arabic and broken English, the
catch of light on dirty window-panes, motes of
dust continually descending in shafts of sunshine.
On one corner, the face of the Sphinx stared into
nothingness. Opposite, a young movie star called
Basma turned her large eyes and seductive smile

on passers-by. Everywhere, the intricate turns and twists of Arabic letters graced the square. Past and present joined forces at every juncture. Time was nothing here.

He passed shop doorways throbbing with the latest Egyptian pop tunes, walked past a beggar with his hand outstretched, and gave him money, one Egyptian pound. Not a lot of money, he thought, only a few pennies in English terms. But a little went a long way here.

He looked at his watch. Half past two. It should start to cool down in a little while, but for the present it was hot, dusty and noisy, and there was no getting away from it. Most Cairenes lived their lives in single rooms, whole families were crammed into ridiculously tiny spaces where babies cried, old men and women clung to lives of misery, and young men and women coupled in the shadows silently, without joy. In the Islamic City of the Dead, on the edge of the living city, the poorest lived in the tombs, sharing their meagre existence with the long deceased.

He took out his mobile and tried Emilia's number. No reply. He rang the main switchboard.

'I'm afraid she's in a meeting, sir.'

'That's all right. I'll ring later.'

He put the mobile back in his pocket. It was all right: the embassy was still standing.

Back at the university, a stack of post was waiting for him from the morning. Miss Mansy popped her head round the door of his office to say his four o'clock class on seventh-century South Arabic verb forms had been cancelled.

He stepped into the corridor just to watch the secretary's rear end move back down the corridor. It was generally reckoned she had the best backside in Cairo, and in a city where most of the women still covered themselves from head to foot, that was something to be treated very seriously. Some of the Egyptian students got themselves into enormous entanglements and suffered unending pangs of love for Miss Mansy. She, however, had long since made up her mind to entangle an American professor or a rich man who would take her away from life as a secretary in a university department.

Goodrich closed his door and went reluctantly to his desk. He didn't know what he'd do if Miss Mansy left or was snatched by Sociology or English. They all wanted her because, sex kitten or not, she was the best secretary in the university. She had a degree in Arabic, which she could speak fluently in five dialects and in the modern literary form, and she'd gone out with single male members of staff from several departments. A treasure. Irreplaceable. And sexier than a tribe of monkeys.

Goodrich sighed and sat down in front of his post. It had been accumulating for several days now, and he hardly knew where to start. He fished in his desk drawer for his letter opener. As usual, the mail was stunningly dull. Anything of interest nowadays came via email. There were several book catalogues, including one of antiquarian books neither he nor the university could afford.

Jack had been the AU's professor of medieval Arabic for five years now. The job had come out of nowhere following Emilia's posting to the embassy. Before that he'd been happy in London, where she'd worked at the Foreign Office. The job in Cairo had been a promotion for her, and going with her had been perfect for him. His lectureship at the School of Oriental and African Studies had been headed nowhere. Money was short, as it was throughout the university sector, departments elsewhere had been cut, and at forty he had little hope of a senior lectureship, much less a professorship.

He'd come into academia late in life. His first love had been the army, which he'd joined at seventeen, moving three years later from his local regiment, the Royal Anglians, to the SAS. Before being sent to Iraq during the first Gulf War, he'd studied Arabic for several months at the Defence School of Languages in Buckinghamshire, and he'd come top of his class. His teacher thought he had an aptitude for it. By the time the war ended, he'd seen enough brutality to last a lifetime. His youthful enthusiasm for matters military had given way to something softer, a love of learning, and, in particular, Arabic culture.

He'd met Emilia during a launch party for an exhibition of Koran manuscripts he'd helped organise at SOAS. He'd been nursing a vodka in a remote corner of the room when she'd come up to him and started a conversation that fifteen years later showed no signs of ending. They'd slept together for the first time that same night, and that also showed no signs of fading out.

He moved on to the next layer of mail. He scrunched up a heap of advertising circulars and tossed them unread into his wastebasket.

Almost at the bottom was a letter from his friend, the scholar and bookseller, Mehdi Moussa. Like all of Mehdi's letters, it was written in the most exquisite Arabic penmanship, in the *ruq'a* script. The language was flowery, based on all the best classical models. After several lines using the most convoluted of phrases taken from al-Hariri and anyone else with a good prose style, Mehdi got to the point.

Dearest Professor, the letter read, *I regret to make such demands on your time. However, if it is at all possible, I would be very happy for you to come to my shop, if possible on Monday afternoon about five. I have something to show you. For the moment, I am not showing it to anyone else, partly from friendship, partly to protect myself. I know I can trust you, hence this invitation and this special opportunity for you to examine what I will show you. I assure you it will be no waste of your time. As the proverb says: 'Believe what you see, and set aside what you have learnt'.*

If you cannot do this, I shall have to go quickly to someone else. But I would much prefer it if you were the first to see and the first to comment. I will wait until six o'clock, and if you do not come by then, my course is set.

Jack laid the paper on his desk with a sigh. No doubt the old boy had found him another manuscript of the *Kitab al-Bukhala,* a ninth-century text the bookseller greatly favoured. But even if it was something worthwhile, he didn't think there was much he could do about it: the departmental budget was thinner than usual, and he was sure the ever-present need for basic equipment would outweigh another manuscript or lithograph. On the other hand, Moussa was a shrewd operator. He knew his clients' budgets down to the last piastre. He wouldn't be offering to show something he didn't think he had a chance of selling, and he had identified Goodrich as his first choice for customer. Jack cancelled a class for that afternoon, and looked forward to his meeting with the bookseller. Not even in his most mangled dreams could he have guessed what would come from it.

Chapter Five

THE EGYPTIAN

The al-Manar Prayer House
Ishaq Alley
Imbaba, Cairo
Monday, 18th September
3.00 p.m.

In the streets outside, children played on rubbish heaps, families were crowded thirty to a room in makeshift apartment blocks built from mud and brick, and on the narrow, festering alleyways, the ground moved like quicksand, shimmering with the bodies of ten million flies. In silence, their wings made a song, a serenade to squalor and neglect. Thick black smoke from local factories filled the torrid air. Imbaba bred disease. Disease and religion.

Back in the nineties, Imbaba had been a virtual state within a state. Wits had called it the Islamic Republic of Imbaba, and that had been near enough the truth. In its complicated web of narrow alleyways, walled-off cul-de-sacs and tall apartment blocks groups of radical Islamists had held sway, imposing the strict laws of the Koran, taxing Christians, punishing criminals and feeding the poor. They had seemed untouchable. Then, in a rapid series of raids, the security services had come in and flushed them out, arresting every man with a long beard and shaven head, any woman in a heavy veil, and flinging them into jail to rot or be tortured.

Now, well over a decade later, they were back, but not as before. These new militants were clever. They used mobile phones and laptops, they had spies everywhere, and they acted behind the scenes. They weren't interested in running Imbaba: they planned to rule the world. Their work was done quietly in cells, they recruited only the most dedicated, they punished disobedience and treachery by instant death. Every Friday, they would meet for prayers in little rooms away from prying eyes. When they met for other purposes, they did so in secret, in hidden places that could only be reached through a maze of stinking alleys, or tunnels dug deep beneath the ground.

Places like this prayer room, tucked away at the back of a cul-de-sac in a cluster of apartment blocks called Hayy Fatima. The room was on the ground floor, in an apartment that acted as the HQ of a cell belonging to a small but dangerous organisation named simply al-jaysh: The Army. The walls were thin, and sounds came from the apartments upstairs – a baby crying, a couple arguing, a teenager's radio. From outside came the roar of a moped, then the shouts of boys running home from their lessons at the local Koran school. Some had already found a rag ball and started playing football.

Nine men squatted in a rough circle on a floor covered in cheap carpeting. They were visibly poor, but unlike so many on the streets outside, their clothes were spotlessly clean, their beards were neatly trimmed, and their heads freshly shaved. Men like these lived simply, emulating the humble lifestyle of the Prophet, who slept on a straw mat and ate a handful of dates each day, washed down with water. They wanted to be like him. He was their model in everything. Their love for him knew no bounds. They had sworn solemn oaths to defend his honour with their lives. One man stood out from the others. He dressed the same way they did, he wore his hair and beard like theirs, and held a plastic rosary in his right hand just as they did. But nothing about him was the same. No one would have questioned for a moment that he was their leader. It was in his eyes, in the set of his mouth, in the way he sat up straighter than the rest, in the calm he radiated. His fingers did not fiddle with the beads as some of theirs did. He did not fidget. His stillness was the stillness of a marble statue. Only his eyes moved, and they moved slowly, taking in each man in turn, as though he was one of the twin angels sent to question them in the grave. He was forty years old, and his face bore the traces of a life spent fighting with al-Qaeda in Afghanistan and Iraq. His name was Muhammad, like the Prophet, and his family name was al-Masri: The Egyptian. Muhammad the Egyptian. Everyman. A simple enough name. But not a simple man.

Despite his name, Muhammad al-Masri was not just anyone. Papers long in the possession of his family made that clear. He was a living descendant of the last of the great Abbasid Caliphs, the rulers of the Thousand and One Nights, whose palace in Baghdad had once been the wonder of the world. Muhammad's ancestor had been killed by the Mongols when they sacked Baghdad in 1258. He had been trampled by horses while rolled inside a carpet, so the superstitious conquerors did not shed a ruler's blood.

Alone of the Caliph's family, one boy, Ahmad, had escaped the pillage and destruction. Ahmad had fled the burning City of Peace and headed for Cairo, bearing with him documents that proved his lineage. Those were the papers that had been handed down to Muhammad al-Masri, given to him by his father before he died several years earlier. Among them was a will and testament in Ahmad's hand, appointing his son the next Caliph, and his sons in direct line after him until God took the earth back to Himself.

Muhammad considered himself and was believed by his followers to be the true leader of Islam, the man who would restore the Caliphate and launch the last jihad against the infidel West. He would finish the task started by the Prophet back in the seventh century, to bring all nations

47

under the rule of the one God.

He lacked just one thing, one thing that would permit him to make a public proclamation of his true identity and call for Muslims from round the world to join him in his sacred mission. He had known of it for years, and now he thought he knew where he could find it. He closed his eyes, muttered a short prayer, then opened them again. 'God be praised,' he said. 'Sixty-one died in the explosions today. Each of our martyrs took unbelievers with them. The unbelievers are in Jahannam, the deepest pit of hell. The martyrs are in paradise, drinking wine that does not intoxicate, among virgins with skin the colour of honey.'

One after the other, the assembly cried out *Allahu akbar.* 'God is Greater'. One of the martyrs, a boy of sixteen, Hamid, had been recruited by their cell, the core cell of the movement. His family would be well looked after. Al-Masri's followers might look poor, they might meet in a shabby room in a slum, they might live humble lives; but the organisation had wealthy backers, pious men and women who could afford to bankroll an ongoing terror campaign. The Koran does not just call on believers to fight in the holy war: it asks them to spend their material wealth to allow others to join the struggle.

'But God requires more of us than this. The Americans, the Jews, the Crusaders everywhere still cast their shadow over the believers. Killing some here and some there is not enough. Destroying the twin towers was not enough. We have to strike a blow that will bring them to their knees. We must lay their cities waste, just as God wiped out Sodom and Gomorrah. We must send their kings and presidents to Satan. It will soon be time, my friends. You will see it with your own eyes.'

He smiled, and when he did his stern face became a different face. It was not a politician's smile. It had no side to it. No one could resist its openness, its unfeigned sincerity. Muhammad al-Masri was dangerous precisely because he was not like a politician. He would never compromise, never negotiate, never promise more than he knew he could give.

'Now,' he said, 'it's time for your reports.'

One by one, the group provided feedback on the cells they ran, not just in Imbaba but across Cairo. Al-Masri's cell was the leadership group, composed of his lieutenants, one of whom was his younger brother. To all other members of the movement, he was a shadowy figure. None of his followers except for these eight men had ever seen his face. Everywhere, he was known only by the name Muhammad. His true identity was a closely guarded secret.

It was Rashid who noticed it first. It happened gradually: a dimming of sound. The baby stopped crying, but that was only natural. The radio was switched off, but perhaps the teenager's mother had lost her patience. The voices of the quarrelling couple faded away, but all arguments end sometime.

As Rashid listened, he noticed that no fresh sounds had replaced those that had been there just minutes earlier. He realised he hadn't heard a moped or the cries of the boys at play for some time.

He put a hand up to silence the man next to him, who was giving his report.

'Listen,' he said. 'Can you hear anything?'

Nothing.

They looked at one another. There was just silence all round them. They knew what it meant.

'Quickly,' shouted al-Masri. 'To the other room. Hurry!'

Without panicking, they filed into the next room, which was furnished like a regular living space. A shuttered window gave onto the alley outside. Rashid rushed across and removed a metal disc, exposing a hole through which he was able to look outside.

'Police!' he hissed.

Outside, a squad of armed police and security service officers were lining the cul-de-sac. They carried sub-machine guns and wore body armour. Rashid could see they were ready to attack any minute.

One man had already opened a false wall and was taking guns from a space behind. He handed them to the others.

As he did so, one of the policemen opened fire. A row of bulletholes crashed through the shutter, and a bullet took a man called Mustafa, piercing his forehead and spreading his brains across the wall behind. The others threw themselves to the floor, and, as they did so, all hell broke loose outside. The shutter was peppered with bulletholes, then the holes were torn to shreds by each successive round of bullets, until the shutter fell to pieces and they were firing through an open window, smashing plaster from the walls.

50

Rashid crept to the window, raising his Kalashnikov in one hand, and fired blindly through the opening, burst after burst of fire. There was a cry outside, then another, and the firing into the room halted. Inside, a second man went to the door that led into the corridor outside. He fired straight through the thin wooden panelling, tearing it to pieces. His bullets found their targets in the bodies of the security troop that had been waiting to break in. Three men died when hot lead slammed into their unprotected faces, others took bullets in their arms and legs. The militant went on firing, pausing only to reload his weapon.

While this was happening, the man who had been handing out weapons went back to the opening in the wall. From it he took out nine suicide belts, each one packed with gelignite and connected without wiring to a button that would ignite the explosion. While Rashid and the other man kept up a steady round of fire to force the police back, the others stood and stripped off their *galabiyyas*, tied the belts round their waists, and replaced their outer clothes. They placed the buttons on their closely wound turbans.

Al-Masri made to don a belt too, but Dawoud, his second-in-command, tore it from his grasp.

'Not you. You are the Commander of the Faithful. You have a mission to complete. They will start lobbing grenades in here any moment. You and your brother have to get out of here now. We'll do the rest. Please hurry.'

Rashid would become Caliph should his brother die. Al-Masri bowed to the inevitable. He went to his brother and told him to hand his gun to the man next to him. Rashid had been rigorously trained. He would never disobey Muhammad.

'We have to get out of here,' said al-Masri, 'otherwise everything is lost.'

Taking his brother's hand, he led him back to the prayer room.

In the living-room, the firing stopped. Dawoud had torn off his white turban and now held it out of the window as a flag of surrender.

'We're coming out,' he shouted. 'We'll give you our weapons. See.'

Dawoud and his six companions threw their sub-machine guns through the window. They clattered on the fly-infested dirt path below.

One by one, hands on heads, they followed their weapons, clambering through the opening into the alley. As far as they could see, men in body armour waited for them, guns raised. Within seconds, they were surrounded. The police moved in to arrest them and, as they did so, all six reached for the buttons in their hands.

In a confined space, even a single suicide belt can do fearful damage to human flesh and buildings. As the six terrorists stepped into paradise, the cul-de-sac and everything in it was all but vapourised. No one in the vicinity survived; few of the victims could even be identified as human. The heat of the explosion turned their blood to powder and their flesh to gel. The sound could be heard across the vast city. On his way to the book-seller's, Jack Goodrich heard it and shuddered. His wife Emilia heard it through the shaking windows of her office. His daughter Naomi heard it at school.

Chapter Six

THE ANGEL OF DEATH

Al-Azbakiyya
Cairo
Later that afternoon

It was half past three when Jack turned up at the little book emporium in al-Azbakiyya. He parked his Fiat in the multi-storey that had been constructed on the site of the old Opera, after it burnt down in 1977, and headed east on foot towards Maydan Ataba.

He walked carefully, watching out for holes and cracks in the crumbling pavements. Nowadays, he only came here for two things: to buy books from Mehdi Moussa and to take Naomi to the puppet theatre that plied a thriving trade on a corner of the old Azbakiyya Gardens. The Gardens had once been a rival for any of the gardens in Paris, but over the years they had been neglected, the grass had withered, and most of what had been green space had been concreted over. Now a fence with barbed wire cordoned off most of it.

The rear of Mehdi's shop, Dar al-Kutub al-Manar, was situated in a little alleyway of mainly domestic premises. The only windows were on the second storey, ancient grilles made up of lattices of turned wooden rods, from which the women of

53

the house could look out onto the street without being seen. On the ground floor blank wooden doors barred the way into the premises behind.

Two small boys of ten or so, the same age as Jack's daughter Naomi, dirt-stained and nimble, played football with a bundle of rags tied with string. One of the boys, Jack noticed, had real flair, and his little friend, quick as he was, had difficulty in keeping up.

'Who do you want to play for when you grow up?' asked Jack. Every boy in every alley, every street urchin trying to thrust a pack of stale Marlboros on you, every self-appointed tourist guide hovering by the pyramids nursed a single dream, to play professional football. Even in the most downbeat alleyways, the beautiful game ruled. The ambition, the hunger, spurred by desperation.

'Zamalek,' the boy shouted back, without taking his eyes off the ball.

'I'm an Ahli fan myself.' Jack smiled. The boy scored a goal, sniffed, and gave him the finger.

'Watch what happens this Saturday at the Stadium,' Jack said. 'Ahli are going to take Zamalek down. You want to watch what their new coach does. Vingada. He's a genius. I'm expecting great things.'

'Can't watch no match,' the boy said. 'Got no money, not for Cairo Stadium, not for nowhere. Bloody foreigner, what did you think? I never set foot in the place, never will, not unless I get picked for Zamalek.'

Jack reached impulsively into his pocket and took out a wad of Egyptian pounds.

'Here,' he said, thrusting the money at the boy

with the golden feet. 'This is for both of you. It'll get you into this Saturday's match, maybe the one after that as well, if you don't spend it on sweets. Go to the match on Saturday. If Zamalek win, you can have tickets for the week after as well. What's your name?'

'Darsh.'

Jack nodded.

'What about you?' Darsh asked.

'Me? My name's Jack. Now, I can't hang around. Enjoy the match.'

He went past several doors until he found Mehdi's, a narrow green-painted wooden portal that led to a flight of equally narrow stairs.

Upstairs, Mehdi was waiting for him in a room lined with books: old books, lithographs mainly, and perhaps one hundred bound manuscripts.

The Egyptian was quite unchanged. Jack guessed his age to be somewhere between seventy and ninety. The old man contradicted all his guesses, however, by looking as fit and spry as a sixty-year-old. He was dressed in traditional style, a long *galabiyya* that fell to his ankles, and a tightly wound white turban that indicated his status as a member of the class of learned men and religious leaders. He stood up as Jack came in.

'*Ahlan, ahlan.* Welcome. How are you? Are you well? Is your family well?'

Goodrich smiled and took the old man's hand in his.

'God be praised,' Jack said. 'I'm well. My wife is well. My daughter is well. How are you?' He didn't ask after Mehdi's wife or family, because that would have been impolite. The heavy emphasis on privacy was a Muslim thing, an Egyptian thing, and a family thing – areas from which Jack kept a discreet distance.

Jack slipped off his shoes and put them to one side. The bookseller handed him a pair of light slippers that would do minimum damage to his fine antique Persian carpets.

'I have fresh tea ready. Come and have a cup. You must be parched.'

A pot of green tea stuffed with fresh mint leaves sat on Mehdi's desk.

'Just what my pancreas needs,' thought Jack, imagining the heavy lumps of white sugar that would have gone into the pot along with the mint. There were little sweet cakes on a plate next to the pot.

They drank from Persian tea-glasses with worn golden rims, rare specimens that Moussa's grandfather had been given – along with the carpets – by his good friend the Iranian ambassador, in the closing years of the nineteenth century.

The hot liquid entered Jack's bloodstream, sending his blood-sugar levels dangerously high while soothing him immensely. He realised he'd been on edge all day, even before the first bomb went off. He and Emilia had rowed the night before, which hadn't helped his composure. He wasn't sure they were over it yet. With Emilia, there was no way of knowing. It would blow over in the end; they loved each other well, and let very little intrude on that.

'You seem rather thoughtful, my friend,' Mehdi said, pouring fresh tea into Jack's fragile glass.

'I'm sorry. I was thinking about today's bombings. They make me uneasy. What if they attack the embassy while Emilia's in it? What if someone blows himself into eternity while Naomi's walking past?'

Naomi was Jack and Emilia's only child. She'd been born in London ten years previously, and was growing at the rate of about six inches a day, or so it seemed. They'd enrolled her in a British school in Zamalek, which was a short drive down the Corniche from their home in Garden City. Today, it was Jack's turn to pick her up: she was getting out later than usual following a long practice for her music exams, and it'd be almost dark when she finished. Long ago, she had chosen to learn the *oud*, a stringed instrument that'd formed the model for the lute. To her parents delight and bemusement, their child was turning into a little Egyptian. She already spoke fluent Arabic, and she'd made more Egyptian friends than British or American. But it was her parentage and her pale skin that put her at risk from extremists.

'I understand,' Mehdi said. 'We all worry. It's perfectly natural. But there's very little point. It doesn't make the bombers go away.'

'So we should just go walking round without a care in the world?'

'Did I say that? Jack, surely you remember the story about Azrail, the Angel of Death, how he met a man called Abu Hamza in the bazaar in Samarqand? The man saw him and shivered when the angel turned and faced him, for the angel gave him such a look as might curdle any man's blood.

'But, to Abu Hamza's surprise, the angel looked away again and passed on by...

'And later that day, Abu Hamza met a genie in

the road, and the genie asked where he would like to be transported. So, he said "Baghdad" in the hope of escaping the messenger of death and enjoying the high life in the imperial capital. Moments later he found himself standing in the great throne-room of the Caliph Harun, when whom should he see standing beside the throne and eyeing him greedily but the Angel of Death himself, black-faced Azrail?'

Jack finished the long-familiar story.

'And the Angel approached Abu Hamza and said, "I was astonished to see you this morning in Samarqand, for God had told me to look for you this evening in Baghdad..."'

Mehdi smiled and drained his glass. He set it down on the inlaid table and sighed.

'Now,' he said, 'I have something to show you.'

'You'll have to be quick,' Jack said. 'I have to pick Naomi up from school in about an hour.'

Mehdi took a little wooden rosary from a pocket and began to turn its beads through his fingers. He was worried about something, Jack thought. The bookseller remained silent for several minutes, allowing their conversation to fade.

'Jack,' the old man said, 'tell me, what would you give to make a discovery that would crown your career? More than that, a discovery that would challenge half the world and maybe change it.'

Jack laughed, a little nervously.

'I'd give the traditional arm and a leg. Or maybe just my right arm. Or years off my life, perhaps. If I had plenty of money, I'd give you whatever you asked. I don't know. What's this discovery worth anyway?'

Mehdi replied drily.

'When you see what I have to show you, you will understand. I asked you the question prematurely, but I wanted to know just what you'd be willing to relinquish, what you would sacrifice. Because you *will* have to sacrifice something for this. What it is worth in money is beyond calculation. That scarcely comes into it. But it may cost you everything else: your career, your family, your unbelief, whatever you hold dear. You are the only unbeliever I would ever say these things to. That's why I chose you. But you are under no obligation to say "yes".'

Jack stared at his friend.

'What have you got? The original manuscript of *The Thousand and One Nights?*'

Mehdi shrugged, but gave nothing away.

'It's best you see for yourself,' Mehdi said 'Step this way.'

Chapter Seven

FROM HERE TO ETERNITY

Jenin, The West Bank
The same day

Samiha had been awake since dawn. She had performed the ritual prayer before sunrise, and had just finished the noontime prostrations.

There was no prayer-mat in the room, just a

towel, but on one wall an arrow in red marker ink showed the direction of Mecca. The room itself was almost bare. A low bed without sheets or blankets had been pressed against one wall. A wash-stand and a ewer held the water she had used for her ablutions. They were the only objects in the little apartment, unless the squat toilet and its water jug in the next room could be counted.

She sat on the edge of the bed and tried to arrange her thoughts. Sometimes she'd had brief fits of trembling, making it hard to stand or stop her hands from shaking. But each time she had pushed desperate thoughts to the back of her mind and concentrated on the mission in front of her.

On the bed beside her lay a pad of paper and a plastic pen. She had written her will and testament as instructed, and said her farewells to her mother and her children, while saying nothing concerning what she was about to do.

Samiha had two boys: Adnan, who was eight, and the baby, Nabil, eighteen months old. She would never see them again. Inside, she was both sadder and happier than she had ever been. Sad, because she would never see her children again, happy because she would die and be done with grief and shame. Today, her name would be cleared and her family's honour restored throughout Jenin. She would become a martyr, a heroine among her fellow Palestinians. Better still, she would go straight to paradise and live there for all eternity. Assuming there was a paradise, which she doubted. She prayed because it was part of the routine of life, and out of a certain piety, but

60

she doubted everything she could neither see nor touch.

She was wearing a smart outfit, a long black jacket and a skirt that ended mere inches below her knees. Yesterday, a barber had cut her hair short, in a style common among young Israeli women. She felt ashamed to be going onto the streets without a long dress and a head covering, but her expensive suit was essential. At the checkpoint, they'd treat her as what she was, a Palestinian human rights lawyer headed for Haifa to take part in talks with Israeli prosecutors and representatives of the rights group B'Tselem. She was to attend as the representative of a young Palestinian man currently held in the interrogation unit in Kishon Detention Centre near Haifa.

The meeting was not a fake. It really would take place at seven o'clock that evening, in a room in Haifa City Hall in Hadar Hacarmel. But she would never get there. Instead, she would make her way to the nearby Haneviim Tower Shopping Mall on Rehov Haneviim. Once there, she would press a button at her waist and turn her body into shrapnel, her splintered bones hurtling across the mall in order to kill as many Jews as possible.

The very thought made her sick, but she knew she had no choice in the matter. The guilt would not be hers, she persuaded herself, but that of those who had threatened her children and sent her on this mission.

If she felt guilt, it was on account of her brief affair with Aziz Daraghma, head of the al-Aqsa Martyrs Brigades unit on whose behalf she was to turn her body into a bomb.

61

Six months earlier, her brother had been martyred fighting for the al-Aqsa Brigades, a wing of al-Fatah. 'Aziz had come to the house several times to express his condolences, and had lavished special attention on her. She regarded herself as an emancipated woman, she was never alone in the same room with him, she was flattered by his attentions. One month after that, her husband, Abd al-Sami', had been arrested once again for drug-dealing, and was now doing time in Ramallah's Ayalon prison.

'Aziz's attentions had become more insistent. He was a powerful man, and now he made his visits by night. No one complained. Her mother had wanted her to come back to the parental home, but Samiha had insisted it was her duty to remain in her husband's place, to keep it clean and comfortable for him on his return from prison, even if he was the worst bastard she'd ever known. On the third day, 'Aziz had talked her into bed. Within days, she had fallen entirely under his spell.

Every time they made love, she felt shame and guilt, coupled with fear of what might happen should their affair be discovered. And every time he kissed her or stroked her breasts or ran his fingers gently between her legs, she was like jelly, and, for the first time in her life, had cried out loud with passion. He told her that the Prophet had said a man should give his wife orgasms, and each time she had reminded him she was not his wife, that he had another wife living streets away; he had merely smiled and kissed her again.

Then, two months ago, her bleeding had not come on time. She had waited, and still it had not come, and a second time, and she knew she was pregnant, though she did not dare go to a doctor to be sure.

She told him, and he grew angry and told her he could have nothing to do with her or the brat she had conceived. And she knew she was dead, that one of her brothers or cousins or brothers-in-law would be sent to kill her for bringing shame on two families. They called them honour killings, but they never killed a man, not even a rapist, and she wondered what honour there was in them.

Finally, he came and offered her a way out of her dilemma. She could carry out a martyrdom operation. She hated the Zionists, didn't she? She wanted to expunge her husband's dishonour and remove the taint she had laid on her mother and sisters, on the memory of her dead father, didn't she? She didn't know that she hated anyone, but she had said 'yes'.

And then she had had a miscarriage. She pleaded with 'Aziz to release her from her pledge, but he said word of her dishonour had reached many ears, and that, one way or another, she would die.

There was a knock on the door, then a second, then a third. She got up and opened it.

Her cousin Marwan had been chosen. He stood face to face with her, but he did not smile the way he used to smile.

'Peace be with you,' he said. That was all. He didn't mean it.

It was another part of the routine.

Without asking permission, he entered the room. He carried a large bag. She knew what was in it, and for a moment her knees almost buckled. She took a deep breath and tried to smile. The martyr's smile, they called it. She would have to wear it on her face when she reached the checkpoint in the security wall, the bright yellow gate that would take her through the chain-link fence out of the West Bank into Israel. As a child, she'd sat in a darkened cinema, watching in fascination as Judy Garland set off on the yellow brick road. Now, she too was off to see the wizard.

He set the bag on the floor, his distaste for her visible on his face. Marwan had been her child-hood friend, and for a long time she had been his parent's choice as a marriage partner for their son. But she had persisted in her desire to go to Ayn Shams University to study law, whereas Marwan had gone into his father's agricultural business in his teens, and had sought a younger bride, a girl that wouldn't say boo to a chicken.

From the bag, he took a video camera and a tripod. She remained standing, not knowing the right thing to do in these circumstances. Satisfied that the camera was properly positioned, he set up the tripod to face the wall.

She did not dare speak to him. Her old friend had become her enemy. He would almost certainly have been the one sent to cut her throat if this had been an honour killing. He would have used his knife on her as though slaughtering a goat, and thought no more of it than that. A woman was of little importance, how much less was the life of a dishonoured woman worth? Her lover would go unpunished, a hero among his people. It was the way of things, as it had always been.

With the camera in place, he returned to the bag and took a Palestinian flag from it. This he pinned to the wall facing the lens, to serve as part of a backdrop. Beside it he tacked a yellow al-Aqsa Brigades banner. On both flags ran the words 'There is no god but God, Muhammad is the Prophet of God', the Muslim testimony of faith, the *shahada*. *Shahada* also meant martyrdom, another way of bearing witness to God's unity. The wall was already full of tiny holes where previous flags had been tacked to it.

At last he turned to face her.

'Take off your skirt and jacket,' he said.

She looked at him aghast, and for a moment she thought he might try to rape her before he filmed her. Then she realised what he wanted, and her knees became weak again, and she almost gagged. But she thought, I will show no weakness, I will not let this man see how afraid I am.

Without once looking at him, she unbuttoned her jacket, a Dior jacket bought from Fatah funds derived from European aid money. She wore nothing beneath but a lace bra. Next, she unzipped her skirt and let it fall. Beneath it, she wore stockings and briefs. Her skin felt hot from blushing. She remembered how, as adolescents, she and Marwan had never been allowed to play together unless she was accompanied by a close relative. Now she was half naked in front of him in this anonymous room.

The room and the apartment were rented by her former lover, not as a place for assignations but as a location in which to house suicide bombers during the night and part of the day before they turned themselves into human bombs. Here they were filmed while they made their final statements to the world, here they were given their suicide belts, here they received their last instructions, and from here they left on their homicidal missions.

Marwan reached inside the bag again. He had seemed wholly indifferent to the sight of her almost naked. She knew she had a good body, one that men desired. What would make a man look at her and turn away? she asked herself.

He stood up, and in his hands he was holding the suicide belt. This one had been specially designed for her. It would cover the area between her breasts and groin, but had two extra sections to fit round each of her thighs, ending some inches before the hem of her skirt.

'Put this on,' he said. He did not offer to help her.

She did as he said, feeling the rough cotton grate against her bare skin. The belt was heavy. Instead of being formed into sticks, the urea nitrate explosive had been formed into thin discrete vertical strips that wrapped round her without unduly increasing her girth, closely fitting the contours of her body, like a slim corset made by an expert tailor.

Wearing the suicide belt, she thought about the explosive and what it would do. 'Aziz had told her that it contained thousands of tiny plastic balls. They would tear flesh from bone, he said, and, better still, they would not show up on an x-ray.

She dressed again.

'Now put these on,' her cousin said. He held out a plain grey overgarment and a long headscarf in the colours of the Palestinian flag, black, white, green and red.

As she struggled into the shift-like covering, Marwan returned to the bag and took out a rifle, a Kalashnikov AK47, the terrorist weapon of choice. Emotionless, he handed it to her. She stood, self-conscious and afraid, in front of the flags, holding the Kalashnikov as an emblem of her membership in the world's most exclusive club. She was no longer a woman, a mother, a sexual being, no longer even human: they had turned her into an object, a deadly weapon.

He stepped behind the tripod and switched on the camera, watching her through the viewfinder, making sure she was in perfect focus. She read from the text 'Aziz had prepared for her.

'My name is Samiha Diab,' she began, her voice faltering, not like her voice at all.

'I am a Muslim, a Palestinian, and the mother of Palestinians. By the strength of God, I have volunteered to seek martyrdom in the path of this holy war, to turn my body to shrapnel to kill the Zionist oppressors. I shall become a knife thrust into the heart of the colonisers, a lance thrown by the people of Palestine into the mouths of those who hate us.

'I know I shall enter paradise, and I know that when my body explodes, it will cast the unbelievers into the fires of hell, where they will remain for eternity.

'I ask my mother and my dear sisters not to mourn my death, but to rejoice that I have been made a bride of Palestine and that my earthly body has been sacrificed on the sacred altar of the Palestinian people. And I call on my children, Adnan and Nabil...'

Here, her voice wavered and her eyes clouded with tears. She fought her emotions and got her voice back under control. The text was blurred, but she knew it by heart anyway.

'I ask my children, when they are men, to become fighters for Palestine, to rise up and drive the Jews into the sea and to make this land a Muslim land once more.

'And I call on my sisters in Islam to consider the fulfilment of martyrdom and to embrace it for themselves. Each one who steps forward in the path of God and makes her body a missile in the face of the Jews, the descendants of apes and pigs, shall put on the bridal dress of the martyr and go down in the history of Palestine as a heroine...'

She continued in the same vein for a minute longer, her image and her words swallowed by the camera, to be used as a tool of al-Aqsa Brigades, Fatah and Hamas propaganda.

Marwan zipped up the sports bag.

'This way,' he said, leading her downstairs into the street. There were people everywhere. Women and children moved to and fro, buying bread for the evening meal. Young men lounged on street corners, smoking and watching the passers-by. Bunting flapped in a gentle breeze: green for Hamas, black for Islamic Jihad, yellow for Fatah and the al-Aqsa Brigades. On the walls, posters displayed the faces of young martyrs who had given their lives for Palestine. An old woman hobbled past, remembering a past too distant for blood.

A car was waiting by the kerb, a black VW, not too old, not too new, a vehicle that would not draw attention to itself. Behind it sat a battered SUV, Marwan's vehicle.

A driver waited behind the wheel of the Volkswagen. Samiha recognised him at once. He was a clerk from her law office, Muslih Shalabi.

Marwan watched her get into the VW, and nodded to the driver. The car pulled out into the light traffic and headed for the nearest gate.

Chapter Eight

THE SWORD OF ALLAH

Cairo

Jack followed Mehdi to a back room. For the first time since he'd been coming here, he noticed a small door set in the rear wall. The old man took out a key and turned it in the lock.

'After you,' he said, showing Jack through. As he did so, he switched on a central light.

Jack gasped as the room came into focus. Near the ceiling, broad bands of ornate Arabic calligraphy ran round the walls. Verses from the Koran, he saw at once, but so elaborately written as to be almost illegible in parts. Lower down, the walls had been decorated with mother-of-pearl inlays that made up the shapes of lozenges, diamonds, and circles in complicated patterns, the individual lines lacing and interlacing through one another. Among these were set panels in blue and white ceramic, probably Iznik ware from Turkey. Jack guessed that the room must date from the late seventeenth century, about one hundred years after the Ottoman Turks had begun to rule Egypt.

The only light to enter the room came from two exquisitely turned lattice windows. Jack imagined the wives of some ancestor of Mehdi's sitting in the room on plump divans, dressed in the bright colours of the harem, fanned by a couple of Nubian slaves, either eunuchs or women, and looking out onto the street through these windows from time to time, hidden from the lustful gaze of passers-by. He wondered what they had dreamt of, for this and the public bath were almost the only spaces they had in which to live out their enclosed lives. He'd heard that some rich husbands prided themselves on the fact that their wives never set foot outside their house until they were carried out in their coffins.

The room was almost bare of furniture. In one corner stood an inlaid mahogany chair, and a small set of antique shelves against one wall held forty or fifty leather-bound volumes, including several copies of the Koran on the top shelf, since the holy book must never sit beneath other books, or below waist level, or on the floor.

In the middle of the room stood a wood and brass table, and on top of it was balanced a large Ottoman box.

Mehdi stepped up to the box and took a heavy-looking key from his pocket.

'Ignore the box,' he said. 'It's just an old thing

my grandfather gave me. I don't think it's worth very much, but it's just the right size to keep my little treasures in. Don't judge the contents by their container.'

He lifted the lid. Jack half expected a genie to emerge in a puff of smoke. Instead, the bookseller reached inside with both hands and brought forth a long object wrapped in plain white cloth along whose edge was a woven band with lettering in gold.

'A *tiraz*,' Jack said. 'This is pretty rare. It must have been well preserved.'

'To save you trouble,' Mehdi said, 'I've examined it already. The cloth probably started life as an honorary robe before being trimmed down to its present shape. The Arabic writing clearly dates it to one of the early caliphs, in the early part of the eighth century. That confused me at first, made me distrust what my eyes could see. Now, I'm sure the cloth is a late addition. But the object inside is much earlier, I'm sure of that too.'

Jack's eyes widened. Surely that wasn't possible. Almost nothing had survived from the earliest days of Islam.

The old man unwrapped the cloth very slowly, taking great care not to tear it. It was already in a bad state of repair, having rotted completely away in places, and showing brown stains on others.

Beneath it was a much older-looking cloth, a little coarser, red-striped, ragged and stained. The stains were stains of age, but it was impossible to tell without proper testing whether it was actually older than the outer cloth or had just been more exposed to the elements at one time.

One thing was certain: it did not appear to have originated at a caliph's court. Jack felt a chill go through him. He thought he knew exactly where it had come from and who had worn it.

The cloth fell away to reveal a long, thin object made of what seemed to be iron or steel, rusted in places, pitted in others, but still perfectly recognizable as a curved short-bladed sword. There was an inscription along the blade, in what looked like an early form of Arabic lettering, hard to decipher. The handle was missing, but the tang remained to show its approximate dimensions. Two central holes indicated where the wood or wood and cord handle had been fastened.

It felt heavier than its ancient appearance suggested. With a proper hilt, he judged it might once have been a powerful weapon in the right man's hand. Mehdi lifted the sword carefully, a hand at each end, and handed it to Jack.

'Here,' he said. 'Try it. It won't break.'

Experimentally, Jack took it by the blunt end and hefted it gently, slicing slowly backwards and forwards through the still air, without intent.

He looked round at Mehdi.

'Why are you showing this to me? I'm not an expert on Islamic arms or armour. You need someone like Jim d'Souza at Sothebys, or maybe Andy Gould at the British Museum. He's so good, he could probably tell us who owned the sword and what he ate for breakfast.'

Mehdi nodded.

'I know that. I met Gould three years ago when there was an exhibition of Fatimid glassware at the Cairo Museum. You were in the States with your family. But I think you are the one who will tell me the identity of the swordsman. I've tried to read the inscription, but it's beyond my powers. You may be able to decipher it. First, there are other items in my box. Forgive me if I seem like one of those street magicians we used to see at Tanta. Be patient.'

So saying, he reached inside the box again and brought out a leather scabbard, very plain and disintegrating in places: it seemed about the right length to have held the sword. After it came a pair of worn leather sandals with a double thong. And after them, the golden bangles, dented and stained with age.

Mehdi next lifted a flat, almost rectangular object out of the chest. Like the sword, it was wrapped in a scrap of the red-striped cloth. Inside were several sheets of vellum, probably made from gazelle skin. Jack scanned a few lines and realised that what he had in front of him was part of the Koran. A partial copy, but old. Very old. And the red-striped cloth and the bangles... He felt the chill within him deepen. And he remembered Mehdi's words: 'What would you give...? What would you give...?'

'These will require your expertise,' Mehdi said. 'And so will this.'

He brought a light cedarwood box from the bottom of the chest. It was an old box, finely worked, with well-formed Kufic letters made from ivory running in bold patterns all over it. He set the box on the table and removed the lid, which came away completely from the tray underneath. From this he took a sheet of parchment almost as long

73

and wide as the box itself.

'Here,' Mehdi said, his voice hushed for the first time. He held the sheet in both hands as though it was the most fragile and the most precious of all things, before setting it gently on the table. From somewhere underneath the table, he took a large desk lamp, which was plugged into a socket in the wall. When he switched it on, the light in the room grew markedly in intensity.

'Sit on this chair,' Mehdi said, dragging a desk chair towards the table before Jack could catch him and take over. And so Jack sat, all unknowing of what was to come, while the old man hugged a secret smile to himself and prayed his guest would see the truth.

Jack adjusted the lamp in order to shine its light on the parchment at the best angle. The writing was crude but legible, and was done in a version of an ancient script which had been used for some of the earliest known manuscripts of the Koran. When he thought about it, the style was very similar to that used on the vellum sheets. They might have been written by the same hand. With closer examination and possible comparison with the very few Arabic documents known to have survived from that period, he reckoned he could assign a fairly accurate date.

But the manuscript itself did the work for him. There were several lines of pious remarks and some honorifics, all in a style very different to that of later centuries. Then came the name of the person to whom the letter was addressed, and he knew his date to within a few years. The letter had been written between 644 and 656 AD, the brief twelve years of the reign of the Caliph Uthman, the third of the Prophet's Companions to succeed him as leader of the Muslim community. Uthman himself was the letter's addressee, God's Deputy on earth, Commander of the Faithful.

O Commander of the Faithful, Sword of Allah, Destroyer of the Infidels and Hypocrites, and Slayer of the Apostates – may God curse them and return them to Hell – greetings and praise, then congratulations and benedictions upon you from this humblest of God's servants.

When the Prophet, peace and salutations be upon him, died, there occurred rifts and divisions within his community concerning the matter of his successor. As is well known, during this confusion the possessions of the Prophet were at great risk of being stolen and dispersed among the Muslims, even of falling into the hands of the unbelievers.

Before he died, the Prophet gave into my keeping many of his most precious belongings. By precious, I do not mean that they had any value in the eyes of the world, but that they were dear to him and dear to his Companions. I have wrapped them in cloths and placed them in the rush basket that accompanies this letter. You will, of course, recognise many of them. To start with, there is the Prophet's sword, known as al-Adb, which he used at the battle of Uhud, together with its scabbard. There are also some verses of the Koran that I wrote at the Messenger's dictation, and that he kept by him. These were among the first revelations, as you know.

75

After his lamented death there was doubt about the succession, which was soon followed by the wars of apostasy, in which so many of the Companions and reciters of the Koran perished. So I kept these objects and wrapped them in cloth and kept them hidden and safe in my dwelling here in Medina. They have remained in safe-keeping until now, but I did not judge it prudent then to reveal their existence, thinking of the evil uses to which they might have been put.

But now you have placed in me a most sacred trust, namely, to serve God and you, His Caliph, as Master of the Public Treasury, and I feel it only proper to return into your keeping this blessed inheritance from the Chosen One, our Prophet Muhammad. You must make use of these things as you see fit and as it pleases God.

May Allah bring you peace and justice, and may He give you long life and many sons.

The servant of God and His Prophet,
Zayd ibn Thabit

Reading the name, seeing the identity of the writer, Jack felt a pang of something in his heart, something he could neither name nor properly understand. Moments later, he almost burst out laughing. The signature might as well have been 'James, the brother of Jesus' for its likeliness. He remained silent for several minutes, and Mehdi did and said nothing to bring him back to himself.

Jack read through the letter again, already noting finer points about the calligraphy and the grammar. It passed for the real thing. Everything about it said it dated from the reign of Uthman. If it did not turn out to be a forgery in a laboratory test.

But Jack did not think it was a forgery. He'd seen the red-striped cloth and the bangles. The Prophet's favourite wife A'isha, who outlived him for so many years, had married him in a dress of red stripes brought from Bahrain. During the battle of Uhud, while sword blades red with blood had gathered light from a hot sun, she and Umm Sulaym had tucked their dresses above their ankles, showing their bangles, that tinkled as they ran from soldier to soldier with water.

And then he looked a second time at the sandals. Of course. He remembered. The Prophet's sandals had been made after the Hadhramaut pattern, with two thongs instead of one.

He read the letter a third time.

'Where did all this come from?' he asked, without raising his eyes.

'They were found in a house in Medina, in the old Sunh district, near where the Caliph Uthman and other Companions of the Prophet had their homes. There was a flood, and the owner of the house had to dig out a cellar in order to wall it up more thoroughly. While one of his sons was digging, he broke into a small alcove that had been bricked up. This was well below the level of the present house. From Medina, these objects made their way to me.'

'I'll need more details in due course. Before that, what do you want from me? I'm not even sure I can be of any use to you, Mehdi. If these objects are genuine, if the letter really was written by Zayd ibn Thabit, I don't have to tell you just how big this could get.'

'I intend to sell everything from this trove, but not to a private individual. They must be kept together, and they must go to a museum, where they can be put on view for the public, whether Muslim or non-Muslim. But no museum or university will take them unless they are sure of their provenance and their authenticity. Do what you need to do. Examine what you need to examine. Then report back to me.'

'Have you a deadline?'

'The people who sent this box to me are growing impatient. But take your time.'

He hesitated. His hand went to his cheek, rubbing it slowly. A nagging tooth, perhaps. Or some anxiety.

'Jack,' he began, hesitantly. 'I have heard that rumours are getting around. Rumours of a sword of the Prophet. I made the mistake of showing the letter briefly to a sheikh at al-Azhar.'

Al-Azhar, a university based in Cairo, was the leading seat of learning and religious authority in the Islamic world.

'You may know him,' Mehdi went on, 'Omar Shaltut.'

Jack nodded. He knew Omar. Not a man to be trusted, he thought, but undeniably an authority on early Islam.

'I think he has betrayed me,' Mehdi continued, 'and that it's only a matter of time before someone tries to get their hands on these things. But I don't want to rush you. I want the right answers, whether favourable or not. In some ways, I'd be glad to hear they're all forgeries.'

'I'll have to think about it. It's a huge under-taking. I'll have to think about what it could involve.'

'I understand. But please don't take too long.'

'Will you be here tomorrow afternoon? Yes? Then I'll pop in about this time and let you have my decision. Or my recommendations if I decide not to go for this. I'll need to take the letter with me, if you don't mind. And the sword too, to see if I can read the inscription. I want to examine them both before I decide what to do.'

'Tomorrow will be fine. I know you can be trusted with them both.'

Mehdi handed him the letter in its box. He then took the sword, without its cloth, and placed it in a long bag he had bought for this purpose.

Jack got to his feet. He swayed for a moment, and realised his legs had grown weak with excitement. For if he was right and these objects were genuine, they would prove the most significant artefacts ever uncovered in Islamic history. He had only to associate his name with them and his career was made for as long as he lived and probably long after. He almost gave a skip as he headed for the door.

Chapter Nine

BROTHERS IN ARMS

In a tunnel deep beneath Imbaba, Muhammad al-Masri and his brother Rashid heard the explosion as they crawled out to safety. They muttered prayers. And as he prayed, al-Masri vowed that the time had come to make his bid for the Caliphate.

The tunnel went south across the Shari Sudan into the Suhafiyin district, where it emerged inside a baker's shop belonging to a close associate of al-Masri's. A controlled explosion caused the tunnel to collapse from the centre back to Imbaba, bringing with it a row of shoddily built apartment blocks.

Salman, the baker, hustled the brothers into a van and drove them across the river, east to Bulaq, where they had another safe house. As they drove, Muhammad turned to his brother.

'Rashid, I have an important task that must be carried out by you. No one else is to know about it. Is that clear?'

Rashid nodded but said nothing.

'I want you to retrieve some items from an old bookseller. This man is a scholar, a sheikh, a pious man. But he knows too much for his own good. You have heard me speak of the sword of the Prophet, the one named al-Adb. Omar Shaltut has told me that this man has the sword and some items that were passed down with it, together with a letter from the Prophet's secretary. He is planning to sell them to a museum. We have to stop him and take the sword. It is what I've been waiting for. I will be Caliph in more than name, once it is in my hands.'

'It's as good as done. And the old man?'

'His name is Mehdi. Mehdi Moussa. I'll tell you where to find him. Kill him. Not a word of this must reach anyone before the time comes.'

Chapter Ten

DEATH AND THE MAIDEN

Highway 66, northern Israel

Once through the checkpoint, they would head north-west towards Haifa, coming into the city from the rear of Mount Carmel.

As the tightly clustered buildings of Jenin fell away, the chain-link fence appeared ahead, its yellow-painted gate visible in the dying light. Lights had already been switched on all round the checkpoint. Driving slowly into the short corridor that led to the gate, the driver stropped half-way and they both got out. Two Israel Defence Force guards stood on each side, young men, one wearing a *kippa*, the others bare-headed. Four men, no women. Samiha breathed a sigh of relief: their intelligence had been correct after all. Female

81

soldiers could search a woman, male soldiers were under strict orders not to.

While her driver was frisked, Samiha held out her ID papers with a letter from the Misrad Ha Mishpateem, the Israeli Ministry of Justice. The letter identified her as a trustworthy lawyer cooperating in the defence of Palestinian suspects. The awful thing, she thought, was that she had been exactly that: a hater of violence and a realist who saw that cooperation and mutual recognition, not suicide bombing, were the ways forward.

The soldier she'd handed the letter to went into a little booth and made a phone call. Two minutes later, he came back and handed her her papers.

'They say you're to go through. The official I spoke to is a man called Moshe Harel. He'll ring this post to confirm your arrival at the meeting, and to tell me when you have left. Make sure your driver stays in the building at all times.'

They drove on in silence, and with every stretch of road she watched her life shorten like a string that scissors cut into ever-shorter pieces.

A short drive took them to Megiddo Junction. She'd passed through here many times in the past, visiting Palestinian prisoners in the large military prison nearby. To her surprise, instead of heading further along highway 66 past the Megiddo and Mishmar Ha'emek kibbutzim, her driver swung the car left onto the Wadi Ara highway, a major link between Afula and Hadera on the coast, well south of Haifa.

On their right, lay the green and brown patchwork of the Jezreel Valley, dotted with red and white rooftops – red in the Arab towns, white

82

in the Israeli settlements. On either side, olive groves clustered round little farms. In the near distance, a substantial town grew on the horizon.

With over forty thousand inhabitants, Umm al-Fahm was the second largest Arab town in Israel proper. Samiha had often spent time here with the friends and families of young men she'd been hired to represent. It was an Israeli town only in the sense that it was physically within the narrow boundaries of the Jewish state. In reality, it was a hotbed of Islamic radicalism. Nowadays, Jews stayed away, following attacks by residents at the beginning of the second intifada. The war in Lebanon had made matters even worse.

'Why are we going down here?' she asked. 'It will take us out of our way. We're not supposed to deviate.'

He shrugged, but did not answer.

They passed two Village Patrol policemen, but no one stopped them. Further on, as they approached the entrance to the town, a jeep with Border Guard troops on board rushed past them, and, for a moment, Samiha felt her heart leap to her mouth. She wondered why she would not have welcomed them, taken advantage of an opportunity to hand herself over and endure a prison term instead of death.

But she realised that, if she'd been contemplating surrender, the time for it had been back at the checkpoint. She had her children's future to think about. A martyr's children received privileges, a martyr's family were given hard cash, more money than most people dreamt of, a flat payment of twenty-five thousand dollars plus three hundred and thirty dollars a month for life. Not only that, her death would expunge her shame and remove the dishonour her reputation would've brought on Adnan and Nabil. What choice did she have, after all?

They passed into a maze of winding alleyways, through which the car crept, moving more deeply into the heart of the town, past a small market-place and on through a tangled residential district.

'Where are you taking me?' she asked.

He did not reply, but moments later they came to a large doorway blocked by a heavy metal shutter. As he halted before it, the door slid upwards, allowing the car to glide through into a small courtyard.

'Out,' he said. 'Quickly.'

Another door opened in a side wall, and she saw a woman in a headscarf, beckoning her inside.

The door closed behind her, and she was ushered upstairs and into a small room, where a woman of about her age was sitting on a chair, dressed in her underwear – a padded bra and thick tights. She did not smile as Samiha came through the door.

The woman who had shown Samiha up came inside too, and shut the door behind her. As far as Samiha could tell, she was around forty, and her outer garments clearly spoke of her religious views. Her face might have been beautiful once, but neglect and frown lines gave her a serious and sour appearance.

'Take off your clothes,' she said, 'and give them to Hiba. The belt as well. Be careful as you take it off.'

'I don't understand. What's going on?'

'We don't have much time,' the woman said. 'You are no longer taking part in this mission. Hiba will take your place. She will attend your meeting instead of you...'

'But...' Samiha was already unbuttoning her jacket.

'Hiba is a graduate. Like you, she speaks fluent Hebrew. She will say you were taken ill at the last moment, she will have your papers, and five minutes into the meeting she will detonate the belt. The men in that room have all been involved in the prosecution of Palestinian freedom fighters. We will be better off without them.'

Samiha put the jacket on an empty chair and unzipped her skirt. The woman helped her remove the belt. Hiba stood and, again with the woman's help, fastened it round her body and thighs. It fitted her perfectly, as did the jacket and skirt. Her hair, like Samiha's, had been cropped. An over-garment and headscarf lay on the floor beside her, and she started to put them on. She was quite pretty, thought Samiha. Did she have parents, a husband, children? she wondered. Or was she just another of God's virgins, preferring death to sex?

'The mission is no longer your concern,' the woman continued. 'Put your clothes back on while I explain what has been arranged for you.'

Samiha shivered slightly, partly because she was wearing so little, partly at the thought of what they might now have in store for her. She took the skirt and pulled it over her hips.

'You will carry new papers,' the woman said. 'Your name has been changed. You will travel on a forged American passport under the name of Samiha Brookes, an Arab-American who has been visiting Haifa on business. We'll give you full details later. A separate car will take you to Haifa this evening, where you will embark on the Salamis Lines ferry, leaving at nine o'clock exactly. The boat is scheduled to arrive at Limassol tomorrow morning at eight o'clock. You will be met at the port and be driven to Larnaca airport, where you will take the next Helios Airways flight to Cairo.'

'Cairo?'

'Don't interrupt. A woman'll meet you at Cairo airport. Her name is Fatima. Don't worry about finding her, she will find you. What will happen to you after that, I neither know nor care. Everyone here will be delighted to see the back of you.'

'And if I decide to stay in Cyprus?'

'You will be killed. And your children will be killed. Now – your car is waiting downstairs.'

Chapter Eleven

PRIME TIME

Zamalek
Cairo

Jack was twenty minutes late arriving at the school. But late arrivals were never a problem, given that everyone knew the dire state of Cairo's roads, not to mention the dire state of AUC professors' minds. He had been so intensely preoccupied with what he'd just seen and read that it was a miracle he hadn't had an accident.

Naomi was waiting for him in the headmistress's office, quite unconcerned by his non-appearance. She was reading her birthday present, a copy of Perrault's *Fairy Tales*, with illustrations by Dulac. To Jack's great amazement, he'd stumbled across an original Hodder edition from 1912 at a stall in the book market in Azbakiyya Square, in excellent condition and going for a knockdown price. Conventional stuff, he thought, but as long as it kept her away from the banalities of Harry Potter he was happy.

'You're getting on well with that,' he said, bending to kiss her. 'Where are you now?'

'Beauty and the Beast. I don't understand how Beauty can love the horrible monster.'

'Oh, you'll find out. Ask your mother. She loves me.'

'You aren't a horrible monster.'

'Oh, yes I am. You've told me so yourself, more than once.'

'That was before, when I was quite young. I'm much more grown up now, don't you think?'

'You are ten, and when you are twenty, you'll still be calling me a horrible monster. Did everything go well in school?'

'Miss Maxwell lost her temper and told us all to sit without speaking for half an hour. It was awful.'

'Well, I'm sure she had her reasons.'

The little girl grimaced and put the book into her satchel. She had long blonde hair like her mother, and was destined, like her, to be a beauty. She had also inherited from Emilia her strange eyes: the iris of the left eye was sea green, that of the right aquamarine. What Jack liked most about her was that she had poise. She never slouched, she walked with conscious grace, and even when she played with other girls, she never quite lost herself in the play.

'That's what you always say,' she said. 'You never back me up.'

'I do when it's necessary. But your mother works with diplomats, so we all have to behave in a diplomatic fashion.'

'What's a diplomat?'

'Something far removed from a ten-year-old girl. Come along. Mummy will be home before us.'

He got her to the car, and they drove home. About three streets from their apartment, the engine died and would not be resurrected. The petrol tank was half full, so he reasoned it must be the engine.

'Come on,' he said. 'We'll walk the rest of the way.'

Garden City

Emilia was waiting for them, as he'd predicted.

'You're late,' she said, letting them in. 'I was getting worried.'

He kissed her gently on the lips, and she responded with a flutter of the tongue.

'Something happened,' he said. 'I had to see someone. It was important. And the car broke down. I'll ring Jimmy Chow this evening.'

Naomi hurried past, eager to catch the latest episode of *Angelina Ballerina* on satellite.

'Was it anyone I know?'

'You know Jimmy.'

Jimmy Chow was a Chinese-Egyptian and the hottest motor mechanic in Cairo. He had a little workshop in Ma'ruf Street, in the centre of an area devoted to car repair shops. Here he fixed the cars of everyone they knew, and charged a fraction of the big garages and the franchises. He'd pick the car up from where it gave out this evening, and have it back by noon if the problem was a simple one.

'I didn't mean Jimmy,' Emilia said. 'The person you saw this afternoon. Do I know them?

'Just Mehdi,' he said. 'Mehdi Moussa.'

'The bookseller? I hope you haven't been spending money.'

He shook his head.

'I thought it might have been a woman. Speaking of which, how is the luscious Miss Mansy? Has she found a man to love yet?'

'I don't think love comes into it, darling. There's sex, I suppose, but like a good Muslim girl she displays it but gives nothing away. I think she's discovered that academics here earn less than bus drivers, and that what she really needs is a job with a big business or a foreign company.'

'She shouldn't rein in her ambitions so much. She could be a film star. The next Basma, who knows?'

'She's too intelligent for that. People look at her backside and think she's a tart, but she's actually very bright, brighter than most students I've taught.'

'And do you look at her backside?'

'Of course I do. It helps keep things in perspective. I know a better bottom to compare it to.'

She smiled and kissed him on the lips again. This time her tongue penetrated beyond his teeth. They hadn't made love in days, he thought, but he knew she liked to keep him guessing.

'Since I can hear no screams from her bedroom, I imagine Naomi has caught Angelina and her ballet class. Dinner is almost ready.'

'Anything special?'

She shook her head.

'Maryam made some *mulukhiyya* with rice and aubergines.'

'I'm a bit fed up with *mulukhiyya*,' said Jack.

'You haven't had it for weeks. Anyway, it was Naomi's choice.'

Angelina Ballerina came to an end, and Naomi was coaxed from her bedroom with the promise of food. Jack dined on *mulukhiyya*, and found the aubergines exceptionally well cooked and delicious. Naomi had three helpings of the soup, two of rice, and one of the aubergines.

About halfway through, Naomi put down her spoon.

'Dad, will you take me to McDonald's at the weekend?'

He looked at her in horror.

'Sweetheart, you were there only a month ago. And you had a birthday two weeks after that. Ramadan starts next week. You'll get to eat at all your friends' houses. After that, it's 'Id al-Fitr.

You can stuff yourself silly then.'

'A'isha gets to stay up late every night during Ramadan, and she gets up early for a special breakfast every morning. She gets fat and nobody says a word to her about it. Muslims have a lot more fun than we do.'

'Darling, when A'isha grows up she'll have to fast all day during Ramadan. You wouldn't like that, no food, no drinks.'

'I like Ramadan,' she said. 'We're all going out with lanterns. Every night. We've been singing *Wahawi ya Wahawi* every day at school. When can we go for my lantern?'

'Do you want to go with A'isha?'

She nodded.

'I'll ring her mother,' Emilia said.

Naomi jumped up and down.

'All the best lanterns will be gone if we don't go soon.'

'Don't worry,' Emilia said. They'd had much the same discussion every year since Naomi had become aware of the Ramadan tradition that sent children out on the streets each evening, carrying lanterns and singing traditional songs. Back home, she'd have been worried sick, but Cairo was the safest city she knew. Children didn't get murdered or abducted here.

'Anyway,' Naomi said, 'that wasn't McDonald's last month, that was Pizza Express. And we had my birthday at Hardee's.'

Jack couldn't concentrate on Naomi or McDonald's for long, because his mind was over-active, focussing on the enormity of what Mehdi had shown him. It was in its bag in his study now,

91

along with the letter that confirmed its authenticity. The Sword of the Prophet. The real sword, not a fake. He'd seen reputed swords of Muhammad in different places, some in Istanbul, and the one kept in the Husayn mosque in Cairo. Fakes, all of them, he had no doubt. But what he'd seen today was different.

'What's up, darling? You look preoccupied.'

'What?' He came out of his reverie and saw Emilia looking at him across the table, concern in her eyes. 'Sorry,' he said. 'I've some problems at work.'

He had decided not to tell her about the sword until Naomi was safely in bed. Knowing his daughter as he did, he was certain she would demand to take the sword to school, to show her teacher and her class. He shuddered at the thought, and at the row that would come when he said 'No'.

'Don't we all?' said Emilia. 'Anyway, you've just missed seeing us women sort things out. Your daughter and I...'

'You mean "My daughter and I"...'

'Quite. Whatever. She and I have decided that McDonald's is on this weekend, Saturday night, to be precise. Do you plan on joining us, or do you have too many of these problems?'

He wriggled.

'Mehdi asked me to look at a couple of items...'

'Tell me something new. Jack, this is your daughter. You need to get to know her better. Take Saturday night off. It'll be good for your soul.'

'McDonald's?'

'Don't think of it as junk food. Consider it

prime time with your only child. This one, sitting next to me.'

'That means I have to...' He thought rapidly. 'Yes, I know, I'll spend tomorrow working on Mehdi's stuff here at home. I'll get my lecture ready on Sunday. Could you...? Would you mind taking a note to Mehdi Moussa tomorrow morning? He's still at al-Azbakiyya.'

'Jack, that's blocks away. It's bad enough getting through the traffic to the embassy every morning. And who's going to take Naomi to school?'

'I'd have taken her, but the car won't be ready that quickly. Jimmy's picking it up later tonight. He'll call for the keys. But he won't work on it before the morning, and it could be a lot later if he has more urgent jobs ahead of it.'

'You win. I can make a detour down Sheikh Rihan, and then up. It may not be too hard getting to Zamalek on 26 July Street. But if the car's ready by the afternoon, you're picking her up from school and delivering her to her music class.'

Naomi went to bed early. Jack wanted to show Emilia the sword, but she pre-empted him by suggesting an early night for them as well.

'I'm going up,' she said. 'You can follow me if you like.'

All thought of the rusty sword vanished in keen anticipation of what might happen in the bedroom.

Emilia went into the bathroom to remove her make-up. Minutes later, she opened the bedroom door. Jack. who'd been undressing, looked up. She was completely naked.

'Jack,' she said, 'I don't care what you've been

thinking about since you came home this evening, I just hope it's good when you decide to tell me. If it's Miss Mansy, I will divorce you and take our hamburger-eating child with me. If you have developed a fancy for men, and Mehdi Moussa has become the focus of your amorous intentions, I will cut off your penis and bury it beneath the nearest obelisk.

'In the meantime, however, I would like your undivided and horny attention for the next twenty minutes or so. I feel an urgent need for sex, and I hope you do too, in view of what is now on offer and what the alternatives are. Any sign of mental displacement, however well meant, will result in fluffy slippers, a thick dressing gown, and something ridiculous on my head. And face cream. You will lose your chance, perhaps for ever. Now, which is it to be?'

'I love you,' he said. 'I am not gay, I am not in lust with Miss Mansy or her backside, and I am wearing the absolute minimum of Ali's after-shave. If you would sneak a peek, you'd see I'm enjoying a very large erection at this moment because you are astonishingly naked and remarkably beautiful...'

'And sexy...'

'...and I love you and...'

Suddenly, she threw herself at him, and they fell laughing onto the bed.

'I love you too,' she said. 'God knows why, but I love you to bits.'

Chapter Twelve

TALONS FROM HIS WORST
NIGHTMARES

**The Goodrich house
Garden City
The following morning
Tuesday, 19th September**

He spent the morning first on the sword, then on the letter from Zayd ibn Thabit. By the time he'd translated it to his satisfaction, his desk was covered with dictionaries, most of them huge Arabic to Arabic dictionaries compiled during the Middle Ages. He had also used editions of the best pre-Islamic and early Islamic poetry as references for the more obscure vocabulary. Whatever doubts he might have started the task with were quickly dissipated. Either the letter was a remarkably clever forgery or it was the real thing. He was confident it was the latter.

The inscription on the sword had not proved too hard in the end. It read very simply: *My name is al-Adb. I am the Sword of the Prophet and the Slayer of the Pagans.* Jack was now certain it was genuine.

By half past ten, he'd started to wonder why Mehdi had not called him. The bookseller had a mobile phone and Jack's home number, and Jack knew how eager he was to get this thing moving. At ten thirty-one, Jack picked up the phone. He dialled, but there was no answer.

He punched in the embassy number and asked for Emilia. It was possible she'd been held up and hadn't made it to the bookseller's. He asked to be put through to her desk, but the voice that came on the line was a man's. Jack recognised the speaker as Simon Henderson, Emilia's boss. They'd met several times over the years.

'Hello? This is Emilia Goodrich's desk. She's not here at the moment, but maybe I can help you.'

'Simon? This is Jack. What's wrong, how come Emilia's isn't there? She was planning to head to work when she left this morning.'

'Jack, hello. Look, I was planning to call you, but something important came up and I had to put it off. I thought Emilia might have been with you, that she was sick or hung over or something.'

'She's never hung over, Simon. And she wasn't sick when she left. She took Naomi with her. I asked her to take a message for me, then she was due at your place.'

'There's been no sign of her at the embassy.'

Jack's heart skipped several beats.

'Maybe she went straight to a meeting you didn't know about. She could be in there now.'

Simon gave a short, mirthless laugh.

'Her meeting this morning was the one I had to be at, the important thing that came up. Have you checked Naomi's school?'

'No, I haven't. You're right. Maybe something

96

happened to Naomi, maybe Emilia had no time to ring. I'll try them. But I may need to get back to you at some point.'

'I'm here all morning, Jack. And if something is wrong, I'm here permanently. I mean that. Now, try your daughter's school.'

The school knew nothing.

'What do you mean, you know nothing? Either my daughter is in her class or she isn't.' He was on the verge of losing his temper or bursting into tears. Inside, he felt anxiety building like an inflating balloon.

'Wait. I put you through to Mrs Crane-Johnson. Mrs Crane-Johnson is headmistress. She can speak to you. Wait, please.'

He waited, and every second his brain was on the edge of panic. Had there been a suicide bombing this morning in town? Wouldn't he have heard it if there had? All his old fears rushed back like treacherous friends. He thought of switching on the radio, but it was in the kitchen.

'Professor Goodrich? I'm sorry you were kept waiting. What can I do for you?'

'Is... I'm sorry ... is my daughter in school this morning?'

'Don't you know? Didn't you drop her off?'

'Why would I be making this telephone call if I knew where she was? Her mother has gone missing, and I want to know where my daughter is.'

'Could your wife have taken her somewhere? Shopping, for example. Some of the mothers are terribly naughty and take their girls...'

'Will you please check your records or ask her

97

teacher or do something for fuck's sake?'

He felt near to breaking point.

'Professor, I'm shocked at your language. We don't...'

'Mrs Crane-Johnson, I can walk to the school in less than fifteen minutes. Much less. Believe me, you do not want me anywhere near your school at this moment. Now, find out where she is.'

He heard the crash as she dropped her receiver. Less than a minute later, she was back on.

'Professor, I have the school roll in my hands. Glancing at this morning's entries, I find that Naomi has not registered for school today. I trust you'll be bringing her in later.'

'Will you please check in the classroom? She may have come late and still be unregistered.'

The reluctance in her voice was palpable.

'Professor, I have already spent quite some time assisting you. You may not know it, but I have a school to run, staff and pupils to supervise and motivate. If you're incapable of ensuring the whereabouts of your own child, it's your responsibility, not mine. I'm sure she's perfectly all right. You're fussing unnecessarily. This is Cairo, remember, not Chicago.'

It took him less than fifteen minutes to walk there. She called security, but this was Cairo, not Chicago, and by the time it took the school janitor to find the office, Jack was in Naomi's classroom, talking with her teacher, a gap year girl from Northampton called Janice. Janice hadn't seen Naomi all day, had no idea where she might be. No, none of Naomi's small circle of friends was missing.

98

'Can I ask them if they can guess where she might be? Can you point them out?'

He recognised most of them from parties and outings. They gave him what they could, which was either nothing or fantasy. There had been no arrangements, no plans to play truant together and go to McDonald's or the zoo.

He used his mobile to ring back to the embassy. Simon Henderson picked up immediately.

'Any news?'

Jack explained. He told Simon where he'd sent Emilia with his message.

'I can get people there in minutes,' Henderson said.

'Let me get there first. It's easy to get confused. There are no street numbers. Come alone. Wait for me next to the cigarette seller at the top of the street.'

Switching off, he headed back to the headmistress's office. He thought he was having a panic attack. Mrs Crane-Johnson was sitting behind her desk. She looked frightened.

'I want your car.'

'What? You can't possibly take a car. You're not insured...'

'My car is being repaired. But I need to get to an address in al-Azbakiyya in minutes, so I want your car.'

'You can't have my car or anyone else's. If you so much as...'

'This may be nothing, or it may be a matter of life or death. Get in my way, and I will hurt you. Now, please let me have the keys.'

She hesitated another five or six seconds, then

99

dived into her handbag, brought out her car keys, and dangled them limply in front of him. He reached out, snatched them, and was off.

The traffic was heavy, but he made his presence felt, and at the cost of several dents and scrapes on the headmistress's Renault, reached al-Azbakiyya in ten minutes.

Everything seemed normal when he reached the alley. He had left the car on a nearby street and gone there on foot. He walked down from the far end, eyes peeled for signs of trouble, but quite unsure what to look for. He went on past Mehdi's rear entrance to the other end, and walked about a little. In a street near the alley he found Emilia's white Volvo. The key was still dangling from the ignition.

He rang Mehdi's number from his mobile, and again there was no answer. He walked back to the door. As he drew near, he saw the two boys playing with a new football. He called the boy he'd spoken to previously.

'Hi, Darsh,' he said. 'How are things?'

The boy shrugged.

'That's a nice ball you've got. I hope you left enough money to get into the match on Saturday'.

Again the shrug.

'You don't seem so talkative today.'

'I told my mother I'd been talking to you. She said I should watch myself. She said you bloody foreigners can't be trusted.'

'Darsh,' Jack said, reverting to the informal style of the boy's name. 'Did you see anyone go into Mr Moussa's shop this morning? A woman with a little girl, perhaps. An English woman in a red suit. The girl was wearing her school uniform.'

Darsh pondered this question for what seemed an age. Nearby, his companion kicked the ball up against a wall. The ball was plastic, a luxury in these alleyways, and it required much greater skill to control it than just kicking a ball of rags around.

'Yes,' said Darsh. 'I remember a woman. I think there was a girl, maybe a couple of girls, I didn't notice.'

'How long? Can you remember? An hour? Two hours?'

Darsh looked at the Englishman, his eyes wrinkled with an effort to understand. The boy had never owned a watch, his family didn't have a clock. Hours meant nothing to him.

He shook his head.

'Dunno,' he said. 'Ahmad and I have been out since after breakfast. They turned up a bit after that. She weren't the old man's first customer, though. There was a guy went in just before her. One of those Jihadi types. Beard and skullcap, white *galabiyya*, arrogant as hell. Didn't even look at us. Thought we was dirt.'

Jack felt the tightness around his chest increase to such an extent he thought he was about to have a heart attack. He had to tell himself all might yet be well, that there was bound to be a good explanation for Naomi's and Emilia's absences, for the silence on Moussa's phone. The man might have been a buyer, no more than that. Perhaps even a member of Mehdi's sufi brotherhood.

'Did they come out again, Darsh? Think hard. Did you see the woman and the little girl come out?'

101

Darsh shrugged.

'Dunno. Don't think so. I had to go off.'

'You've been very helpful, Darsh. Enjoy the match. I'm afraid I have to go.'

He shook the boy's hand and walked down to the bookshop. The door was shut, and no amount of ringing the bell brought anyone to open it.

He decided not to wait for Simon.

He called to Darsh.

'Listen, Darsh,' he said. 'I think something may be wrong with the sheikh. Do you understand?'

The boy nodded. He knew the appearance of a beardie often spelt trouble.

'I'm going to break the door down. Yes? Keep an eye out for me, and if I don't come out soon, tell your father or your mother to call the police.'

Without further hesitation, he put his shoulder to the old door. It snapped open on the third attempt. He stepped inside, and the door banged gently shut behind him, unlocked but still intact. He stood still at the bottom of the stairs, listening for sounds of anything that might tell him what was going on, but there was only the uncertainty of silence. It draped itself around him like a cloak for his anxiety.

He climbed the stairs and entered the room at the top of them, the book-lined room in which the majority of the sheikh's transactions were done. It looked as if a storm had hit it, upending furniture, shattering glass, scattering books and papers everywhere.

Glancing round, he saw that the door into the back room lay half open, although the only light was still the muted glow that filtered through the ancient windows.

'Emilia?' he called, and again several times. 'Emilia, can you hear me? Are you there?'

There was no reply. This time he called out in Arabic.

'*Ya Mehdi! Ayn anta?*'

Still nothing. His heart was beating like a drum at dawn. Something clawed at his stomach, something with talons from his worst nightmares.

He went up to the door and tried to see inside, but the half darkness was only partly relieved by the light coming from the front room. Gently, he pushed the door open, and it turned on stubborn hinges, away from him. He could make out the table on which Mehdi had placed the box during their interview less than twenty-four hours previously.

He stepped inside. And it seemed to him, as he turned to view the room, that each second that passed was stretched and drawn like the frames in a film played in slow motion. And that his eyes had grown detached from his heart, and his heart from everything, and that in this detachment he saw without seeing and understood without a connected heart, understanding yet not understanding.

Emilia and Naomi were lying together, as though placed there by a careless lover, their limbs at awkward angles. Darsh had been mistaken, there was just one girl, just Naomi. Emilia was on her back, her face towards the ceiling, eyes wide open. Naomi lay face downwards, her arms straight out, like a tiny female crucifix. Mehdi lay several feet away. Their throats had been cut from side to side, who could say in which order, and about their heads three pools of congealing blood lay like three great red flowers in bloom. Emilia's skin was already pale, so drained was she of blood, and her whiteness stood out against the Persian carpet underneath like a bouquet of white lilies against the petals of deep red roses. Naomi had dropped her school satchel at some stage, and her books and papers were swimming in the blood, and her name on the leather satchel was obliterated by the thick red liquid.

'Jack? Where are you? Are you in here?'

He looked round to identify the speaker. In reality, his mind was somewhere else, at another end of the universe.

'Simon?' Some earthly part of him recognised the man standing in the doorway. He made no sense of the fact that Simon held a gun in one hand and walked carefully towards him.

'They're in here, Simon,' he said. 'Don't hurt them. Don't hurt them, Simon.'

And then he screamed, and his mind shut down. They took him out like that, silent now, like someone who will never speak again. Then went in a second time. Not the Cairo police. Not the Egyptian security forces. But men and women from the British embassy, come to take away one of their own. And to find a killer before he killed again.

PART TWO

Chapter Thirteen

A HIGHLAND REFUGE

Bailebeag Cottage
Loch Killin
Scotland
Saturday 2nd January

Nearly four months had gone by like ghosts, phantoms of a future come into the world lifeless. Simon Henderson had taken care of everything. The bodies had been taken back to England and buried beneath an ancient oak in Durham, Emilia's home town. Grief had deprived Jack of every fortitude. He had said farewell to Emilia when he identified her body in the mortuary in Cairo. But Simon Henderson had told him he should not see Naomi, that things had been done to her that he would not specify, things that made it inadvisable for Jack to say his goodbyes. It had left a barrenness in him, an empty space into which an unbearable guilt had seeped, like poisoned water filling a cellar.

About a week after the funeral, he had said goodbye to Emilia's parents and had travelled as far as London with his own. They remained silent throughout the journey, as they had mostly done during the first days of mourning. Their granddaughter's death had aged them visibly. This sort of death they could not understand, this sort of loss was more than their old hearts could bear. And Jack had been locked in his own unbearable prison of loss, knowing that, outside its walls, there was nothing, and that he could not live with nothing.

While his parents had set off back home to Norwich, Jack took a train to Scotland, all the way north to Inverness, then a bus south to the Monadhliath Mountains, where he rented a cottage overlooking Loch Killin. It was the only plan he had, to take himself away from humanity and sit in his depression day after day while looking out at the dark waters of the loch. It was more than deep enough to drown a man, and there were days when he stood in his doorway and thought of the freedom that would bring him. But he knew it wasn't death he sought, but freedom from his grief. At night the moon haunted him.

It was deep winter by now, and heavy snow lay on the Grampians and on the neighbouring hills. He had stocked up enough food and fuel to see him through to spring, but there were moments when a sort of cabin fever took hold of him and threatened to overthrow his sanity even more surely than the grief.

Within a matter of weeks he had read all the books left in the cottage, and written painful thoughts down on every scrap of paper its drawers had offered. The CD collection was abysmal, and there was no TV. Every day now, he listened to Radio 3 and Radio 4, depending on his mood. But the music on one made no impression on him, and the plays and talks on the other left him cold. He craved silence above everything, but silence tormented him after its own fashion.

Christmas passed without celebration. No carol singers came out to his isolated cottage, no traders called to sell him turkey or Christmas pudding. But he lay awake all Christmas night, and continued through the day, unable to control the sudden bouts of tears that dogged him until well after midnight.

Hogmanay came and went without his noticing the date or knowing what year it was. From time to time he heard the news and knew the wars in Afghanistan and Iraq were continuing without sign of an end in sight, that the Iranians were still building nuclear weapons, and that Hamas was still firing rockets into Israeli towns.

Just after eight o'clock one evening, shortly after Hogmanay, when it was pitch dark outside, there was a sound of knocking on Jack's door. Nervous, he would not open the door thoughtlessly to a stranger. His lights were all lit, however, so he could hardly maintain a permanent silence. When the second knock came, he went to the door and shouted through it.

'Who's there? What the hell do you mean, coming round here after dark? What do you want?'

The voice from the other side was muffled.

'Jack? Are you in there? I need to speak to you.'

'Who the hell are you?'

'This is Simon. Simon Henderson from the Cairo embassy. Can I come in? It's freezing my balls off out here.'

He was about to send Simon packing when he remembered him at the funeral, and before that the kindness of everyone from the embassy, and how Simon had taken charge of everything.

'OK,' he shouted. 'But you can't stay overnight. I haven't got the room.'

'Thank you.'

Jack unlatched the simple wooden door and opened it to let Simon in.

Henderson was dressed in an enormous, bright yellow down jacket that gave him an appearance not unlike the Michelin Man. On his head, he wore a woollen Scandinavian-style hat with pom-poms, and mufflers over his ears; his hands looked like giant tomatoes in their bright red ski gloves. Over his shoulder, he carried a little rucksack. His face was red, and his moustache was thick with ice.

Jack had to work hard to fit the image in front of him to the man he'd known under very different circumstances – and in very different clothes – in Cairo.

Once inside, Simon got himself up against the fire. Even though he'd dressed well for the weather, he was shivering from head to foot. The Scottish mountains are unforgiving, even to those who approach them well prepared.

'You could have chosen somewhere warmer,' Simon said, his teeth rattling together as he spoke. 'A Greek island or the South of France.'

Jack sat on a chair on the other side of the fire. He nodded, to himself more than to Simon.

'I thought this was a good idea at the time. Emilia and I used to come here for holidays, mainly in the Cairngorms just to the east. And there's Loch Ness to the west – we went Nessie

110

hunting one year and she took a photograph of a huge log. But, to be honest, I don't give a damn where I am. Why should I?'

'It's your time of grief, Jack. I hope I never go through that, and I hope I die without putting anyone else through it. Hell, what do we know? We can't control these things.'

He paused, as though unsure of himself, then spoke again.

'But now it may be time to make a fresh beginning for yourself.'

Jack looked at him angrily.

'Jesus, you diplomats can be totally naïve at times. You all seem to live in Nutwood. Rupert Bear and the Grand Vizier.'

'I suppose that's right. But it doesn't help to be too naïve in our business, as you will shortly discover. There's more to us than embassy parties and being unctuous to dictators, and you for one should know it. You knew Emilia, for one thing, and you know she didn't step out of a Rupert annual.'

'You're right, I'm sorry. I haven't spoken to anyone for quite some time.'

'So I can see. Don't worry, you'll get the hang of it again. But before we come to that, you don't happen to have a coffee-maker in here, do you? Or instant. Instant will be fine.'

Jack got to his feet. His sudden anger had left him. Simon Henderson wasn't responsible for the deaths of his beloved Emilia and Naomi. Perhaps he'd come to tell him they'd tracked down her killer or killers.

'Actually,' he said, 'instant is all I have. I bought

111

a giant jar of Nescafé when I got here. I've scarcely touched it. All I want to do these days is sleep.'

'Well, that may change when I've told you one or two things. Let's have the coffee first, though. I've been on the road for hours. And make a strong one for yourself: I want you awake. There's a lot to talk about.'

The warmth of the room had begun to bring some life back to Simon's body. He removed the jacket, hat, mufflers and gloves, and allowed the fire to act directly on him. He was a tall, thin man, whom most people would have taken for an architect or designer. Under the down jacket, he wore a good tweed suit that had probably come from Henry Poole or Anderson & Sheppard. As always, he looked full of good health and vitality. Jack knew little about him, but Simon's bearing almost shouted Sandhurst. What had impelled him to move into the diplomatic corps?

Jack made two large mugs of coffee, poured in powdered cream, and added several spoons of sugar to his.

Simon had moved to the kitchen table, and Jack sat down facing him.

'OK,' began Jack. 'What's this all about?'

Simon sipped his coffee and grimaced at the taste of the artificial cream. He did not answer right away. Instead, he stirred the coffee, watching the liquid spin. A second sip tasted the same. He put the mug down and looked up.

'Jack,' he said, 'I have some difficult news for you. In a way, it's good news. But you should prepare to be upset all the same.'

Jack flinched. He couldn't even think what might have happened to make him more upset than he already was. Something that had brought Simon Henderson all the way from Cairo to the wilds of Scotland.

'Just get on with it,' he said.

'Very well. Jack ... Naomi is still alive.'

He didn't take it in at first. It sounded like a sick joke.

'Could you... Could you say that again?'

'Naomi, your daughter, is alive.'

'That's not remotely funny, you bastard. You identified the body, you were at the funeral. My daughter is dead. I don't know what brought you here, I don't know what sick sort of diplomatic mind-game you're playing, but this conversation ends here. I want you to leave. Just get out and head the fuck straight back to Cairo.'

He stood abruptly, knocking his chair onto its back. It would have given him the greatest pleasure to smash Simon's head against the floor as well. Henderson was just another upper-class twit, the sort he'd learnt to despise in the army, a Hooray Henry who thought Britain still ruled the world and behaved as though he was personally responsible for keeping everybody else in their place.

Simon took another mouthful of coffee and put his mug down again.

'Sit down, Jack. Put your chair back to the table and sit down. I'm not going anywhere. Nor are you.'

'I said I want you out of here. By God, I could snap your neck with one hand, you little swine.'

113

'If you do that, you won't know what this is about, Jack. I told you, this is good news. Mostly.'

Simon's command of the situation had a calming effect on Jack. He'd learnt something else in the army, and that was how to obey orders, mostly from men like Henderson. He picked up the chair and put it next to the table.

'Now, sit down and listen to what I have to say. Try not to interrupt. Keep your questions till later. And have some coffee. You need to concentrate.'

Jack did as he was told. But he swore to himself that he would hurt Henderson if the conversation grew any more bizarre.

Chapter Fourteen

FIONA

'Jack, the body I identified, the body we saw buried alongside Emilia – that was not Naomi's body.' He held up a hand. 'No, just let me finish. Something terrible happened. The body you saw on the floor at Mehdi Moussa's, the little girl in the school uniform next to Emilia, wasn't Naomi. Does the name Fiona Taggart mean anything to you?'

Jack's mind fumbled through clouds of confusion in search of the name.

'Yes,' he said. 'Yes. She was in Naomi's class. They were quite alike. I remember her now, she used to come to the house. Emilia sometimes

114

ferried her to school if her own parents weren't around...'

The bad penny began to drop. But if the body was Fiona's...? It made less sense than ever.

'The body belonged to Fiona. The reason I identified her as Naomi was, first of all, because there was absolutely no reason to think that the little girl lying next to Emilia's body could be anybody but Naomi. Secondly, although I'd met Naomi a few times, I'd only seen her briefly and, as you say, she and Fiona Taggart were quite alike. More importantly, Fiona's killer had done things to her, to her face. The face was badly mutilated. That was why I insisted I do the identification instead of you.'

Jack stared at him. It still made no sense.

'I don't understand,' he said. 'Where was Naomi? And surely the Taggarts would have noticed Fiona was missing.'

'That was the heart of the mix-up. The Taggarts weren't in Cairo, they weren't even in Egypt. Jill Taggart's mother was seriously ill, thought to be dying. They'd both gone back to England the day before. They left Fiona with the maid, a woman called Wafa. They'd done it before for shorter breaks, and they didn't expect to be away more than a week to ten days. In fact, they were away for three weeks, and busy, first with the hospital, then with the funeral.'

'It still doesn't make sense. Wouldn't this Wafa have reported Fiona missing when she didn't come back from school?'

Simon sighed and drained the rest of his mug.

'You're right, she should have done. But she

115

didn't. You know how things are in Egypt. Wafa was frantic with worry. She knew that, if the police came, she'd be arrested and blamed for whatever had happened. As time went by, her first mistake turned into a big lie. The school phoned and asked where Fiona was, and she said the child had gone to England with her parents. When the Taggarts rang – which wasn't too often, I have to say – Wafa would say Fiona was asleep or at school, and they were too harassed to think anything was amiss.'

'But that was months ago. Didn't they report this when they got back?'

'Of course they did. They hauled Wafa to the police station, where she's still being kept, and the story came out. But nobody made a link to Naomi's death, not till recently. I had a copy of Emilia's office diary, but I had only glanced through it. There was an entry to say you were due to pick Fiona up on her way to school that morning.'

Jack stared at him. His brain had almost stopped working. He couldn't take this in.

'We swapped,' he said. 'I had to stay in. She went instead. But she didn't say anything about Fiona.'

'She probably only remembered about it when she was on her way. She must have picked Fiona up and taken her with Naomi to Mehdi Moussa's.'

'It still doesn't make sense. If it wasn't Naomi, then where the hell is Naomi?'

'I don't know. Not exactly, that is. What I do know is that the killer took her. He knew who she was. He must have asked their names, Emilia's perhaps, then the little girls'. Fiona had to be killed because she might have recognised him or been able to give a description to the police. But he took Naomi, and he still has her.'

'But...'

'We found this in your office a couple of days ago. Your secretary had left your mail untouched. When I realised what must have happened to Naomi, I went through all the mail that had gone to your home address, then everything waiting for you at the university. This was what I found.'

He handed an envelope across the table. Jack took it and removed a folded sheet of cheap blue writing paper, the sort you could find at any street corner paper stall or *suq* bookseller. It was covered in fine lines of hastily written Arabic.

Professor Goodrich. If you wish to see your daughter again, follow my instructions to the letter. Bring the sword of the Prophet and the letter of Zayd to the Husayn mosque tomorrow and leave them in front of the mihrab. *Leave at once. Do not mention this to anyone: if we so much as suspect that the police are there, your daughter will die like her friend, but her death will take days, not moments.*

Jack put the letter down. Emotions had begun to surface, emotions he could scarcely handle.

'Then she's dead. If I'd known of this... Sweet Jesus.'

'Actually, we don't think she's dead, Jack. For one thing, we have a rough idea who's been holding her. We just don't know where to find them. The Egyptians are looking for them too, but they've gone underground. They know you still have this sword and letter.' He paused. 'By the way, I take it they are genuine?'

I ... I haven't really had time for a full investigation. But I'm sure the letter's the real thing. And the objects Mehdi showed me with the sword, plus the inscription...Yes, I'm ninety-nine per cent sure they're all genuine.'

'You can tell me about that later. The point is that they want this sword desperately, they think you have it, but they don't know where you are. I know, your parents know, but I haven't passed that information on to anyone else. All the same, they will be looking for you. And they will keep Naomi alive until they can offer you an exchange again.'

'You talk about "they". Who are they? What do they want?'

'I told you. They want the sword.'

'Then give it to them.'

Simon rubbed his hand across his face. He'd known this wasn't going to be easy.

'It's not that simple, Jack. Hear me out. We don't know precisely who these people are, but we're building a picture and we don't like what we see. The Americans are helping us. The Egyptians too, but they're playing their cards close to the chest as usual. Before I say any more, there's something I need to tell you. You've already signed the Official Secrets Act, am I correct?'

Jack nodded.

'When I was in the SAS, I worked with MI6 in Iraq.'

'Good. You know the score. Jack, I'm with MI6 in Cairo.'

'I'd rather guessed that. But if you're with intelligence...'

'Emilia was too. Quite right. We agreed she would never break cover to you. Partly because your old SAS connections might have created a conflict of interest, but mainly because she had a much higher security clearance than you. She was afraid to risk creating a barrier between you both.'

'Higher than me? How's that? She was just your secretary.'

'Actually, Jack, she was my boss. She ran the intelligence section in the Cairo embassy. I've taken her place.'

'Why are telling me all this, Simon? All these revelations. First Naomi, now Emilia. What's it all about?'

'Jack, we need you to help us. We need to find whoever is behind this group and stop them They have something belonging to you, you have something they want badly.'

'How bad is that?'

Simon stood and went to the fireplace. The fire had burnt down and it was growing chilly again. He bent and took an armful of logs and tossed them on the embers. Jack watched him in silence.

'Sorry,' said Simon. 'I'm still a bit parky.'

He returned to his chair.

'Do you have the sword with you here, Jack? Can I see it?'

'I didn't know what else to do. It got packed with my other things. There was just so much going on. It came over with other things the embassy sent. The letter as well.'

'So it's still safe?'

'I put it in a drawer, and I haven't looked at it or the letter since then.' He leant back in the chair, then straightened and got to his feet. 'Come over here,' he said.

There was a dresser at one side of the little kitchen.

Jack opened a drawer and took out the sword, which had been kept with its scabbard. Next to it was an envelope containing the letter from Zayd ibn Thabit. He took all three items across to the kitchen table and laid them there.

Jack explained how they had come into his possession and recounted the testimony of the letter from Zayd. He also told him about the red-striped cloth and the Hadhramaut sandals, as well as their significance.

They went back to the living-room and sat down at the fire. The logs had caught and were sending bright flames up towards the chimney. For minutes, they sat watching the flames grow in strength. The wind had caught in the chimney, puffing and blowing, and from time to time sending down a gust that knocked the flames into a sudden panic and sent a million sparks roaring upwards.

Ill at ease, Jack got to his feet again and went to the window, pulling back a curtain and looking out into the darkness and the snow in it, made visible by the light that came from the room. He was tired, and he realised that his self-imposed exile was about to end. Simon Henderson hadn't come all this way, through a freezing Scottish winter, just to pass the time of day. He'd dealt with the Secret Intelligence Service before. He

120

knew they weren't pussy-cats.

'Simon, how did you know about the sword?'

Simon shrugged.

'You told me yourself, Jack. Shortly after the murders. You said you had something belonging to Mehdi Moussa, a sword belonging to the Prophet, or so you thought. After you came here, I began to pick up references to a sword. One of our informers told us about an Islamist group who were asking questions. It's the people who have Naomi. They want your sword. It says so in that letter. What it doesn't say is why they want it. They want it for a specific purpose.'

'Which is?'

He went back to his chair and sat down. The coffee had made him restless, that and the news that Naomi was alive and being held hostage.

Simon took his eyes from the fire.

'This group has been working under deep cover for years, and we're only just starting to realise how powerful it has become. Its leader is a man called Muhammad, not the most helpful of names from our point of view. But this Muhammad is a rather important man. He has documents which claim to prove he's a descendant of the last Abbasid Caliph. He intends to proclaim himself as the new leader of Islam, whereupon he will launch a jihad against the West that will make al-Qaeda seem like choirboys. But he can't do that until he has one thing. He needs the sword, Jack. He needs to stand up with the sword of the Prophet in his hand. When he does that, fighters will flock to him from every corner of the Islamic world.

'He's out there now, Jack. We've seen his

shadow, felt his hand, smelt him crossing our paths. He's looking for the sword, he'll stop at nothing to get it, and if he chooses to order a jihad, there will be a bloodbath the like of which mankind has never seen.'

'A bloodbath? You mean a terror campaign?'

Simon did not answer at once. When he did, his voice had changed.

'Not quite. The thing is, we think he is trying to put his hands on a nuclear device. A bomb big enough to wipe out a city, perhaps. London, possibly, maybe New York. And that may only be the start.'

Chapter Fifteen

WHISKY GALORE

The Road to Loch Killin
The same evening

Years in the mountains of Afghanistan had taught Rashid what it meant to be cold. Scotland was cold, but not as cold as the high reaches of the Afghanistan border on the Hindu Kush and the Himalayas. Off the main highway, night had come down like the black wings of Azrail, the angel of death.

He stopped briefly to study the track ahead. Switching off the headlights, he got out of the car and let his eyes adjust to the darkness. He'd come through a long stretch of pines, but now the way before him lay open. As his night vision improved, he saw what he'd come looking for: two tiny lights up ahead. The lights remained steady. Not a vehicle, he decided. The lights of a dwelling.

He decided to leave the car and go the rest of the way on foot. Taking snowshoes from the boot, he slipped them on, then fished out the sniper's rifle he'd brought for the job, together with the Colt pistol he used as a back-up.

He took a breath of cold mountain air and told himself it was all but over now, and that the sword would be in his hands before midnight. He'd ring his brother once it was in his hands. There'd be no need to keep the girl any longer. Muhammad would cut her throat and throw the body in the Nile.

Bailebeag Cottage
The same evening

'What about Osama bin Laden?' Jack asked. 'Isn't he still in Afghanistan? He wants to bring back the Caliphate. Won't he have something to say about this competition?'

'Bin Laden's dead, Jack. The competition is close to taking over. With the sword in his hands, Muhammad will control every radical Islamic group in the world. He already has followers deep inside al-Qaeda, Hizbullah, Hamas, the Muslim Brotherhood – just about everywhere.'

Simon seemed about to go on, but he faltered and grew silent.

Jack picked up a long poker and used it to rearrange the logs on the fire. Sparks rushed upwards like demons out of hell. Sap ran out of the largest log and ran spitting into the flames.

'Jack,' Simon said, 'there's something else. I'm not sure how significant it is, but you should know it anyway. This man Muhammad had a grandfather who was an associate of Hajj Amin al-Husseini. Ring any bells?'

Jack shook his head.

'Somebody I should know?'

'By name, yes, you probably do. He was the Palestinian leader back in the twenties through to the forties, the Grand Mufti of Jerusalem.'

Jack nodded.

'Yes, of course. I know who you mean now.'

'You know that Husseini became a close ally of Hitler and spent most of the war helping the Nazis and planning the extermination of the Jews in the Middle East? That he wanted to build a concentration camp in Nablus.'

'Vaguely.'

'He was a bad lot. He helped organise the pro-Nazi coup in Iraq in 1941. A year or two later, he set up a Waffen SS Division of Bosnian Muslims who went on to slaughter ninety per cent of Bosnia's Jews. They became favourites of Himmler. Had their own military school in Dresden.

'Well, after the war, Husseini was branded a war criminal, but he escaped through Switzerland and France and turned up in Cairo, along with a lot of other Nazis. He was welcomed as a hero, and when Nasser took control, Egypt became a safe haven for dozens of war criminals. Of course,

Nasser himself had started life as a member of Young Egypt, the biggest Arab Nazi movement.'

'Where's this all leading?'

'Husseini stayed in Cairo till the early sixties. He kept busy. In 1951, he arranged the assassination of King Abdullah of Jordan. He worked with his Nazi friends to spread books like *Mein Kampf* through the Arab world. It's still a bestseller.' Jack frowned.

'I know. You see it everywhere on the bookstalls.'

'The Mufti was born in Jerusalem, but he'd studied in Cairo, at al-Azhar, and he had family in Egypt. You'll have heard of one of his close relatives at least: Yasser Arafat. Now, here's the thing. This man Muhammad seems to be a member of Husseini's family as well. Emilia thinks ... sorry, thought ... thought he had links with Nazi circles in Cairo. Still has them.'

Jack found this hard to believe.

'Nazis? Surely they're all dead?'

'Not quite all. Alois Brunner, Eichmann's assistant, still lives in Damascus. In the Meridian Hotel. There are others in other Arab capitals. Several lived in Baghdad under Saddam Hussein. Saddam was brought up by an uncle who was a ringleader in the Mufti's 1941 pro-Nazi coup. Husseini himself only died in 1974. Fascism is alive and well in the Middle East, Jack. Have you never seen film of a Hizbullah rally? Or Hamas? Using the Hitler salute? All those posters with "God Bless Hitler" on them? Emilia thought that there were children of ex-Nazis still active in some Arab countries, and that the circle that started around Husseini in Cairo was in its third generation. And she thought Muhammad was their great white hope.'

'Why are you telling me all this?' Jack asked.

'Because you need to know. You have the sword. You know the background. You speak fluent Arabic. You know how to take care of yourself. And you have a closer link to these people than anyone in UK or US intelligence.'

'For God's sake, Simon, I'm just an academic nowadays. I gave up fighting years ago. I didn't really like it that much. My expertise is in obscure texts in medieval Arabic. I'm a nerd, Simon, a dull citizen of the unexciting city of scholarship. I can't be of the slightest help to you.'

'On the contrary. All that makes you convincing. You have a perfect background. Not cover, a real life lived in universities, real contacts in several Muslim countries, a real knowledge of these matters. I want to give you the chance to take revenge for Emilia, and to get Naomi back. I want you to act as bait. Let word get out that you have the sword. Then we'll see who comes sniffing round.

'Pack the sword and the letter up safely, Jack. Make sure no harm comes to them. We're going back to Cairo. One of the senior people in the embassy has opened up a channel to the Saudis. That's another reason we need the sword so urgently.'

'The Saudis? I don't see the link.'

'Isn't it obvious? The Saudi dynasty claims to lead the Islamic world because they control the twin holy cities, Mecca and Medina. This chap Muhammad threatens to upstage them, put them out of business entirely. He may even launch a jihad in Arabia, maybe take control of Mecca. That way he'd get his hands on the oil money, and make himself look all the more like the real article. The Saudis want the sword. With it, they'll come out on top.'

'The Saudis finance terrorism, Simon.'

'Let us take care of that, Jack. You need to concentrate on getting Naomi back.'

'You'd best stay the night, then. We can leave in the morning.'

Simon shook his head.

'Pack your things now, Jack. There's no time to lose. We're leaving here tonight.'

Chapter Sixteen

A SHOT IN THE DARK

Loch Killin
12.21 a.m.

Darkness lay on the earth like a conjuror's blindfold. The only light in the frozen world was the yellow beam of the torch Simon carried, its batteries growing weaker now, as they made their way down towards the narrow road somewhere below. Jack had been driven here in his landlord's car, and had no other means of transport. He carried a rucksack on his back. The sword and letter were inside, together with everything else he'd scrabbled together before leaving: his wallet, his passport, his favourite photographs of Emilia and Naomi.

Snow was still falling, driven into their bare faces by a strong wind from the north, a wind that carried snow clouds from the Arctic, cold and bitter. The thermometer outside the cottage had read minus ten centigrade – no record, but little comfort for anyone out in it. Both men knew that, if they got lost and were forced to spend a night and more outside, they could lose their lives to the cold.

The snow was eighteen inches deep, more where drifts had formed. Jack had fetched two pairs of snow shoes from the lean-to where the cottage equipment was stored, along with a walking pole for each of them. It was slow going, but steady. They oriented themselves at first by putting the cottage at their backs, but before long it was out of sight, beyond the reach of Simon's torch.

Suddenly, the snow stopped. Above them, a mighty rent had opened in the heavens, and in its emptiness they could see the moon, two days past its first quarter, surrounded by stars. This heavenly light was reflected in the snow at their feet. Visibility increased dramatically, and with it, their anxiety about finding the path back to the car diminished. Simon switched off his torch.

The going was easier, since they could now see the way ahead, but it was no better underfoot. The deep snow forced them to lift their feet high at every step, the snowshoes clumsy and dragging. All around them, tiny crystals sparkled in the moonlight.

Without cloud cover, the temperature dropped further, freezing the surface of the most recent snow. They saw the road ahead, marked by snow poles. It would still be several miles until they reached the car, but at least they could stay on a straight path.

'Simon, there's something I have to know. You were impatient to get away tonight, said you didn't want to wait till morning. Why the hell are we out here in the dark?'

Simon slowed to catch his breath.

'You said you had nowhere to put me up.'

'I was lying. You knew that. Why tonight? Why not first light?'

Simon came to a halt. His breath lay on the chill air like candy floss.

'OK, you deserve to know. I think I was followed out here. I made some standard manoeuvres, tried to lose him, but I can't be sure I did.'

'Followed? By whom?'

Simon shook his head.

'No idea. Somebody who wants to catch up with me. There have been a few times before. I think it's someone from the Islamist group I mentioned. Someone we don't want to meet.'

Their pace quickened. The freezing air penetrated to their lungs, constricting and hurting them. Their breath came in short gasps. By now, their legs were tiring. Unaccustomed to walking on snow, both men's muscles protested at the unusual punishment laid on them. Jack felt as though an iron bar were tightening about his chest. His head ached, and his eyes stung from the bitter air. His outdoor clothing had never

129

been intended for conditions quite like these.

They reached the first snow pole. Judging by the slope, the best way forward was to their left.

'Let's rest a bit,' Jack said. 'My legs are seizing up.'

'There's nothing to sit on.'

'We can clear a space.'

Minutes later, they had scooped out enough snow to expose a dry circle on which Simon placed a canvas square from his rucksack. Just getting off their legs was an enormous relief, but as they rested they grew colder.

'We can't stay here long, Jack,' said Simon. 'If we fall asleep, we'll be dead by morning.'

'Another five minutes, then we'll move on.'

Simon turned his head to nod, and, as he did so, he caught sight of something on Jack's parka. A second passed as he realised what it was, then he was on top of his friend, pushing him back into the snow.

'What the...'

Jack barely got two words out before there was a hissing sound, followed by a cry from Simon, and the sensation of his body slumping heavily onto Jack's. A series of hissing sounds followed, and Jack knew at once they were under fire from a silenced rifle.

'Simon? Are you OK?'

For several moments, there was no answer. Then, in a dramatically weakened voice, Simon whispered, 'I've been hit... Stay down ... as close to the ground ... as possible, keep ... behind the snow we piled up.'

Jack rolled Simon off his back, then helped him

down behind the bank of snow. He lay down beside him, and as he did so heard another hiss pass over his head.

'There was ... a red dot ... on your jacket,' Simon said. 'He targeted you ... with a laser sight. He'll be wearing ... night-vision goggles ... as well.'

Every word seemed strained through blood and pain. Jack was terrified. He'd been in combat before, but this was different. Out here, without a flak jacket or helmet, without a weapon with which to shoot back, he was helpless. What if Simon should die, what if he was left alone out here with a gunman in pursuit? Where would he go, what would he do?

'Where were you hit, Simon? Can you tell?'

'In my side ... it hurts like hell. We've got to ... get out of here...'

'Let me see.'

He picked up the torch, a heavy-duty Maglite.

'Don't ... switch on ... the fucking flashlight, for God's ... sake.'

'I have to see how badly you're wounded. I've done First Aid under fire before.'

'This is ... past First Aid.'

'Let me be the judge of that. I'll use the moonlight. Let me open your jacket.'

Against Simon's protests, Jack unzipped his parka and pulled it back. Simon flinched as the cold hit him like a sledgehammer across his chest.

With such restricted movement, it was hard at first to make out anything. Jack used his fingers, probing gently. They came away wet and sticky with blood.

'I have to staunch this bleeding.'

131

Inside his parka, Jack wore a woollen scarf. He unwound it from his neck and placed it over Simon's wound, then took the long cord that ran through his hood, cut it with his Swiss Army knife, and used it to tie the scarf round Simon's chest.

'Exit ... wound...' murmured Simon. 'Have to ... plug it...'

Jack removed his parka and the two sweaters he was wearing underneath. Gritting his teeth against the biting cold, he unbuttoned his shirt with shaking fingers, then put his parka back on. Removing Simon's down jacket, he ran his hand round the man's other side, his fingers slipping in blood, until he reached the exit wound, a gaping hole that told him Simon would die if he could not get him to a hospital quickly.

He put a rolled-up sweater over the larger wound, then bound it in place with the shirt, using the sleeves to hold it in place. He started to put Simon's jacket back in place. As he did so, Simon cried out several times, as his body started to lose the numbness he'd experienced after the first impact.

'Jesus God! Take that off. It's fucking killing me!'

'We have to stop the blood. If you lose too much, the cold will kill you fast.'

'It'll ... kill me ... anyway. Listen, Jack ... put your hand in ... my pocket, the ... right-hand pocket. There's a gun...Take it and use it ... if you can.'

Jack fished in the pocket and drew out a heavy pistol.

'It's an H&K ... USP Compact ... short barrel ... easy to fire... Takes nine millimetre rounds ... left pocket.'

Jack reached inside the other pocket and brought out a small box of bullets.

'Already ... loaded. You know ... how to use it. Same pocket... Car keys.'

Simon was growing perceptibly weaker by the moment.

'Don't tire yourself,' said Jack. 'I'll call for help on my mobile.'

'Get ... rid of it... Can't let ... authorities know...'

'We have to get you into an ambulance.'

'I won't ... make it.'

There was another hiss and the sound of something hitting the ground a few feet away.

'He's ... moving in,' croaked Simon. He felt his voice dying, knew it would give out in minutes.

'I'll get you to your feet. We can still make it.'

'Don't be ... a fool. You've ... got to ... get out of here ... avenge Emilia's ... death. Naomi ... you have to find ... Naomi. He ... wants the sword, he ... knows you have it. Find the Caliph... Go straight ... to Cairo... Take the sword... Find Scheherazade...'

'Who is Scheherazade?'

'Find Scheherazade... Now go!' Simon's voice picked up strength. 'Crawl as far as you can. When you can, run as fast as possible...'

'But...'

'Don't argue... Go. Find Scheherazade.'

Jack hesitated only moments longer. Even if they sent a helicopter for Simon, he'd never make it to a hospital, and even if he got to an operating theatre, it was almost certain they would never save him.

He got to his knees and started to crawl, dragging his rucksack with him. As he started to move, Simon let out a great yell of pain and got to his feet. He moved for several seconds, as though trying to run. Jack looked back once, and saw the fatal red dot fix on the yellow surface of Simon's jacket. The next moment, he heard the bullet slice the cold air. Simon jerked backwards and lay still. Jack crawled on. His parka was off-white, and against the snow it provided a small degree of camouflage.

The problem was how to get up any real speed on the snow. The snowshoes dragged him back, but without them he would sink too deeply. His pursuer had night-vision goggles and could spot him with a laser device. There was little chance of his making it to the trees, let alone to Simon's car. Cairo was the remotest of destinations in a world that had shrunk to a few yards of snow.

As he crawled, he constantly looked round to see if a red dot had alighted on his clothing. Once, he saw it appear on the snow behind him. He stood then and stumbled forward, using the downward slope to ease his progress. The snow-shoes caught in the snow, tripping him and throwing him forwards several times. He heard a crack and a bullet rushed past, missing him by an inch, or so it seemed.

An idea leapt from nowhere into his mind. Without thinking it through, he used his knife once more to cut the cord that ran through the bottom end of his parka to tie in front. He whipped it out and knelt to remove his snowshoes, his fingers fumbling from cold and fear. Using the cord, he lashed the snowshoes together vertically and stuck them fast in the snow. Removing his parka, he took the gun, bullets, and keys, and transferred them to his trouser pockets.

Hurrying now, he slung the parka over the tottering structure he'd built from the snowshoes, hood on top. The cold bit even more sharply than before, without any outer covering to protect him from it. If he didn't get to the car quickly, he would die from hypothermia.

Leaving the parka in place, he moved, step by infuriating step further down the slope. Glancing back, he saw the red dot appear on the front of the parka, then a bullet ripped through the cloth, dislodging it, sending it and the snowshoes backwards onto the snow.

As the bullet struck, the light began to change. In the sky, the stars were going out. Moments later, dark clouds swallowed the moon. The night was pitch black again.

Jack knew the darkness would provide only temporary cover. The gunman's night-vision capability would soon compensate for the loss of moon- and starlight. Maybe it was time to let his pursuer know he could fight back.

He took the handgun from his pocket and pointed it roughly in the direction he thought the shots had come from. He didn't want to hit anyone, knew he couldn't get even close; he just wanted to say, Back off, I've got a gun. For whatever that was worth.

Closing his eyes tightly, he pulled back on the trigger. There was a loud explosion, and for a moment he was back in Kuwait.

The gunshot echoed off the sides of Carn Easgann Bana, the tall hill to the south whose lower slopes he was skirting. Silence fell. He guessed that the marksman, if he had been tricked into thinking he'd hit him, would be coming down to investigate, but that the gunshot would have warned him to be cautious. No doubt he'd find Simon's body first, before venturing in Jack's direction.

He didn't want to risk going back for the parka, fearing he might lose it in the dark and stumble into Simon's killer. The reality of what he'd just witnessed, of the situation he now found himself in so unexpectedly, the truth about Naomi, all came down on him like a heavy weight landing on him from above. In a sense, he felt betrayed – betrayed and cursed and unloved, as though the universe had set its face against him, as though God or fate or love had rejected him.

The cold had penetrated to his bones. He feared that, if he stumbled, he might not be able to get up again, and if the assassin didn't get him, the naked air would.

He crashed into the first tree, almost stunning himself. Using the branches of the pine to hold himself upright, he steadied himself and got his breath. As he stepped away, he saw the red dot land on the tree, then saw needles and bark leap into the air as another bullet struck. He dodged round the tree and got himself into the little wood. They were Scots pines, as far as he remembered.

Getting behind one tree, pressing himself in as far as he could get, he took out the gun again and aimed back along the path. It seemed ridiculous, like a scene from a bad Western, as if he'd become the Lone Ranger, firing off rapid shots from his six-shooter while Tonto scouted through the forest for a way out. Except that Tonto now lay dead in a pool of frozen blood.

He was forced to keep close to the road instead of burying himself in the woods. Simon's car was here somewhere, and he could never hope to escape without it. He pressed on, passing through the tangle of pines like a bull charging. The going was much better here beneath the trees, where no snow had fallen; but the trees themselves impeded his passage, their branches slashing his face and arms like stinging whips.

He had almost given up hope and was beginning to succumb to the cold when he saw something up ahead. Simon had left his parking lights on, to warn any oncoming traffic of the car's presence out in this fierce darkness. The SUV loomed through the trees like a harbour far out at sea, like Stornoway emerging from behind the midnight waves, a beacon in a vast coldness.

The Range Rover was a brand-new 2006 update of the MkIII, a powerful cross-country vehicle fitted with snow tyres. All that was in his favour, but against him was the fact that the SUV was facing the wrong way. Simon had left the vehicle unlocked. The first thing Jack did on getting in was to turn on the engine and the heating. Still shivering, feeling as though he'd never get warm again, he slipped the automatic into reverse and put his foot on the accelerator. Hemmed in by the woods, a U-turn was out of the question, and a three-point turn would take for ever, or hold him even more tightly. As he drove, the interior started to warm up.

Moments later, he slammed on the brakes. Right behind him, another vehicle sat on the road, its road lights dark, its interior unlit. On either side, the wood extended right to the borders of the road, leaving no space for two vehicles to pass. He was trapped, and the man who had come to kill him was already in firing range.

Chapter Seventeen

A GAELIC PSALM

Loch Killin
The same morning

He drove forward several yards, then used Command Shift to move into manual. With a deft movement born more of fear than skill, he slipped back into reverse and gunned the engine. The rear of the Range Rover – a heavy vehicle weighing in at almost five and a half thousand pounds – crashed hard into the car behind. The blow crushed its front bumper and radiator as the momentum knocked it back and sent it sliding along the track with increasing speed. With its wheels locked, the car in the rear had no choice but to slide across the frozen ground underneath. Behind it, the ruts made by Simon's car and by the gunman's vehicle helped the locked vehicles to pick up speed, all the thrust coming from the Range Rover's powerful engine, a 4.4 litre V8 that produced four hundred horsepower.

The Range Rover's reverse lights were still working, throwing out enough light to give an impression of both sides of the track. He drove using the rear mirror, glancing from time to time at the road ahead, brilliantly lit by the headlights. And as he did so one more time, he realised how very stupid he had been. His hand went out to find the switch to turn off the lights, trying now this, now that button. Looking up again, he saw the red dot on the windscreen, right in front of him. He ducked instinctively, in time to hear the cracking sound as the bullet destroyed the windscreen.

Keeping his head low, holding the wheel as straight as he could, he fiddled for the light switch and found it. One click and the headlights died. The lights in the rear continued, and he now used them to help steer. A second bullet screeched past his ear, and he remembered that his assailant had night-vision goggles.

He stopped dead and bent down to fumble for a control that would open the bonnet. After some frantic searching, his fingers came in contact with a handle on the right-hand side. He pulled it and felt something give.

Jumping out, he raced to the front of the car, found the release, and pushed the bonnet up. Two bullets struck it, but went no further.

Quickly, he got behind the steering wheel again.

He ploughed on, for what seemed an age, concentrating on just one thing – to push the car behind in a straight line. The bonnet acted as a shield, deflecting fire from the rifle, now receding further and further into the distance. Inside, the front of the Range Rover was covered in tiny fragments of windscreen glass, and his own body had been flittered with tiny shards. He could feel them prickle across his upper body, amplifying the sharp stinging of the cold, now raging through the smashed windscreen.

When he next looked, the trees had vanished. Moments later, the road surface changed from soft to hard. The car he was pushing ran straight for a few seconds as he pushed down gently on the brakes. Away from the shelter afforded by the trees, snow slowed both cars down, and they finally came to a halt several yards on the far side of the road, in what was, if he remembered, a turnip field. The other car went on for ten yards more before coming to a complete halt.

There was no time to waste. Taking the pistol, he leapt from the Range Rover and made his way to the car behind. Four shots wrecked its tyres. Finally, he thought, he had a chance.

He put down the bonnet and got back into the SUV. Driving back onto the road, he turned left using full headlights. He knew where he could find clothing and a car in which he could drive the twenty-five miles that would take him further north to Inverness. To spare himself the full blast of the icy wind that came in through the space where the windscreen had been, he drove slowly.

Angus Gilfillan's house was half a mile past Whitebridge. The old man and his wife were the caretakers for Bailebeag Cottage. Even with snow on the ground, they had seldom failed to turn up to bring him fresh provisions and clean the place from top to bottom. They supplemented his diet with eggs and milk and butter, to which Ailsa added cakes and biscuits of her own baking. This largesse extended only as far as their tenant. For themselves, the Gilfillans were a dour Protestant couple who sang metrical Gaelic psalms once a week at a little church in Inverness and sought to find God's ways in a world changed beyond belief.

Jack had come to love them both dearly during the few months he'd been living in the cottage. They were unfailingly kind, always concerned about his welfare, all the more so after he told Ailsa about Emilia and Naomi, and showed them both photographs of his dead loves. He'd been reluctant to speak of any of it at first, but patient Ailsa, sensing something deeply wrong, had prised his secrets from him bit by bit with a skill that surpassed that of the best therapist. Once he'd opened up, he'd used her shamelessly as his counsellor, unburdening himself of agonies, agonies that never ceased to lose their horror, yet somehow hurt less in the presence of her calm, unshockable nature.

Angus was the silent partner, never given to idle talk. But in his way, the old man had been of almost greater help to Jack than his wife. Like her, he was unflappable. What little he did say was often profound and always wise. For some reason, his references to the Bible and Christ were few, as though he recognised that raw religion might alienate his sad tenant. His own life had been hard, but he seemed to have come through poverty and hard work without a single scar.

Between them, the Gilfillans had never once been to the cinema, never owned a hi-fi, never watched television, never attended the theatre, never listened to any but sacred music, never wasted time on a jigsaw puzzle or Monopoly, let alone games of chance, never tasted wine or whisky, and never read a novel or a poem other than the works of Robert Burns. They were, in their quiet fashion, fanatics, living lives closer to the Reformation than the present day. And yet, an act of terror would have been as unthinkable to them as the commission of adultery, or the worship of idols.

When Jack banged on their front door it was something like three o'clock, and the night was still as black as tar. He hated waking them and, he guessed, frightening them; but what choice did he have? Anyone else, however well meaning, would have called the police, and that was the last thing he wanted at the moment.

Several minutes after his first knock, Jack heard Angus's voice, challenging yet more cowed than he'd ever heard it.

'It's me, Angus, Jack Goodrich from Bailebeag. For God's sake let me in.'

There was a sound of a key turning and a bolt being thrown back. The door opened and Jack saw Angus, his thin white hair fanning out from his head as though he'd received an electric shock that very moment. The caretaker's sleep-filled eyes widened until they appeared to be twice their normal size.

'Professor Goodrich! Good heavens, what brings you here in the middle of the night?' He paused suddenly. 'But look at you, man. Look at the state you're in. You must be frozen to death. Come inside with you. I'll poke the fire and Ailsa will get some hot water on.'

Jack didn't argue. He had to return his body to a sensible warmth before frostbite set in, or worse.

Angus helped him to the little parlour and pulled a chair up right in front of the fire. It had been banked down for the night, but Angus took the long poker that stood by the hearth and opened it up again, then tossed on fresh coals from the scuttle.

'It will fetch in a few minutes. Dinna sit too close, it will do you no good to lean over it.'

'Will you draw the curtains, Angus? All the way. Don't let a chink of light get out. And do the same upstairs, if there's a light in your bedroom.'

Angus stared at him for several moments, then turned and hurried upstairs. His wife was already sitting up in bed, having guessed that something serious must be afoot.

'What is it, Angus?' she asked as he entered the bedroom. 'Is it Ian Stewart, the poor man? Has the cancer beaten him at last? Is that Jean knocking on the door?'

He told her who it was.

'The poor devil's near tae death,' he said. 'There's a risk he'll lose his toes and fingers if we don't do something quickly. I'll run a bath and get him in it before the cold in him goes any deeper. While I do that, you'd best stay here and pray for him. He'll need his Creator tonight, that's for sure.'

The curtains had been drawn at bedtime, but Angus went across and pulled them tighter, just to be sure. He had no idea why this was necessary, but the professor had insisted on it.

Ailsa, a thin woman dressed in a heavy flannel nightgown, her grey hair hidden under a plain white cotton cap, glared at her husband.

'I'll pray while I make a pot of hot tea for him tae drink for when he comes out of the bath. Be sure he doesn't stay in it for more than fifteen minutes. And you'd best fetch him down some warm clothes tae put on while the water's running.'

'He'll need more than tea, woman, if he has an empty stomach, which I'm sure he has. I expect he could do with some hot food as well, something light, a few eggs maybe. A cheese omelette, that will see him right.'

Half an hour later, Jack had been bathed, warmed, and fed, and was feeling drowsy. But the thought of sleep appalled him. He knew that if he slept now, anything might happen. What if the killer tracked him here? The snow had stopped falling some time ago, and the SUV tracks would be unmistakable.

'I have to leave,' he said. 'I have to get to Inverness tonight.'

'Man, you must be mad. Here, get this whisky down your throat. It's entirely medicinal and is kept in this house for no other purpose.'

144

'I've had enough whisky for tonight, thanks.'

'Is that what happened?' asked Ailsa, concerned to know how this strange Englishman from Bailebeag Cottage had arrived at her door half dressed, shivering, and waking God's ain folk at past three in the morning. 'Were you drowning your sorrows in drink, was that it?'

'I'm past that, Ailsa,' Jack said.

'Why didn't you just call by and sit up for a talk?'

He looked at them both, wondering what he might have dragged them into, all unknowing. Frail, good-hearted, simple people whose knowledge of the world was severely limited. How could they even start to understand fears like his, the empty spaces of hatred, the wastes of disillusion, the world turned enemy, God-deserted, beyond the reach of their faith and their prayers?

'A man is trying to kill me,' he said, wondering how he could cushion what he said. They had a right to know, he thought. He had brought this on them.

'He's out there now, somewhere. He is probably the same man who killed my wife, and I have now learnt that he kidnapped my daughter. He has already killed someone tonight, and he means to kill me as well, if he can find me.'

Not for a second did either of his listeners show or express disbelief. Neither Angus nor Ailsa had ever told a lie in their lives, and they did not question what Jack had just told them.

Angus got to his feet.

'I'll ring the polis. They can send a bobby in from Fort Augustus or Inverness, they'll be here

145

in a shake of a lamb's tail if I ring them now.'

'Sit down, Angus. And you, Ailsa. If you bring in the police, this man will kill them sooner than let them take him alive. He's an expert marksman, and he is quite ruthless. I have something in that bag so important to them they will hunt me from one end of the earth to the next to get it. I have to take it back to Cairo, where it came from, I have to prevent more deaths.'

He stood and went across to the window, drawing the curtain back by just a fraction. Outside, it was still pitch dark. He saw no sign of anything moving, but had not expected to. Not yet.

'If the police get involved,' he said, 'I will be caught up in their enquiries, and the killings will continue. I may be able to do something to stop them, if only I can get out of this place safely and leave the country without being arrested.'

Ailsa whispered a short prayer before speaking.

'Are you trying to tell us you've done something the police would consider ... criminal?'

Jack shook his head.

'No, but I've been attacked and almost killed. The police will not understand exactly what happened out there tonight. There's one man dead, and if they investigate him, they'll find he worked for the British Secret Intelligence Service, what you probably call MI6. The man who killed him is a terrorist. It could take the British police years to sort it all out, and while they do that more deaths will follow as sure as day follows night. If this man gets his hands on the object in my bag, thousands of people will die.'

He paused. They said nothing. He had brought

them into his world, a world that was as alien to them as their kirk would be to him.

'I need to borrow your car, and you will have to help me hide the Range Rover I came in. If you can find somewhere where it will never be found, so much the better.'

'Can't you drive it yourself?'

'The windscreen's smashed. I'll leave your car in the park at Inverness airport. I'll telephone you as soon as I can, to let you know the bay number. I know that will put you out badly, but I can't lose any more time. Are you willing to help me?'

He looked round, letting the curtain fall back to where it had been. The old couple were sitting with their heads bowed. Angus prayed, at first in a soft voice, then loudly, calling on Jesus to keep Jack safe, calling on God to punish murderers and terrorists. He finished and looked up. Centuries of Presbyterian resilience in adversity glimmered in his eyes.

'There's nae much petrol in the tank,' he said, 'but she'll get you tae Inverness. Where will you go after that?'

'Better I don't tell you, in case you're asked by the police. There's a body up there beyond the woods, but if more snow falls, it may as well lie there till Spring.'

'You can't mean that, surely,' exclaimed Ailsa. 'It would be a terrible sin tae leave a human being out there all that time, unburied.'

'Pray for him, if you like. I'll contact his people, and they'll doubtless send someone to take him away.'

'If they will do that, we'll wait,' said Angus. 'He

can't come tae much harm frozen out there. But it's a sin tae leave him alone. We'll take your car and send it down to the bottom of Loch Ness before first light. I'll take it down tae Foyers, it's verra deep there.'

Jack smiled for the first time since seeking shelter in the little cottage, almost a bothy. Loch Ness averaged a depth of six hundred feet and could swallow all the Range Rovers in the world without even hiccupping. He hoped Nessie wouldn't mind.

While Angus started his old Volvo and got the interior and the driver's seat to warm up, Jack took the Range Rover in order to get it off the road. There was an old building at the back that had served once as a barn, and the SUV fitted into it with plenty of room to spare. Angus promised he'd take it out later. This far north, the sun wouldn't rise till almost 8.30. Foyers wasn't far away. There was plenty of time. Jack worried that there might be more than one killer out there, but he said nothing to alarm the Gilfillans further.

He wanted to hug them, but they were made of sterner stuff than that. Jack, after all, had had years living in Egypt, throwing off his English reserve. They had stood in frosty churches churning out the eerie psalms of the far north: shaking hands was the height of intimacy permitted in such surroundings, and even outside their home they stuck to their principles. Ailsa handed him a pack of cheese sandwiches she'd made in the kitchen, with a flask of milky, sugared tea.

'God go with you,' said Angus. Ailsa repeated the blessing in Gaelic.

Jack felt overcome with emotion, moved by their simple kindness. He hoped their God would look after them as they deserved.

'Stay inside,' he said. 'Don't open the door to anyone. When you've dumped the car, find an excuse and go and visit some friends or relatives. Don't come back home for a week or so. This will pass, but you shouldn't take risks.'

They reassured him that they would be careful, that all would be well, that Jesus would preserve them from harm, and he set off with their homely voices in his ears and several layers of Angus's clothes covering his body. The threat of frostbite had subsided, and although he still had some pain in his fingers, the gentle immersion in warm water seemed to have worked well.

He put down his foot and sped up the road to Inverness.

Chapter Eighteen

A LIGHT IN THE DARKNESS

Loch Killin
Later the same morning
4.55 a.m.

There was no public transport on the east side of the loch. That was why Angus and Ailsa Gilfillan had their ancient Volvo estate, which they used to move equipment and church members from

149

place to place. But the Volvo was in Jack Goodrich's hands and God's keeping this morning, and Angus had no choice but to walk the three miles back from the spot where he'd dumped the Range Rover. It was still too dark to see an inch in front of his face, but he knew the road well and had his old Ever Ready torch to see him safe home.

He'd done what the professor had asked him to, certain he'd done the right thing, although it had seemed a criminal and ungodly waste of an expensive car. The steep banks beyond Foyers had allowed him to send the SUV as near to the bottom as was possible this close to the shore. He'd left the engine idling with footbrake and handbrake both off, then dropped a heavy stone onto the accelerator and jumped back as the car picked up speed and drove itself down into the loch. No doubt it would provide a fine toy for the monster down there. He'd never doubted Nessie's existence, though he and his fellow Rechabites had long debated its ancestry and meaning in the Lord's world, concluding that it was a creature of the devil best left to the Stygian doom in which it had swum from the first days of Creation.

During the last mile, he began to flag at last. All he wanted now was to get home, and eat a hearty bowl of porridge.

He thought it a little odd at first that there was a light ahead of him, then realised it must come from his own cottage. Hadn't Professor Goodrich told them to conceal any lights behind the curtains? It occurred to him that Ailsa must have left the light shining in order to guide him back safely in the dark. He'd get in quickly now, he thought, and draw the curtains again.

She was sitting in a high-backed chair in the kitchen, and a strange man was standing beside her, holding a pistol to her temple. She was terrified, he could see that right away, and no wonder. Her lips were moving silently, in prayer or fright, and he saw how her bladder had given way, and he felt ashamed for her and angry with the man; he wanted to hold her, reassure her, tell her everything was going to be all right, except he knew nothing would ever be right again.

It comforted him strangely, seeing the man there, his eyes like a marauding fox's, bright and malevolent, as full of hatred as his own eyes were full of love, for it meant he'd done no wrong in helping Jack Goodrich, committed no crime in sending that great ugly beast of a car to the bottom of Loch Ness. What he had done wrong was to leave Ailsa here unprotected while he'd gone out. Now a man was holding a gun to her head, a man who'd already killed someone tonight, a secret agent of some sort, if the professor was to be believed, which he clearly was. The gunman was dressed in one of those enormous parkas they sold in Inverness, like an eiderdown quilt with sleeves and a hood.

He smelt something on the thin cold air – tea and the smell of food heated up from before. She must have offered the stranger food, seeing him come in cold and hungry, or perhaps he'd pulled the gun right from the start, ordered her to feed him. Angus had no gun himself, and could not have used it to kill a man. Unless perhaps now,

now he saw Ailsa threatened, and the man's eyes on him, so cold.

The stranger might have been a Gypsy or an Arab or an Italian, Angus thought, desperately trying to relate the killer to what he knew. He remembered that Jack Goodrich had lived in Egypt, that his wife and daughter had been killed there. Well, the wife at least: it now seemed the daughter had been abducted. By this man, Professor Goodrich had thought.

'Would you like to explain just what it is you're doing with that gun in your hand so close tae my good wife's head?'

The gunman looked at him as though he wanted an excuse to pull the trigger or turn the gun on this old man who'd broken in on him.

'Tell me where he is, where he went to. Your wife has shown me round your house, and I've seen for myself that he's no longer here. If you do not tell me the truth, I will kill her. I do not make a pretence. I have killed many times, hers will be the least death to me. I swear before God that I will kill her. Tell me where he has gone.'

Angus felt a great calm as he spoke. God was with him, he thought, as was only right in these last moments.

'Where has who gone? There's only been Ailsa and myself here this night.'

'You're up very early for a man who's been with his wife all night.'

'This is farming country. We rise early as the Lord intended. Please put down your gun. You are frightening her.'

'I will put down the gun if you tell me where

152

Goodrich has gone. I may decide not to shoot her, I may hurt her first. If you lie to me, I will hurt her. Would you like that on your hands, old man?'

'You are badly mistaken. No one of that name has been here tonight. No one but herself and myself.'

'I followed his tracks here, tracks made by the car he' – he paused, seeking to incriminate Jack – 'the car he stole from me. You've been harbouring a criminal, a madman. Just tell me where he is.'

'I saw tracks as well, mister. Outside, where you would expect tae see tracks. They head on up the road. I canna say where they're headed. There's lots of roads that way.'

'He turned in here first. I've seen the tracks leading into your shed.'

'Those are my own tracks. I took the car out and left it with a friend. I walked home. I do that most days.'

'I told you I would hurt her if you lied. You must be taught a lesson.'

Suddenly the gunman grabbed Ailsa by the wrist and pulled her, ignoring her protests, to the other side of the kitchen. They ended up next to the stove.

When Ailsa had made him tea in a vain attempt to calm him down and get him talking, the killer had seen her place her old-fashioned kettle on the gas hob. Now, he put his gun down and turned the knob to full. Blue and yellow flames leapt up.

Gripping Ailsa further up her forearm, he thrust her hand into the flames and held it fast. She screamed and screamed again, and there was a smell of charring flesh on the air, and he kept her hand fixed hard in the flames until the skin started to turn bright red, then black. Angus made a move towards him, but the stranger already had his gun in his other hand again and was pointing it straight at Ailsa's head.

'I'll tell you where he is!' shouted the old man, desperate to spare his darling wife a moment's more pain.

'Tell him nothing!' she cried, fighting her pain until it overwhelmed her. A moment later, she had fainted away.

The gunman took her hand from the flames and let her fall senseless to the floor.

'Best to tell me now, while there's time to take her to hospital,' he said. 'Goodrich is nothing to you. Not family, not a friend. Tell me where he is going.'

'You ken well enough,' answered Angus, frantic with concern for Ailsa. They'd been married for over fifty years, his own hands tingled with the pain in hers.

'I know the direction, but it's too late for me to catch up with him now. He must have told you his final destination.'

'Why would he tell me that? Look, you've hurt my wife, she's badly burnt. Let me ring for an ambulance.'

'No need,' said the killer.

He put the gun back in his right hand, pointed it at Ailsa, and shot her in the head. Her body jerked violently and was still.

Angus went numb with shock. His God had deserted him, the promise of a lifetime spent in prayer, wrapped in psalms and sermons, had

154

been broken and lay as lifeless on the kitchen floor as his murdered wife.

'You may as well kill me too,' he said. 'For there's not a word I would utter now unless to call God's curse on your head. You will burn in hell for what you've done, and neither God nor I will have the slightest pity.'

A thousand yards away, on his death bed, old Ian Stewart lay wide awake, riddled with cancer. Beside him, his wife Jean crooned to him, old songs, 'Mo Shuil Ad Dheidh'; 'My Love is Like a Red, Red Rose'; 'Will Ye No Come Back Again?', songs they'd known when courting, and now him dying in their bed, and his hair white against the cotton pillow, long now, for he hadn't wanted it cut and would never have it cut again.

The second shot rang out crisp in the early morning air. She wondered who could be out at this hour. There had been all that shooting earlier. It was still too dark to see a rabbit or a hare. Unless it was one of those poachers who had things they could see in the dark with? What puzzled her was that it had not sounded like a shotgun. A pistol maybe? Was that what they used nowadays?

Jean finally got to her feet and went downstairs. He liked a little tea and digestive biscuits around this time. There'd be another pot later for the nurse, young Mary McGregor, who would be here in about an hour's time. She hoped Mary would have the morphine with her. He'd need it badly before the day was out.

She laid a tray for them both, napkins and

155

doilies as was their habit, biscuits for him, oat cakes for her. She'd have her full breakfast later, after Mary got here.

The kettle had just boiled when she heard the knock on the door. She straightened her hair and went to open it, wondering who it could possibly be at this time. Perhaps Ian's little angel of mercy had made it out earlier than she'd hoped. Who else could it be, after all?

PART THREE

PART THREE

Chapter Nineteen

THE WINDS OF PARADISE

Cairo
Monday, 4th January
8.45 a.m.

Muhammad al-Masri was tense with excitement. Not many hours ago, his brother had told him he'd finally tracked the Englishman down, tracked him like a desert fox to his lair. The sword would be in his hands any time now, and word would go out at once that the Caliph, the Shadow of God on earth, lived. Sword in hand, he would launch the last jihad against the powers of the earth.

The door opened and a small boy came into the room. He was a boy of average height, aged about twelve, with jet-black hair and ears that stuck out on either side. He was wearing a blue school uniform that was about one size too big for him, and his unease was clear. His name was Farid, and he had volunteered to be a martyr. He'd come to Cairo from Gaza, where children put on mock suicide belts at the age of four, dressing up, not for play, but to become accustomed to the thought of wearing the real thing once they come of age.

Al-Masri welcomed him with a beaming smile.

'Farid,' he said. 'You look very fine in your new clothes.'

Farid looked blankly at him.

'If I'm to die, sir, I want to die a Muslim, in Muslim clothes.'

The older man shook his head and smiled again.

'The moment you enter paradise, Farid, God will know you are a Muslim. Many wear the clothes of a Muslim, but have the hearts of non-believers. You have the heart of a true Muslim, the heart of a *mujahid*, the heart of a martyr. The Prophet himself will be there to greet you. The angels will sing your praises throughout eternity.'

Farid, who had heard about paradise every day since he could speak, brought things down to earth.

'What about my parents, sir? Will they be looked after? And my brothers and my sister?'

Al-Masri nodded. It was routine practice to take financial care of the families of martyrs.

'For the rest of their lives. You have my word.'

Farid knew that his older brothers, Walid and Nasser, and his fourteen-year-old sister Fatima, who would soon be married, were themselves enrolled on al-Masri's roll-call of future martyrs. He thought of the happiness when he would meet them all in heaven.

'Is it time yet?' he asked, fearing his courage would fail him. Al-Masri glanced at his wristwatch.

'Yes,' he said. 'It is time.'

Farid felt the cool winds of paradise rushing

towards him. In minutes, he would make the transition from human being to martyr. The Caliph himself had told him you took a single breath in this world, and the next in paradise, or that it was faster than taking a single step from one side of a straight line to the other. In less than a second, his pulverised and bleeding flesh would be resurrected in a martyr's immortal body, a body of paradise. In a celestial palace, he would never sicken or grow tired or old or die a second time.

If he was honest, he felt sick. All he really wanted was to go back to his mother. God alone knew how he'd said goodbye to her an hour ago, and her neither knowing nor suspecting. He felt panic rising inside, terror that he was about to die, and what if it was all for nothing?

The school building was just across the road. Cars were drawing up at the gates, depositing children, and driving away again. Other pupils arrived on foot, all wearing uniforms just like his, girls as well as boys. They belonged to a wide range of nationalities, but most of them seemed to be British. This was the British School in Cairo, an old institution in the wealthy quarter of Zamalek, founded to teach the sons and daughters of expatriates. As the years had passed, many middle-class Egyptians had started to send their children here, some Americans, some Jews, and expat Europeans like the Dutch or Danish, who didn't have schools of their own.

Three days earlier, a British attack near Basra had killed thirty insurgents, including the leading al-Qaeda organiser in Iraq. He had been a personal friend of al-Masri's. They had trained and fought together, first in Afghanistan, then in northern Iraq. Today, the Caliph would take revenge for his friend's death. This would be a blow the British would never forget. After this, they would leave Egypt in droves.

The man standing next to Farid was a university lecturer, a close associate of al-Masri's whose brain was behind much of the group's strategy. He spoke excellent English, which he'd learnt at Cairo University.

Choosing a moment when the entrance to the school was packed, he walked Farid across the road and went up to one of the two teachers standing by the small wrought-iron gate, ticking off students as they went in.

'Excuse me,' he said.

The teacher, who had been talking to a teenage girl, turned and smiled. She was new to the school and just starting to familiarise herself with the pupils and their parents.

'Yes, of course, Mr...?'

'Sabri. Tariq Sabri. This is my son, Farid. Farid has just been enrolled in your school, and this is his first day. He's a bit nervous. I wonder if you wouldn't mind showing him to the morning assembly, and after that ... to wherever he will need to be. He's starting in the second form.'

'Has he seen Mr McKenzie?'

'Two days ago. Everything's in order.'

Pupils had started to hurry. Assembly was due to start in a couple of minutes. The teacher, Miss Evans, took in the situation and reached for Farid's hand. Farid drew his hand back, and she smiled. He did not smile back.

'I won't eat you,' she said.

Turning to the supposed Mr Sabri, she smiled again.

'Assembly's about to start. Mr McKenzie doesn't like stragglers, and we don't want young Farid here to get off to a bad start, do we? Perhaps I'll see you again. If Farid's in Form Two, he's sure to be in one of my classes.'

Sabri shook her hand, then bent down and whispered in Farid's ear.

'God has blessed you already, Farid. When you get to paradise, ask God to grant me the same blessing. The martyrs are waiting for you. God is waiting for you.'

Rising, he smiled at Miss Evans. The next moment, he was gone, and the teacher was hurrying Farid along to the assembly hall.

Farid's head was racing with conflicting emotions. He wanted to be with his mother, but he could not face the shame if he backed down. Everyone he'd ever known had lauded martyrdom as the highest of human aspirations. His own heroes from childhood on had been, not footballers but shahids, suicide martyrs from Gaza and the West Bank. There were posters of them on his bedroom wall, the way an English boy might have pictures of David Beckham or Wayne Rooney on his. He knew their names and how they had died.

The suicide belt, taped to his naked waist, chafed as he ran. Snatches of prayers tumbled through his increasingly chaotic thoughts. He fought back tears, for martyrs never cry. The

163

teacher thought him simply frightened by being rushed into a new school, among so many strangers. She decided to take him under her wing.

With the help of prayers he'd recited since childhood, and others he'd learnt from al-Masri, he drove the negative thoughts out of his head. It was time to concentrate, time to focus his mind on the act of jihad he was about to carry out.

Miss Evans ushered him through a double door and into the assembly hall, a square room built to accommodate the three hundred or so pupils of the senior school, along with staff. The headmaster was standing on the stage, dressed in an academic gown, tufts of white hair sprouting on either side of his head. A row of teachers sat behind him on chairs, and to one side the school music group was preparing for a rendition of 'Abide with me'. It was a scene that might have been found in any private school in Britain, though the range of nationalities was greater.

Miss Evans, worried that she herself would be the last on stage, spotted an empty chair towards the middle of the room, among the second formers. She hustled Farid there and told him she would come for him after assembly, then rushed off towards the stairs leading to the stage, with the eyes of the headmaster on her all the way.

Farid made his way to his seat, watched by curious eyes. The moment he sat down, he felt contaminated. All around, there were unbelievers with blond hair and white faces, next to darker-coloured pupils who might have been Muslims from unreligious families. The boy next to him looked Chinese, and he knew the Chinese were idol-worshippers. Another boy wore an Indian-style turban, and one of his teachers had told him Indians who weren't Muslims worshipped the Golden Calf. There were girls in short skirts, girls older than himself, who should have been married by now but who were sitting with boys. Some even wore make-up. It was a den of vice, and he knew God would thank him for destroying it.

The music started, and at a signal from the headmaster, the whole school stood. Farid alone stood without a hymn book, had no idea what a hymn book was. All at once, they began to sing.

Farid slipped his right hand into his jacket pocket. His finger found the button connected to the belt. He took a deep breath and let it out again. The last thing he saw was a girl in the row in front of his, who had turned to smile at him, and the last thing he felt was the touch against his finger as he pressed the button down hard. He didn't hear the explosion, didn't see the blood, didn't feel the shock-wave. His angels were calling him to God.

Chapter Twenty

EYELESS IN CAIRO

Cairo
Monday 4th January
10.00 a.m.

He arrived in Cairo with the clothes on his back and the bag he'd taken from the cottage. The day before, he'd caught the 9.00 a.m. Inverness flight to Heathrow by a margin of ten minutes. The plane had stopped in Edinburgh, but he'd reached Heathrow with plenty of time to transfer to Terminal 4 and book a seat on an Egyptair flight to Cairo that arrived just before 10.00 that night. On both flights, he'd done his best to snatch some much-needed sleep, but the confusion in his mind made it impossible to relax properly. When he did sleep, his dreams were sick and ugly, filled with dread of past and impending death. Stepping down from the plane, he felt for a moment as if he was arriving home, except that he wasn't. He had no home now. The person most perfect in the world to him now was in forced seclusion somewhere, out of reach and in the greatest danger.

He'd telephoned the Gilfillans from Heathrow, but there'd been no reply. He'd worried about it all the way to Cairo, and had woken this morning with a niggling sense that something was wrong.

While in Heathrow, he'd made a call to the 24-hour helpline for his London bank and discovered that he'd become rich overnight. The money for Emilia's insurance – a considerable amount – had come in about one week ago; but before that an even larger amount had been sent from an organisation he'd never heard of, Millennium Insurance 6 Ltd. He'd asked the operator to investigate the payment, thinking it a massive error on someone's part, but she reassured him it had come directly from Coutt's Bank in London on a draft authorised and signed by a director of the company, whose initials were SH.

It was only after hanging up that the initials of the fake corporation and director added up. Generosity following the death of a valued employee? Or a fund to draw on in his search for his wife's killers? Either way, the two sums meant he'd never have to work again, something of an irony since he'd probably be as dead as Emilia and Simon in the next few days.

Thinking it over, he rang the Garden City branch of Citibank, where he and Emilia had done most of their banking. Another large sum had gone into their account there several days earlier. Obviously, Simon had been thinking ahead. He imagined a future of form-filling and corridor-treading ahead of him before remembering that life was short, and his life likely to be shorter than most.

He was staying in the cheapest hotel he could find, the New Palace on Soliman El Halaby, between Ramses railway station and the Egyptian Museum. It was a legend among backpackers: he

167

could have had a bed in the male dormitory for the equivalent of two and a half dollars, but settled for a single room at the outrageous price of four.

With all that money sitting in two bank accounts, he could have stayed at the Four Seasons or the Nile Hilton without blinking at their prices. What a mistake that would have been, he thought. Downtown in this backpackers' paradise, he could remain anonymous. Any of Cairo's upmarket hotels served as a meeting place for people he'd prefer to avoid, and their guest lists would be computerised and vulnerable to prying eyes.

He'd checked in under a false name, Jim Corbett, and had avoided handing over his passport by means of a substantial bribe to the desk clerk. As soon as possible, he'd arrange for a forged passport in Jim's name, in order to start building cover for himself as a first-time Brit tourist come to explore the sights. That was the plan, at least, though God knew how he was supposed to go about it. Starting tomorrow, he'd look for a cheap room to rent, somewhere no questions would be asked.

His own house was still there in the cool green suburb of Garden City, within walking distance of the embassy; but he was sure it would be the last place he should go, that if anyone was still on his trail, that was exactly where they would look. It was probably being watched at this very moment, he guessed. In any case, it held too many memories, too many regrets. He'd find a place somewhere out of the way, he'd be out of the hotel by tomorrow night. But today, he had other things to do.

He'd woken at dawn to the long-familiar tones of half a dozen muezzins chanting the call to prayer. Most of them were recorded and played over loudspeakers. One in particular crackled the whole way through. But the meaning was clear enough: it's time to get up and pray. 'Prayer is better than sleep' they chanted. He wondered again about the Gilfillans, tried to figure out where they might be. He hoped Angus had managed to get rid of the SUV.

His first goal was to find Scheherazade, whoever she was, and to do that he imagined he'd have to get to someone at the British embassy, someone who'd worked with Simon Henderson, someone who'd worked with Emilia, maybe someone who'd met Naomi and remembered her and what had been done to her and her mother. He could think of plenty of people he'd met at parties and receptions, plenty of Emilia's co-workers, but he had no idea who was just plain embassy or consulate, and who was MI6/SIS.

Before heading for the embassy, he decided to buy himself some clothes. Staying anonymous was going to be a problem. To get money, he'd have to turn up at a branch of his bank, but he wanted to avoid the one he'd always used.

He could see complications ahead, especially if he turned up dressed as he now was and asked to withdraw a large sum from a wealthy account. Equally, he couldn't arrive at the embassy in his present clothes. Fortunately, he'd lived in Cairo long enough to know how to get round obstacles. It was what expats were good at. They knew the right people, whom to ask for what in which ministry, where to find the best deals, whose brother knew whose cousin. The problem was, he couldn't do anything of the usual expat things, couldn't use any of his regular contacts. It came to him forcibly that he was on his own.

His dilemma was simple: if he wanted to blend in with the rest of the city, he needed to preserve his downmarket image, perhaps even try to pass himself off as an Arab or, better still, a pale-skinned Circassian from Jordan. An unkempt look would improve his chances of being believed, but by the same token, it would almost certainly see him stopped at the embassy gates by a polite but firm guard.

The cheap shower gave him alternating bursts of hot and cold water, but it was enough to take away the grime of travel. Drying himself with a tiny towel, he dressed as well as he could. As he did so, he wondered about the explosion he'd heard an hour ago. Where had it been? Had anyone been killed this time? Or injured?

Stepping out of the hotel onto the raucous street plunged him at once into the whirlpool of insanity that was Cairo. Dust from the city's cement plants coloured the air a toxic grey-white. Sand blown in from the Western Desert added a pale ochre hue. Exhaust fumes from cars, buses, and motorbikes belched out across every street and every intersection.

De-sensitised by his time in Scotland, where the air was as pure as it gets, his nose and throat immediately responded to the morning smog by seizing up. He knew that, by the end of the day, he'd be coughing up smut and blowing blood from his nose. His doctor had once told him that breathing in the polluted atmosphere of Cairo was the equivalent of smoking thirty cigarettes a day. Given a few days, he'd readjust; but nothing would ever take the pall of dust away.

The sound of the city was overpowering after the deep silences of the lakes and mountains. There was a constant blare of motor horns, as drivers leant their hands on them in the vain belief that loud noises could increase their speed. Every inch of Cairo was in permanent gridlock. Whether you drove an old banger or rode in the back of a limousine, you'd move at a snail's pace. The only thing the limousine had in its favour was air-conditioning.

Chapter Twenty-One

AN ASSISTANT CHARGÉ

Cairo
10.35 a.m.

He used the ATM at the branch on Gezira Street in Zamalek. The old joint account had never looked healthier. To avoid drawing attention he withdrew just enough to buy clothes and other necessities.

He did his shopping in the Khan el-Khalili, a noisy, bustling, chaotic fourteenth-century bazaar that catered for practically every modern need. The huge indoor market was a rabbit warren of tiny shops and kiosks that sold everything from books to respectable ladies' nightwear, to tourist gewgaws, to every style of men's clothing except the fashionable.

Passing the perfume sellers around Muski Street, he made his way toward the tailors' shops west of Maydan Husayn, the old square that had once been the centre of medieval Cairo.

Jack blended in easily here, knew several of the shopkeepers by name, and had the patience to strike a bargain. Every stop was punctuated by a glass of mint tea or a tiny cup of coffee, and because Jack spoke fluent Arabic, there were long chats to be had into the bargain. Haggling was essential: without it the shopkeeper would lose face and the customer feel cheated even when he hadn't been. With much hand-shaking and banter, he bought a European-style suit made-to-measure, tailored to a better fit on the spot, a few shirts, a garish tie, new shoes, and extra underwear.

He wore his new clothes and had the rest sent to the hotel by a boy. With the new suit, he looked every bit the businessman. Not very prosperous, granted, but respectable enough. He'd get into the embassy, but knew that he'd have to put on Egyptian clothing as soon as possible. A short walk took him to another shop, where *galabiyyas* were sold in every possible shade of brown and grey. He bought a grey one, and another boy was found to carry it and a grey skullcap back to the hotel, ready for his return.

172

In a different part of the Khan, he found a barber willing to trim and shave him. While he was being seen to, a man in a light gabardine *galabiyya* came in and sat on the bench opposite. He glanced at Jack from time to time, but never caught his eye: he was puzzled, Jack imagined, by the fact that he did not look like a tourist, but was clearly not an Egyptian. A shoeshine boy came and polished his shoes for a few pennies. He was followed by a fortune teller, who promised to tell Jack's future.

'No, thanks,' he said, thinking that the last thing he wanted was to know what might lie ahead.

He took a cab to the embassy in Garden City, promising the driver extra payment if he got there before noon. They plunged into the traffic, which had started to lighten as the time for noon prayers approached. The streets were lined with the flags of a dozen or more countries displayed on lamp-posts, and he remembered that it would soon be the Muslim New Year.

As he stepped out of the cab, he looked up over the security barrier at the imposing façade. The long white building with its tall windows and gleaming pediment spoke of the days when Egypt had been a British colony in all but name. Most of the other embassies seemed gimcrack beside it. It had once been the hub of government in the country; but even if those days of glory were gone, the diplomatic corps still presented a brave and aloof face to the world.

He showed his maroon passport at the barrier and again at the main entrance. A woman in a grey suit appeared and escorted him into the building. He did not recognise her. At a desk in the lobby, he gave his name again, showed his passport a third time, and asked to speak to someone on what he called a security matter of some importance.

'Just a moment, sir.' The desk clerk, a young black man, picked up his phone and pressed a four-digit number. He spoke quickly and inaudibly, then put the phone down.

'Will you please wait on one of those chairs over there, Professor. Someone will come down soon to speak to you.'

He went to the chair and sat. And sat. Time passed slowly, and no one came. A clock ticked somewhere, and after he'd been sitting twenty minutes, sounded the quarter hour. On the wall behind the receptionist, two electric clocks silently displayed the current time in London and Cairo. Once, he went back to the desk, only to be told to be patient. They were checking details upstairs, the clerk said. He would be seen shortly. Jack noticed that no one had smiled at him since he got to the embassy. No one had asked if his business was urgent.

He half expected to see a familiar face; but, although several members of the embassy staff passed through the lobby, passing up and down the broad staircase, no one recognised him, and he recognised no one. The lobby was cool and echoing. Even time seemed frozen there.

A man in a well-pressed black suit came down the stairs and walked purposefully towards him. His hard-soled shoes clicked on the marble floor.

He was smiling, and as he came nearer, he stretched out a hand. It was not a real smile, Jack could see that at once, and when the man took his hand, it was not a real handshake, but a quick squeeze followed by immediate withdrawal.

'Professor Goodman, am I right? Malcolm Purvis, assistant chargé d'affaires.'

'Goodrich,' said Jack. 'My name's Goodrich.'

'Oh, right. Sorry about that.'

His face suggested irritation at his gaffe, and indifference to its effect. He did not seem too pleased to see Jack. Perhaps he'd been called away from lunch or an important meeting. His eyes were set too close together, as though there wasn't enough room for them in his pale patrician face. The lips were thin, the manner assured, the hair cut to the regulation public school length and style.

'Will you come with me, Professor?' he asked. 'I need to hear about what has brought you here. Really, you should have gone to the consulate. They can answer most of your questions. If it's about domestic security.'

'That's not my concern, thank you. I came here about...'

'Let's wait till we get to my office. Idle talk and all that.'

Jack followed him in silence up the stairs and down a long corridor to a door marked 'Assistant Chargé d'Affaires'. Purvis showed him in and pointed him to an armchair while he himself took his place behind a wide mahogany desk. He lifted a piece of paper that was lying on a blotting pad, and fixed his attention on Jack.

'Professor, the note that was passed to me said you were making enquiries about two individuals who, you say, worked or still work in this embassy. The names were Simon Henderson and Emilia Goodrich. I presume the woman is a relative of yours, perhaps your wife. I've looked right through our database, and I'm afraid I can't find any record of those names. Are you sure you haven't made some mistake? Perhaps you could spell the names for me again.'

Jack wrote them down on a pad of paper, just as he had done before. Purvis tapped at his keyboard, his nimble fingers entering and retrieving data. After a couple of minutes, he looked at Jack again.

'Are you sure you aren't making some sort of mistake, old chap?' he asked. 'These names just don't appear. But I have a James and a Susan Henderson.'

'What does he look like? Can you print me out his picture?'

Purvis shook his head.

'Sorry. Security, you know. Details of embassy personnel cannot be divulged to anyone outside.'

'What about my wife? Emilia Goodrich. She worked with Simon. Perhaps I should explain that they belonged to the SIS.'

Purvis threw him a withering smile.

'I'm sure you're mistaken, sir. You've been reading too many spy novels. The SIS works from London. There's no bureau here in Cairo, I can assure you.'

'My wife was murdered several months ago here in Cairo. I've since been told that the people who killed her have taken my daughter hostage. Simon Henderson was shot in the early hours of yesterday morning. SIS will need to be informed.'

'I'm sure they will. You just have to pick up a telephone. By the way, did you shoot him? Is that what you've come to tell me?'

'I want to speak to someone who knows me. Get Richard Bailey down here right away. He'll vouch for me. He'll tell you who I am.'

Richard was an old friend, stretching back to the days just after the Goodriches had arrived in Cairo. He'd been their guide to the city for the first twelve months or so. Jack had always thought that Richard worked with the embassy's Trade and Investment Section. Now he couldn't be sure.

Purvis took several seconds to make up his mind, then picked up the telephone and rang a number.

'Richard? This is Malcolm Purvis. Look, would you mind dreadfully dropping whatever it is you're doing and come to my office? Super. I've got an old friend of yours here. So he says. No, I want it to be a surprise.'

He replaced the receiver.

'He'll be right down. Just stay there. I've a report I need to finish.'

The chargé went back to work on his computer. Minutes passed in silence, broken only by the tap-tap-tapping of the soft keys.

The door opened and Richard Bailey stepped into the room. Jack felt a wave of relief pass through him. He got to his feet.

'Richard, thank God you're here. I've been getting nowhere with this friend of yours. He can't

177

even find Emilia's name in his bloody computer...'

Richard looked straight at him, but the expression on his face did not change. Instead, he looked at Purvis.

'Malcolm? You said it was an old friend. I've never seen this character before in my life.'

Purvis shrugged.

'Says he knows you. Says his wife worked with SIS out here. She was killed a few months back, so he says. Somebody else he knows was shot yesterday. I don't know what to make of him.'

'Richard,' Jack protested, standing and grabbing at his friend's arm. 'You know perfectly well who I am. Your wife Nancy was one of Emilia's best friends. You were all at the memorial service here in the embassy. They killed Simon Henderson. They tried to kill me.'

Richard turned back, taking Jack's hand off his arm. His face was emotionless.

'Sorry, chum, but I don't know you from Adam. I expect you've got the wrong Richard Bailey.'

But Jack could tell Richard was speaking under some kind of strain. There was something like fear in his eyes. Jack recognised it: he'd seen it often enough in the eyes of men in combat. This was more muted, but it was the real thing.

Bailey turned to Purvis and said, 'Best get someone to take this chap out. He shouldn't have been let into the embassy in the first place.'

'Richard, wait...' Jack pleaded. But Richard was already on his way out, and Purvis had lifted the phone and was asking security to send someone up.

'Professor,' Purvis said, as though by way of

mitigation – a skill drilled into him in his years mastering the art of being a diplomat – 'I realise that the death of your wife must have placed a huge strain on you, and I respect that. But ... I have the impression that this intolerable stress must have affected you in some way. To be utterly frank, your story does sound implausible. Rather far-fetched, if you don't mind my saying so. I don't think I can help you any further. If it's not impertinent, I would recommend getting medical help. The consulate can help you out there. Do feel free to come back at once if you come up with the sort of evidence I would need to take this to my superiors. But this really is as far as I can take the matter.'

Five minutes later, Jack was on the street, more confused and frightened than he'd ever been in his life.

Chapter Twenty-Two

ONE THOUSAND NIGHTS AND ONE NIGHT

Cairo
5.45 p.m.

He spent the rest of the afternoon sorting out his bank account, withdrawing more money from the ATM to see him through the coming week, but not enough to draw attention to himself.

By the time he got back to the hotel, it was growing dark. A new day had begun. After so long in Scotland, he had returned to a place where the day ended and began with the setting of the sun. Somewhere, the first muezzin lifted his voice, almost obliterated by the sound of the traffic. Moments later, a second voice lifted, then a third, until the loudspeakers of Cairo's fifteen thousand mosques cancelled the traffic, as though calling darkness down on the sprawling city.

He simply could not understand what was going on. After Emilia's murder and what he had thought to be Naomi's too, he had thought he could never be more miserable, or less enchanted with life. His thoughts had lost all clarity, his limbs had grown listless, he'd wanted nothing more than to bury himself away from people, and to sit for endless hours immersed in a world of negative emotions. Many times he'd thought of killing himself, of walking out of the cottage into the snow, of lying down and letting death come to him inch by inch, forcing him into a sleep that would slip into death without his noticing. But he'd soon realised that these thoughts did not mean he wanted to die: he just wanted a way out of the misery.

His desperate flight through the snow had taught him how much he wanted to live, and Simon Henderson's encouragement had awakened him to the fact that, above all else, he wanted to take revenge for the deaths of his wife and his old friend, and to see Naomi's face again.

Tonight, however, he had fallen back into a state of depression, finding himself up against what seemed to be impossible odds. It was not just the indifference and lying he'd encountered at the embassy, it was more a sense that there was positive hostility towards him. How he'd provoked such hostility was still totally unclear to him.

He went downstairs to use the public telephone, and rang the Gilfillans. Still no answer. He thought they might be at church. They went to their wee Free kirk on several days of the week, to run a Bible class, a parishioners' Fellowship, and a meeting of the elders. And, then again, Jack thought, perhaps not. He put down the receiver and thought hard. He rang his parents in Norwich. No answer there either. That was stranger, he thought. His mother and father didn't do much outside except shopping.

Finally and reluctantly, he rang his sister in Nottingham. He and Sandra hadn't spoken in years. She'd always resented his move to Cairo, leaving her, as she used to say, with the responsibility for their ageing parents.

'The Metcalf household.'

Sandra had always been stuffy about how she introduced herself.

'Sandra,' he said, 'it's me. Jack.'

There was an appreciable silence. To his surprise, when she spoke, her voice was softer than his memory of it.

'Jack. I'm so sorry. I was going to write, but Mum and Dad said you didn't want to be disturbed, and they wouldn't give me your address.'

'That's all right,' he said. 'I really wasn't in a fit state.'

'It's terrible, what happened. Is there anything

181

I can do to help?'

'Talking to me is enough.'

'Where are you, Jack?'

'I was in Scotland after the funeral. But I came back to Cairo this morning. I can't explain, it's very complicated. But I'm all right, as all right as I'm likely to get.'

They talked about the murders, and he told her that Naomi was probably alive, but being kept hostage, and, when that was done, they spoke about Sandra and her husband, about the past, about the futility of things. Then it was time to get to the point.

'Sandra, there are some things I need you to do.'

'Anything. God, Jack, you must have thought I was a bitch. Mum and Dad showed me photographs of Naomi, I couldn't believe what a lovely little girl she was. I can't imagine how you feel. I should have been a proper aunt to her, sent her presents, written to her. God, I'm so sorry. I pray you find her safe.'

Sandra had never had children. Her lack had become a central focus for her life. She and her husband, Derek, a bank manager, had been through every possible form of IVF, and still her womb remained lifeless.

He told her about the Gilfillans, gave their address, and asked her to ring the police in Inverness or Fort Augustus.

'And I'd like you to check on Mum and Dad. They aren't answering the phone. These days, I get anxious. Can you let me know they're all right?'

'What's your number?'

'I don't have one. I left my mobile in Scotland. I'll buy one here and ring you tomorrow.'

'OK, I'll do that. Is there anything else I can do? Do you need money?'

He laughed.

'Sandra, that's the last thing I need. I suddenly became very rich. Insurance and ... something else. Think about something you really need, something you and Derek could do with, to make your lives better.'

Her reply, when it came, was almost a whisper.

'A baby, Jack. That's all we've ever wanted.'

'I can't work miracles.'

'I'm not asking for a miracle. There's... There's a new treatment available in Italy, but it costs a fortune...'

'Find out about it, tell me how much it costs. Maybe you can have a miracle after all.'

They talked a little more, then he hung up. It was the most expensive phone call he'd ever made in his life. At least something good had come out of it all, he thought.

He left the hotel in order to find a place to eat. He would have eaten a snack in the hotel, but found himself suddenly ravenously hungry and in need of sustenance. He could devour a bowl of *kushari*, he thought. It occurred to him that, if he went to his favourite *kushari* restaurant on al-Tahrir Street, he could pop in to the university later and check whether there were any letters or emails waiting for him – something, he now realised, he ought to have done sooner. The keys to his room were still on the key ring he'd taken all the way to Scotland, and now back to Cairo.

He put on his *galabiyya* and headed downtown, looking much like any other pale-faced Egyptian on the street. No one so much as gave him a second glance. The cool evening air prompted him to walk; with the heat taken out of it, the air was almost breathable. On the way, he stopped at one of Cairo's numerous mobile phone shops and bought a Motorola V620, identical to the one he'd had before, and whose features he knew by heart.

The evening was wearing on by the time he finally reached the restaurant, named al-Tahrir after the street. He usually came here for lunch on working days, and the staff knew him. It was reckoned the best *kushari* restaurant in the city – he made a point of never going anywhere else. A large bowl of *kushari* came to only three Egyptian pounds. It consisted of macaroni, rice, lentils, chick peas, and fried onions, covered in a spicy tomato sauce. Jack washed it all down with a glass of Kakula, the sickly sweet local version of Coke.

Eating allowed his mind to work on the problems now facing him. He went over each individually, trying to see how, if at all, they were connected. If the embassy wouldn't give him assistance to find Naomi, he was sure the Egyptian police and security services wouldn't either. They'd be sure to check with the embassy, and it didn't take a genius to work out the answer they'd receive. He simply did not understand why the embassy had behaved the way it had, or why Richard Bailey, once a good friend, had betrayed him in such a crass and unfeeling way. He went over every possibility, but nothing made sense.

He gave up in the end. When he looked around, he noticed a man staring at him. Smiling back, he was surprised when the man did not nod or acknowledge him in any way. He thought the man looked vaguely familiar. Then he realised that he must look a little odd with his English face on top of a very ordinary *galabiyya*, set off by the little grey skullcap.

His stomach full, he felt a little improved in spirits. The Kakula gave him a sugar buzz that was not altogether unpleasant, even if it was corroding his insides. This stuff was ten times worse than the real thing. It was time to check his mail, he thought. He paid his bill and left.

The AUC's Arabic Department was situated on the Greek Campus, where all the Arts and Humanities units were centred, along with the library. Since he was already on al-Tahrir, he walked east as far as Yusuf al-Jundi, a much narrower street. He'd gone about half-way to the entrance into the Social Sciences building when he remembered where he'd seen the man in the restaurant before: he'd been the man in the gabardine *galabiyya* at the barber's, the man who'd kept casting glances in his direction.

At that moment, the street lights went out. Blackouts were not uncommon in Cairo, but, looking back, he could make out a glow of lights on al-Tahrir. He realised there was no one else around. He'd just have to get to the entrance as best he could.

Footsteps sounded on the street behind him. He didn't think there was any reason to be afraid: muggings were rare in this almost crime-free city.

But they had been known to happen, and students were often vulnerable targets.

'Who's there?' he called. The footsteps halted. There was no answer. He repeated the question. It seemed very quiet here, only yards away from the growling street. He walked on further, cursing himself for not having bought a torch somewhere.

He called out again. 'Who are you?'

Still no reply. Still an uncanny silence. He saw something flicker in the darkness. Just then, he heard footsteps coming from the opposite direction.

This time he hurried to the doorway, pushing hard to let himself in. The door was locked. It was never locked this early, never. The footsteps approached together now. Slowly. Cautiously. Not students, he was sure of that: they all carried little torches. Not passers-by: there was no reason to come down this way unless to find this entrance or get into the network of alleyways that clustered round the university's press office further down on Muhammad Mahmoud Street.

There was a scraping sound, and Jack saw a flash of light as the first of the unseen figures struck a match, then the red glow of a cigarette, floating in the darkness like Mars in the night sky.

He challenged them again. No answer was returned. He could hear the second man breathing, a low rasping sound. Soft footsteps this time. He would have to make a rush at the right moment, dash past the first man and make it back to al-Tahrir, where the crowds would swallow him up in seconds.

'If it's money you want,' he said, 'you can have what I've got on me. There's no need for trouble.'

Suddenly, he screwed up his eyes as a bright light blinded him. One of the men was holding a torch pointed directly at him. As he turned away from the beam, he saw the first man, a dark figure briefly glimpsed in the darkness before the light was taken away from him. In those few moments, Jack saw that the man was carrying a knife in his right hand. A broad-bladed knife. He was a big man, Jack saw that too, and there wasn't enough space to run past without his being able to catch Jack with his hand or slash out with the blade.

The man with the knife spat on the ground, then snapped at Jack.

'Give us the sword, Professor, and you won't be hurt.'

'I don't have the sword,' Jack answered. He raised his arms, showing that he carried nothing.

'Then take us to it. We'll let you go once we have it. We'll let your daughter go. You have my word.'

'The word of a kidnapper? The word of a murderer?'

'If you don't take us to where the sword is hidden, your daughter will die slowly and painfully. That's a promise.'

As the second man held the torch beam steady, the first moved in quickly, ready to use the knife to disable his opponent. Jack slipped in under the blade and threw himself at the man in a rugby tackle. His attacker was taken completely unawares and went over with a crash. Jack got to his feet again and prepared to make his dash for freedom, but the man with the knife, though winded by his fall, jumped up even faster, the knife still fast in his fist, ready to slash out.

There was a cracking sound. As Jack watched, the knife fell from his attacker's hand and clinked on the ground. The man shook violently. The cigarette fell from his lips. Blood came from his mouth, black and thick in the torchlight, like calligrapher's ink. Jack heard him gurgle, then saw him fall in front of him and lie still.

The torch wheeled about and caught a black-clad figure just emerging from the alleyway opposite the doorway. In the newcomer's hand was a stubby weapon, a handgun. Before the other man could throw his torch to one side and make a run for it, he too was hit, a single shot to the head, followed quickly by a second as he lay flat on the ground. Jack recognised the double tap, a technique used by special forces all round the world.

The figure in black turned to Jack.

'Are you all right?'

Numb, he nodded. Words were beyond him.

'Then let's get out of here,' said the rescuer, who had been swallowed up once more by the darkness.

'What's going on?' asked Jack, still bewildered, and still frightened. 'Who are you?'

'I'm Scheherazade,' the figure answered. 'The police will be here any minute. It's time to go.'

Chapter Twenty-Three

IN THE CITY OF THE QUICK
AND THE DEAD

Cairo
11.00 p.m.

'This way, quickly,' whispered Scheherazade. Jack followed, and together they hurried back down to al-Tahrir Street, the thoroughfare from which Jack had just come.

As they came out onto the bustling street, the darkness of the back alley gave way to bright streetlights. Cairo's famous nightlife was still in full flow, and many bars and discos would go on until one or two in the morning. The Egyptian capital, as Jack had often reflected, had more right to be considered 'the city that never sleeps' than New York or Paris.

Even though he'd just heard her voice, when Jack turned to look at his rescuer, he was surprised to see that Scheherazade was a woman dressed in a black veil that shrouded her from head to foot. At that moment, she turned to face him, and, as she did so, he saw her slip the gun inside the folds of the veil before placing a pair of dark glasses over her eyes.

'Thank God you're wearing a *galabiyya*,' she said. 'Just behave like an Egyptian man,' she said.

189

'Act as though I'm your wife, keep me several steps behind you, and for God's sake don't hold my hand. Remember you're back in Cairo.'

'How could I forget?' he asked, looking round.

'Keep walking towards the square, but hail the first empty cab that comes past.'

'What...?'

'Keep quiet and listen to me. There are others out here. We've got to give them the slip. You heard him just now – they think you have the sword or know where it is. Some of their best people are on the street tonight. Hail the cab and tell the driver to head for the Mamluk tombs. He's to go directly to the Shafi'i mausoleum. Tell him you don't want him to pick up any more passengers, say your wife doesn't want any man who's not her husband sitting next to her. I'm told your Arabic is good. If it isn't good enough for this, tell me now.'

'Ya mrati,' he said in reply, 'tsharrafna.' Pleased to make your acquaintance, wife.

She laughed, a light, pleasant laugh that took him aback. It was the first glimpse he'd had of what she might be like beneath the black shroud. Coming after the ruthlessness she had displayed in the alley and the briskness in her voice, it was something of a surprise. How intriguing that she was called Scheherazade. It was the name of the princess from the Thousand and One Nights who had saved her life by telling a different story to the Sultan Schahriah every night.

A black and white taxi came past, driving slowly, on the look-out for passengers. Jack stuck out his arm and was about to shout out their destination, as was customary, but Scheherazade put a hand on his arm and hissed loudly.

'Don't call the destination, for God's sake. Anyone might overhear.'

Jack just waved his arm, flagging the driver. The cab stopped anyway, and Jack told the driver where they wanted to go.

'No problem, sir. Get in.'

As they sat down, the driver switched off the tinny radio, which had been playing the latest hit by pop idol Amr Diab. Women in full veils and their husbands weren't likely to take too kindly to music of any description. Cairene cabbies never read maps and often have to stop to ask directions from pedestrians (who never read them either); but they can size up their passengers with a quick glance and bend their behaviour to suit their tastes, personalities, and beliefs.

They pulled away from the kerb. As they did so, a man standing by a fast-food stall jotted down the cab's number before it moved off into the night. He also made a note of the fact that the car's rear bumper had fallen off.

The journey passed in silence, after a few tries by the cabbie to get into conversation with Jack. From the *maydan*, they headed directly south on Qasr al-'Ayni, passing Garden City and its embassies on the right (with the Nile just out of sight beyond), then skirting Roda Island as far as Majra al-'Uyun, where they turned sharply, heading east, down to the underworld.

Southern Cemetery
Cairo
11.40 p.m.

In the sky above them, stars like glowing grains of desert sand danced to unheard music in the light of a waxing moon now almost at its full. Down in the city's heart, astrologers watched the constellations as keenly tonight as they had done since antiquity. Jack placed no trust in heaven or man. What weak or formless trust he might have had before had died utterly in the past few months. He felt no pain on that account, but sensed the opening in him of a place of emptiness that neither the bright stars nor the vast yellow moon could fill.

Here, in Cairo's vast southern cemetery, centuries of Muslim tombs provided accommodation for both the dead and the living. For generations, the guardians of the tombs and shrines, the families of the deceased, and, more recently, the poor with nowhere else to go, had bedded down each night with their buried ancestors.

The taxi dropped them outside the tomb of Imam al-Shafi'i, the ninth-century founder of one of Islam's four great schools of law. This was one of the holiest places in Cairo, a site to which very few tourists ever penetrated. Jack paid the cabbie and watched him start back towards the city. As his rear lights twinkled and disappeared into the distance, Jack's eyes adjusted further to the moonlight and the drifting stars.

'Stay here,' Scheherazade said. 'Don't move. Let's see if anyone followed us.'

They stepped back into the shadows by the side of the tomb. Music came from nearby, Abd al-Halim Hafez singing *Gana el-hawa*, a pair of loudspeakers blaring the song across the night of the cemetery. In the midst of death, a love song. 'Love came to us, came to us; Love captured us, captured us...'

'There's a wedding tonight,' said Scheherazade, 'a couple of streets away. The groom is Gamal Lutfi. Sixty years old, a famous lecher. He makes a living selling retreaded tyres on Ahmad Maher. A stingy old bugger. He has three wives already, and tonight he has a new virgin for his exclusive use. Her name's Khadija. I've seen her a few times, she comes from a street not far from here. She's fourteen, stunning, and has as much choice in the matter of her marriage as a cat has over who buys her from the pet shop. He's strong as an ox, so even if she outlives him, she'll be in her thirties or more, too old to make a decent marriage elsewhere.'

'The old story,' Jack said. It felt weird, talking like this to someone he'd not been introduced to, someone whose face he had not even seen.

They waited for a full half hour. One or two cars passed by, but all stopped to let off wedding guests, and drove away again.

'I'd better know your real name,' said Jack. 'Calling you Scheherazade is a bit ... inhibiting.'

'Call me Jamila,' she answered.

'And who exactly are you, Jamila?'

She laughed softly.

'Wait till we get to where we're headed. I don't think we've been followed, do you?'

'Not as far as I can see.'

'In that case, come with me.'

She headed off towards a narrow alleyway on the other side of the street. There were streetlights even here, lights that used electricity that had been routed here along with water, gas, and other utilities by the city council. There were post offices in the northern and southern cemeteries, as well as police stations and bus stops on the wider thoroughfares; a few doctors had opened clinics to treat the inhabitants. Some people lived their whole lives here, others struggled to break free. Some were the legal guardians of the tombs they called home, others squatters who'd been forced out of housing complexes elsewhere and driven to this region out of necessity.

Away from the main streets, the alleyways they walked through were pitch dark, and Jamila used a torch to find her way across the maze of shortcuts and narrow passages that wound between the tombs and graves.

Finally, she stopped outside an imposing portal and pushed open the rusty gate that guarded the mausoleum behind.

'This is the tomb of Sidi Ibrahim Nour,' she said. 'A very important Sufi. A major saint. In his day, anyway. There used to be a celebration of his birthday up to fifty years ago. Nobody much comes here now. We'll be safe inside, until it's time.'

'Time? Time for what?'

She laughed again.

'Don't be so impatient. All will be explained.'

They passed inside. She reached for a switch on

the wall and in a moment a naked light bulb flared into life on the ceiling. It only gave out thirty watts or so, just sufficient to make things visible.

They were standing in a covered courtyard with doors on either side.

'That's Ibrahim on the left,' Jamila said. 'His main wife is on the right. Several of his male relatives share the tomb with him, and she has her mother and sisters with her. Of course, there was never any question of letting them all stay together. Men and women stay separate even in death. Too much chance of hanky panky, I suppose. He has a dome, she gets a flat roof. He has sex with seventy-two houris, she gets fucked by him once a century if she's lucky. Our rooms are this way.'

Jack listened, astonished. How come he'd been rescued by the only veiled woman in Egypt who picked up strange men and talked with them about sex?

Rooms had been built round the mausoleum for relatives of the dead to stay in when they turned up for the annual mourning rituals. Jamila led him through a narrow doorway into a small chamber that was lit by a bare bulb, just like the courtyard.

He tried to suppress a yawn, but it came anyway. He was beyond tired now. The only real sleep he'd enjoyed had been on the plane. In the hotel, plunged back into the smells and sounds of Cairo, and no longer certain of who he was and where he was supposed to go, he'd slept only fitfully.

'You can get to sleep soon,' said Jamila. 'Before

you can do that, we have to talk about a few things. And we have to put in an appearance at the wedding. Let me get this bloody rag off first, though.'

She unfastened the long black *milaya* that covered her from head to foot, threw it onto a chair and removed the veil that covered her face. The glasses had come off earlier.

She let out a heartfelt sigh of relief.

'You can't imagine how much I hate wearing that stupid outfit,' she said.

Underneath, she was dressed in a thick blue sweater and jeans. Her black shoes were Nike trainers.

Jack wondered at her transformation. The black cockroach who'd found him and led him here had become a woman whose long black hair and smiling face immediately turned her into someone he'd like to know. Her eyes were huge, her smile a little lop-sided, and her nose just a bit too small; he thought her amazingly pretty.

The room she'd brought him to clearly served as a combined living room and kitchen. He'd been in tomb houses like this many times before. From time to time he'd visited the Northern Cemetery to study inscriptions on the walls of the mosques and mausoleums of sultans and princes. He'd found the poor people friendly and ready to help him, even if he was a foreigner and an unbeliever.

'Your name does you justice,' he said, hoping the compliment would not offend her. Jamila meant 'beautiful'.

She reddened and, without replying, motioned

him to a padded chair.

'It's freezing in here,' she said.

There was a large Calor gas heater in one corner. Jamila rolled it nearer to where Jack was seated and used a match to light it. The panels in front began to turn red and a perceptible heat fanned out.

Jamila went across to a small propane stove on a waist-high bench.

She used an old saucepan to heat a mixture of water, ginger, and sugar. She stood with her back to him, humming along to the wedding song that still came across the midnight streets, Amr Diab again, singing *Qalbi ikhtarak*, 'My Heart Chose You'.

'It's not all that likely, is it?' he said. 'That she chose her husband-to-be.'

'What do you think? Her father sealed her fate in some back room with the old lust-machine.'

'I hope she's a virgin.'

The importance of virginity could not be exaggerated. Later on, the bride and her new husband would retire to the bedroom, and several minutes later she would hand out a pair of bloodstained knickers. Whether it was human or chicken blood would never be asked, but the knickers would be paraded through the neighbourhood to loud cries of joy from the neighbours, who had been waiting for this evidence of the bride's chastity. Her family could rest tranquil, knowing their honour was intact, and the bride could breathe a sigh of relief, knowing that an absence of blood might have led to her death at the hands of any member of her family.

197

'God help her if she isn't,' said Jamila. 'One of her brothers could have been screwing her for years, but if she doesn't bleed tonight, she'll be the one they stab to death.'

She finished heating the drinks and poured them into a couple of ceramic mugs that had 'University of Cairo' written all over them. With a smile, she carried them to a little brass table that sat between the chairs. Her skin was like velvet, and her eyes were as black as the night sky. For a moment, a shadow seemed to cross her face, then it vanished as if it had never been.

She sat in her chair and picked up her mug. Steam rose from it, mixing with the cold air in the cold room.

'Don't they wonder why you're here on your own?' he asked. 'Women who wear veils don't go out in public without a male relative to keep an eye on them.'

She shook her head.

'I told them my husband was away, but would be returning in a short time. Any time I've had to go out, I've had one of the women accompany me. People aren't that fussy round here, not like up town or in places like Shubra. But that's why we have to show up at the wedding, even if it's only for half an hour. Now you're here, everybody has to know you're my husband.'

'But ... who exactly is that? Do you have a husband?'

She laughed softly and shook her head.

'No one but you, I'm afraid.'

'I'll need a cover story.'

She took a deep breath, like someone coaching

a slow child.

'Your name is Ayyub. You've been in Ismailiyya for three months, working at your cousin's bakery because he needed help. You belong to a Sufi fraternity in Imbaba, and you're a good Muslim. After that, talk about the football results. Ahli won last week, seven-four. Keep off politics, and you'll be fine.'

Jack groaned and picked up his mug. The liquid was still too hot to drink, but he tried sipping it anyway.

'Do you have any news?' he asked, his impatience getting the better of him at last.

'News?'

'About my daughter. About Naomi.'

She shook her head.

'Same as before. She's still with this group. They won't harm her so long as they think she's useful to them.'

He told her the details of Simon's death and the chase through the freezing snow. The man with the night-vision goggles, the bullets hitting their target, the trees on all sides.

'I've never seen snow,' she said. 'But I've seen photographs. I'm sorry about Simon. He and I were very close.'

'You mean...?'

She shook her head and then looked at him. This time she did not smile.

'Not like that,' she said. 'But he taught me all I know. When it's time, I'll grieve for him. But not now. We have important things ahead of us. More important than you may guess. Where did you leave the sword?'

199

'It's in a left-luggage locker at the railway station. I couldn't think of anywhere else to put it. I want to fetch it tomorrow and put it in a safer place.'

'You are not serious?' she asked.

He nodded. There'd been so little time. But the lockers at Ramses Station weren't the most secure of places to leave anything valuable.

She shook her head and gave him a look that made him wish he'd put the damned thing in the national vault.

'How did you know where to look for me?' he asked, to change the subject.

She pursed her lips.

'Simon and I had a firm arrangement. Phone calls at set times while he was in Britain. I knew he'd run you down to some little place in Scotland, and that he was planning to take you out and get you back to Cairo on the first available flight. By dawn British time today, I knew something bad must have happened to him. He would have rung, no question about that.

'What I didn't know was whether something bad had happened to you as well. I reckoned that, if you'd got out, he'd have sent you here anyway, so I checked the airline passenger lists through my computer and there you were, like a sitting duck. I think your attackers must have tracked you down the same way. They'll have guessed you would try to get into the university and covered all the entrances.'

She sighed. Inwardly, she was still fighting back tears for Simon. She'd known him for years. In a different world, they might have been lovers.

'I didn't think of that. I lost you for a while. I'd no idea which hotel you'd gone to, or whether you'd gone back to your house in Garden City or decided to stay with friends.

'But I guessed you'd go to the embassy. Simon had given me a password to access the embassy mainframe computer, so I kept checking with them and going to all the hotel guest lists through the day. I got lucky. A man called Purvis from the consulate had flagged up a notice that you'd visited them. It included your hotel name. They also noted that their security people were to put a trail on you.'

'Is that who...?'

She shook her head.

'I don't think so. I got to the hotel, found out you were in your room, then followed you when you came out. You had me behind you all the way to your restaurant, then to the university.'

'Why didn't you just introduce yourself?'

'That would have been a mistake. I knew somebody from British intelligence might be trailing you, but I couldn't pick them out. If I'd approached you then, they'd have known, and I knew there was a more than even chance that, if they knew, someone else would too. They mustn't find out we're together.'

'But why would MI6 be stalking me? And why did that nerd in the consulate deny all knowledge of Emilia and Simon?'

She stopped talking. For long moments the shadow returned, a thin veil of sorts, heaviest around her eyes. Was her bright façade just that, a façade? Jack wondered. Was that engaging smile just a front for something else?

'Jack, there's something you should know. Osama bin Laden is dead. Did Simon have time to mention that?'

'Yes.'

'Did he say that the man who leads the group who are holding your daughter plans to take Bin Laden's place?'

'Yes. As a new Caliph.'

'What he won't have told you is that a group of Foreign Office appointees within MI6 have seen their chance to cut a deal. The FO thinks they can pull off a coup. If they can lay their hands on the sword, they'll use it to make a bargain with this man. It's the old "covenant of security" trick again. If he promises to guarantee there will be no terror attacks on the UK mainland, he can have the sword and welcome. And if he becomes Caliph in more than name, Britain will be ahead of the game.'

'Jesus.'

'If only he was, Jack. If only he was.'

'If they want the sword, why didn't they just ask me?'

'Because they know or guess Simon Henderson spoke to you and told you what they're up to. If they'd come right out with it and asked for the sword, they wouldn't have known what you would do, who you would take it to. They don't know where you've hidden the sword, and they can't risk letting you know they want it. You can be sure they've been following you, and I think it's likely they plan to hand you over to al-Masri's group.'

She glanced at a clock on the wall.

'We'll talk more about this later. Now, I'm going to make some very strong coffee, and when it's inside you, we have a wedding to go to.'

Chapter Twenty-Four

TAXI

Al-Tahrir Street
Half an Hour Later

Amin Yunus was tired. He'd been up since early morning, but he still hadn't earned enough to feed his family. The couple he'd left in the City of the Dead had paid well, but he needed a few more fares before he could go home to sleep. He had decided to head back here to al-Tahrir Street in the hope of picking up some tourists from the bars. A couple of tourists would do the trick very nicely, he thought. He could overcharge them handsomely and they wouldn't even notice. He might even make enough to pay for a new bumper.

Al-Tahrir was his usual beat. Because it was such a good place for picking up tourists, only a small number of drivers were allowed to ply for trade here. As he cruised the street, a man on the left flagged him down. He drew up by the kerb, and the passenger got into the front seat. As he did so, two more men opened the rear doors on either side.

'Where to?' he asked.

'You tell us,' said the man in the front seat.

'I don't understand.'

'You were seen earlier picking up a man and a woman. He wore a *galabiyya*, she was in full hijab. Remember them?'

'Of course. What's it to you?'

One of the men behind leant forward and whispered something in Amin's ear. The cab-driver went pale.

'What... What do you want to know?' he asked. His voice was trembling. The people in his cab weren't the sort of people he wanted to mess with.

'Where did you take them? That's all we want to know.'

He told them. As he did so, one of the men in the rear seat took out a mobile phone and made a call.

'Thank you,' the first man said to the cabbie. 'Now, get out of the car.'

'But ... this is my car.'

'Didn't my friend behind you explain how things stand? You'll get your car back. Now, save your life and go home to your family.'

He opened the door and got out. His knees almost buckled beneath him. The man in the passenger seat shuffled across and took the wheel. He closed the door and moved the car out into the traffic. Behind him, the man with the phone was already giving directions.

Amin watched the rear lights vanish. He knew he'd never see his car again. He would take nothing home tonight. Nor any night to come. The men who'd taken his car had sentenced him and his family to a living death.

Chapter Twenty-Five

THE CRIMSON AND THE WHITE

**Southern Cemetery
Cairo**

The celebrations had started at sunset and would continue till two or three in the morning. No one in the quarter would sleep tonight. No one but the dead. The couple had been married hours earlier in a simple ceremony in the bride's house, where her father had signed a contract in her name before the local sheikh. She'd seen her husband for the first time then, had caught sight of the warts on his hands as he signed the papers, had watched his rheumy eyes stripping her naked. Something had died in her then. The rest of the day had been spent at home weeping, waiting till almost midnight, when she joined her husband in the wedding procession.

The party had started before that, once the sun went down. The darkness would be filled with a mixture of music and ululations from the female friends and relatives of the bride.

Jack had been at dozens of weddings like this in almost every part of Cairo, but never before in

the City of the Dead. Uptown, the lavish weddings in the grand hotels cost more than the
house the couple planned to move into. Tonight's
bride would not have a new home, but would join
her husband and his other wives in his old place.
The wedding party had not been organised by
caterers: it was a home-made affair, in which
family and neighbours joined together to create a
celebration they would all remember till the next
one. He led Jamila through the entrance to the
party enclosure.

A wide alleyway between two rows of tombs
had been cordoned off for the occasion with the
bright red tent hangings that came out for all
local celebrations, from the Prophet's Birthday to
parades of little boys about to be circumcised.

Rows of coloured lights had been strung in
loops from end to end, others had been woven
through the branches of winter trees. The
loudspeakers that blared out the music were the
size of small trucks. Everywhere, little gas heaters
struggled to take the chill off the night air.

The bride and groom sat in isolated splendour
at one end of the enclosure, raised up on high-
backed gilded chairs set on a platform surrounded by plastic flowers. They'd arrived at about
half past eleven, greeted at the alley by ranks of
women in bright ankle-length dresses and hands
crimson with henna, their voices shrill like the
cries of long-necked birds, uttering the ululating
warbling that started at the backs of their throats
and echoed across the tombs.

Jack looked up to where Khadija the bride sat
rigid on her throne, like a tiny painted doll, her

child's body swathed in a voluminous white wedding dress several sizes too large for her, that served for every bride who married in the vicinity. Her husband, who'd done this before, beamed at his milling guests. The old goat was tense with the thought of taking Khadija's virginity later, and hoped none of his other wives would kick up a fuss afterwards.

Everyone was here. In Egypt, a wedding invitation is like an order from the President. No one says no unless they're already on their deathbed.

At the bottom end, the male guests sat on wooden chairs or rose from time to time to dance with one another. There was no mixed dancing, practically no mixing of the sexes whatever. At the other end, women in their festive outfits called to the bride to join them in their dancing, but she shook her head, frightened of making a fool of herself. At home, she liked to listen to pop music; but she'd been told her husband hated loud music of any description and wouldn't let it be played under his roof.

Jack hadn't eaten since his meal at the restaurant, had hardly eaten all day. The smell of cooking wafted across the cold night air and assailed his nostrils. The wedding feast was being cooked on little propane stoves in several of the nearby kitchens. Great pots three feet wide were filled with lamb, chicken, rice, macaroni and eggplant.

On tables in the enclosure, plates of salad, fried patties, and honey-drenched *kunafa* teased the guests, who were getting hungrier by the minute. Small children, thinking themselves invisible, sneaked under the tables and reappeared to snatch fistfuls of sweet filled pastries, while a flustered woman flapped her hands in vain to shoo them off.

As Jack and Jamila started to head for the platform, in order to offer their congratulations to the bride and groom, the recorded music was switched off and an ensemble of traditional musicians shuffled up to a low stage, carrying drums, *ouds,* a reed flute, and a violin tuned to the Arab scale. They were no sooner seated than they started to drum, scrape, and blow, playing a traditional wedding song, *Arustak al-Halwa,* 'Your Bride is Sweet'.

Jamila had come without her face veil. She caught sight of old friends, who turned as her name was mentioned and rushed over to her.

'Jamila, dear, where have you been all evening? I looked for you everywhere. We thought you weren't coming.'

The welcome came from a large Nubian woman who lived two tombs away. She had a gap in her gleaming white teeth, and the palms of her hands wore patterns of henna like a lace glove. Other women joined her, waving their fingers at Jamila, asking why she'd turned up so late.

'My husband just got back a few hours ago,' she said, shyly indicating Jack, who squirmed and smiled back nervously and muttered a few words of greeting. The less he said, the better, he thought.

Once the women had had a chance to look him over and congratulate Jamila on his return, he was sent off in the direction of the male contingent.

'I don't want you hanging around,' Jamila whispered. 'The other women will only get jealous because you're so much nicer looking than their husbands, and that means the evil eye, and, frankly, we can do without that.'

'You don't believe in that old superstition?' he said, though he'd never met an Egyptian who didn't.

She shooed him away and he slunk off to the male area. At least he'd been seen, placed in the mental space occupied by 'Husband', and was now no longer the subject of speculation. The coffee he'd drunk before coming out had given him an unwelcome buzz. He dreaded to think what his head would be like when he woke in the morning, if he woke at all. The kid on the platform had looked almost as young as Naomi, and the thought of her being bedded by the brute next to her made him seethe. The thought prompted darker thoughts, thoughts about Naomi – where she was being held, whether she was still alive, and whether they had raped her.

He made his way further down the enclosure, and every inch of the way he was followed by curious stares. He'd been marked down for a stranger the moment he set foot in the place, though the welcome given to Jamila by the women would have done much to offset suspicions. He didn't look particularly Egyptian, however: with his light skin and offbeat accent, he was often mistaken for a Circassian from Jordan or Syria. Outsiders weren't welcome in close-knit communities like this, and he'd have preferred to avoid getting drawn into conversation. One slip could be

209

enough to turn this into a very difficult situation.

Women and girls had started to bring the steaming pots of food from their kitchens. Jack sniffed the air and welcomed the distraction as much as he welcomed the prospect of a late supper.

There was a lull in the music as the *oud*-players retuned their instruments. It was difficult to keep them in tune in the cold air. Somewhere in the road outside, a car drove up and stopped. A second car followed it, and a third. More guests had arrived.

The band struck up again. Food was being served on plastic plates. Children were skipping about, trying to help themselves. Glasses of fruit juice were being handed round. The groom was telling his bride to sit up straight and smile. More pots were brought in and set on trestles. A group of women enticed Khadija to step down and join them as they ate. Her sister was there, and from one side her mother appeared, carrying a heavy clay dish. The music rose and fell. The bride's grandmother stood and performed a short dance, and her friends, a bunch of tough old hags, clapped as she lifted her feet on the hard earth.

The tent hangings opened at each end of the enclosure, then two others on either side, where they met in the middle. The newcomers had arrived. Preoccupied with the food, no one noticed them at first. They were men, and they were dressed in long black robes, and as they came into the enclosure their eyes darted from left to right, searching for something. Or someone.

Jamila was the first to pay real attention to

them, and when she did, her blood ran cold. These weren't wedding guests, these weren't kids from another quarter who'd come to gatecrash. She looked down through the enclosure, desperately hunting for Jack. It didn't even occur to her to ask how they had found them. What mattered was how to get Jack and herself out of here.

The men in black were mingling with the crowds. Here and there, guests had started to notice them and to realise they weren't here to take part in the festivities. No one needed to be told what they were. They'd been known to disrupt wedding celebrations before, considering the music and dancing – however unmixed – a sin against their puritan vision of Islam. Groans went up here and there as guests anticipated an end to the evening's festivities.

Jamila knew better. She made her excuses and hurried in search of Jack, weaving her way among young girls swaying in a slow dance. Damn it, she thought, where is he? She knew that, if she could pick him out among the crowd, so could they. She should never have brought him. And she should have brought a gun with her.

Jack didn't see the men at first, then he glanced up and caught sight of Jamila hurrying in his direction. There were shouts as some of the guests saw her pushing her way into the men-only section. She ignored them and hurried past, her eyes trying to follow the movements of the men in black robes while sifting through the guests to find Jack.

Then she saw him, waving to her, perplexed by her intrusion into male territory. She ran towards him, and he saw the expression on her face and knew something was wrong. He looked round and saw a man in a black beard and robe coming straight for him, and all at once realised the man was holding a gun, a short sub-machine gun like an Uzi. Then two more men were making for him from the other side, and Jamila was shouting above the hubbub of voices and the sound of the lutes.

'Jack, get out of there now! This way!'

He started to run towards her, but a stack of chairs was blocking the way. Pushing them aside, he stumbled, and, as he did so, the first man reached him and grabbed him by the shoulder, then moved in to get a firmer grip. The other men were only yards away, and others were coming from different directions. People were shouting now, and the musicians faltered.

The man closest to Jack managed to get his free arm round Jack's neck. That was his mistake. All Jack's fighting instincts, honed by years of training and combat, snapped into play. He sank into the grip, dropped one arm and suddenly came round, using the man's waist as a pivot, destabilising him and bringing one leg across his assailant's, throwing him heavily to the ground. The weapon he'd been holding came loose and clattered to the floor. Jack reached down and lifted the man before he could get his bearings, then struck him hard on the neck, dropping him. As the others came within reach, Jack grabbed the gun. He recognised it straight away as a Chinese Uzi clone. Nothing like as good as the original, but a lot better than nothing.

As he straightened, a man he hadn't seen came right up behind him and put the barrel of a gun to the nape of his neck. Someone screamed. Then more screams started. Jamila appeared in front of Jack. As she did so, the other two assailants raced up to him.

'The gun, Jack! Throw it to me!'

He didn't hesitate. As she caught it, she turned and opened fire, killing the two men next to her, knowing the man with the gun at Jack's neck wouldn't dare shoot him.

She turned and pointed the gun at Jack's captor.

'Walk away,' she said.

'I will shoot him,' the man said. 'I have shot infidels like him before. He's nothing to me.'

'He's everything to you. If you shoot him, you'll never find the sword. I don't know where it is. He hasn't told me.'

She could hear feet running towards her, someone barking out instructions to encircle her and Jack.

The gunman hesitated for a fraction of a second, and Jack swivelled on one foot, grabbed the gun barrel, and kicked the man hard in the balls. He screamed and fell to the ground, clutching his private parts and yelling.

The others were almost on them. The man in front had his gun at waist level and was aiming at Jamila. Jack raised the Uzi he'd just snatched and fired at him, riddling his chest with a long burst of 9mm bullets. Blood spurted, splashing guests as they panicked and ran in every direction. Jack swore as he saw more gunmen headed for them, knowing he didn't dare open fire for fear of hitting innocent bystanders.

Jamila looked round. There was a gunman at each entrance. Then she remembered another way out.

'Quickly!' she shouted. 'Follow me.'

They ran together now. A man stepped out in front of Jamila, pointing his gun at her chest, but she went on running, struck sideways with her weapon, and broke his jaw. He fell to the ground writhing in pain.

They ran to the women's section, dodging chairs and tables, knocking them back into the path of their pursuers as they passed.

One of the men behind them opened fire, missing them and hitting a group of frightened women who had been running out of the way. Three of the women died instantly, their festive clothes soaked with blood.

The astonished bride and groom were transfixed, horror-struck as their wedding party became a scene from hell. Little Khadija sat frozen to the spot. She knew she should run, but in her wedding dress she could only take tiny steps. Gamal, her husband, sprang into action suddenly. He could see people running in their direction, a man and a woman, followed by gunmen. He leapt from his chair and jumped off the platform, leaving his young bride to fend for herself.

'This way,' shouted Jamila. 'There's a way out behind the platform.'

Two more pursuers had started to fire at them, hoping, perhaps, to disable them in order to prevent their escape. Bullets hit anyone too slow or feeble to get out of the way.

As they came level with the platform, Jack could see no sign of an exit on either side.

'We have to climb across,' said Jamila, panting. 'There are steps at the back.'

Jack jumped up, then held out a hand to pull Jamila up beside him. As she saw them leap to the stage, Khadija screamed and started up from her chair, hampered by the crazy folds of her wedding dress. She screamed again, shouting at the gunmen, telling them to stop, to leave her alone. And as she cried out to them, confused and frightened, an Uzi stuttered and a garland of red flowers exploded on the sequinned dress, tearing her from shoulder to hip. Bullets pierced her heart and lungs and stomach, tore through her kidneys, ripped her liver to shreds, destroyed her short life, and shattered what few sad dreams she'd ever had. As her family had prayed, her wedding night was crowned with blood.

Jamila bent down to help her, but Jack had seen the full extent of her injuries. He pulled Jamila back to the steps. Moments later, they were on level ground again, tearing a path through the hangings.

After the lights in the enclosure, the alleyway was dark.

'We've got to get out of here,' shouted Jack.

Jamila pulled him towards the nearest doorway, but he shook his head.

'They'll scour the place. Bring in reinforcements. We need a car.'

'This way,' she said, remembering the direction

from which she'd heard the cars arrive.

They stumbled forward, but behind them light appeared in the opening, and men with guns started to make their way out of the exit. Someone tore part of the hangings down, to make room for the others.

Jack glanced round and saw them, silhouetted against the light. He was still in darkness where he stood, just out of reach of the weak lights from the enclosure.

'Get down,' he called to Jamila.

He knelt on one knee, raised his gun, and opened fire. He had no way of knowing how many he hit, but a series of cries were enough to tell him he'd put several out of action.

Jamila had run forward to a crossroads where the alley was crossed by a wider road. A single streetlight cast a weak glow on the roadway.

'Jack, as fast as you can, they left their cars here!'

He fired another long burst, then got to his feet and ran to the junction. Behind him, an Uzi stuttered, and he sensed bullets whizzing past on his left side.

Four vehicles had been left in the middle of the road.

'They left the keys,' Jamila shouted. She was already in the driving seat of the first car. Turning the key, she started the engine and waited for Jack to join her. He rushed across to the open door.

'Get out and cover me,' Jack said.

She was beside him in a moment.

'Stay behind this car,' he said. 'Use it as cover,

and keep them off as long as you can.'

Firing from the alley started again, and this time there was more than one gunman. Jamila crouched behind the bonnet of the middle car and fired back, using their silhouettes as targets, hitting at least one.

Meanwhile, Jack went from car to car, taking keys from the ignition. It was normal for drivers in Cairo to leave keys in their cars: vehicle theft was scarcely heard of. He rammed the keys into a pocket in his *galabiyya*.

'Let's get moving!' he shouted. Jamila began firing again, but the gun jammed. She swore and tossed the Uzi aside.

They ran for the front vehicle. Jamila jumped into the driver's seat. Jack was still clambering into the passenger seat when she gunned the car forward into the night. Firing erupted all round them, shattering the rear window. Then their attackers were just shadows in the mirror. Moments later, they'd been swallowed by the darkness.

Chapter Twenty-Six

BLESSED BY MADNESS

Manshiyat Nasr
Cairo
The following morning
10.10 a.m.

He woke from a dream without form or pity, as though he'd been blessed by madness. Emilia had broken free of her grave, shrouded in white, longing for revenge. He'd watched her break through the earth, as though he himself was chained, watched her white face stir with mischief, her bitter eyes, her lips spitting soil and blood. And then his chains had broken, and he'd been running, and with him a city was in flight, while fast behind them his dead wife hurried in close, mocking pursuit. The sky had been red, and he'd noticed that blood was pouring from his ears, pouring from the ears of everyone in that maddened flight. He was deaf, then he could hear again, and all he could hear were the sharp cries uttered by Emilia, and when he looked behind the people of the city had joined her and Naomi stood at the front, crying for her mother. The people wore white shrouds covered in ashes, their eyes were bloodshot, their mouths were red and open like wounds, they were cawing like

218

crows, while a dead grey ash fell from the sky, and he woke, screaming.

'Jack? Jack, are you all right?'

He'd been shaking, throwing his arms about, uttering a sound less human than animal. Someone held his arms, and was making soothing noises, shushing him into silence.

'Jamila...?'

'It's all right, Jack,' she said. 'You're safe. We drove out here last night. Don't you remember?'

Sleep had not rested him. His red-rimmed eyes darted round the room. It held no furniture, just this bed. The walls were made of dried mud, and on one wall hung an icon of the crucifixion. The wall opposite held an icon of the Virgin, a cheap print pinned directly to the mud.

It all came back. From the southern cemetery, a broad highway had led them to the east side of the citadel, and on their right they'd found a narrower road leading up into the Muqattam Hills. It had been a short journey, and it had brought them to a place Jack would never have thought of entering, a place he'd often heard about but never visited in all his years in Cairo.

In the Muqattam foothills lived communities of Coptic Christians, outcasts who eked out a hard living as Cairo's refuse collectors. They roamed the streets of the city, piling all manner of garbage on their donkey carts. Back in the villages that dotted the hills, they turned Cairo's cast-offs into gold. They were the original recyclers, and in their yards heaps of accumulated rubbish were sifted and resifted, and finally made useful again. They sorted and crushed plastic to serve as sandals, baskets, cutlery, and anything else the city's handymen could fold and twist and cut the raw material into. They washed and crushed tin cans, and somewhere else skilful workers would transform them into boxes, suitcases, car parts, and television antennae. Old clothes became rag rugs. And what was left went to the pigs at the back of the village, pigs whose succulent meat was prized by the Copts and the expatriate community if by nobody else.

Jack sniffed. In the village – a grim place called Manshiyat Nasr – everything and everyone stank. There was no escaping the smell of raw garbage, or the constant buzzing of flies.

'You'll have to get up,' Jamila said. 'The family needs their house. I've paid them well, but their children have been up all night, and they need their bed.'

'My head feels as though they've stuffed it with garbage.'

'You even look like garbage. You need a shave and a bath.'

'What time is it?'

'It's after ten. You needed to sleep very badly. I let you lie in.'

'We have to get to the station. We have to get hold of the sword and put it somewhere safe.'

'Eat something first. We weren't followed here.'

In the next room, a woman in her forties was preparing eggs. Her children were all outside, picking through a rubbish tip behind the house.

They ate together, sitting on a bench that ran along one wall, holding their plates on their laps.

'My mother used to come here,' said Jamila.

'She was a social worker. There was a project to educate the children, but it never came to anything.'

'Does she still come?' asked Jack through a mouthful of egg.

'She died,' said Jamila, and he sensed a sadness in her voice that had not been there before. 'Fifteen years ago. I was fourteen. I mentioned her to a few people today, but no one remembered her. Social workers come and go, but nothing really changes.'

'We can't stay here,' he said. 'Word will get round. Someone will hear there's a reward for the person who can take Muhammad al-Masri's people to us.'

'We leave here in a few minutes,' Jamila said. 'We have to find somewhere more secure, somewhere we can operate from in relative safety. Finish your breakfast, and we can be on our way.'

'How are we going to get to Ramses station?'

'In the car,' she said.

He shook his head and took a sip of coffee that tasted as if it had been brewed seven times.

'No good. They'll be looking for it everywhere.'

She smiled.

'They won't find it. It already has fresh number-plates – I saw a stack of them outside. The man who lives here has been putting red stripes on the car. Welcome to the criminal class, Jack. You are now the official possessor of an untraceable stolen vehicle.'

Chapter Twenty-Seven

AN ARYAN CHILD

Muhammad al-Masri's Bunker
Shubra
Cairo
Late morning

They let her spend time with the child whenever she was allowed a break from work, which wasn't often. Her duties kept her pretty much occupied for most of the day, but recently that had been slackening off as the project came closer to completion.

The little girl was beautiful and sweet, thought Samiha. In spite of all that had happened to her, she was a delight to be with. She still considered her own two boys to be the most wonderful children in the world, but if she'd been blessed with a daughter, she'd have wanted one like Naomi. The boys were headstrong from the influence of their father and the macho society in which they lived, but this English child had a different kind of spirit. Her prettiness belied inner strength that few adults possessed. Samiha admitted to herself that she had come to love her. Knowing how fragile Naomi's life was, that love had been intensified to the point where she could not bear to think that further harm might come to her.

The al-Masri brothers were Naomi's greatest danger. Neither of them wanted her here, and Samiha knew that the only reason the child hadn't been killed long before this was that she was being held as a hostage who could be exchanged for the sword they believed to be in her father's possession. No, thought Samiha – there was another reason. Some of the key figures in the bunker were unlike any Arabs she'd ever known. Several had blond hair and blue eyes, and Naomi was a favourite of theirs. They called her an Aryan child, and sometimes they brought her sweets. Samiha had no idea where they came from. They had Arab names and spoke fluent Arabic with Egyptian and Syrian accents; but on a few occasions she had overheard them talking together in low voices in German.

She had arrived in Cairo at almost the same time as Naomi, and had seen her in her first, terrified state. The other women had been harsh with her, but Samiha had shown her kindness from the start, and gradually Naomi had become her responsibility. She'd been in floods of tears for weeks, and it was a long time before Samiha was able to get from her the truth about what had happened. She remembered that she'd been incandescent with rage for days afterwards, and had scarcely been able to control herself when dealing with the people round her, above all with Muhammad al-Masri, who scared her to death every time he checked on what she was doing.

Like Naomi, she knew her life was at risk daily. She too was an outsider, her history making her vulnerable to any and every accusation of

223

disloyalty. She worked hard to convince them that she had seen the error of her ways. She prayed all five prayers each day, and attended al-Masri's sermons every Friday. If it hadn't been for her desperate wish to see her children again, her hope that one day she might be able to take them away from Jenin and give them a good life elsewhere, she could not have coped.

In the course of her work, she'd discovered most of the details of the plot that al-Masri had concocted. From his bunker beneath the streets of Cairo, his tentacles were reaching out to vast distances. He had people working for his cause throughout the Islamic world, contacts to the regime in Iran, to the leaders of Hizbullah and Hamas, and, she was now certain, to the remnants of the al-Qaeda leadership in distant Afghanistan. Al-Masri had already taken control of almost three-quarters of al-Qaeda's networks in Europe, America, and the Middle East.

Her task, one to which she was perfectly suited, was to create companies through which he could carry on his scheme beneath a veneer of respectability. There were major front companies now in France, Britain, the Netherlands, Germany, and the US, as well as a host of Islamic charities from Morocco to Pakistan, through which money was being funnelled to his operations. Her particular suspicions surrounded two small airlines al-Masri had bought along with airfields in the Netherlands and Germany. She thought she knew what these were being used for, what they were shipping, and who operated them on the ground. Drugs, she knew, were being brought

224

in by carefully staggered and well-routed stages from a variety of locations.

Heroin came across the Indian Ocean to Hadhramaut in Yemen, from where it was moved to Saudi Arabia and the Gulf States. She had help set up front companies in Dubai, who laundered money through real estate transactions, shipping the money on to al-Masri's accounts in banks in Germany. Poppy paste was smuggled from Afghanistan to Tajikistan, from where it was slipped across the Russian border, and then on into Europe. The idea wasn't just to make money from the sale of drugs, but to help weaken the hated unbelievers, to sap their strength and courage through corruption of their young.

She hated the trade, hated what drugs did to people, but she was powerless while she worked under close surveillance in the bunker. She had sworn that, if she ever got out, she would use her in-depth knowledge of the network to bring it crashing down. Everywhere, she had laid subtle traps that the drug enforcement agencies could use to trigger total collapse of the trade run by al-Masri's organisation.

But it wasn't the drugs that made her lose sleep at night. The secret flights and clandestine shipments by sea and road carried other goods as well. It was only in the last few days that she had begun to add it all together, and, if what she feared was true, a great darkness was yawning, full of greater danger than she had thought possible. Not for the first time, she cursed her powerlessness, trapped here in a city she did not know.

The door of her little office opened and she

turned to see Naomi standing in the entrance. Her heart leapt as it always did to see the little girl. Like anyone brought up in a country where virtually the whole population had black hair, Samiha found Naomi's blonde hair endlessly fascinating. The eyes, each a different colour, were like nothing she'd ever seen. And when Naomi smiled – which wasn't often – her whole face lit up.

'Come in,' she said.

'I was told I could come to see you,' Naomi murmured. She had learnt to keep her voice low in this dreadful place, where everyone but her friend Samiha was stern and grim-faced, and all the women wore veils. 'I wanted to bring you a present.'

She held out a piece of paper on which she had been writing a poem. Samiha had been teaching her to write poems in Arabic. She had wanted to teach her to draw, but the woman who supervised her had insisted that the Koran forbade all artistic representations. The only artistic skill allowed was calligraphy, and Samiha had done her best to impart her limited ability to Naomi, who was proving a fast learner.

The poem was about Naomi's father. A sad poem that ended on a note of despair at the thought of never seeing him again.

When Naomi finished reading it, tears started down her cheeks. At moments like these, Samiha thought her own heart would break. Gently, she wiped the tears away and told Naomi to shut the door.

'But we're not supposed...'

'It's all right, child. I have something to tell you.

226

It won't take long. It's a secret. You must keep it to yourself. It could make trouble for both of us if you tell anyone.'

Naomi shook her head.

'I won't tell. I promise.'

'Good girl. Now, come over here and sit on my knee.'

Naomi did as she was asked. Samiha put her arms round her.

'Now, darling, listen carefully. I have some news for you.'

'Bad news?'

'No, dear. This is good news.' She took a deep breath. 'I've been looking in the computer, the main one everybody uses down here. I found out that your father has come back to Cairo. He was in a faraway place called Scotland, after your Mummy died.'

Naomi looked at her open-mouthed.

'Has he come to get me?' she asked, her lip trembling.

'I don't know, love. If he knows you're alive, he'll hunt for you everywhere. You can be sure he will.'

'But... But what if he can't find me?'

Samiha felt words drain from her. How on earth would anyone find this place? But she smiled bravely and whispered in Naomi's ear.

'I don't care what it takes, Naomi; but if I can get us out of here, I'll take you straight to him.'

As she pulled back, the door opened and the man Samiha knew as al-Masri's brother, Rashid, stormed in.

'I've been searching for the child everywhere. You know she's not supposed to be here during the day. You pamper her.'

Samiha was afraid of him, almost more than she feared his brother, but she snapped back.

'She's done no harm. She came to see me because I've been teaching her some verses from the Koran. What is wrong with that?'

He did not answer, but snatched Naomi's wrist and yanked her towards the door. She cried out in pain.

'Stop it! You're hurting me.'

Rashid paid no heed. He looked at Samiha with contempt.

'You're wasting your time. What use is the word of God to a Christian brat? My brother needs her now. Don't come to find her. You'll see her again when this is over.'

Without another word, he pulled Naomi through the door and slammed it hard behind him.

Chapter Twenty-Eight

HEAD LINES

**Bab al-Hadid/Ramses Station
12.04 p.m.**

It was the winter tourist season and, in spite of the bombs, Europeans, Australians, South Africans and Americans were flocking like birds to Cairo to take advantage of cheap travel offers.

In Ramses Station, they boarded the luxury trains to the beaches of Alexandria in the north or the monuments of Luxor and Aswan in the deep south. The prices were to them the greatest bargains they had ever seen. Students and backpackers went one step further and boarded third-class carriages filled with live chickens, snotty-nosed children, and *fellahin* going home for a few days to the villages they'd left years earlier in search of riches in the big city. The concourse resembled King's Cross early on a Friday evening, except that there were no queues anywhere, just rugby scrums as passengers pushed their way through to the platforms. More flags had been draped inside and outside the station. Tourists huddled together, trying to find their own flags among the forest of banners.

Jack bought himself an orange juice at a stand about fifty feet from the luggage lockers. It was likely that the terrorists would be looking for a couple, so he and Jamila had slipped in through different entrances. She had the key. Once they could be confident the coast was clear, she would move to the locker, retrieve the bag with the sword and letter, and head back the way she had come. He would watch her the whole time, then follow at a safe distance until they got to the car. His assailants of the night before had left two handguns in the car, Walther P99s, and these were now nestling in Jack's and Jamila's waistbands.

He saw her hesitate as she scoured the entrances to the platforms, trying to pick out anyone doing the same thing. She'd said they might have a lot of men on the streets this morning. For two years now, she had been investigating the group along with Simon, who had employed her precisely because he'd doubts about some of his MI6 field agents. She'd told Jack the group was already large and was getting bigger, and that it could put dozens, even hundreds of militants on the streets at any time. She'd warned him to put out of his mind any thought that their opponents would always be as easy to spot as the ones the night before had been. For all she knew, any watchers in place at the station might look like businessmen, railway staff, students, shoe-shine boys, even tourists. What they'd to identify was anyone who might be taking a greater interest in passers-by than seemed normal. All through the concourse, men and boys followed tourists, offering to carry their luggage, or change money, or be their guides for the day. Could it be one of them? Jack asked himself.

Glass in hand, he strolled a little closer to the locker area. He'd done nothing to change his appearance. His darkening beard helped him look a little more Egyptian with each day that passed. The crumpled clothes he hadn't changed since putting them on the day before let him blend in with the less than immaculate world of the average Egyptian male.

There was a small news-stand near the juice stand, and Jack walked over to it. He glanced at the headlines from *al-Ahram*, *al-Akhbar*, and the English-language *Daily Star*. Each one carried the day's lead story, the inexplicable shooting at a wedding in the southern cemetery. There were photographs of the carnage. Khadija, the bride, would be buried later today. Her distraught husband posed for the cameras, his cheeks wet with the tears of a newly-wed.

Just as he made to look up again, Jack's eye caught the right-hand column of *al-Ahram*. There was a photograph in it of himself, one he recognised straight away as his mug shot from the university website. It appeared in a box with the heading 'Advertisement'.

He handed some coins to the vendor and walked off with the paper in his hand.

The Arabic text was straightforward.

To Professor Jack Goodrich of the American University. We have something of yours that you need very badly. You have something that belongs to us. Please ring our telephone number to arrange for a swap. We guarantee your safety and the safety of someone close to you. The number is: 401 9354.

Jack folded the paper. When he looked round, he saw Jamila heading for the lockers. Quickly, he checked to see if anyone was visibly following her. He drew closer and saw her reading the numbers. Suddenly, she stopped and bent to insert the key into the tall locker to which it belonged. The door swung open, and she reached inside, drawing out the bag. In a single motion, she swung the bag onto her shoulder and started to move quickly – but not too quickly – out of the station. Jack stayed at a distance, but kept pace with her, monitoring the concourse as she passed through it.

She had almost reached the entrance when Jack saw a man detach himself from the wall to their right. Looking round, he saw two more pushing their way through the jostling crowds, sending ripples of protest through the tide of passengers. Jack slipped his hand into his pocket, in which he had cut a hole to allow him easy access to the pistol in his waistband. The man near the entrance was making straight for Jamila, and Jack saw him put a hand into his own pocket and take something out.

'Jamila!' he shouted. 'Watch out!'

She looked round, saw the man, and started to run for the exit; but as she did so, three more men appeared, blocking her way.

'This way,' shouted Jack.

She was beside him in seconds, but their pursuers were closing in on them from both sides. Jack knew that, if he opened fire here, he'd have the police hunting him as well as the Caliphate group.

Rather than try to outrun them to the main entrance, where others might be waiting, Jack took Jamila's hand and ran with her in the direction of the platforms.

On platform four, the 12.15 Ordinary train for Alexandria was about to leave. The gate had been closed, but Jack leapt over the metal barrier, before turning to help Jamila, who was hampered by her long garments. Their pursuers were gaining on them. Jamila's gown caught on a protruding piece of metal. Jack found the spot and freed her, and she jumped down to the platform.

'Hurry,' he said. 'The doors haven't closed yet.'

They ran together, and a man in the rear carriage held the door open for them. As they staggered in, Jack saw the men behind already climbing over the barrier, then hurrying for the train. He slammed the door in their faces and, as he did so, there was a sudden jerk. The train pulled away.

'Hold this door,' he told Jamila, then struggled into the packed carriage, tripping on boxes and bags and howling children. A fat woman was blocking the aisle as she fiddled with a package on the wooden seat next to her. Jack pushed her onto the seat, crushing the package, then sprinted to the end of the carriage.

When he got to the door, it was wide open, and two more jihadis were struggling to haul themselves aboard. The train was picking up speed. Jack grabbed a stanchion to steady himself, then kicked out, a high kick that took the nearest man in the throat, just beneath the chin. He fell back, grunting with pain, lost his hold, and crashed onto the platform with a sickening crunch.

His companion still had a hand round a stanchion. He used his other hand to draw a pistol, but the train was rocking, and he wasn't steady yet. He fired wildly, but the shot went wild. Jack grabbed him by the wrist, dislodging the gun as he spun his attacker through ninety degrees, dislocating his shoulder, then hurling him backwards into space. Seconds later, a passing train hurtled over the track he'd landed on. Jack got hold of the door and closed it.

He walked slowly back through the carriage, aware that every eye was on him. No one dared protest. The women all looked away, not wanting to catch his eye. Some of the men glared at him, but Jack glared back, and they thought better of whatever it was they'd been planning to say or do.

He went back to the open space next to the door, where Jamila was waiting.

The train was running faster now, but it was an Ordinary, an old train that would amble through the Delta for hours before it got to its destination.

Jack had no way of knowing whether other hunters had entered the train higher up, but if that was the case, they'd surely be making their way back down to the rear carriage by now. If they started firing, there would be another massacre insides such a crowded space.

'We've got to get off,' said Jamila, who'd been thinking the same thoughts.

Jack nodded. He dashed back into the carriage and found the first communication cord. Muttering apologies, he leant across an old woman and a girl, grabbed the cord, and pulled it down hard. Seconds later, the driver applied his brakes and the train screeched to a halt, throwing standing passengers to the floor.

Jamila already had the door open when Jack returned. Taking care to check for trains in both directions, they jumped down to the clinker-strewn rail bed. They were still well within the city, in the northern end of Bulaq, Jack guessed, not far from the railway bridge that crossed the Nile into Imbaba before the line turned north and set off for Alexandria.

They scurried across the tracks, terrified that a Turbotrain might come out of nowhere to hurtle down on them at great speed. The way remained clear. No one climbed down from the train to chase them. They reached the other side and clambered over a wall onto a sloping bank. In front of

234

them lay the houses, markets, and workshops of Bulaq. Jack could hear the sound of metal being worked. Beyond that'd be the old clothes markets for which the quarter had become famous. They would find a taxi there without difficulty.

Jack stopped Jamila and asked her for the bag. He unzipped it. The sword was still inside, wrapped in its cloth. Near it, the letter was intact.

He breathed a sigh of relief, then zipped the bag again. So far, so good, he thought. But now he had a telephone call to make.

Chapter Twenty-Nine

AT THE FOOT OF THE PHARAOH

Central Cairo

When they got back to Ghamra Street, where they had parked the car near a police station, it was no longer there.

'Someone must have recognised it after all,' laughed Jack. 'Or else the police have impounded it. Either way, we're stuck until I can buy a new one. I don't want to waste time now, I've got to make this phone call.'

They walked the short distance back to the railway station. It was probably the last place their pursuers would think to look. Jack found a row of telephones. He didn't want to make a call from his mobile, which could be traced. He fancied a credit card might prove a risk as well. Jamila went off to fetch some change, while Jack cradled the bag with the sword.

He got through on the first ring. They'd been waiting.

'This is Jack Goodrich,' he said. 'I was asked to ring this number.'

A man's voice answered, unfriendly and guarded.

'What a happy coincidence, Professor; I've been looking for you everywhere. My name is Muhammad. No doubt you have heard of me. I have to say I'm very angry with you. You and your companion have caused a great deal of damage. When I finally meet up with you, as I intend to do, we shall have words. But for now, you may consider yourself safe. You have something I want very badly. When it's in my possession, I may calm down a little and choose to exercise mercy. You will be allowed to go where you please, once my task is done. But we'll cross that bridge when we reach it.

'First, there is something you need to see. It may help persuade you to hand the sword to me. In fact, I'm sure it will. Can you please tell me where you are right now?'

'Where's my daughter?' Jack demanded. It was all he could do to stop himself losing his temper completely, but instinct told him the man on the other end would simply put the phone down on him. 'If you've harmed her in any way, I will make you suffer for it.'

'Rest assured, she is in safe keeping for the pre-sent. You'll see that when you pick up what I plan to give you. I asked you before – where are you?'

'Do you take me for a complete idiot? Your people have already tried to kill me more than once. Tell me where this thing is, and I'll pick it up. Put it in a public place, and keep your thugs away.'

There was a protracted silence, then al-Masri spoke. His voice was colder than ever.

'Very well. I will do as you ask, since you clearly do not trust me. Be at Ramses Square at three o'clock. It's an easy place to get to, and very public. There will be a container at the foot of the new statue. No one will be watching. You have my word. You may pick up the box and leave.'

The line went dead. Jack tried to ring again, but there was no answer. He hung up and told Jamila what had happened.

'Ramses Square is just over there,' she said, pointing out of the station. 'Did he know you'd come back here?'

She looked round nervously, sure they'd been watched, then dismissed the thought.

'Let's not hang around to find out. I've thought about how to do this. We need to get a cab to al-Azbakiyya.'

Al-Azbakiyya

The driver dropped them on the street that led to Mehdi's old shop. Jack paid him generously and asked him to wait for them.

The alleyway was as he remembered it. Its image had been stamped indelibly on his brain, and he felt his breath shorten as he walked down it. He

237

knew that, if he stopped and closed his eyes, it would all flash before him again – the dark stairwell, the book-lined room, the bodies, the blood. Jamila looked at him and took his hand.

People were passing up and down the alleyway, but near the shop Darsh was squatting on the ground, fixing the inner tube of a bicycle tyre.

They went up to him, and at first the boy did not recognise Jack, who had changed visibly since his last visit to the alley. Then Jack spoke, and Darsh recognised his voice.

'It's you,' he said. 'You were here before. Your friend, the old man, he was killed. There was a woman killed too, and a little girl.'

'The woman was my wife,' said Jack, and he saw Darsh flinch. 'The little girl was a friend of my daughter's.'

'I'm sorry,' Darsh said. 'I'm sorry your wife was killed.'

'Thank you,' said Jack. 'Now, Darsh, I have a job for you...'

Ramses Square
2.50 p.m.

For years, the granite statue of Pharaoh Ramses II had stood at the centre of the square named after him, facing out on a pool of water, a maze of flyovers and walkways, buses, cars and pedestrians. For over three thousand years, Ramses had endured the blistering sun and desert wind. But life in the sprawling square opposite Cairo's main railway station had taken its toll. Over time, he

238

had started to corrode, his stone flesh eaten away by traffic fumes and the eternal smog of pollution. In 2006, he'd been taken away and stored in the new Grand Museum, where he was to be given a setting worthy of his dignity.

Experts had debated for many months what they would replace the old statue with. The square, hardly a place of beauty, surrounded by tall buildings, lit by night with glaring neon signs, felt forlorn without the statue. In the end, someone had come up with a clever idea: why not replace the Pharaoh with the replica of the statue that had been made to test ways of transporting the original. No one knew the difference, and pretty soon everywhere went on with the replica much as they'd gone on with the real thing.

While Jamila took Darsh to a tea-shop for a drink and pastries, Jack headed down to the north end of Talaat Harb Street, where he quickly found a large camera shop. In the back, they sold a wide range of binoculars. He'd used military glasses in the SAS, and knew what he was looking for. He found the most expensive pair in the shop, a Leica Duovid, which gave ten times magnification plus an option to zoom to fifteen times. It would serve his purpose perfectly.

He got back to the square with time to spare. Using a forged passport Jamila had located for him, he booked himself a room half-way up the multi-storey Everest Hotel, right next to the al-Fath Mosque, whose minaret was the tallest in the city. The Everest looked directly across the square to the statue. Like all the rooms on that side, there was a small balcony, from which Jack could see everything happening in the square below.

He rang Jamila on her mobile. It involved little risk, since he'd be expected to be somewhere in the vicinity. They'd agreed to speak briefly, and to use simple code.

'I'm in place,' he said. 'Is Mercury all right?'

He'd decided to call Darsh Mercury, the messenger of the gods.

'Very well.'

'I have everything in sight. Checking location now.'

He closed the call.

With great care, he scrutinised the area for some distance round the statue. The pedestrians on the narrow pavement that circled the statue and the pool were walking, and the traffic was running fairly smoothly. They wouldn't be at the railway station, it was too far from the statue. The area round the statue offered no hiding places. He zoomed in, but nothing had been left on the plinth at Ramses's feet, which was raised up above the pavement by about ten feet. Steps provided access to the plinth on the statue's left and right, and behind it. It was always possible that someone was waiting out of sight at the statue's rear, but if they came forward, he would see them. There were five minutes to go.

He kept the binoculars trained on the base of the statue and waited. Moments later, a man stepped off the pavement, ran up the steps to the statue's left, and deposited something on the plinth. Within seconds, he had scurried away, down the steps, onto the pavement, and across the road, weaving through the cars and buses

240

with the ease of someone born to it.

Jack followed him as far as he could, then the man went out of sight. They'd be watching for Jack now, he thought, or for Jamila. He rang her number again.

'Ramses just had a devotee. Send Mercury over.'

In the tea-shop, Jamila switched off the phone and turned to Darsh.

'It's time to go, Darsh. Don't run until you're near the statue, then go fast, as if you're Abdel Halim Ali in centre-forward position going for a strike. Zamalek are one down, and there's just five minutes to go.'

He grinned.

'We'll find you where we arranged,' she said.

And he set off, walking away from her into the bustle and noise of the square.

Jack had picked up Darsh now, and kept the binoculars focussed on him all the way across to the central reservation. Darsh ambled along, just another Arab street boy on the scrounge, looking for a tourist to hassle or a stray dog's tail to pull. Boys like him were the wallpaper of the Cairo street. They passed everywhere, an irritant to foreigners, with their 'Mister, mister, you need guide, mister?', invisible to most Egyptians. No one gave Darsh a second glance. There were a million boys just like him. They dressed in hand-me-down clothes, they were always dirty, hungry, and unschooled, and nobody cared.

Jack watched him as he strolled through the constipated traffic, arriving on the inner pavement, and walking nonchalantly to the steps. He didn't draw attention to himself by glancing

241

round, he climbed the short flight of a dozen steps cool as a penguin, and he tossed a handball against the side of the plinth.

As the ball bounced back, he caught it and suddenly jumped up, snatched something lying on the top, leapt down again, and ran hell for leather. He ran as if Ramses Square was a soccer pitch and he had a clear run towards the other side's goal. On the road again, he swerved through a tangle of cars, mopeds, and motorbikes, then dashed towards the railway station, where he vanished into the crowds outside.

Desperately, Jack scanned and rescanned the area around the statue, Sweeping his glasses backwards and forwards, scrutinising everyone he saw, expecting all the time to see someone start off after the boy. But no one leapt forward. Not near the statue, not on the other side, where Darsh had performed his disappearing act.

He put down the binoculars and rang Jamila.

'I think Mercury is safe. Let's get over there before anyone starts looking for him.'

Jamila was waiting for him at the entrance to the hotel. He still had the bag with him, but by now he was growing desperate for a safe place to leave it.

Darsh would not be waiting for them at the station. He had simply used the crowds there to hide himself. From the station, he had headed back round the east end of the square to the back of the statue, and had walked slowly down Kamil Sidqi Pasha, a street that ran straight from the rear of Ramses Square, slicing apart the Ghamra district to the north and Bab al-Shariyya to the

242

south. He found a café, one that Jack had told him to head for, and stepped inside. The owner glared at him and started to throw him out, but Darsh showed him money. At a table near the window, he ordered a Coke, using money Jack had given him.

The café sat in the cheap tourist district where hostels and bargain hotels jostled with low-priced eating houses catering for the battalions of students and backpackers who came to the city with a handful of dollars and empty stomachs. Jack had spent a lot of time round here, when he helped out foreign students who came to spend a year or so at the American University. He'd told Darsh to look for the Semiramis Café and to wait for him and Jamila to turn up. They arrived on foot. Crossing the square by cab would have taken too long. Darsh was on his fourth Coke, sucking the black liquid down through a straw that had been in many mouths through the years. He'd never drunk so much pop in his life, and never Coke, and his bowels were starting to regret it.

While Jamila stood outside to keep watch – she wouldn't have been welcome inside anyway – Jack hailed the boy and sat down next to him.

On the table sat a white cardboard box. It was about eight inches long and six wide, and had been securely sealed with parcel tape. Jack didn't touch it. He'd been taught long ago that you don't open suspicious parcels without great care – especially boxes sent to you by someone who's been trying to kill you. He took a wad of notes from his pocket and handed it to Darsh. It was more money than the boy had ever seen, more than his parents would ever have seen. As he took it, his eyes went wide. So much money, he thought, for such a small job. If it hadn't been for the woman being there, he'd have suspected base motives.

'Thank you, Darsh. You may not know it, but what you just did was an enormous help to me. You need to go home right away. Al-Azbakiyya's not far from here. I'll get a taxi for you outside. Finish your Coke, then go home and put the money somewhere safe. I have things to do, and you may not see me for a while. But when I come, I want to talk to your parents. I want to pay for you to go to a proper school, and later test out for Zamalek, get onto their youth squad. You have talent. You should use it.'

Darsh pushed the Coke bottle aside and said he couldn't manage another drop.

'That's OK. You've had too much. We...'

At that moment, the door of the café opened, and Jamila came in. Jack took one look at her face, and knew there was trouble.

'Get Darsh out the back way, get your packet, and let's get the hell out of here.'

Chapter Thirty

CROSS-DRESSING

Jack snatched the box from the table and put it in the bag alongside the sword, then slung the bag over his shoulder.

'Darsh,' he said, 'you heard what she said. Go

244

out the back way now. Hide somewhere for an hour, then go home. Don't argue. It's dangerous for you to stay here.'

Darsh stood, puzzled, but not alarmed. Out on the street, he'd learnt how to look after himself. If someone was after him, he'd soon lose them.

Jack handed cash to the owner, enough to secure Darsh's exit and, he hoped, buy some silence. Darsh thanked Jack again, and ran off.

Jamila had changed her clothes at the café in Ramses Square. She was now wearing a jacket over designer jeans. Over her head she wore a scarf from a dull little shop that sold conservative women's clothing. The *milaya* was in a shopping bag she'd picked up from a street seller.

She led Jack from the café onto the street, then drew him quickly to where a small Peugeot cab was waiting.

'Get in,' she said.

'What's happening?' he asked.

'They're on the street. The place is swarming with them. I've seen them stopping people and asking questions. One went right past here a few minutes ago. Let's get moving.'

The cab pulled smartly away from the kerb. Jack glanced through the window.

'Where exactly are we headed?' he asked.

'Urabi Metro Station,' she said. 'It's the fastest way out of here, and it will take us where I want to go anyway. With any luck, they won't see us go in, and they won't know where we've gone.'

'Which is where?'

'You'll see,' she said, not wanting to say anything in the cabby's hearing.

They travelled fast down Gumhuriyya, then turned sharp west on Rihani. The station was right in front of them.

'Leave us off here,' Jamila said.

The driver swung within inches of a row of brightly decorated vegetable stalls and pulled up sharply.

'Give him enough to keep his wife and children in luxury for the next year.'

Jack grinned, but Jamila frowned back.

'I'm serious. We have to get out of this cab quickly, and I want to give the driver a good reason not to open his mouth later.'

Jack took out a wad of dollars and shoved them at the driver.

'You never saw us,' said Jamila, switching to Arabic. 'If my husband or anyone else asks about us, you never set eyes on either of us.'

The man's eyes bulged. He nodded, unable to speak. What did he care if they were running away? Let God take care of the matter, as was His prerogative.

'*Shukran*,' he managed to mumble. 'Thank you very much. I won't say a word.'

They got out and started to walk away. Jack saw the red 'M' of a metro station ahead, and realised Jamila was heading for it. They had hardly taken half a dozen steps when there was the sound of screeching brakes behind them. Their heads turned along with one hundred others.

A silver Mercedes – the type Cairenes called a Powder, because only drug dealers can afford one – had blocked off the cab they'd just vacated.

Two doors opened – one smashing into the cab as it was flung out – and a couple of men in suits jumped out.

One man, dressed in a black European suit, with brushed-back grey hair and wearing sunglasses, rushed round to the other side of the cab, hauled the door open, and dragged the screaming cabbie onto the pavement, knocking over a stall selling cabbage.

Jack watched horrified as the grey-haired man took a pistol from his pocket and held it to the cabby's throat. A woman screamed. The man who'd been driving the Powder also produced a gun, with which he menaced the onlookers. Some went on standing, staring as the drama unfolded in front of them, like a colony of meerkats watching as a hyena creeps their way. Others took to their heels, weaving through the crowded street without pausing.

The first gunman shouted in broadly accented Arabic at the cab-driver.

'Which way did they go? Which way?'

Terrified for his life, the cabbie pointed. Jack saw him lift his hand and was sure he would identify them in the next instant, but instead, the cabbie had the presence of mind to point in the opposite direction.

They ran, blending with the other pedestrians escaping the men with guns, knowing they had to get to the metro and board the first train.

Suddenly, an old man near the car shouted to the gunmen.

'I saw them go that way. A man and a woman. That way.'

He pointed to the spot where they had last been seen.

The gunmen exchanged glances and started for the pavement. As they did so, the grey-haired man in the black suit turned, gun still in hand, and lifted his weapon. The shot tore through the cabby's head. The high-velocity round shattered the skull and sent brain matter and blood in a crimson spray that covered the cars and the onlookers. The cabby's body collapsed like a doll from which the stuffing has suddenly been taken, and as it crashed to the ground, it was accompanied by a shower of crisp fifty dollar bills.

They reached the metro entrance.

'Which platform?' Jack shouted.

'South,' said Jamila, leading him down.

As they reached the platform, a train was standing, its doors still open. People were still going in. A last, desperate dash took them inside the nearest carriage. The doors closed, and the train began to move. Someone hissed at Jamila for not taking a women-only carriage. She hissed back. As it pulled away, Jack saw the two gunmen arrive on the platform and stare at the outgoing train in mute frustration.

'It would help if I knew where we're headed,' said Jack. 'What if we get separated?'

'We're going to change at Sadat.'

'Change for where?'

'We're taking Line 2 to Shubra al-Khayma. Don't worry, this was my back-up plan all along.'

'We could have changed at Mubarak instead.'

'Mubarak's in Ramses Square. They could be thick on the ground. This is longer, but we stand a better chance of missing them.'

'They shot him,' Jack said, his voice dull. 'The driver.'

'They'd have shot us as well,' Jamila said. 'Just be grateful we escaped. Now, keep quiet and put this on.'

She took the long black *milaya* out and passed it to him. He hesitated for only a moment, then pulled the shapeless garment over his head. It was a tight fit on him, but no one would look too closely. Jamila tugged and straightened it. Once it was straight, she took out her head and face coverings and performed the same trick with them. The other passengers, all men, watched Jack's transformation without a word. It all made perfect sense, of course: a beautiful young woman absconding with her lover, pursued, no doubt, by a jealous husband. Some shook their heads, but they were all thinking the same thing: *Lucky bugger. I wish it was me.*

Jack wondered where Jamila planned to go in Shubra al-Khayma. Shubra and its northern extension, Shubra al-Khayma, formed one of the poorest quarters in the city. With over a million inhabitants crammed into a modest space, it was crowded, dirty, and a breeding-ground for religious extremism. Not the sort of place for a man to be found cross-dressing.

The sound of the engine altered. They were coming close to the next station.

'We can lose them if we get out here at Nasser,' he said.

'On the other hand, we could walk straight into them. The shooters from the Mercedes will have telephoned to everyone near a Metro. They may have people at Sadat too, but that's the only place we can make a change now. There'll be people on every platform, and some of them will get on board this train, and we won't know if they're among them till it's too late.'

He looked at the repeated flashing of light against the carriage windows.

'There's no way out, is there?'

As he said this, the train drew in at Nasser station. The platform was crowded. Jack saw some men wearing dark glasses: gunmen or ordinary Egyptians?

'Quickly,' hissed Jamila. 'Give me the bag with the sword. It looks awkward on you.'

He passed it to her, and she slipped it over her shoulder.

At the doors, a mass of passengers had become entangled with one another, some trying to get off, others trying to get in.

'OK,' she said, 'get off and find a women-only carriage on Line 2.'

Using his strength combined with his appearance as a veiled woman, Jack forged a way through the crowds. Jamila followed in his track, clutching the bag with the sword and the mysterious box.

They hurried to the eastbound platform for Line 2. The next train would take them one stop east, then turn sharp north. Shubra al-Khayma was ten stations away. The end of the line.

She saw the assassins right away, the two men who'd killed the cab-driver. But they were looking for a veiled woman with a man, not a veiled and unveiled woman together. She saw the grey-haired watcher catch sight of Jack and nudge his partner, a young Chinese-looking man. Jamila made a point of taking Jack's arm, as though she was out shopping with her mother. The men returned their gaze to the platform, and, as they looked in the other direction, a train came in. Jack and Jamila made for the second women-only carriage and slipped inside. Moments later, the alarm sounded and the doors slid together. The train was on its way towards Shubra al-Khayma again. The last thing their pursuers expected was that they'd stay on the train and travel further.

Chapter Thirty-One

ADVENT

Shubra al-Khayma
Cairo
That afternoon

They could smell the quarter even before they came out of the Metro station. The air was rank with all the normal smells of Cairo, but ten and twenty times intensified. This was one of the most crowded urban districts in the world, a rattling, jumping fuse-box of people and animals, the abrasive smells of spices alongside the stink of raw sewage.

They were swept up at once into the craziness of

it, dodging the micro-buses that sped up and down the streets, weaving past mopeds and rusty cars, every step taking them deeper into a hive of narrow streets and noxious alleyways that intersected a world of tenements, railway yards, sweatshops, mosques and churches. Above their heads the spaces between the rooftops on either side were filled with electric wires stretched out like overheated spaghetti, washing that hung from poles and lines as though put there to welcome heroes home from war, metal awnings, lamps, and the ubiquitous green flags of the Muslim Brotherhood, proclaiming 'Islam is the Solution'. It wasn't hard to see what the problem was.

They kept up the pretence that they were mother and daughter. Several times, Jack sensed eyes on him. He knew he had neither the shape nor the gait of an Egyptian matron. Worse still, Jamila was attracting the wrong sort of attention from many of the men they passed. This was a conservative part of the city, a place where radicals and terrorists grew like weeds in the parched soil of defeated hopes and wasted longings.

'We have to get off the street,' he said. 'Before somebody gets the wrong idea.'

'I didn't plan it this way,' she said. 'Just keep walking. It isn't far from here.'

Just what 'it' was he dared not think.

Outside a mosque, children were rummaging in a heap of rubbish, a hill of discarded items from which they would salvage anything that might be sold for a few piastres.

The stone came out of nowhere, striking Jamila on one arm and bouncing off onto the squalid street. When Jack looked round, he saw a young man bending to pick up a second missile, and near him another with a stone already in his hand.

The first man straightened and looked directly at Jamila.

'Hey, sister. Your pussy's just like honey.'

It was a common enough insult, but Jack had to restrain himself from ripping off his veil and laying into the little rat. A second stone caught Jamila on the hip, and a third struck her temple, drawing blood.

He was going to throw caution to the winds and hit back hard, when out of nowhere an old woman appeared beside the youths who'd thrown the stones and laid into them with a heavy stick.

'Who do you think you are?' she shouted. 'What do you think you're doing? Throwing stones at young girls, shouting things you should be ashamed to mention. *Ekhs alayk!* I know who you are, Hamid Mansi. You too, Farid Dabbash. If you don't clear off this minute, I'll have a word with your fathers. Now, get out of here.'

Their heads bent low, the two boys crept off, urged on by cries from other passers-by. The old woman watched them go, then vanished back to wherever she'd come from.

'Let's get out of here,' said Jack, taking Jamila's arm again.

'This way,' she said, turning into an alleyway festooned with Ramadan lanterns that had been up since the last fast.

Jack noticed a Coptic church on their right, and realised they had crossed into a Christian section. About one million Copts lived in Cairo, and

253

many of them had their homes in Shubra and Shubra al-Khayma, cheek-by-jowl with fundamentalists who treated them like dirt and tried to burn down their churches from time to time.

Jamila led the way round to a street behind the church, and stopped outside a blue-painted door. Looking round to make sure no one had followed them, she banged loudly on the door with her fist.

Half a minute passed, then the door swung open. A middle-aged woman dressed in black stood staring at them.

'Jamila!' she cried and rushed to embrace her. Jamila put her arms round her and hugged her, then kissed her, first on one cheek, then on the other. They were clearly old friends.

When the hug session came to an end, Jamila stepped back and introduced Jack.

'Shadia,' she said. 'This is Jack. We need to stay with you for a few days.'

'You'd better come in, both of you.'

Jamila was about to step forward, when she remembered how Jack was dressed.

'Shadia, I don't want to confuse you, but Jack is a man. He's a Christian like you. He comes from England. Jack is an English name.'

'Of course it is, of course it is,' Shadia said. 'You'd better get in here before people notice.'

Next thing Jack knew, he was in an upstairs room surrounded by a family of ten or more.

'You'd better get those things off,' laughed Jamila. 'Then I'll introduce you properly.'

Jack removed the head covering first, then the all-enveloping *milaya*. There were four children present, and they burst into fits of laughter, never having seen a man dressed as a woman in their lives.

'Shadia, everyone – allow me to introduce my friend Jack Goodrich. Jack is a professor at the American University. He speaks perfect Arabic and is a very great authority on the ancient language. Now, Shadia...'

The woman who had let them in stepped forward, still grinning at the sight of a man emerging from a veil like a butterfly from a chrysalis. Looking at Jack again, she had second thoughts about the butterfly. A moth, maybe.

'Professor Goodrich,' Shadia said, 'let me introduce everyone. These are my six children. The two little girls are Marie and Irene. Stand up, girls.'

Two girls stood up, one three years old, the other about five. They smiled shyly, then burst into uncontrollable giggles.

There were two more girls, Marina and Hannah. When Jack asked, Marina said she was eight, Hannah told him she was twelve. After them came two boys, John and Pierre, fifteen and seventeen respectively.

'This is my sister Noha,' Shadia went on, pointing out a woman in her thirties, 'and my brother-in-law Boutros. Boutros is an accountant. This is Mr Zakhary and his wife Mary. They live in the apartment upstairs. Mr Zakhary is a teacher at St Sergius school.'

The Zakharys were in early middle age, both a little frayed round the edges, their faces somewhat sad, their eyes braced against something unseen, their manner slightly brittle. But they stood and shook hands and smiled. Jack reflected that it was hard being a Copt in Cairo. In recent years, attacks on Christians had grown in pace with the rise of Islamic radicalism.

There was no more room on the cushioned benches on which everyone sat, but Shadia shooed the younger children onto cushions on the floor, allowing Jack and Jamila to sit down. No one asked why Jack had been wearing a woman's outfit.

As they sat down, the door opened and a man stepped inside. He wore the long beard and robes of a Coptic priest, and at first struck Jack as a stern patriarchal figure come to discover vice among them. But his fears were dispelled in the next moment, as the two youngest girls, Marie and Irene, got to their feet and ran to the man with cries of delight. He swept them up, one in each arm, and kissed them.

As they calmed down, the priest caught sight of his new guests.

'Jamila,' he said, 'how lovely. It's been a long time.'

She got up, gently nudging Jack as she did so, prompting him to rise.

'Joseph,' she said. 'You're looking well.'

'Thank you. I always feel well when I see you. How is your father?'

'He's well,' she said, 'but still single. I try to find girlfriends for him, but he's not interested. Maybe you should speak to him some day.'

The priest smiled.

'What can I do? He misses your mother, even

256

now. She was a wonderful woman, I don't think he'd be satisfied with anyone else. Now, speaking of girlfriends, may I assume you have brought this gentleman here to introduce him as your fiancé?'

Jamila went red.

'I barely know him, Joseph. I ... I knew his wife, though. Let me introduce you both.'

'Jack, this is Father Joseph Yaqoub, Shadia's husband and the father of the children you just met. Joseph, this is Professor Jack Goodrich of the American University.'

On hearing Jack's name, the priest's eyebrows went up.

'The Professor Goodrich of early Arabic studies?'

Jack nodded.

'I'm honoured to meet you. The pre-Islamic poetry is one of my hobbies. Well, more than a hobby. I greatly enjoyed your book on the Hanging Poems. It's an honour to have you in my house.'

'It's an honour to be here. I didn't think anybody had read my books and articles.'

'You have fans out here, Professor, believe me.'

A sudden cloud passed over the priest's face.

'Professor Goodrich, please forgive me. I don't know how I can have been so insensitive. Please tell me if this is a terrible mistake, but I seem to recall hearing that something bad had happened to your wife and ... was it your son? There was nothing in the papers, but someone I know mentioned something...'

His voice fell away.

'No,' said Jack. 'It wasn't a mistake. My wife

257

was ... killed some months ago. Here in Cairo. My daughter...' He thought of the priest's young children and hesitated. 'My daughter is alive.'

The priest held out both hands and folded Jack's in them. He said nothing, but his look went through Jack like a soft jolt of electricity.

The girls were sent off to play in another room, and Father Joseph joined them on the banquettes.

On the walls were several icons and a colour photograph of Pope Shenouda III, head of the Coptic Church. Jack had often been in Coptic homes before, but those had been middle class. This was a much poorer household, its piety more evident, like the shack belonging to the Zabbalin.

Joseph spoke to his wife, and she went out.

'I've asked Shadia to make some coffee for you. You both look a little dusty and in need of refreshments. You'll have to excuse us, but it's the Fast of the Nativity now. It started last November, and we'll go on fasting till Christmas Day, except the children.'

Of the many things Jack was grateful for, one was that he'd not been born a Coptic Christian. The Copts fasted for two hundred and ten days a year, and placed special emphasis on Lent. On fast days, they ate nothing from dawn to sunset and avoided all animal products – meat, fish, eggs, butter. It was a hard regime. The very thought made Jack's stomach rumble. The Coptic Christmas Day was six days away, on the seventh of January.

'No,' he said, 'please don't make an exception of us. If you're fasting, we can fast too.'

Jamila, who had given up observing Ramadan

at the age of sixteen, cast Jack a look that might have killed a lesser man.

'I insist on it,' said Joseph. 'I expect you are an Anglican. Anglicans do not fast in our way. Say nothing more. You are my guests, and very honoured guests at that.'

Coffee and little Christmas cakes came five minutes later, and Shadia joined them on the bench, a low seat that ran round three sides of the little room.

They talked about general matters, the Yaqoub family and what they had been doing since Jamila last visited, her father and other members of her family whom the Yaqoubs seemed to know.

Jamila explained to Jack that the two families had become close several years earlier, when her father had taken on a commission to build a new church for Father Joseph's congregation in Shubra al-Khayma, St Sergius – the church they had just passed.

The visitors made their excuses and left. Soon, only the Yaqoubs and their two boys were left.

'I'm sure you're tired, boys,' said Joseph. 'Why don't you join your sisters?'

'We'd rather go outside,' said the older boy.

'Just be sure to take it easy. You can't afford to use up too much energy during the fast.'

The boys shook hands again, kissed their father and mother, and left. Father Joseph glanced at his wife, who said she had to attend to the evening meal. She stood, shook their hands, and followed her sons.

'We need your help,' said Jamila.

'Yes,' said the priest. 'I'd already gathered that.'

Chapter Thirty-Two

THROUGH A GLASS DARKLY

Shubra al-Khayma
4.30 p.m.

They told Father Joseph everything. To have kept the truth from him would have been treacherous. If they wanted him to shelter them, it had to be with his clear understanding of the danger they were courting, danger that might rebound on him and his family should anything go wrong. When they had finished their narrative, the priest fell silent. He and his family had known Jamila for many years, and he trusted her. He knew Jack's reputation and did not think he would invent something like this.

Jack showed him the sword and the letter. The priest read it and nodded.

'Yes,' he said. 'It seems authentic. The vocabulary, the script.'

Jack took the cardboard box from his bag. He was itching to see what was inside, but knew he could not afford to be careless.

'Father,' he said, 'I need to take this box somewhere to open it safely. I don't know what's inside it, and it could very well have been sent to kill me. I know how to disarm it if it is an explosive device, but I have to take it somewhere safe.'

The priest grinned.

'I can do better than that, my son. Bring your box to the church office and I'll show you.'

Terror attacks had made Coptic Christians security conscious. Priests went on training courses, parishioners were told how to keep an eye out for potential threats, and charities in the States paid for equipment to detect bombs and weapons.

The office was at the back of the church, and they entered it through a separate door. On a small table stood a MailGuard x-ray device, a basic model designed for mailrooms in small organizations. Father Joseph switched it on, and Jack slipped the box inside.

On the screen appeared two outlines: a hard rectangular object with two symmetrical holes, immediately identifiable as a video cassette. The other object was about two inches long and less than half an inch wide. At its centre were the jointed phalanges of a human finger. A child's finger.

Jack closed his eyes and fought down the bile that had curdled his stomach. Father Joseph crossed himself and muttered a brief prayer.

'You go out, Jack. I'll open it.' Jamila tried to get hold of the box, but Jack snatched it away.

'Scissors!' he shouted. 'I need scissors.'

The priest gave him a pair and Jack used them to tear open the box.

Inside was a second, smaller box, and inside that was the finger wrapped in cotton wool, the dried blood on it still fresh, the bone protruding

261

slightly from one end.

There was no way of knowing for sure whose finger it was, but Jack did not have to guess. He wanted to scream. All the old nightmares danced through his mind at once, the horror of blood, the clamour of ghosts, all that dim garbage of the brain.

He looked up, and realised he could scarcely see for tears. Someone took his hand, and bit by bit he grew calm.

'What's in the video?' he asked.

Jamila and the priest exchanged glances.

'I have a video player in the next room, Jack,' said Father Joseph. 'Let Jamila and myself watch this. I think you understand why.'

'No,' Jack said. 'I want to see exactly what I'm up against.'

They went next door, and Father Joseph inserted the cassette into the machine. The TV screen was dark, then it flickered into life. The camera had been placed on a tripod, and the scene it recorded was steady. A bare room with concrete walls. A lightbulb dangling from the ceiling. The hum of something like air-conditioning. It was like a scene from a film by Andy Warhol. There was nothing human in it. Just concrete and light.

Then, abruptly, the sound of a door opening. A little girl in a dirty, crumpled dress was pushed into the centre of the room. Someone – the cameraman or another man outside the scene – told her to stand still. In spite of the dirt on it, Jack recognised the dress. It was the regulation dress for the junior school Naomi attended. He

262

looked at the child's face. It was his daughter ... and it was not his daughter. It was Naomi ... and it was someone else entirely, a child he'd never seen before. Her long blonde hair had been cut short. It was lank, unwashed, and ragged. Her vivid face had grown haggard. She had lost weight, a stone or more. Her eyes, her bright-coloured, scintillating eyes, were dead. Lack-lustre. A ghost's eyes, without animation, love or hatred. She stood in the centre of the room alone, and he thought she would cry, but she just stared at the camera stony-faced.

A man came into the room from the same direction as Naomi. A man of average height, bearded, good-looking but for a row of smallpox scars on his forehead. He was dressed in a white *dishdasha* and wore a skullcap. Turning to the camera, he stared into the lens unsmiling and arrogant.

Jack could feel his heart beat in his chest, like the wings of a trapped bird, banging wildly for its release. His blood had turned cold. He could see Naomi shiver in the thin dress, and he knew she was cold. Not air-conditioning, then, he thought, but air. He guessed the room must be located somewhere underground, and he realised she could not have been far from Ramses Square.

The man took a microphone from the camera-man.

'If you are watching this, Professor Goodrich, you will already know what is about to happen here. Permit me to introduce myself. My name is Rashid, and I am the brother of the man you know as Muhammad. You escaped me in

Scotland, and you have evaded my people here in Cairo. I underestimated you. You are more resourceful than I could have imagined. And that is why your daughter will have to suffer.

'You have a sword that does not belong to you. It was given to you by a man to whom it did not belong. It belongs by right to my older brother Muhammad. He is a direct descendant of the last true Caliph, the last successor of the Prophet, peace be upon him. Return the sword to him and you will see your daughter again alive.

'If you do not return it, the next parcel you receive will contain her head. To show you I mean business and that the finger in the box really does belong to your child, I shall show you how it was obtained.'

He stopped speaking, and someone pushed a wooden table in front of the camera. A second person entered and stood behind Naomi. Without warning, he grabbed her round the upper arms and rammed her forward, using one arm to flatten her left hand on to the table top, holding her by the wrist.

Rashid laid the microphone on the ground and straightened. He reached inside his robe and took out a short-bladed knife, a hunting knife or something of the sort. He stepped over to Naomi's left side and took hold of her wrist while the other man used both arms to secure her firmly from behind.

That was when she broke. When she saw the knife. She screamed, and the scream tore through their ears. Father Joseph uttered an inaudible prayer.

'Daddy!' she screamed. 'Daddy! Please help me! Come and get me, Daddy! Don't let him hurt me.'

Rashid showed not the slightest compassion for her cries. And he did hurt her. He splayed her fingers, placing the little one in isolation, and he cut down with the hard edge like a chef slicing through asparagus. Next moment, his white robe was splattered with blood and Naomi's finger was rolling on the table.

Jack passed out. He dropped from the chair, hitting his head on the floor. Father Joseph switched off the video and, with Jamila's assistance, helped Jack back onto the chair.

He came round quickly, and when he was able to stand, they got him to his feet and walked him slowly back to the Yaqoubs' house. Shadia took him in and showed him to the boys' bedroom, where he was ordered to lie down. He was shuddering. Every so often, a fit of shivers would take him. Shadia wanted to get a doctor, but Jamila wouldn't let her. There was too much risk.

As Jamila prepared to close the door, Jack looked up at her.

'I've seen men torn apart before this. Limbs torn off, heads smashed. I thought I was inured to it...'

'I'd hate you if you'd done anything else. No one should see what you just saw. I found it hard to take, and she's not my daughter. Have some rest, Jack. Save your strength till later.'

Father Joseph was waiting for her in the corridor.

'Father, we need somewhere safe to stay. That

265

means being anywhere but here. You and your family are at risk every minute we're with you. You've seen what they're capable of, what that man is like. Can you think of anywhere?'

He led her downstairs.

'You're right,' he said. 'You can't stay here. I have to think of Shadia and the children. But I can't let you and Jack go out on the street. They'll have people in Shubra al-Khayma. I've heard of this man's brother. Muhammad al-Masri. They call his group Ahl al-Janna: the People of Paradise.'

He paused.

'Jamila, I don't think he will be content with the status of Caliph. I fear he means to announce himself as a new prophet. The Prophet of the Last Days. He will need this sword of yours to help him convince men. If he succeeds, they will flock to him like bees to the Queen.

'As for you and Jack, there's a crypt underneath the church. There are some coffins, but not many. I can screen them off. The entrance can be hidden. Your father designed it like that: mobs like to desecrate the dead. You and Jack can stay there while you sort this out.'

She took his hand.

'Thank you, Father. We wouldn't survive long on the street. Perhaps you can take us there later. But now I have to go back to your office.'

'Whatever for?'

'To see the rest of the tape. He wants to offer Naomi for the sword. He'll have more to say.'

Jack had largely recovered when she got back, though his spirits were lower than she had seen them. She told him of Father Joseph's offer. He just nodded, as if it were all one to him whether they found a hide-out or not.

'There's something else,' she said. 'There was more on the tape. Rashid wants you to leave the sword in the zoo. You're to go in through the entrance on Charles de Gaulle, near the French embassy, and make for the hippopotamus lake, which is just inside.'

'Yes, I know it. I used to take Naomi there.'

'He wants you to leave the sword in a bag at the foot of the iron bridge over the lake.'

'When? Today?'

'No, tomorrow at noon.'

'Why so long?'

'I don't know. He says there'll be an envelope taped to the front of the bridge. This will contain directions to wherever Naomi has been left. Take the envelope and leave the sword and Zayd's letter. No one will touch you.'

'And you believe that?'

He wanted Naomi back immediately, wanted to rush her to a hospital.

Jamila shook her head.

'I have to go all the same,' he said. 'You understand that, don't you?'

'I would do the same in your place. Anyone would. Your duty is to that little girl.'

'I can't help her if they take me prisoner as well, or if they kill me.'

'I could go.'

He hesitated.

'No, they may recognise you by now. They'll have watchers all over the place.'

'What about Darsh?' she asked. 'He was in and out like lightning today.'

Jack shook his head.

'It's too great a risk. It very nearly went wrong for him today. There must be another way.'

There was a knock on the door. Father Joseph came in.

'I wanted to see how Jack is getting on. And to ask if there was anything else on that tape.'

'Sit down, Father,' said Jack. 'Perhaps you can help solve our dilemma.'

Jamila explained.

The priest listened carefully. He looked at Jack, then back to Jamila.

'Neither of you can go,' he said. 'You need to take them by surprise. The zoo will be crowded tomorrow. A Coptic priest won't be noticed. I'll leave the sword where they suggest, and I'll take the envelope. Until then, I shall pray for your daughter's delivery. You are welcome to join me in the church.'

That night, Jack rang home. He wanted to know if Sandra had contacted the Gilfillans, and he was anxious about his parents.

He took out his mobile phone and keyed in his sister's number. It rang three times, then a man's voice answered.

'Derek Lassiter. Who's this?'

'Derek. How are you? This is Jack.'

There was a spluttering sound at the other end.

'Jack? Who the fuck do you think you are, ringing this number, cool as a cucumber? "How are you? This is Jack." Gives you a thrill, does it, just ringing my fucking phone number from God knows where, jaunty as a lark, how are you, how's Sandra?'

'What's up, Derek? Has something happened? Can I speak to Sandra?'

'Just put her on, shall I? Here, Sandra, love, it's that sweet little brother of yours, he wants to talk to you about mummy and daddy and those nice friends of his, what was their name, the Gil-fillans?'

'Shut up, Derek and tell me what's going on.'

'Are you for real? "Tell me what's going on"? It's too late for the butter-wouldn't-melt-in-my-mouth treatment. They're on to you, lad. You'd better forget all this blarney, all this "what's going on"? nonsense, find the nearest police station and hand yourself in pronto. Before you do any more damage, if you catch my drift. Unless you're planning on a trip to Nottingham. Is that it, is that what's coming next, Sandra and me? Because I'm telling you now, if you turn up here, I'll twist your fucking head off. Understand?'

Jack cancelled the call. His hand was shaking as he did so. What had happened?

The oldest of the two boys, Pierre, was planning to go to university later in the year. He had a small computer in the room he shared with his brother, and an Internet connection.

It took about one minute to find out what was wrong. Jack's father and mother had been found murdered in Norwich. Two couples and a single man had been killed in the same manner in Scotland, and Jack's name had been linked to each of the crimes. He was the UK's most wanted criminal. A manhunt had started in Britain, and officers from Norfolk and Scotland had been sent to Cairo in search of him.

Chapter Thirty-Three

A BRIDGE TOO FAR

Cairo Zoological Gardens
Duqqi
12.00 noon
The Following Day

One hundred years earlier, Cairo Zoo had been the fourth best in the world, a jewel on the Nile's west bank, planted with trees and shrubs and plants from India, Central Africa, and South America. The green expanse had started life as the Gardens of Delight, reserved exclusively for the concubines of Khedive Ismail's Harem. Giant ferns grew alongside a profusion of pagodas, kiosks, gazebos and belvederes spread across an archipelago of islands intersected by lakes and miniature meandering canals. It had been a place of refuge for citizens sweltering in the summer heat.

Today, it was much fallen from grace. Its glories were still there, but the zoo was shabby and down -at-heel. There were signs of neglect everywhere. The old walkways of red, white and black pebbles, with their intricate mosaic patterns, were worn with the passage of millions of feet, and those that had deteriorated too far had been replaced with concrete. Railings showed signs of rust, the gazebos needed fresh coats of paint. Worst of all, however, were the conditions under which the animals were kept. Restricted in narrow pens, teased by the public, subjected to the constant din made by passers-by, they seemed tired and sad.

Jack had found himself a vantage point on a knoll overlooking Gustave Eiffel's ironwork suspension bridge, which lay immediately to the north of a lake in which two hippos rested, up to their eyes in mud. From here, with the help of his binoculars, he could see everything that happened at the bridge entrance.

Jamila checked her weapon. It worried her that once the ten bullets that remained in the magazine were finished, she had no easy way of replacing them. She was sitting in a Peugeot that Jack had hired that morning. She had parked it close to the entrance, about half a block away from the French embassy. The engine was running, and her pulses were racing, for she knew just how easily this could go wrong. She looked at her wristwatch. Almost twelve.

Her mobile rang. She opened it and Jack's voice came through.

'A man in a *dishdasha* has just taped something to the left-hand post. Father Joseph has seen him, but he's waiting for him to get clear. Keep this line open.'

The priest was several yards below where Jack sat, standing still like someone admiring the

271

scenery. His older son, Pierre, was waiting nearer the zoo entrance, beside the cages where the lions paced angrily round and round their tiny concrete boxes, glaring from time to time through rusty bars at the crowd. In another section, a keeper was letting a string of foreign visitors handle the lion cubs, who endured the cuddling with stately indifference.

Father Joseph moved forward at a walking pace. He would not act till the last possible moment. If there were watchers, they would not be expecting a man in a priest's cassock and high hat.

He stood for several moments next to the green bridge, as if admiring it, then let the small bag he'd been carrying in one hand drop to the ground, while snatching the envelope from the pillar. He did not run, trusting that anyone watching would still be waiting for someone quite different to arrive. Without looking round, he made off along the lower path that went directly back to the lion house.

'He has the envelope,' said Jack. 'I can't see him any longer: there are too many trees in the way.'

'Get back to the car now,' ordered Jamila.

The priest thrust his way in among the crowds gathered in front of the lion house, to where Pierre was waiting. They grazed one another, and, as they did so, the envelope made its way into Pierre's hand, then vanished inside the pocket of his jeans as he walked away from his father, turned, and headed for the entrance.

Father Joseph followed him. Jack had taken a different path from the bridge, and was now at the lion house. He caught sight of the priest's distinctive garb through the crowd, then lost him again.

Pierre made it through the exit without incident. No one knew he had the envelope, no one was interested in him. He walked briskly to the car and got into the back.

'My father's on his way,' he said.

But as Joseph reached the way out, two men stepped out from the crowd and grabbed his arms, one on either side.

'I think you should come with us, priest,' one of the men said, pulling Father Joseph away from the entrance towards a path leading towards the south end of the gardens. 'We want to have a word with you.'

As the man yanked on Joseph's arm, someone came up behind him and the last thing he felt was a hand on his neck and fingers pressing hard on his carotid artery. He collapsed like a rag doll. The other man swung round, bewildered, and Jack moved on him before he had a chance to react. A sharp chop to his Adam's apple sent him down beside his companion.

'Quickly, Father, let's get out of here.'

They were in the car, pulling fast away from the kerb and well out of sight before any of the Ahl al-Janna could emerge from the zoo. They headed back to Shubra al-Khayma. It was ten minutes past noon.

Jack read the message in the envelope as they drove. It was brief and to the point.

Professor Goodrich. If you have left us what we seek,

273

and if we are satisfied that it is the real thing and not a replica, go to the main entrance of the American University at three o'clock. Your daughter will be waiting. There is no god but God, and Muhammad is his Prophet.

There was no signature.

The main entrance to the university was in the Ewart Building, on Sheikh Rihan. Within a block each way stood the Egyptian Parliament building, the Ministry of the Interior, and the Central Government Building, the notorious Mugamma. The Honeycomb, the modernist structure that housed the US embassy, was visible above the rooftops two streets away to the south-west.

Jack and Jamila had paid a hefty 'tip' to a traffic cop on Qasr al-Ayni and asked him to keep a watch on their car, which was waiting for them just round the corner. Jack's plan was to run Naomi straight to the city's best public hospital, Qasr al-Ayni, just over a mile south along the street of that name.

His nerves were in shreds. If anything happened to Naomi now, if she were snatched from him just as he had come to hope he would really see her alive again, the blow would be more severe than that first discovery of what he had thought was her body swimming in blood. There had been bad dreams all night. Sleeping beneath a church had done nothing to lighten his anxiety.

By three-fifteen, Naomi had not appeared. Jack went inside once, to see if she'd been left in the entrance hall, but he found only students and administrative staff moving from room to room, appointment to appointment. No one recognised him.

He came out into the open air again. Still no sign of her.

By half past three, he was in despair. They waited till four. Then five, then six, then seven. It had been dark for a couple of hours.

'I think we have to leave, Jack. Something has gone wrong. We'll buy all the newspapers tomorrow. They're bound to get in touch. Perhaps they want to authenticate the sword and the letter. They probably have someone from al-Azhar working on it now.'

Jack shook his head. He'd known the sword was real the first moment he set eyes on it, accepted that the letter was genuine after one reading. It wouldn't take another scholar this long.

'She's dead,' Jack said. 'I can feel it. They used her to get the sword. For all I know, she was killed the moment the camera was shut off yesterday. They never had any intention of handing her back.'

Jamila didn't know what to say. She felt crushed by the thought of Naomi's death, and she could only guess what it was doing to Jack.

'Let's go back to the car,' she said. 'There's nothing more we can do here.'

PART FOUR

Chapter Thirty-Four

PERSEPHONE IN EGYPT

The al-Masri Bunker
Shubra
2.00 p.m.

Naomi was in a lot of pain. The only painkiller they kept down here was paracetamol, and it did absolutely nothing for the agony she was going through. Samiha had done her best to staunch the bleeding with bandages and cheap antiseptic cream, but the wound would not dry up, and she had to change the bandages at regular intervals, causing yet more pain.

Samiha had sneaked away from her computer to be with Naomi. She had never been so angry or upset in her life. The blinding cruelty of severing a child's finger made her head swim. Hurting adults was bad enough, but to wound a child deliberately and without remorse seemed to her the very height of evil.

Naomi had grown feverish overnight, and since noon she had been getting sicker by the hour. Samiha knew nothing of medicine, but instinct and experience with her own children told her that Naomi might not live long if she didn't get to a hospital quickly. But it was impossible even to dream of it. Unless...

She decided to go back to Rashid and tell him firmly that something had to be done as fast as possible, or the child would die.

'Naomi,' she said, 'try to be brave a little longer. I'm going to ask if they'll let me take you to a hospital. I won't be long.'

'Don't ... leave me ... Samiha,' Naomi murmured, barely able to get the words out. Her voice was weak and flat, and she had started to drift in and out of consciousness.

Samiha squeezed her good hand and went out of the room.

It was considered improper for a female to interrupt members of al-Masri's inner core. The men had important business, God's business, to attend to, and it was a sin to distract them from their sacred responsibilities. But Samiha had vowed to save a child's life, and nothing could frighten her any longer.

Rashid al-Masri was in the room he used to sleep, work, and pray in. It was much larger than the cramped cells occupied by Samiha or Naomi. Samiha knocked, and when he said 'Enter' she marched in, determination vividly displayed on her face.

He frowned.

'Who asked you to come back here?' he demanded. 'Is something wrong?'

'Yes,' she said. Despite the pounding of her heart, her voice was steady. The least sign of weakness would give him an excuse to dismiss her. 'Something *is* wrong. The child is dying. She needs help. She needs to be taken to a hospital urgently.'

His eyes narrowed. Samiha had often noticed

the cruelty in them, a coldness of intent that told her he would stop at nothing. On the few occasions she had seen his older brother, she had seen the same thing, but intensified. Rashid would kill or torture any human being who crossed his path or endangered his cause; but Muhammad al-Masri would sacrifice the human race on the altar of his warped devotion to the God of Battles.

'What's that to me?' he snapped. 'Or to you, for that matter? I told you to take care of her. If she's dying, it's God's will. If she's in pain, I'll come there when I have a spare moment and put her out of her misery. Now, get out of here.'

She felt a wave of nausea run through her stomach.

'What do you mean by that?' she asked.

'Isn't it obvious? The little bastard is of no further use to us. We have the sword. It has been examined and pronounced genuine by a sheikh from al-Azhar. We have the letter that went with it. That has also been examined by the sheikh and certified authentic. The child is of no consequence. If you're too squeamish to cut her throat yourself, I'll do it. But I have more important things to occupy me for the present. Get out and don't come back unless it's to tell me you've taken care of the problem.'

He stood and glared at her until she left the room. He did not touch her: that would have been improper. It was then, after so many months, that she came closest to breaking down. If it had not been for the knowledge that Naomi's life now depended on her more than ever, she would have

281

collapsed. But to do that would have guaranteed a knife through the child's throat, and probably one in hers afterwards. Samiha swore to herself that, while she still breathed, she would stop that happening.

She decided that only the boldest of actions would help her pull off the impossible. Back in her own room, she burnt half a dozen data CDs with files from her hard drive. They went into the plastic bag the CD box had come in. Then she rummaged in the drawer where she was allowed to keep a few changes of clothing; there she found a *milaya* for herself and a plain headscarf that would fit Naomi if doubled. Finally, she took the heavy pottery bowl in which she kept dried figs, emptied it of its contents, and put it in the bag next to the discs.

Back in Naomi's cubicle – for it was little more than that – she got the little girl dressed. There had been strong black coffee on a stove in the galley kitchen near her own room, and she forced two large glasses of it down Naomi's throat. It tasted vile, and Naomi choked as it went down; but she was too far gone to fight back, and Samiha knew it would help keep her alert. If Naomi lapsed completely into unconsciousness, it could prove fatal.

As the child came round a little, Samiha bent down and told her what they were going to do. Naomi nodded and promised to cooperate.

'Do you understand what I need you to do, Naomi?'

'Yes. I'll try very hard.'

They went up to the next level, and headed for

the office used by the woman in charge of all female workers. Fatima Kassab was a thin-lipped, sharp-eyed woman whose main task in life was to make existence hard for other people. Not the tiniest seed of kindness had ever lodged in the hard rock that was her heart. She liked to make the women in her charge cry. She used sin as a weapon with which to beat them, and when that did not work, she slapped their faces until she drew blood. No one got on the wrong side of her, not even the tough male fighters who guarded the bunker. Samiha knew that convincing her would be the hardest part of what she had set out to do.

'What do you want?' she snapped as Samiha came in. She looked at Naomi, and Samiha could see her bristle with distaste. The unbelieving child had angered her sense of propriety from the day she first set eyes on her.

'I've been sent by Rashid,' Samiha volunteered. 'The child is dangerously ill, and he wants her taken to the nearest hospital without delay. Her father has something else the Caliph wants; he didn't hand it all over, but if the girl dies, he'll have no further reason to negotiate. Rashid told me to get your permission and said I was to take her since she knows me.'

'What's wrong with the brat anyway? Why should she be sick? She lost a finger. So what? I've seen men survive arms and legs being blown off.'

Samiha bit back the retort she so badly wanted to make.

'She's a child, not a man, and her wound hasn't been treated. It has become infected, and that's causing the fever. She's seriously ill. If we don't hurry, she could die. Didn't the Prophet say "Allah has not created any disease without also creating a medicine or a remedy for it"?'

Fatima hesitated. She didn't dare disobey a direct order, let alone disagree with a Prophetic Tradition, but she only had this on the word of a woman she neither liked nor trusted.

'I'll go down to see him first,' she said. 'I'd like his personal approval.'

'I'm sorry,' said Samiha, knowing she had to be bold or suffer the consequences. 'He gave express orders that he is not to be disturbed until after the Asr prayer. He's in a foul temper. I don't advise interrupting him, and I don't think you should mess things up at this stage.'

The overseer looked hard at Samiha. When she thought about it, the child did look seriously ill. She was as white as a ghost, and her bandages were soaked with blood. There was no particular benefit to Samiha in bringing the child to her, or in taking her to hospital, except that the Palestinian had a soft heart. Softness of heart, in Fatima's opinion, was the greatest of weaknesses.

'I'll take her,' she said. 'There's a clinic not far from here that we sometimes use. It's run by our people.'

'Is it far? She can't walk very well.'

'In that case, we'll take a taxi. Let me get some money to pay for it. You can go back to your room.'

'I'm sorry,' said Samiha, 'but the Caliph's brother gave strict instructions that I was to stay with the girl all the way. Look at her. She's moaning. She's almost delirious. If she panics on the street, she could attract unwanted attention. She knows me. I can keep her calm. You can come if you insist, but I have to go with her.'

Fatima felt rushed, but she made up her mind quickly. Punishments for disobedience could be severe, even for someone as loyal as herself. She preferred not to take the risk.

'Let's go,' she said.

A narrow concrete staircase took them to a higher level again. Guards watched them as they made their way to a door. Fatima asked one of the guards to let them through. She was well known to them, and they opened the door, pulling aside bolts and pressing digits on an electronic pad. The door opened slowly, moving into the wall on tracks set in the floor and ceiling.

They stepped out into a furnished room in what seemed an ordinary apartment. More armed guards watched them come through. The door started to slide back into the wall, coming flush with it so that no sign of it appeared on the outside.

Fatima explained her journey to the guards, who let her pass with Samiha and Naomi. Another door led into a hallway that was set on the ground floor of a tenement. The entire building was occupied by members of the Ahl al-Janna, as was much of the district in which it was set.

The street leapt at Samiha like a monster from a nightmare. For months, she had been shut away from the sights and sounds of the everyday world, cocooned for most of the time in her tiny room that resembled a monk's cell more than anything. Apart from mealtimes (when the men and women ate in separate shifts) and trips to the female bathroom and toilets, she had slept and worked in her room twenty-four hours a day.

Now, traffic surged down a narrow street, and the pavements were filled with jostling crowds. Three million people lived in Shubra, as many as in Lebanon. It was the size of a small country, but packed into these streets and alleyways. In reality, the street was not that big, the traffic was relatively light, and the pedestrians were not that great in number. But to Samiha it was the most frightening place she'd ever set foot in.

Holding Naomi between them, they set off in search of a taxi. Naomi flinched from the cars and the passers-by, and stumbled from time to time. Samiha prayed that the neighbourhood would be suitable for her plan, otherwise this would turn out badly in the end. It was no longer a matter of fixing a wounded hand or giving antibiotics for a fever: if they returned to the bunker, Rashid would see to it that both she and Naomi would pay for this deception with their lives.

Fatima insisted that they had to walk to an intersection with Shubra Street, which ran directly to Ramses Station. They'd find a cab there, she said, and the clinic was not far.

Suddenly, they passed the mouth of a narrow passageway between two tenement blocks. This was what Samiha had been waiting for. She squeezed hard on Naomi's arm, praying the child would respond. They had passed the passageway and, for a moment, Samiha thought Naomi was too far gone to play her part. Then the little girl cried out in pain, a genuine cry, and said she was going to be sick.

'Quickly,' said Samiha, 'in here.' She drew Naomi back into the passageway. But for the sound of traffic, it was as if the street had been snatched away. Sunlight struggled to find its way through the narrow gap above, and the alley was in a state of permanent twilight. Fatima, who had Naomi's other arm, had no choice but to follow, scolding the child for holding them up.

Naomi threw up on cue. It wasn't difficult: she had already been sick several times before in her room.

'Hold her,' said Samiha. 'I have something in here to wipe her face with.'

She fumbled in the bag and, as Fatima turned her back on her and bent to grab Naomi, Samiha took out the heavy bowl and crashed it on Fatima's head. One sickening blow, and a second in quick succession before she fell.

Checking no one was around, Samiha bent to feel Fatima's pulse. She was alive, but unconscious. Moving quickly, Samiha stripped the prostrate woman, pulling off her outer garments and headscarf, then her underwear, until she was completely naked. She stuffed the garments into the bag. For a pious woman like Fatima, being found naked on the street was worse than death. Samiha guessed she would hide in a corner somewhere and wait for dark and well beyond before moving. If she moved at all.

Fatima had brought a small amount of money with her to pay the clinic. Samiha found it and put it in her own pocket. She hoped it would be enough to pay for a cab.

The junction was just ahead. Samiha gave Naomi her bag to hold, then picked the child up and took her in her arms. She felt as light as a baby.

The first cab pulled over.

'Take us to the British consulate,' Samiha said as she settled into the back seat, with Naomi stretched out beside her.

The driver looked back at them.

'The child looks ill,' he said. 'Don't you want a doctor?'

Samiha shook her head. She knew she couldn't trust a doctor round here. Someone in the consulate would know. Someone in the consulate would help her reunite Naomi with her father.

Chapter Thirty-Five

GEORGINA

3.45 pm.

Samiha's heart sank when she drew up in front of the embassy. The driver told her the consulate was inside the same building, but it was such an imposing building, she thought, a proud, arrogant building, and she had no idea where to go and whom to ask for. She was sure her English wouldn't be adequate, or that they would turn her and Naomi away the second they looked at them. Naomi was shivering, and Samiha was scared she might die then and there.

She paid the driver and got Naomi out onto the road right in front of the security gate. Two uniformed guards with guns eyed them suspiciously.

She went up to the guard on the right-hand side and spoke to him in English, a language she read well but had hardly ever spoken since university.

'Please,' she said, 'I need help. For the little girl. She needs to be taken to hospital. Somewhere safe. She's in great danger. Can you help? Can anyone inside help?'

The guard eyed her coldly. Another dirty Gyppo beggar, he thought. There was no charity in his heart. He'd been in Afghanistan and Iraq, and he'd lost whatever charity he'd once had.

'Just fuckin' *imshi, bint,*' he said, without even asking himself why this particular beggar spoke such good English. 'Go on, hop it. Scarper, or I'll have my mate here teach you a lesson you won't fuckin' forget. Get out of it! Scram!'

He took his weapon in both hands in order to frighten her.

Samiha pulled off Naomi's headscarf.

'She is an English child. Her mother is dead, and she doesn't know where her father is. Look at her. She is dying. She must be taken to a hospital.'

The guard did a double take. Even he could see that Naomi was not Egyptian. Her blonde hair and white skin – her tan had long since vanished in captivity – made the woman's story seem convincing. Unless the Gyppo had stolen the kid and was trying to con a reward out of the embassy.

289

He bent down to Naomi, and saw she flinched when she caught sight of his sub-machine gun.

'What's your name, love?'

Naomi was lapsing into semi-consciousness again, but her new surroundings and the sight of the guard roused her sufficiently to answer.

'Na ... omi. Naomi ... Goodrich. My ... father is ... Professor Goodrich. I live in ... Garden City.'

'What's wrong with her?' asked the soldier, straightening up.

Samiha showed him the bandaged hand.

'She's got a blood infection. The fever is burning her up. She will die if the wound isn't treated.'

Seeing the bandage and the blood thickly caked on it, the guard woke up to the seriousness of the situation. He hurried to his sentry box and used the phone there to ring through to the consulate.

Half a minute later, a woman came tearing out of the front entrance and down to the security gate. She was a young staffer from the consulate, still green behind the ears and eager to help. Her name was Georgina Moffett-Petrie, she was twenty-three years old, she loved animals, and she had been in Cairo six months.

Samiha explained the situation to her, and she grasped the problem at once. One of her dogs had been badly injured when she was eleven, and there had been a mad dash to the vet's. She thought quickly, and turned to the guard.

'Have you got the key to your Land-Rover, Sergeant?'

Her father was a colonel, and she knew how to speak to the lower ranks.

'Yes, ma'am, but we're not allowed...'

'Bugger what you're not allowed. I'm allowing you. This is an emergency, and I'm taking this child straight to the Anglo-American, and I'm not waiting till someone gets an official car out of the park. Hand the keys to me now.'

'Ma'am...'

'Sergeant, if you don't hand those keys over, you'll be up on a charge and headed back to Afghanistan before supper.'

The sergeant didn't know if consular staff could put him on a charge, but she sounded as if she could, and it wasn't worth the risk. He fished in his trouser pocket and pulled out the keys.

'Help me get her over to the jeep, miss,' she said to Samiha.

They got Naomi in the back, and Georgina climbed into the driver's seat.

'I'm coming as well,' Samiha shouted, and she climbed into the back beside Naomi, taking her hand and reassuring her that all would be well now.

The Land-Rover had a blue light and a siren, and after a bit of fumbling Georgina found the right switch and turned them on. The military appearance of the jeep helped her forge a path through the afternoon traffic. They drove up a stretch of the Corniche with the Nile on their left, then west across al-Tahrir Bridge onto Gezira Island. Naomi was shivering more violently and threw up again. Georgina drove without hesitation. She could have found the way blindfolded: one of her regular duties was visiting UK visitors and expats in hospital, and the drive was imprinted on her brain already. She pulled onto a little road that ran north of the Exhibition Grounds. Behind them, the Cairo Tower rose over six hundred feet into the air. Lights were coming on along the river as twilight soaked into the city. Ahead, the sun went down behind the pyramids like a smoking brand.

The road led straight to the hospital entrance. Staff had already been alerted by the siren, and a trolley was waiting to take Naomi off to the small room where they handled the occasional emergencies that were brought to them. It was a small hospital, but well equipped.

'I don't know to thank you,' said Samiha, when Naomi had been rushed off. 'You've saved her life.'

'Let's hope so,' Georgina said, though she was still worried about the little girl. She had seemed extremely ill. 'Look, I think you'd better tell me all about what happened. I assume it was an accident, but if her parents aren't around... Are you the nanny?'

Georgina had to explain what a nanny was. In her world, perfectly respectable girls were nannies, even Princess Di had once been a kindergarten teacher, so the fact that Samiha spoke good English did not seem particularly odd.

'No, I'm not a nanny, but I've been looking after her for several months. It isn't easy to explain.'

'I have time. At least it keeps me out of the office. I have the most tedious job on at the moment, arranging an orientation session for some new arrivals. Perfectly ghastly. I did one a month ago, and they did nothing but moan about the price of rents and the food. Let's find the cafeteria, if there is one.'

Over a series of coffees in the small room that served for visitors, Samiha told Georgina as much as she thought advisable and made up enough to fill the gaps – about Emilia Goodrich's murder, which Naomi had seen at first hand, about Professor Goodrich's trip abroad to a week-long conference, about her being a friend of the family who'd been asked to look after the child, about an accident while she'd been away shopping. She said nothing about Muhammad al-Masri or the group he belonged to, or her own background, or the suicide bombing she'd been scheduled to carry out. It took a long time, but Georgina was a good listener.

An Egyptian doctor in a white coat and with a brisk manner came into the room and eyed them up and down. Samiha with an Arab face and hair tucked away under a headscarf, Georgina with curly blonde hair, green eyes, and Western clothes.

'You seem too young to be the child's mother,' he said, addressing Georgina, having already dismissed Samiha as unimportant.

'I should think so,' replied Georgina. She had already learnt that Arab men could be rude to Western women, even doctors. 'And she isn't my sister. I'm from the British consul. Samiha here is a friend of the child's family. She brought her to me and I brought her here.'

The doctor looked as though he might explode. He turned his rage on Samiha, snapping at her in Arabic.

'And how long did you wait before bringing her here?' he asked. 'I've had to put her on fluids and intravenous antibiotics. She may not pull through. The infection has been developing for something like twenty-four hours.'

Samiha argued with him briefly, trying to explain what had happened, without being able to tell the truth. She knew that, even if she did come clean, no one would believe her.

Georgina brought the discussion back to English.

'Can we see her?' she asked.

'Certainly not, but I would like the parents to get here as quickly as they can. If the child dies and they aren't here, I can't be answerable for that.'

'I think you'll find I have every legal right to see the girl,' retorted Georgina. 'I'm a consular official and she's a UK citizen.'

'Come back later. Come back this evening. She has to rest now. It's a bad infection. She may not live.'

'Thank you,' said Georgina, 'you've made that perfectly clear. We'll come back later.'

'Before you go, see someone at reception about the bill. There's a one thousand Egyptian Pounds deposit that has to be made now.'

Georgina saw to the payment, then took Samiha back to the car.

'Let's go back to my office,' she said. 'We need to talk some more.'

The guards had changed, and Georgina had no trouble bringing Samiha into the embassy. The consular section had closed to the public at 1.30, but some staff were still at their desks. There was a problem with the new biometric passports, and they were working late to solve it.

Georgina's office was a cubby hole located between a toilet and an ancient air-conditioning system. She squeezed in behind her desk and woke up her computer.

'If you can find room, take a seat,' she said. 'I won't be a moment.'

Samiha, worried sick about Naomi, found it hard to conceal her nervousness. She dragged a small overstuffed armchair out from behind a heap of files and sat in it. She was starving, and the coffees she had drunk had made her jittery. *She may not live...* The doctor's word spun in her head like splinters of broken glass.

'Can you tell me where exactly Naomi's father is?' Georgina asked. 'Is he in this country?'

Samiha felt helpless. Her lies were bound to catch her out.

'I don't know where he is,' she said. Her hands would not be still. Her brain buzzed with fear and uncertainty. Naomi might die. She herself was adrift and alone in a strange city, without friends or money. The only embassy that might help her was that of Israel, and she knew her name would set alarm bells ringing if she turned up at their door.

'I don't understand,' said Georgina. 'You say you're a friend of the family and you were asked to look after Naomi, but now you say you don't know where her father is?'

Georgina felt her sympathy for the Arab

woman evaporating. Something was going on here, and she wanted to get to the bottom of it. She was sure Samiha was lying about something.

'It was last minute,' Samiha said, struggling to keep her story straight. 'He forgot to leave a phone number or an address.'

'I find that hard to believe.'

'Nevertheless, it is the truth.'

Georgina frowned.

'Stay there,' she said. 'We need to sort this out. I'm going to look Professor Goodrich up on the computer. What is his first name?'

Naomi had told Samiha her parents' names very early in their relationship.

'Jack,' she said. 'Her mother's name was Emilia.'

Georgina started typing.

It took about five minutes. When she looked at Samiha again, her eyes had lost all of their earlier friendliness.

'Can you tell me exactly what is going on?' she demanded.

'I told you,' Samiha began, 'there was an accident.'

'You've been lying to me from the beginning. When did Professor Goodrich leave Cairo?'

'Almost a week ago. He should be back soon.'

'What is his address? You said you were a friend of the family. I presume you've visited him at home.'

Samiha had no answer. She was flat out of lies.

Georgina went on, inexorable.

'Would it interest you to know that Professor Jack Goodrich had a meeting in this building last Thursday? It seems he came with a ludicrous story about a sword, claimed to know people who'd never set eyes on him, and wanted to see someone from our intelligence services. And that's far from the end of the story. It now appears that there are two British policemen in Cairo who have come to arrest the professor on seven counts of murder, including his own parents. He is a wanted man. And I think you are involved in this somehow. I think he attacked his daughter, and that you are covering for him. Everything else you've told me is just a tissue of lies.'

Samiha put her hands over her ears to blot out the litany of accusations. She closed her eyes hard against the light that eemed to call her a liar. Tears had started to ooze through the closed lids. She tried to hold them back, but they kept on coming, and within moments she was racked by deep, convulsive sobs, then weeping uncontrollably with loss and loneliness and the dreadful knowledge she carried of what Muhammad al-Masri planned to do.

Georgina let her cry. She felt nothing for her, and she wondered just how deeply Samiha was involved in the murders. What she did care about was Naomi, so she waited to hear what Samiha would have to tell her.

It took a long time for Samiha's sobbing to stop. In the end, she cried herself out. She looked at Georgina with red-rimmed eyes. She had lost track of everything: who she was, where she was, where her life and her children had gone. She was empty, a hollow shell that had once held a human being, a mother without sons, a wife without a husband, a Muslim without faith, a woman without hope.

She began to talk. From that first day in Jenin to the present moment. The suicide belt they had strapped to her, Nabil and Adnan, the journey to Israel and on to Cairo, her first meeting with Naomi, their escape.

At first, Georgina listened with only half a mind. She had a party to go to, diplomats to take care of, local dignitaries to impress, and she was tired of Samiha and her deceptions. But as Samiha's story progressed, she began to listen more carefully. Half-way through, she understood the mistake she had been making.

Her brother Ben had served in Iraq with the 1st Battalion Staffordshire Regiment. After his tour of duty, he'd been given leave to recover from wounds sustained during a firefight in Basra, and he'd come home to Akenside, their country house in Needwood Forest. She'd taken time off work to help with his recuperation, and she'd spent several weeks there, taking walks with him, watching him fish in the Trent, carrying his bream and carp back for supper, talking to him in the library, chatting over lunch, listening to him talk about the war.

For the first two weeks, he'd sung a single song, to her and to her parents. His light wounds apart, things had gone well for him in Iraq. He spoke of the fighting spirit of the regiment, the camaraderie among officers and men, the importance of the job they'd been sent to do. It had sounded like a good war, and he was desperate to get back to Basra and his men.

Her father had taken her aside one day and

said, 'Georgie, keep an eye on him, will you? Wait till he's ready. He won't open up to me, not in a million years. He'll talk to you, though. Be sure you're there when the time comes. Don't let him out of your sight. I'm going to take your mother away for a few days. See what happens then.'

It had taken two days. They were walking the dogs, two Labradors, Finn and Finbar, and he'd been cracking jokes, a soldier's jokes, a bit off colour, a touch racist, a little maudlin, when he'd just stopped dead in the middle of the lane and gone into a sobbing jag that took half an hour to control. She'd held the dogs by their leashes and watched him, saying nothing, not even touching him, crying herself from time to time out of sheer pity for what she still didn't know and could only guess at.

He'd recovered and they'd walked back home in silence. She took him to the library and poured him a whiskey, raw, in a large glass, then poured one for herself.

He didn't stop talking for five hours. He'd told her the truth, and every time she had looked into his eyes, she'd seen the rawness of that truth mirrored in them. He spoke of the horrors he'd seen, the ghastliness of some of the things he and his men had done, the hatred the Iraqis had shown for them, the fear that was with them day and night.

She looked at Samiha and saw that same look, that same haunted perception of horror and beastliness and the world's cruelty mirrored in them. It became impossible to disbelieve her.

Samiha explained everything she had learnt

during the months she'd worked with the Ahl al-Janna. She knew about Jack and the sword, and the reason why Rashid al-Masri had been hunting Jack, and how he had used Naomi as bait. She connected Jack's return from Scotland with a visit made abroad by Rashid shortly before. She told Georgina what sort of man Rashid was, that he was a cold-hearted killer, and that he had gone hunting for Jack. And Georgina believed her. Believed her without reservation.

She went back into the computer to see if there was anything else on Jack Goodrich, and this time she hunted more deeply than before. Her brother, who had taken a course in computer encryption at Sandhurst, and who was something of a buff in his spare time, had taught her more than she was really supposed to know. He'd shown her how to break codes, find and generate passwords, and breach other security barriers. Now she put her pirate skills to good use.

What she found troubled her. MI6 had their fingerprints all over Goodrich. His wife had been a senior intelligence officer here at the embassy, and a man who had worked for her and since been promoted had gone to Scotland to look for Goodrich and still not returned. She formed an impression that the man in question had acted without the consent of his superiors. The professor had been under surveillance after his visit to Cairo on Thursday, but MI6 had lost him that same evening, then picked him up again last night. He'd been followed from the American University, where he'd been seen waiting for several hours.

There was more, however. References to a sword that Goodrich had found or stolen. To a radical Islamic group called the Ahl al-Janna, and to secret meetings with their representatives. There were other files relating to this, but, however hard she tried to hack into them, they denied her entry. She gave up in the end. By now she knew enough.

She pushed her chair back and smiled at Samiha.

'He's in a church,' she said. 'In a place called Shubra al-Khayma. I haven't a clue where that is, but I can find it on a map. They don't know what he's doing there, but they think he still has the sword you mentioned, and they have the church under surveillance. You will have to go there and tell him his daughter is still alive. I'll take you, but I can't get more involved than that. I'm taking enormous risks as it is.'

'Why are you doing this?'

'Because I think you're telling the truth. Because I've seen what was done to Naomi. Because my father and brother are soldiers, and they've always told me never to trust anyone working in intelligence. Because I've met the man who saw Jack here last week, and I think he's a total shit. Now, let's go and see how Naomi is.'

Chapter Thirty-Six

VESPERS

St Sergius
Shubra al-Khayma
Early evening

Georgina walked Samiha into the church. Samiha had never set foot inside a Christian place of worship in her life; she had been brought up to believe they were places where Satan was worshipped, where idols stood above an altar at which the priest drank blood, just as the Jews mixed flour with the blood of murdered children to make Passover bread. If Georgina hadn't reassured her, she would never have crossed the threshold

They entered at the west end, coming into the narthex, which was empty. Three beautifully carved wooden doors separated this narrow area from the nave. From the other side, they could hear voices raised in song. The cantor was singing a Shirat for the month of Kiahk.

Hail to you, O full of grace, the undefiled virgin, the chosen vessel for all the world.

The unextinguished lamp, the pride of virginity, the indestructible altar and the sceptre of the faith.

The words were in Coptic, quite meaningless to either Samiha or Georgina. It was probably the oldest music in the world, handed down from the days of the pharaohs and given new words by the early Christians. The cantor's voice rose and fell, intoning the ancient words syllable by syllable. Then the congregation joined in. A smell of incense wafted through the pierced doorways, frankincense, myrrh, sandalwood and ambergris.

Georgina, who had never been to a Coptic service before, let her curiosity get the better of her.

'Let's slip in and sit at the back,' she said, and made for the nearest door.

Samiha hung back, frightened by the chanting and the overpowering sweet scent, but Georgina took her by the hand and drew her into the nave.

It was like no place Samiha had ever seen or heard of. There was a richness to it, a vibrancy of colour and sound, a shimmering of wood and glass and smoke, a lambency of gold and silver, an incandescence of angels' wings and saints' faces that made her think she had stepped into another realm. Coloured lights had been strung across the nave for Christmas, and in front of the iconostasis that separated the body of the church from the three sanctuaries and the altars there stood a nativity scene.

No one noticed as they slipped into a pew at the rear on the women's side. Georgina felt undressed. There was much standing, occasional sitting, and infrequent kneeling. The liturgy for Vespers went on without pause, a preparation for the Midnight Mass that would last till four in the morning.

At long last, Father Joseph gave the congregation absolution. The assistant priests and altar boys went back behind the iconostasis, while he remained standing, watching his parishioners as they filed out. Georgina and Samiha remained waiting. He went back through the iconostasis, where he and his assistants tended to the altars, offered up short prayers, and checked that all was well for Midnight Mass. They were tired already, and a long day waited for them.

The others left through a rear door, then Father Joseph returned to the nave, where Georgina and Samiha were still waiting. He had thought they had stayed behind to pray, or to make confession. But he didn't recognise them, and that was odd, because Coptic priests are confessors to entire families, and he knew all the families who attended his church.

'Can I help you ladies?' he asked in Arabic.

Samiha stared at him, tongue-tied. Georgina did the talking.

'Do you speak English?' she asked. 'I'm afraid my Arabic's not up to much. It's a terrible shame, and I do promise to buckle down to it when there's time, but...'

All at once, he scented danger.

'I speak a little English, yes,' he said. 'Are you lost? May I be of some assistance?'

She told him who she was. He listened politely, making a connection that troubled him. He wondered who the Arab woman was.

'I'm looking for a man called Goodrich,' Georgina finished. 'Professor Jack Goodrich. I understand he is staying here.'

She saw the priest turn pale, noticed the almost

hidden gesture of his right hand, as he made the sign of the cross.

'It's all right,' she said. 'I've come about his daughter. Naomi.'

She explained as well as she could what had happened. Father Joseph listened warily, aware that excessive trust on his part could put both Jack and Jamila at risk. He had known Jamila for years, and now he had sworn to protect her.

Samiha spoke for the first time, her accent quite distinctive to an Egyptian ear.

'Sir, I have been with Naomi almost from the beginning. I've been looking after her in the place they kept her in. I was their prisoner as well. Yesterday, they cut one of her fingers off, the little one on this hand.' She raised her left hand, and Father Joseph knew she was speaking the truth. He had seen it happen. She went on.

'They left her to bleed. I did what I could to bandage the wound, but she became feverish, and by this morning she was almost dead. I found a way to get us both out. Professor Goodrich should visit her. It may raise her spirits, give her strength. Otherwise, I'm afraid she may die. If you know where he is, please find him and tell him this.'

There was something in her face, something in her voice that convinced him she was no threat to his guests.

'Wait here,' he said. 'I'll bring him to you now.'

Five minutes later, he returned with Jack and Jamila.

Jack spoke with them quickly, astounded by Samiha's story. If anything, he was more suspicious of Georgina, but when she spoke at last his fears diminished. Unlike Malcolm Purvis, she came across as a little naïve and refreshingly honest. Why on earth someone with such an open face had joined the diplomatic corps he could not guess.

'Samiha,' he said, 'I want you to stay here with Jamila. Tell her everything you know, then we'll both speak with you later.'

'I have nowhere else to go,' she said. 'I need your help, and I'm willing to tell you everything I know in return.'

She smiled then. Her face in that moment became a different face. The diffidence, the fear, the unhappiness all seemed to leave it. Jack looked at her and felt some indefinable quality assert itself, a quality that touched him in a way he'd not experienced before. Her transformed face, with its tentative smile beneath enormous sad eyes appealed to him. He wanted to trust her. To like her. To help her.

He smiled back.

'If you've saved Naomi's life, you've already done me the greatest favour imaginable.'

He turned to Georgina.

'Can you take me to the hospital? They may not let me in without you.'

'Of course,' she said. 'I haven't enjoyed myself so much since my Aunt Phylly broke her leg in Gstaad. This is the first time since I got to Cairo that I've felt I'm doing something useful. Bloody useful, from what I've heard.'

Jack smiled.

'More useful than you can possibly imagine,'

Jack said. He would see Naomi, stay with her, and nurse her back to health.

'Let's go,' said Georgina, and they were off.

Naomi lay in semi-darkness in a room on her own. Her temperature had dropped dramatically as the antibiotics fought the infection. She was still on the intravenous drip, but she had fallen into a light sleep some hours earlier. Jack tiptoed in, followed softly by Georgina. A nightlight shone on Naomi's sleeping face and on her left arm, which was lying outside the covers. Her hand had been skilfully bandaged.

He went across to her and bent down to kiss her cheek. Straightening, he saw at once how she had changed. Had he seen her by chance in the street, he might have taken her for another child, a little girl somewhat like his daughter, but less fortunate. She had lost weight, and her face looked pinched and worried. Even in sleep, she frowned.

Seeing her trapped in this no-man's land between life and death, his heart was close to breaking. The grief he had felt thinking her to be dead was reawakened and mixed with confusion, fear and guilt. He looked down at her, and for a moment thought he was watching her asleep in bed in their old house in Garden City. Then he blinked through tears and saw the truth. He thought of Emilia and how she went to Naomi every night to tuck her in before sleep. As often as he could make it, he had been there too, waiting his turn. He remembered Emilia's face and heard her voice whispering to Naomi as she drowsed. And for no reason he could think of, the face of the Palestinian woman he'd just met – he couldn't recall her name – was visible against the darkness. Somehow, it comforted him.

The doctor in charge had made it clear in no uncertain terms that Naomi had to stay with them for at least another forty-eight hours, longer if she did not pick up. Jack sighed. He'd lost her for so long, all he wanted now was to take her back with him, back to the church, back to England. Then he thought of the people who were trying to kill him, and he felt more afraid for Naomi than before.

He laid his hand on her cheek and stroked it. As he did so, her eyelids flickered. She moaned gently, then jerked as she came fully awake. Her vision was blurred at first, but as she blinked her eyes the room came into focus.

'Daddy? Is that you? They killed Mummy. I thought they'd killed you too. Where am I? Am I back home?'

He couldn't speak. Georgina watched, a lump in her throat, as he took her good hand in his and squeezed hard.

'You're in hospital,' he managed to say. 'You've been sick. The doctor wants you to stay for a little while. But I'll come to visit you, I promise.'

She frowned, then smiled.

'Where's Samiha?' she asked. 'She takes care of me. I need to talk to her.'

'Hush,' Jack said. 'Samiha rescued you. She's not here now, but she'll come later. You need to go back to sleep. You have to recover your strength.'

He kissed her again, and she closed her eyes. Moments later, she was fast asleep.

Chapter Thirty-Seven

IN THE SYRIAN PORTICO

The Syrian Portico
A1-Azhar University
Cairo
The same evening

Malcolm Purvis, dressed immaculately in a
£17,000 black vicuña overcoat, pink cashmere
scarf, and polished brogues, looked like an actor
who has strayed onto the wrong set in the wrong
film. He was walking across the main courtyard of
al-Azhar University, and some of the looks he was
receiving would have made a lesser man turn and
leave. A moon cut to the quick, hovered in the sky
above. Lights flickered all round the courtyard,
throwing shadows beneath the myriad archways.

A bearded man, very like the bearded students
milling around them, was taking him to meet his
contact within Ahl al-Janna, the brother of the
little upstart who claimed to be the new Caliph
of all Muslims. Let him claim what he liked,
thought Malcolm, so long as he's useful. Al-
Masri was shortly to take the place of Osama bin
Laden as head of al-Qaeda, and it was Malcolm's
job to keep him sweet, to ensure that Britain was
kept off the list of terrorist targets.

As before he'd driven to a spot near the Khan

al-Khalili, Cairo's enormous indoor market near al-Azbakiyya. From there, the guide had taken him through a warren of ever-narrowing passageways, past tumbled, worn-out buildings with the stench of age deep in their stones and latticed windows, down alleys of mud brick that was slowly crumbling to dust. He had been brought to al-Azhar at last through the Barbers' Gate, into a vast open space flanked on all sides by domes and minarets, some of them floodlit. The Muslim New Year was two days away. There was an air of festivity about.

Here, more than anywhere he'd been in the city, Malcolm sensed himself surrounded by the Orient, by shapes and sounds straight out of the Middle Ages. This was the world's oldest university, the greatest seat of learning in the Islamic world, a maze of little courtyards, prayer halls, and seminar rooms, where learning and piety lived side by side, and sometimes collided.

'This is the Riwaq al-Shuwam,' said the guide. 'The Syrian Portico.' Malcolm had taken a dislike to him, which he tried to suppress. The man wore a cheap suit, the jacket frayed at the cuffs, the collar buttoned but tieless, in the Iranian fashion. He walked awkwardly, and Malcolm thought it was this mild disability, rather than his poverty, that set him on edge. Not that the man had been overly friendly.

He took Malcolm up some steps and knocked at a door half-way along a narrow corridor. A voice answered.

'Come,' said the guide in English. Malcolm noticed that he had sore eyes and that he rubbed

310

them a lot. He made a point of not shaking hands when the man turned to go. It had never occurred to him that the man would not have shaken hands with him anyway, that he considered all un-believers unclean.

Waiting for him was a man of about thirty dressed in the clothes of a religious scholar. He was seated behind a desk completely free from clutter. On its mahogany surface sat a single object, exactly in the centre, a green-covered book with gold lettering. Purvis guessed it was a Koran, but decided he'd make no remark to that effect, in case his host should be offended. You could never be too sure about Korans, he thought.

On the wall were several examples of Arabic calligraphy and a photograph. Malcolm recog-nised it at once: it was a photograph of Hajj Amin al-Husseini, the Grand Mufti of Jerusalem and a much-wanted war criminal. He said nothing about it. It was just as sensitive to mention Hus-seini in some quarters as it was to speak of the Koran.

'Mr Purvis. How good to see you again.'

Rashid al-Masri did not stand and did not offer Malcolm his hand.

'Please, take a seat,' he said. 'I'll sit here, if you don't mind. There's not a lot of space in al-Azhar, you know. It was built for a different age.'

The room was small and gloomy, with a single lamp in one corner and a trickle of sooty daylight that crept through a small window. Despite the weather, it was barely heated. Malcolm, about to remove his overcoat, thought better of it.

'I'll have some coffee brought,' said Rashid,

coming out from behind his desk this time. He went to the door and put his head into the corridor, shouting a name or a command, Malcolm had no idea which. Moments later, a young boy came running. A few words, then the boy was off.

Rashid went back behind the desk.

'Thank you for coming,' he said. 'I am most grateful. Please excuse my English, it is very rusty.'

'Not at all,' Malcolm beamed.

There was too much holiness here for Malcolm's liking. These Muslims took their religion much too seriously, he thought. He felt uneasy, distracted by Rashid's chilliness, a chilliness his expressions of friendship did little to disguise. Malcolm knew perfectly well that Rashid only tolerated him because he thought he could be useful to him. After all, he reflected, didn't he feel the same thing about al-Masri?

'What brings you here today?' asked Rashid. If a snake could speak, his voice would be just like Rashid's. 'I have what I was looking for. I found Goodrich and persuaded him to hand over the sword. It belongs to my brother now. He guards it with his life. It is never out of his sight, not for a moment. He thanks you for your help in finding it.'

Malcolm straightened himself. He realised that he was out of his depth here, that all the ornaments he normally relied on to decorate his sense of status – the vicuña overcoat, the Savile Row suit, the Eton accent – were entirely lost on the man facing him across the desk. He might just as well have turned up in rags. He and Rashid inhabited different worlds, were devoted to different gods, and fought for different ends. Yet they faced one another in this room because, for the moment, their purposes meshed. It might all change. It might be completely different next month or next year. At heart, they were enemies. But even enemies can do one another favours from time to time.

The door opened and the boy struggled inside, carrying a brass tray on which an ornate coffee pot and two tiny cups without handles struggled to keep their balance.

When the coffee had been served and the first sips taken, Rashid repeated his question.

'What have you come to talk about, Mr Purvis? I don't have much time.'

'No, of course you don't. The thing is, now you have the sword and so on, my superiors at the FO would like to be sure that we all see eye to eye. Your brother doesn't present a problem. He can be Caliph and welcome. The UK government won't object. But we do need to be sure that the UK mainland will be safe. In the event of any... You understand, I'm sure.'

This was their first meeting since al-Masri had acquired the sword. Malcolm's superiors knew that this had shifted the balance between them and the Ahl-al-Janna. Now, they needed to know that the Muslim leader would keep his side of the bargain.

'I told you before. My brother will not touch Great Britain if you do not harm him or his movement, and in gratitude for your help. We have no claim on Europe or America, only on Muslim lands. We shall destroy the Zionist state and establish Islamic rule in every country that has already been conquered for the faith. Of course, you do understand that there can be no written treaty between us, only a bond of trust, a covenant of security?'

Malcolm nodded. There was cardamom in the coffee. The smell teased his nostrils. He could feel the surge of the strong, bitter liquid in his veins.

'Quite,' he said, 'quite. Just so. I merely needed to be sure. Will you need more money?'

Rashid smiled. MI6 had channelled quite a lot to the Ahl al-Janna already. British troops would pull out of Afghanistan and Iraq, there would be no more UK votes for Israel at the UN. It was a good arrangement, he thought. For as long as it lasted. Once Israel had been destroyed and every Jew there put to death, the onslaught on Europe would begin. Spain and Portugal, under Muslim rule centuries ago, would be brought back into the fold. The jihad would never end.

'No,' he said, 'no money at this stage. My brother will proclaim himself Caliph at the Islamic New Year, in two days' time. The proclamation will go out across the Internet. Muslims will arrive from every corner of the earth to make *bay'a*. To swear a sacred oath of allegiance. There will be representatives from Britain.'

He smiled, then put his cup on the tray and got to his feet.

'Before you go,' he said, 'is there anything else of interest I should know?'

Malcolm looked at him steadily. The stale air of

learning and holiness was making him reckless.

'Goodrich is in a church in Shubra al-Khayma, St Sergius. We have had men watching the place. I intend to call them off this afternoon.'

'That is interesting. Thank you.'

'The thing is ... some of our police are here in Cairo. They want to arrest him for the murders I told you about. It's rather ... delicate. You see, if they take him back and put him on trial, he may blurt out things that would be better left unsaid. It could hurt both of us.'

'Yes, I see that. I understand. Don't worry – I can take care of that.'

'His daughter has turned up. Damaged goods, apparently. She's in the Anglo-American.'

'The hospital, next to the Tower?'

'That's the one. Bang next door.'

'That's interesting too. Thank you. You have been most ... what is the word? Reciprocal? Now, your guide is waiting to take you back to your car.'

Malcolm was shown out. As the door closed, Rashid leant back in his chair and smiled. He glanced at the photograph of his great-great-uncle on the wall.

The boy came in and took the tray and its contents away. He had been gone only about a minute when there was another knock.

'Come in,' said Rashid, sitting up straight.

The man who came in was something of an oddity. He wore the clothes of a pious Muslim, and his beard and hair were trimmed like Rashid's. On his head, he wore a small black skullcap. The cropped hair that showed beneath it was blond, like the hair of his beard. His eyes were cobalt blue and his skin colouring European.

'*Al-salam 'alaykum,*' he said. He spoke the Arabic without a trace of an accent.

Rashid replied to the formal greeting.

'Please, Kurt, sit down. Tell me your news.'

Kurt sat, and as he did so grinned broadly.

'Our friends from Brazil have arrived,' he said. 'They have brought the trigger with them. Everything will be in place well within schedule.'

'Thank you. That's the news I've been waiting to hear. Where are they now?'

'In the hotel. I'll take them to Shubra later. One at a time.'

'My brother will see them this evening. Thank you for making this possible.'

Kurt smiled again.

'Thank him,' he said, nodding at the picture of Husseini on the wall.

Chapter Thirty-Eight

MIDNIGHT MASS

Later that evening

Georgina, still getting a buzz from it all, drove Jack back to St Sergius. There was an excitement in the air. In a few hours, it would be Christmas. People were out on the streets preparing for the celebration, greeting one another with a warmth that had gone out of the Christmases she had known at home. No one was shopping, no one was spending a fortune on presents that would gather dust at the back of a drawer. She began to think she'd come to the right place after all, that there was a lot more to Cairo than what she had seen or would ever see at the embassy.

As Jack got out of the car outside the church, she lowered the driver's window.

'Professor Goodrich. Before you go, I'd just like to ask... Well, would you mind awfully if I popped in to the hospital from time to time? Just to see how she is...'

He smiled.

'That's kind of you,' he said. 'I'd be immensely grateful. I may be tied up a lot over the next few days. And ... I may need your help again.'

She took a business card from her handbag and handed it to him.

'Here, this has my home number and address. The embassy is shut tomorrow through to Friday. Keep in touch.'

He stepped closer to the window.

'Georgina, I don't know how much you've guessed of what is going on here. If there were time, I'd go into more detail. Perhaps there will still be time for that. In the meantime, it's imperative that not a word leaks out about the Palestinian woman, Naomi, or myself. Are you able to do that? To keep it all to yourself?'

She sneezed, then twice again. It was cold with the window down. Suddenly, she felt very far from home and family. Lovely as this Egyptian Christmas was, she wished there were carols,

317

wished this was an Anglican church with a good choir singing 'Silent Night'.

'I was brought up in an army family, Professor. Silent men keeping a stiff upper lip about dreadful things they'd seen and done. I drank secrecy with my mother's milk. Your secret is safe with me.' She hesitated. 'So long as you're on the side of the angels.'

He looked round, saw the lights, the church tower illuminated. If there were ever angels, it should be tonight, he thought.

'Go home,' he said. 'Get some shut-eye. Maybe you'll see angels in your sleep.'

She drove off and he went round to the rear of the church, to the priests' entrance.

He made his way to the crypt. The assistant priests nodded to him as he passed. Father Joseph had told him they could be trusted. He had told them that he and Jamila were a couple in need of refuge from the church, and they had accepted the arrangement without demur.

Samiha and Jamila were talking as he came in. They broke off on hearing his footsteps. Samiha smiled, and once more he felt a shift somewhere inside his emotions, as if some sort of mutual recognition had passed between them.

There was hot coffee and a plate of *Kahk al-Id*, the Christmas cakes and biscuits everyone would be munching on the next day. Jack helped himself to both. Samiha asked after Naomi, and the note of anxiety in her voice was genuine and somehow reassuring.

'Jack,' Jamila said, after he'd told them how Naomi was doing, 'Samiha here has had access to their computer system, or most of it. They let her see almost everything.'

Jack glanced at Samiha.

'I thought you said you were their prisoner?'

Samiha nodded.

'I'll explain how that happened later. Muhammad al-Masri's brother Rashid told me early on why they'd chosen me. It was because I was dispensable, a fallen woman, someone who deserved to die. They had an accountant from New York and some others, all of whom were there against their will. Once they'd made use of us, it would be no trouble for them to shoot us and dump our bodies somewhere.'

She filled in a little about the work she had done for the Ahl al-Janna. The companies she had set up, in particular the small airlines that had been used to smuggle materials from Iran via Afghanistan and Tajikistan in Central Asia, and on into Europe.

'Several small flights came here,' she said. 'To Cairo. They were never direct. Some came through Turkey, one through Syria, one through Lebanon. The Iranians have had plenty of experience smuggling arms and other equipment to Hizbullah. This was just a stage further.'

She stopped. While she had been in the bunker, she had treated the plot as almost unreal. Knowing she would die before it came to fruition, she had thought of it more as a plot from a film or a book than something that would happen in real life. Now, talking to Naomi's father and this intense Egyptian woman, the reality started to bite.

'What were they smuggling?' asked Jack.

'Weapons mostly. Sub-machine guns, rocket launchers, grenades. These were stored at a site outside Cairo – sorry, I can't remember the name. There were two shipments that originated in a city in Iran. Somewhere called Isfahan.'

Jack raised his eyebrows.

'You're quite sure? Isfahan?'

She nodded.

'That's where the Iranians have their nuclear centrifuges,' he said. 'Where they've been enriching uranium. Do you know what was in those shipments?

She bit her lip, thinking hard.

'Yes,' she said. 'It was something called tritium. Is that right?'

Jamila nodded.

'It would form part of a nuclear weapon,' she said.

Jack was fully alert now. This was beginning to make sense. Too much sense. 'Go on,' he urged.

'There was a special delivery about a month ago,' Samiha said. 'It came from Germany. They bought a little private airport in Wildeshausen, near Bremen. It was to fly smaller planes in and out. I was ordered to create two companies for Wildeshausen. The first holds the airport licence, and the second has a German civil aviation licence. That allowed them to buy materials from German manufacturers without needing to disclose their final destination.

'There were several flights to a small airport just south of Cairo, at Heiwan. Everything was shipped in as car parts for the motor plant there.'

'You said there was a special flight.'

'That's right. About a month ago. It came from Germany as well, but whatever was on it had been flown to Wildeshausen from Afghanistan, through a small airfield in eastern Turkey. They unloaded it at Helwan and shipped it to Cairo the same day. I know it was special, because that was the only occasion on which the Caliph's brother Rashid went to pick up a delivery in person. I traced the cargo back to Afghanistan. They used the same plane all the way. There was no manifest, but I found a report from a man called Hajj Ahmad. He's al-Masri's liaison with al-Qaeda. He was responsible for winning support for the Caliph among al-Qaeda in Afghanistan.'

'What was in the report?' Jack was growing impatient.

'In the Nineties, after the collapse of the Soviet Union, Osama bin Laden bought nuclear weapons from Kazakhstan. He is also said to have obtained some from Chechen rebels, who had stolen two 30kg rucksack bombs in 1991. What was on board the plane was one of these devices, a small weapon that could produce a yield of about one kiloton.'

No one spoke for some time after that. There was no need for words; it almost seemed that to speak would be obscene in the shadow of what Samiha had just told them. When Jack finally broke the silence, it was as if he did so in a different world.

'Samiha, do you have any idea what they plan to do with this bomb?'

Samiha took a deep breath.

'Rashid was always telling people to hurry up,

hurry up. We had to get things ready in time for the New Year.'

'The Muslim New Year?' asked Jamila.

'Yes. The first of Muharram. In two days' time.'

No one spoke for a while. Jack could make no sense of it.

'Where is al-Masri?' he asked.

'Here in Cairo. No one has gone. They stay locked up in their bunker. Muhammad will declare himself Caliph at some point during New Year's Day.'

'What happens before that? After that?' asked Jamila. She had lost her appetite for the sweet cakes on the tray in front of her.

'Something happens in Cairo,' said Jack. 'That's right, isn't it?'

Samiha had not been made privy to their specific plans, but she nodded. She was sure Jack was right.

'Why would they want to explode a small nuclear device in Cairo?' he asked. 'It would kill Muslims more than unbelievers. Or is he planning to hit a Christian district?'

Jamila turned to him, a look of horror on her face.

'No,' she said, and the word came out as a mere whisper. 'That's not it. That's not his plan.'

She hesitated, thinking it through again. She was right, she decided. Otherwise it would have been too much of a coincidence.

'Jack, have you noticed flags all over the centre of Cairo?' she asked.

'Vaguely,' he said. 'I thought it might have something to do with New Year. Or both New

Years – they come so close together for once.'

Jamila shook her head. She had forgotten that Jack had been out of touch for too long, that he hadn't heard news of Cairo in some time. Samiha obviously hadn't had a chance to hear of anything down in her bunker.

'They're not there for the New Year,' Jamila said. 'Not exactly. The flags were put out to mark a conference that starts on Friday, to coincide with the New Year. It's an international conference, and it's to be held at Giza.'

She hesitated. The full implications of what al-Masri planned were just starting to sink in.

'Jack, it's a summit conference. Heads of state from forty-five countries will attend. The US President will be there. Your Prime Minister. The French President. Our President Mubarak, of course. Even the Israeli PM. The Palestinian President. It's a conference on peace in the Middle East. The Americans started working on it after the Israeli-Lebanese war in 2006.'

'And all these people are here?'

'Some are in Cairo already, the rest arrive tomorrow. There's a special Coptic Christmas celebration.'

'Did you say this is being held in Giza?'

Giza is a large built-up area that forms the south-west stretch of Cairo. Beyond it lies the Western Desert. But where the buildings end, the Giza Plateau begins. This is the most famous site in Egypt, one of the seven wonders of the world, instantly recognisable. In a small area about one mile by three-quarters stand the Great Pyramid and its two companions, hundreds of tombs, mortuary temples and causeways. This had once been the great cemetery of ancient Egypt. Here too stood the Great Sphinx, 'the Lord of Septet, the Chosen Place'.

'Not in the city,' Jamila said. 'They've cordoned off the pyramids and tombs, built a luxurious tent city to house the conference. It's a spectacular setting. The more important heads of state, their wives and their ministers have the best suites and rooms at the Mena House Oberoi hotel overlooking the pyramids. Tomorrow, there's to be a formal opening of the Grand Egyptian Museum, attended by a mixture of foreign dignitaries and the great and good from Cairo. People have been selling their children just to get an invitation. The conference will be opened at a ceremony on Friday. They've marked out an area south of the pyramids for it. The Sphinx will be a little to the east. There's to be a grand tour of the Great Pyramid afterwards, for any heads of state who feel up to it. The whole thing's going to be broadcast on television all round the world.'

Jack heard Samiha gasp. When he looked round, her face was drained of blood, and her hand was pressed against her mouth. Her eyes caught his. In that moment, her eyes filled with fear and she became real to him. More than a badly remembered name.

'The pyramids,' she said. 'The Father of Terror.'

They'd been speaking in Arabic. Abu al-Hawl, the Father of Terror, was the Sphinx.

'He used to speak about them all the time. Both of them did, Muhammad and his brother. The ancient monuments, the temples, the tombs with statues and paintings of gods. They called it the pagan past. Like the time before the Prophet came. The Age of Ignorance. Muhammad used to say that when the Caliph ruled again he would do as the Prophet did and destroy all traces of idol-worship. The pyramids would be trampled back to the desert sand. The tombs would be flattened. The Sphinx would be blown into tiny fragments. *Dharratan, dharratan,* he said.'

Jack translated what she had just said into English.

'Atom by atom,' he said, barely audible. A *qunbula dharriyya*, from the same root, was an atomic bomb. Al-Masri's intentions could not have been clearer.

'We have to tell the authorities,' said Jamila. Her pulse was racing, A cold sweat trickled down her back.

'I wish it were that easy,' Jack said. 'I'm a wanted man, and the moment I go near the police or anyone else, they'll clap handcuffs on me and toss me in the nearest gaol. Then they'll throw the key to the crocodiles.'

'I can go,' said Jamila. 'No one's looking for me.'

'You can't be sure of that. We need more information, and we need a way to pass it on without making it seem like some elaborate stunt.'

He looked at his watch. It was well past midnight. From the church above, the sounding of chanting and singing could be heard.

'We need to get some sleep,' Jack continued. 'Tomorrow will be a very long day. We're all exhausted, and we can't afford to be falling asleep

325

on our feet if we're to be effective.'

Jamila opened her mouth to argue, then closed it as she realised he was right.

'We'll speak to Father Joseph in the morning,' she said.

Chapter Thirty-Nine

THE FATHER OF TERROR

**St Sergius Church
4.30 a.m.**

Time passed like a querulous ghost. A sense of urgency removed substance, dimmed the materiality of hours and minutes, destroyed all form. Jamila and Samiha slept behind a curtain on one side of the crypt, Jack behind a wall of cardboard boxes. He dipped in and out of sleep, woken at times by the chanting that seeped down through the ceiling. Each time he fell asleep he dreamt, and his dreams were dark and frightening. He dreamt of Naomi, saw her run naked like a Vietnamese child down a road between a forest of flames, saw her skin burn bright red, then char and turn black and fall away, leaving just bones and a grinning skull. Behind the bones stood the Sphinx, grown seven times its true size, the Father of Terror, its neck circled with skulls, its head crowned with a plume of burning smoke, its eyes red hot, its mouth open like a gate to hell.

326

He started to scream. Then he woke.

He woke to darkness. Someone was beside him, shushing him into silence.

'Jamila...?'

'No, it's Samiha. You're all right. You had a bad dream. But it's all right. You're all right now.'

There was a small lamp beside his mattress. She switched it on, and he closed his eyes against the glare. When he opened them again, she was still bending over him, holding his hand, a look of concern on her face.

'Where ... where's Jamila?'

'Fast asleep. I heard you crying out, so I came over.' She let go of his hand, and for a second he felt a sense of loss.

'I can't sleep without bad dreams,' he said.

'I'm the same. Jamila's restless too. Would you like a coffee? If we can't sleep, we may as well stay awake properly.'

They came out from behind the boxes. Jack sat at the table while Samiha made the coffee. She brought two large glasses to the table. The coffee was black and flavoured with cardamom seeds.

'Do you want to tell me what you were dreaming about?' she asked.

He looked at her, remembered her hand in his, a small hand the weight of dust, and he thought he was still dreaming. The nightmare was starting to fade at last. He shook his head.

'There's plenty to have bad dreams about,' she said. 'My oldest boy, Adnan, used to wake up screaming like you. I had to hold him for a long time every night until he went back to sleep again. I worry about how he's coping now without me.

327

You can't bring up a normal child in Jenin. Israeli troops, Hamas gunmen, posters that turn killers into heroes. They dress the children in suicide belts at school. Mothers put them on their own children. There's a Mickey Mouse character on television that tells children to hate Jews and Americans, and says they have to grow up to be martyrs. It's as if we've all gone mad. And now this.'

She closed her eyes, and images from the past flooded in, faces of neighbours, eyes without feeling behind woollen masks and green headbands, children running from tanks, the faces of her Jewish colleagues every time there was news of another terrorist attack. Old emotions began to surface. She opened her eyes again and the room came into focus.

'I had nightmares in the bunker,' she said. 'Naomi had them all the time. I slept in her room as often as I could. Part of it was a reaction to that time when I thought I would have to go through with the suicide attack. I suppose I was safe enough in the bunker; but I could never rid myself of a terrible fear of Muhammad al-Masri. He's willing to destroy anything that threatens to come between him and his goal.

'Some of the people round him are on a knife's edge. Five times a day they perform ablutions, five times they pray, in the middle of every night, at the coldest time of day, they get out of their beds to pray some more. They spend hours debating how they propose to apply shari'a law once the Caliphate is established. They behave like the humblest and the most downtrodden of

328

people. They dream of death as though it were a blessing, and they are more than half in love with it themselves. But it takes the slightest setback to get them shouting and calling for someone's blood. I thought one of them would come for me one night, to kill me or rape me, perhaps both. I never slept well.'

'I haven't slept properly since Emilia and Naomi were killed,' he said. 'I have nightmares most nights.'

'Did you dream about them just now?'

He hesitated, then nodded. He wanted to tell her everything, and he was afraid of saying anything that might make her get up and leave.

She told him her full story, and he listened. Two strangers moments from death. When she finished, he told her about finding Emilia's body, thinking Naomi had died as well. She was the first person he'd talked about it with in detail. Her eyes were on him all the time.

Just then, as he was drawing to a close, a sound came from the church. A series of bumps, then scraping. Silence, and then someone crying. A woman weeping. And from nowhere it seemed, a man's screams.

They woke Jamila. She fetched the handguns and gave one to Jack.

'Stay down here,' he said to Samiha. 'Jamila and I are trained to deal with trouble.' He tried to sound reassuring, but at the back of his mind he thought they had been trapped.

Jack led the way out into the sacristy, and from there into the sacred space where the three altars

329

stood, in front of the seats on which the priests sat during services. After the quiet seclusion of the crypt, setting foot in the sanctuary was like entering a further dimension of calm. The stillness was arresting. Jack stopped like someone who hesitates on the brink of deep water or a forest clearing. Incense had taken the place of air. Light had been transformed to solid gold. He held his breath, preserving the incense in his nostrils and throat, cedar and sandalwood, frankincense and labdanum, myrrh and fragrant gums.

Jamila came behind him, silenced by the deathly hush pervading the place, by the tranquillity, the fragrance beyond all measure, the sense of sanctity.

He slipped quietly between the *haykal* screens. Gold and precious stones glistened dully behind a haze of coloured incense that lingered from the midnight mass. The faces of saints trembled in the semi-darkness, their eyes fixed on God.

A scream broke the silence, then voices further inside the church, within the nave: a murmur of voices, as if someone was arguing.

They went further, and Jack could make out the sound of a woman crying. No, not just a woman, children as well.

The man screamed again, a scream that seemed to tear the flesh. Then the same man's voice praying desperately, and then silence, and then the scream again, louder this time, much louder, dissolving into pitiful sobs. And the woman screaming now as well, and the children crying out. Jack and Jamila took cover back behind the iconostasis screen. They strained to see what was going on, hampered by the poor lighting and the incense smoke.

Half-way down the nave was the ambon, a marble pulpit raised on several slender marble pillars. With Jamila following closely behind him, Jack crept forward until he could see clearly what was happening. A group of people were gathered at the foot of the ambon. He recognised Father Joseph at once by his clerical garb, then realised that the woman who had screamed was his wife Shadia, and that the children were theirs.

The family was surrounded by a group of six armed men, some dressed in *galabiyyas*, others in leather jackets; all wore skullcaps. One had his hand on the priest's neck and was forcing him into a kneeling position, his head pushed down hard within inches of his knees. A second man was administering the bastinado to the soles of his naked feet, striking again and again with what looked like an iron rod.

A man in the clothes of an al-Azhar sheikh who had been watching from the side put up his hands, signalling to the others.

Jack started as he sensed someone coming up behind him. He spun, bringing his gun up, ready to fire. It was Samiha. He drew her down next to him, keeping her to one side of the screen where she could see through perforations in the wood.

'Do you recognise any of them?' he asked in a whisper.

She looked hard, then whispered in his ear.

'The one in the robes is Rashid, al-Masri's brother, the one I told you about. I'd recognise him anywhere.'

Jack reached into his trouser pocket and took out his knife. Opening it on the main blade, he slipped it back inside his pocket.

Suddenly, Rashid grabbed one of the girls, little Marie, the three-year-old and dragged her screaming in front of her father.

'Let him look at her!' ordered Rashid. 'Let him see what I'm doing. We've wasted enough time here. Let's get this done with now.'

The man who had been holding Father Joseph's neck took his hand away and grabbed the priest by his hair, yanking his head up as hard as he could. Joseph cried out.

'Look at me, priest,' shouted Rashid. 'I want you to understand just what is going to happen here. What will happen to you and your family if you don't tell me where Goodrich is hiding.'

Holding Marie with one hand around her upper arm, he took something from inside his *galabiyya*, a knife with a serrated seven-inch blade. He lifted it and put it against Marie's throat, hard enough to make her bleed.

'I've killed little girls before, and I'll cut your daughter's head from her body without hesitation if you don't speak up.'

The priest looked at him and spat. With the spittle came blood and fragments of teeth. Rashid and his bully boys had been working on the old man, kicking and beating him to force a betrayal.

'If you kill a child, God will put you to burn in the deepest pit of hell, the fittest place for a devil like you.'

Rashid's only response was to shout to one of

his henchmen.

'Bring the older girl as well. When he sees one die, he'll do anything to save the other's life.'

Before the man could grab Hannah, Rashid drew back his arm and in two hard strokes sliced the blade of his knife through Marie's neck. Blood exploded from the wound, spurting fountain-like through the incensed air. An unearthly scream split the church in two. Shadia fell to the ground. Father Joseph let out a cry of such despair that Jack put his hands over his ears to shut it out. Beside him, Samiha turned away and was sick.

Rashid tossed Marie's body to one side, letting her drop to the stone floor, her blood pouring out in a widening pool. In his left hand he still held the tiny head. His robes were red with blood. He threw Marie's head onto Father Joseph's lap. Numb with shock and horror, the priest let it lie there. He was past prayer now, past hope.

Jack crossed to where Jamila was stooping, spying round the narrow doorway of the iconostasis.

They whispered quickly, picking out three gunmen each. Jack would go in first, to give Jamila the benefit of surprise. They checked their weapons. Both had been reloaded when Jamila was cleaning them earlier.

Jack stood and went to the doorway.

Rashid had been given Hannah. Hannah was twelve and quite tall for her age, and she was petrified. Witnessing her sister's fate, seeing the punishment her father had taken, she knew it was a matter of moments before her own head was severed and tossed to the floor.

Rashid held her tightly by one arm and pressed

the blade to her throat.

Jack stepped out from the shadows, in full view of the gunmen and the saints hanging on the *haykal* screen.

'Let the child go,' he said. 'She's nothing to you. You came for me. Here I am.'

As he spoke, he was assessing the distances between the gunmen and the members of the stricken family. He held the gun behind his back. His priority was to get Hannah away from under Rashid's gleaming blade.

Rashid did not even show surprise that Jack had appeared as though from nowhere.

'The child is mine,' he said. 'They are all mine. They are unbelievers. God has told us to slay the unbelievers.'

'Christians are People of the Book. They are entitled to your protection. The child is only a child. The laws of jihad prohibit her murder.'

Rashid laughed. It was a foul laugh without humour in it, and it echoed abominably through the nave.

'The child means nothing to me,' he said. 'Just as your daughter meant nothing to me. When I have finished with you, I will deal with her. You defied me. Your daughter defied me. Defiance is not an option.'

Jack kept his eyes on Rashid, adding up the people he had killed, the extent of his loathing for the man. The killer stood in the nave, smug and arrogant, an abomination in a house of God, convinced of his superiority, the superiority of his God, as though he himself had grown divine after a certain fashion. He had become a god of scorn

334

and anger, a beast of the apocalypse, a divinity without pity or love or agony, beyond reach, beyond humanity. And there was nothing Jack could do. Nothing whatsoever.

Unless... Jack knew that Rashid could snap an order at any moment, and his men would massacre the entire family. He also knew that he and Jamila together could take the gunmen out with a series of well-aimed shots. But what would happen then? He could not shoot Rashid without risking the girl's life.

Rashid made up his mind for him. He turned to the men nearest him.

'Kill them all,' he said. 'Leave Goodrich for me.'

The terrorists raised their weapons, acting instinctively to follow orders. They were well trained, and they were quick. But Jack was quicker still. The first man died with a bullet through his skull before his gun was halfway to its target, the second half a second later, the third as he turned to face the assault, two taps to his forehead. Three more shots rang out a second after Jack's. Jamila had lined up her targets exactly, taking each one down with a shot to the head.

For the first time Rashid looked afraid. He made as if to cut Hannah's throat, then thought better of it.

'If you kill her,' Jack shouted, 'you'll follow her a second later. Hand her to her mother and put your hands on your head. I have questions to ask you. I want you alive, not dead.'

Rashid began to drag Hannah backwards with him. He had a car outside and a driver waiting to take him away. Hannah was limp with fright, but her slim body was nothing to her sister's killer.

Rashid got himself and his hostage as far as the door of the narthex. That was when he cut her throat, throwing her forward in an attempt to create confusion. He was through the door and away as shots rang out behind him. One caught him in the upper arm, making him cry out; but he did not even stumble. Without a backwards look, he ran from the church.

Jack and Jamila arrived on the empty street in time to see him leap into the car. They fired, but the driver had already rammed his foot on the accelerator. The car screamed off into the night.

Chapter Forty

CHRISTMAS DAY

They rushed back inside the church. The nave had been transformed into a charnel house. It was filled with grief beyond measure. Shadia had come round to see her oldest daughter killed as well. Father Joseph, in great pain from his beating, was trying without success to comfort her. She was screaming and tearing her hair. Samiha was doing her best to console the two remaining girls, Irene and Marina, but nothing she could say or do would quiet or comfort them, and she could not imagine how anything in their lives would give them peace again. The two boys sat huddled together on a pew, their arms round one another. The younger, John, wept inconsolably, Pierre had gone pale and had withdrawn inside himself.

Jamila, who regarded them as her second family, was devastated. She felt sick and numb and crazy. Of course, she knew that she and Jack had prevented a massacre of the entire Yaqoub family, but looking at the bodies of Hannah and Marie, seeing where their blood had fanned out across the floor, forming twin pools on which the reflections of the Christmas lights danced in myriad colours, she felt no relief, but a crushing sickness of the soul.

It was only as he stepped back inside the nave that Jack realised the danger had not passed. Naomi was still in the hospital, and Rashid knew where she was.

Leaving Jamila to do what she could with the family, he crossed to where Samiha was sitting with the girls.

'Samiha, I need your help. We have to get to the hospital right away. Before Rashid gets there.'

She got to her feet, and told Irene and Marina she would see them later.

Jack told Jamila to get the family back to their house and to wake the other priests.

'Keep away from the police,' he said. 'They may have been infiltrated. If anything happens to me or Samiha, you're the only person who knows what they're planning for Friday. You have to stay alive and out of their clutches. Find a way to alert someone in authority. Maybe the US embassy. At least get the conference called off.'

Still awash with emotion, she just nodded. A voice told her to get a grip on herself, that stopping the explosion took priority over everything. And a second voice prompted her to break down in tears.

With Samiha close behind, Jack ran into the street. The rental car was still parked where Jamila had left it, and the spare key was in his pocket.

They raced south-west on Abu'l Faraj, waking sleeping children who dreamt of Baba Noel, tearing their silent night to shreds. Just south of the Sinan Pasha mosque, they joined the Corniche and went fast south to the bridge. All the way, Jack prayed to what little there was left of God in him, and all the way he saw Rashid's hand bear down on Naomi's finger, saw the same hand slice Marie's small head from her shoulders, saw the same bloody hand cut a long gash through Hannah's innocent throat.

He drove down the last stretch, eyes straining for a sign of Rashid's presence. But when he got to the front of the building, there were no other cars.

They banged on the front door until a porter answered.

Jack pushed past the startled *bawwab* and strode into the reception area. As he did so, a nurse appeared on the stairs. She looked frightened, then caught sight of Samiha coming through the door.

Before she reached the bottom of the stairs, Jack was beside her.

'I need your help,' he said. 'The English girl,

the one with the wounded hand. Take me to her.'

Stiffly, the nurse, a woman in her forties, shook her head.

'You can't come barging in here at this time of the morning and make demands. Who are you? What do you want with her?'

'I'm her father. Someone is coming here to kill her. I have to get her out of this place.'

'Please, calm down. You aren't making sense. The child is not fully recovered. If you take her away now, she will have a relapse. She will die.'

'I'll deal with that once she's safe. But I'm taking her now, and you aren't going to interfere.'

The nurse pursed her lips and pressed the beeper in her breast pocket. Jack pushed her to one side and Samiha, who had been here twice before, pointed to a door on their right that led to the corridor on which Naomi's room was situated.

As they hurried through, the nurse's voice bellowed after them. They ran. It was the seventh door along. Jack opened the door and went inside softly, not wanting to alarm Naomi.

She was fast asleep. Tiny coloured lights from monitors twinkled like the lights on a Christmas tree. For a horrid moment, Jack was reminded of the lights in the church, reflected in pools of blood. He went across to the bed and shook her gently by the shoulder.

'Naomi. Naomi, wake up.'

She took time to come round. As she did so, he heard something that sent his heart racing. A car was driving up to the hospital. Driving at speed. Moments later, he heard its brakes screech as it stopped outside the building.

Footsteps could be heard in the corridor. Samiha looked out: the nurse was on her way, flanked by a doctor in a white coat and the porter.

Jack remembered that the door opened inwards. The handle on the inside was a long metal stanchion firmly screwed to the edge. There was a second stanchion on the wall next to it, for recuperant patients to hold on to while entering or leaving the room.

'Quickly, block the door,' he shouted to Samiha.

A car door slammed outside.

Samiha lost no time. She caught sight of a broom in one corner, snatched it up, and thrust it through the two stanchions barely in time. Two seconds later, someone pushed the door and found it would not budge. There was a cry of rage. Then more footsteps, one person hurrying down the corridor.

Jack got the window open. The cold night air rushed in.

'Daddy?' Naomi asked. 'What are you doing? Is something wrong?'

'I have to take you out of this hospital,' he said. 'There's a better place, but you need to go there quickly. Don't make a noise. We mustn't wake anybody.'

But Naomi could hear the banging on the door, and she was frightened.

Samiha hushed her and told her everything would be fine. She got her out of bed, then used the top blanket as a shawl to wrap her in.

Jack climbed out. It was just a short drop to the ground. The banging grew louder, then someone threw their full weight on the door. The broom handle cracked.

Samiha handed Naomi down to Jack, then climbed through and dropped to the ground. A second crash came from the room behind, and they heard the broom snap in two.

Jack had Naomi safely in his arms. He and Samiha ran, knowing they ran for their lives. As they rounded the building, they saw a second car parked next to theirs, and a driver at the wheel, visible in the light shed by a nearby security lamp.

'Give me Naomi,' said Samiha, halting to take her from Jack.

The driver was halfway out of the car, reaching for a gun. Jack saw him, drew his own weapon and fired. The man fell forward, one foot catching on the door sill, and crashed to the ground. He was still moving when Jack went up to him, and the gun was still firmly in his grip. Jack stood over him and pumped a single bullet into his head.

Rashid was rushing towards them, a gun already in his hand. He fired at Jack, but the bullet went wide.

Jack threw himself behind Rashid's car. A bullet slammed into the opposite side. Using the car for shelter, Jack crept round to the back, then stood up, his automatic held in two hands and fired.

But he fired at nothing. Rashid had seen how exposed he was and had turned back behind the wall of the hospital.

Jack ran for his own car, pausing to put a bullet into the left front tyre of Rashid's. Samiha had managed to put Naomi on the back seat, and was climbing into the front passenger seat. Jack got in beside her. The key was still in the ignition.

A volley of shots came from the hospital, hitting the car broadside on. Jack started the engine, and slammed the gear into reverse. The car whined its way back, turning through a narrow gyre. Into first gear, and the car leapt away down the drive, then second gear. Shots followed them into the darkness.

As they sped away back down the road that would take them to the river, Jack turned to Samiha.

He started to speak. That was when he noticed the blood on her clothes.

Chapter Forty-One

ON THE RUN

5.20 a.m.

The ambulances were the first to arrive, followed soon after by the police. Jamila had told them to go to the church. She and Father Joseph met them at the entrance. Shadia and the remaining children were being cared for by women from the congregation. A doctor had been called for. Everyone was in a state of tension as word of the attack spread round the waking community. Christmas mass had been cancelled.

Father Joseph introduced Jamila as a Christian and a close friend of the family. He seemed like someone dead. While paramedics bandaged his bruises and contusions, he talked in a monotone to a policeman.

They asked Jamila why this had happened, and she said she didn't know, that the gunmen had been Muslim terrorists, as their bearded faces and shaven heads testified. The bodies remained in the nave while a forensics team started work. Marie and Hannah's remains were dealt with first, then taken away in a private ambulance that had been called for by one of the priests.

'Who killed the gunmen?' a detective asked Jamila.

'I did,' she said. 'I used to work for the security services. I carry a gun for my own protection.'

She gave them the gun and it was bagged and labelled.

'You'll have to come with us to the station,' they said.

'Later,' she answered. 'I can't leave the family like this. I have to see to the children. They know me. Let me wait at least till your crime scene investigators have finished in the church.'

From a remark made by the police lieutenant who was in charge of the case, Jamila realised she was lucky. They were handling this with kid gloves, not the normal treatment for Christians in this city. The moment details had been phoned through, it had dawned on the police captain that being heavy-handed carried enormous risks on the eve of an international conference. The status of Egypt's Copts was on the agenda, and enough questions were already being asked about official treatment of minorities.

Jamila walked back with Father Joseph. He seemed like an old man now, bent and feeble, his spirits torn down, his eyes vacant.

In the darkness, a crowd had gathered and was growing still. Some were sobbing. Others sang hymns. They held candles, and the children, their Christmas ripped apart, stood with them appalled and wondering. Yet others, hidden by shadows, watched and waited.

A bullet had passed right through Samiha's left forearm, causing heavy bleeding. A fraction of an inch further to the right would have severed the radial artery.

Once he was certain they were not being followed, Jack parked on Jabalaya and switched off the lights. Experience in the field had taught him how to use touch to determine the extent of an injury.

'Take off your scarf,' he told her. 'Use it to put direct pressure on the wounds.'

He helped her get the scarf in place.

'Now, hold your arm above your head. I know it hurts, but you have to reduce the bleeding. I can't take you to a public hospital. Can you bear it for a while, till I get help?'

'It hurts like hell,' she said, gritting her teeth. She raised her arm. 'But I can manage if you can.'

His hand was still over hers, helping apply pressure. Her hand was small and, despite the loss of blood, still warm. For a few seconds, he let his hand rest on hers, then took it away.

He took Georgina's card from his pocket and

switched on a little dashboard light. She had told him she lived in Aguza, in a cheap flat that belonged to the British Council, a couple of streets away. He was running out of choices, and both Naomi and Samiha needed urgent help.

Driving fast north to 6 October Bridge, he crossed to the west bank and headed up Nile Street. He knew his way to the Council, but it took longer to find Georgina's street.

Naomi said nothing all the way, and he feared she might have relapsed into unconsciousness. When they finally stopped, Samiha opened her door at once and got into the back with Naomi.

'She's OK,' she said. 'But we have to find a doctor fast.'

A grumpy Georgina answered the door after half a dozen rings. Her face was smeared with cream, and her hair was tousled.

'If it's you, Jamie, just fuck off. What the hell time is it anyway?'

'It's after six,' Jack said. 'It'll be dawn in half an hour. This isn't Jamie. It's Jack Goodrich. I need your help. I've no one else to turn to.'

She yawned and rubbed her eyes.

'Jack? What's going on?'

He told her in as few words as possible. She stared at him in disbelief. Was Jack Goodrich a dangerous man to know after all?

'Naomi's in the car,' he said. 'Samiha has been shot in the arm. I had to take Naomi off the drip. We need to get them both to a doctor as quickly as possible. While we're on the way, I'll fill you in on what Samiha has been telling me about Muhammad al-Masri and his organisation.'

Georgina popped back inside to dress.

As he waited downstairs, Jack watched a grey light come stealthily to touch the faint crescent of the rising moon. Here, away from the endless bustle of the inner city, Cairo seemed peaceful. It was a different world to the one he'd just come from. And he thought how it might all be changed in the twinkling of an eye, how at some unspecified time on Friday the sky above Cairo would turn white. He could be at the pyramids in fifteen minutes, sooner than that if he drove fast and avoided the traffic.

The door opened and Georgina came out, dressed in jeans and a baggy sweater and carrying a hairbrush.

Jack drove back to Nile Street, then north to where it became Sudan Street. A short drive took him across the old railway track into Imbaba, the slum district that had been al-Masri's base until his removal to Shubra.

As he drove, he told Georgina what Samiha had told him.

'It sounds very far-fetched,' she said. 'Like something from a thriller. Tom Cruise or Pierce Brosnan. James Bond. That sort of thing.'

Listening in the back, Samiha interrupted.

'James Bond didn't cut off Naomi's finger. James Bond didn't turn up at the church tonight and kill two beautiful children. He has a bomb and he will use it. You can choose to help us or hinder us. If you hinder us and he detonates the bomb, there's no telling how many people will die.'

Georgina fell silent.

They passed the camel market, then drove to the concrete expanse of the Kit Kat shopping mall.

'I've been here a couple of times before,' Georgina said, instructing Jack to pull over near the mall. 'Doctor O'Malley has his clinic over there.'

Jack carried Naomi while Samiha, weak now from the loss of blood, walked slowly, supporting herself on Georgina's arm. The sky was still full of stars as the moon lifted like a curved sliver of ice, but the eastern horizon was no longer black. Beyond the Muqattam Hills, dawn flickered like a troubled flame. Jack glanced at the soft twilight and thought, not of this dawn but of the one to come.

The clinic was based on the ground floor of a high-rise block inhabited by rural immigrants who were barely on the lowest rung of Cairo's steep social ladder. It had originally been run by Médecins sans Frontières, the international group of doctors and nurses who worked in the Third World, but they had moved out after an attack by members of the Brotherhood, and, after a short gap, it had been reopened by an Irish doctor in his sixties, Pádraig O'Malley.

Pádraig had graduated from the College of Surgeons in Dublin in the days when condoms and *Lolita* were still banned, and had gone on to pioneer birth control in the Republic. Retiring in his mid-fifties, he'd headed for Africa, and had worked in a number of turbulent countries before winding up in Cairo. Overstretched and under-manned, his little clinic was the only lifeline for the poor fellahin from Upper Egypt who'd been drawn to the big city in the hope of a better life. With precarious funding from a number of Catholic charities at home, he bandaged their wounds, filled them with antibiotics, vaccinated their children, and handed out condoms that he kept out of his annual reports to the charities.

He was getting ready for work when they knocked on the door. Within moments, a nurse had wheeled Naomi off to a side room, and the doctor had stripped Samiha's sleeve away.

There were no questions, no arguments. O'Malley had treated more gunshot wounds than he cared to remember, and he had never called the police or the security services. His only concern was to save lives.

While he worked, Jack went into greater detail with Georgina.

'We need to use a computer,' he said. 'If Samiha can break into the one that al-Masri keeps records on, she may be able to determine where the bomb is to be placed and how many kilotons it is. If it's a mini-nuke, it may be one kiloton or less. Cairo will be safe, but everyone at the conference will be incinerated.'

'I have a Mac at home. My brother bought it for me when I got here. Jack, I don't know whether to believe you or not, but if your story is true... Won't you let me go to the ambassador?'

'He'll never agree to have the conference called off on such thin evidence. We need something convincing.'

One hour later, Naomi was improving again. The fever had gone, and Dr O'Malley said she would soon be out of danger.

'The hospital said...'

'Don't waste time on what the hospital said. They're worried willies the lot of them. I've seen more cases like this than they've said Hail Marys. She still needs attention, but she'll be up and running in a day or two.'

'I want her out of Cairo by tonight at the latest,' Jack said. 'No ifs or buts, she has to be on a train to Alexandria before midnight.'

'That may be a tall order.'

Jack didn't argue.

'I'll be back this evening,' he said. 'See she's ready by then.'

Samiha was pronounced able to walk. Her arm was in a sling, but she'd been given a transfusion and had insisted on going with Jack.

Jack handed O'Malley a generous donation.

'Get her ready to leave tonight,' he said, 'and there'll be a lot more. Thank you for what you've done already.'

'Forget the money,' the doctor said. 'If she's fit to leave, she'll leave. If not, I won't let her go, however much you pay.'

Jack looked around. The clinic had been filling up with men, women and children. People without lives desperate to live. People who'd known nothing but pain seeking a moment's relief. The poorest of the poor, the defeated, the humbled, the excluded. And a man who thought he was the shadow of God claimed he had the solution to all their fears and hurts, that he would bring them salvation in the form of a mushroom cloud. Jack shuddered. It was cold in the open air.

349

Chapter Forty-Two

A VIGIL

Jack left them at Georgina's, where she and Samiha planned to start work on the computer search. Samiha was still weak from loss of blood, but month after month of anger and frustration drove her to push herself to the limit in the hope that she might stop al-Masri in his tracks.

'Take care, Jack,' she said. 'Get back here quickly.'

He rested his hand on her cheek and nodded.

'Tell Georgina to take you back to the clinic if you feel ill. I'll be back as quickly as possible.'

The drive back took longer than the one in. The traffic was heavy. On the east bank, he twice passed a line of limousines, one headed for Abdin Palace, the other coming away. The President was receiving his guests.

Crowds still stood vigil outside St Sergius. They no longer held candles, but priests had arrived from other churches across the city and were leading small groups in prayer while acolytes passed back and forth with censers. Jack had expected to see a gaggle of news reporters and cameramen, but there seemed to be no one from the press. He guessed that the authorities had not informed the press corps yet, and that some sort of gagging order had been put on the story: the last thing the man in Abdin Palace wanted was for this to leak out in the middle of the conference. Jamila had told him about a suicide bombing at a school on Zamalek, and the consternation that had caused.

A cordon of police was trying to keep fresh arrivals from drawing closer to the scene. Jack worked his way round them, then past the crowds until he reached the Yaqoubs' house. A smaller crowd had gathered here. They knelt on the street outside the house, whispering prayers, invoking a God who had never seemed more distant than today. A priest carried an icon of the Virgin up and down before them, stopping from time to time to let them kiss it or stroke it with their bare hands. A monk stood to one side, holding a golden crucifix. Jack thought the old women, who made up much of this group, looked cold and hungry; but it was clear they would be there all day.

A heavily built man stopped him at the door.

'I need to go inside,' said Jack. 'I need to speak to Jamila Loghoud. She's a friend of the Yaqoubs. She's with them now.'

'You can't come past,' said the doorkeeper. 'No one's allowed through.'

A long discussion followed, and, in the end, the man went inside, spoke to Father Joseph, and returned to let Jack in.

'He says you can't stay,' the man said. 'He says you'll know why.'

Jack nodded. He knew very well.

A doctor had been to tend to Father Joseph, who was dressed in a loose black cassock. He was in the living-room with the four children and Jamila, along with two priests and an old woman who was introduced as Joseph's mother. The Zacharys were there, as well as Boutros. Jack could hear Shadia sobbing from the next room. Jamila explained that her mother and sister were with her.

He spoke briefly to Father Joseph, and promised to bring his children's killer to justice.

'And I have to take Jamila with me,' he went on. 'I hate to do that when I know you need her so much, especially the children. But we have important work to do. If we don't track this man down, there will be slaughter that will make what happened this morning seem a small thing by comparison. The horror we all feel now will be magnified many times, magnified beyond measure.'

The priest nodded. He was dry-eyed, but Jack could guess what was going on inside. Like himself when he had stumbled on Emilia's body and thought Naomi slain, he knew Joseph would never be the same person again. A man's faith can only stretch so far, he thought.

'Jamila explained all this to me while you were gone. You're right. You have to put an end to it. May God go with you.'

'Father, it may sound trite, but I do understand what you're going through. It would be easy for me to say, it will pass. But I know it will never go away. I have no answer and no cure. Grief does not quench grief. My pain cannot heal yours. But I swear I will exact justice. Marie and Hannah will not go unavenged.'

352

The priest stared at him.

'I do not seek revenge,' he said. 'It is not the Christian path.'

'That is your privilege,' said Jack softly. 'But Rashid al-Masri will die all the same. For what he did to my wife. To my parents. To those people in Scotland. To little Fiona Taggart. God knows how many innocent people he has killed, how many he will kill if he's allowed to go on. I promise this, that I will kill him. Quickly or slowly, it makes no difference. And I will not pray for his soul, for I do not believe he has one.'

Joseph made the sign of the cross.

Jamila said goodbye to the children, and left with Jack. As they went down, he told her what had happened.

'In case something goes wrong,' he said, 'you need to know where to find Naomi.'

He told her the doctor's name and the location of the clinic, but she said O'Malley was already well known to her.

He handed her Georgina's card and told her to keep it safe.

Outside, prayers were still being said. They pushed their way through the crowd and headed for the car. But the crowds outside the church had spilt over the road and were growing in number as more mourners arrived from Misr al-Qadima and other Christian areas. In the mêlée, Jack and Jamila were separated.

He saw the car and Jamila close to it, but as he broke free of the crowd, two men appeared on either side of him, as though out of nowhere.

'Professor Jack Goodrich?'

When Jack looked round, the speaker had already closed in on him. The second man moved in from the other side. The voice had spoken with an English accent.

'Are you Jack Goodrich?' the man asked again.

'Who wants to know?'

The man reached inside his pocket, and for a moment, Jack was sure he was going to take out a gun. Instead, he held out a little wallet with a gold-coloured crest on the inside.

'Detective Inspector Norman Alderton of Norfolk Constabulary. My partner is DI Iain Ferguson of the Scottish Northern Constabulary. May I ask if you will confirm that you are Professor Jack Goodrich of the American University of Cairo, last resident at number seventeen Fouad Street in the district of Garden City, Cairo?'

'What's this about? What the fuck is this all about? Who are you?'

'Will you confirm that your name is Professor Jack Goodrich, as already described?'

'Yes. But why? I've done nothing. Why...?'

'In that case, Professor Goodrich, I have to advise you that you will now be escorted to a nearby police station, where you will be charged on suspicion of murder. Namely, the murder of your parents, Arthur and Nancy Goodrich of the city of Norwich, Ian and Jean Stewart, and Angus and Ailsa Gilfillan of Whitebridge in the Scottish county of Invernessshire. You are also suspected in the murder of Simon Henderson of the British Embassy in Cairo. Pending formalities, you will be extradited to the United Kingdom, where you

354

will be formally charged under English law. You have the right to remain silent or to appoint a lawyer.'

As the first policeman finished speaking, the Scot motioned with his hand and two uniformed Egyptian policemen emerged from the crowd.

A black car drove up and halted beside them. Jack was manhandled into the rear seat, with the two detectives on either side of him. One of the uniformed policemen got into the front seat.

'Get moving!' Alderton called to the driver. He obviously meant business, thought Jack as the reality of his situation suddenly began to bear down on him.

As the car moved off, Jack turned to one side and saw Jamila staring at the car open-mouthed.

In twenty-four hours' time, the International Conference on Peace and Reconstruction in the Middle East would begin.

Chapter Forty-Three

BEHIND BARS

Georgina's flat
6.30 a.m.

Georgina opened the door to find Jamila frantic with worry. She had only met the other woman briefly, not at all long enough to form any impression of her character. She asked her inside, and Jamila lost no time in explaining what had happened.

'I already knew the police were here.' Georgina was growing worried again. She felt she'd been dropped head first into water that was far out of her depth. 'Maybe they really have evidence that Jack did commit these murders.'

'You wouldn't believe that for a moment if you'd been in the church this morning. If it hadn't been for Jack, the entire family would have been slaughtered.'

They talked while Samiha got some sleep. Jamila told Georgina about her own background in the Egyptian security services, and filled in as much as she could about Jack.

'Georgina,' she said after a while, 'we could sit and talk for hours. I could take you on a tour of secure websites, including pages for MI6 Egypt. But every minute we talk, time is slipping past and lives are at risk. We need to get Jack, and we need to work out what we plan to do next. Because, if we don't have a plan, we may as well just leave Cairo and save our own sorry skins.'

'Couldn't we...?'

Jamila smiled.

'Ideas later. Our first priority is to find out what's going on with Jack.'

Georgina, who had handled several cases of British citizens arrested in Cairo, had developed a good working knowledge of the system. While Jamila waited in the street outside, she marched into the central police station in Bab al-Khalq.

Faced with an officious desk sergeant, Georgina rummaged in her handbag and produced her consular pass.

'I want to see a senior officer, and I don't have time to wait.'

The sergeant, not knowing a word of English, was well-versed in the ways of hierarchy. The foreign woman standing in front of him was holding a very official looking card of some kind, and it was not for him to argue. He called the duty inspector, a tall, lugubrious man from the Delta, who had learnt some English at the University of Alexandria.

It took Georgina under two minutes to find out that Jack was in the station, was being questioned by two British policemen, and was due to be flown back to London on the next flight.

'I may need to speak to him before he goes,' Georgina said. 'How long will that be?'

He glanced at a clock on the wall behind the desk.

'In the next hour,' he said. 'The British want to have him on the next flight, come what may. He has killed a lot of people. They say he was responsible for the deaths in Shubra al-Khayma early this morning. A mass murderer. He should never have been allowed into this country.'

She thanked him and left.

Jamila thought quickly.

'They normally take prisoners out through the back,' she said. 'If the press get wind of this and turn up, they'll get him into a car in the yard outside the exit, then move out fast to get clear of the crowds.'

She hurried off to Ahmad Maher Street, about

357

half a mile away, where it was possible to buy almost anything, and returned with a bundle. Grabbing Georgina by the hand, she ran with her down to the Bayt al-Razzaq, just five hundred yards away.

'Let's go in,' she said.

The house was a luxurious eighteenth-century building that was visited by Cairo's more discerning tourists. Inside, Jamila headed straight for the *haramlik*, the rooms where the women of the house had once been secluded. At this time of the year, they were the only visitors. Jamila opened the paper bundle to reveal two *milayas* with scarves and gloves.

Five minutes later, they were standing at the rear of the police station, two veiled women who said to the sentry that they were waiting for their husbands to come out. A hefty bribe got them into the yard.

An hour passed, but no one appeared with Jack. Maybe, Jamila thought, they would leave it till much later after all. Or come out in a minute.

Four hours later, they were still waiting. Georgina had ventured back to the front desk twice, and each time she'd been told 'another hour'. They began to suspect that Jack had already been spirited away in order to avoid the press. Police went in and out of the yard, prisoners were marched out or taken in, relatives took sons and brothers away, a van arrived carrying food, but Jack did not appear. It was already mid-afternoon, and time was running out.

Suddenly, the rear door opened and two men

came out, one a tall European, the other an Egyptian police superintendent. Georgina grabbed Jamila by the hand and squeezed hard. As the men passed on their way out, she whispered fiercely.

'I recognise the man in the overcoat. His name is Malcolm Purvis, he's a diplomat, and I happen to know he works for MI6.'

Jamila nodded. She'd heard of Purvis.

Five minutes passed, then the gate opened and a large black Ford saloon reversed inside. The gate was left open, and the driver stayed at the wheel. Minutes passed. The engine was still purring. Jamila felt her heart beating, knowing she'd only get one chance. She had no idea how many policemen would be guarding Jack, how many would be armed, whether she could do this at all. She'd explained to Georgina what she planned to do. Georgina explained that she'd spent most of her weekends back in Britain with something she called the Territorial Army, and that she knew how to handle herself. Her only problem was that she'd never been trained to fight when wrapped up in draperies that covered her from head to foot.

Suddenly, footsteps sounded behind the doors. Jamila stepped forward to one side, Georgina to the other. So intent was the guard on ensuring no one was blocking the exit, they went unnoticed.

The doors opened with a flourish. A policeman stepped out, then went to the side in order to hold one wing of the doors open. Immediately after him came a whey-faced man in a cheap European suit, then Jack, who was handcuffed to him, and behind them, the other British detective.

They moved straight for the car. The man in the rear went forward and opened the nearside rear door. The first detective told Jack to get inside and, once he was seated, got in beside him.

Jamila and Georgina made their moves. Before the detective could get the door shut, Jamila reached inside the *milaya*, took her gun from the waistband of her jeans, then ran up to the car and pushed her way in. The second detective had not yet reached the other door, where he planned to get in on Jack's other side. Georgina moved in on him and pressed something that felt very like a gun barrel into the small of his back.

'Stay just where you are,' she ordered, using the commanding officer's voice she'd learnt from her father, 'or you will leave your liver, kidneys, and most of your stomach here in Cairo.'

Jamila pointed her gun straight at the first detective's head and told him to move over. Stunned and scarcely alert after so many hours of lost sleep followed by the grilling he'd just been through, Jack barely reacted at first. Then he caught on, and yanked on his cuffs, dragging the other man across the seat towards him and locking the rear door to block the way in for the second detective.

'This is a hijack,' Jamila said. 'Do anything and I will shoot you in the left thigh. Do anything else, and I will put a bullet in your right thigh, and a second in your groin. I have been trained to do this, I have done it before, and, believe me, I won't hesitate to do it again if you try to get in my way.'

Leaving the second detective pounding futilely on the side window, Georgina hurried round the car and jumped into the front passenger seat.

Jamila leant forward and spoke to the driver in Arabic.

'Put the car in gear and slam your foot on the accelerator,' she ordered. 'Drive as fast as you can. I'll tell you where to go later. If you don't do what I tell you, I will shoot you and drive the fucking car myself.'

Whether it was the shock of hearing a woman swear, or the realisation that he'd just wet himself, the driver did exactly what she'd said. The car pushed its way out, scoring a deep gouge against the gate, which the guard was trying belatedly to close in its path. The driver turned right and headed on down the empty street.

Jamila took off her headscarf and smiled at Jack. She spoke in Arabic.

'That's our bit done,' she said. 'The rest is up to you. What the hell do we do next?'

Chapter Forty-Four

THE ABSOLUTE SUSPECT

Georgina's flat
Half an hour later

'They told me I'd murdered my parents in Norwich, then headed back up to Scotland, where I'd killed Simon and the Gilfillans. They'd figured it all out, done the timings, and matched up the bullets. If you can believe it, they even sent some poor sod to fly back and forth between Scotland and Norfolk. I'm the absolute suspect, they're not even looking for anyone else. I told them the truth, and they just laughed in my face. Said it was the most far-fetched story they'd ever heard, that I must have been reading too many thrillers. The Egyptians want me back in Cairo to stand trial for the murders out at the church.'

Jamila watched him talk, not wondering for a moment whether he was telling the truth or not. She knew he was. And she knew that there was no police force in the world that would believe him. As for Georgina, the thrill of the rescue was giving way to severe doubts about the wisdom of getting involved in such a caper in the first place. She could imagine her mother getting wind of it, and the cold voice she could adopt on such occasions. She fancied a prison term would be better than facing that sarcasm.

They had tied up the policeman and the driver, using rope Jamila had bought in the Tentmakers' Market next door to the police station, expressly for that purpose. They were probably still out there now, gagged and bound with knots that would have to be cut apart, lying on the floor of the car, which had been parked in an alleyway off the street. Georgina thought they'd be extremely uncomfortable by now, but knew they'd come to no serious harm. They'd be found in an hour or two, and the British cop taken back to his hotel for a long hot bath and some painful stretching by the resident masseur.

They were back in Georgina's flat. While the

others had been away, Samiha had woken up and found it impossible to return to sleep. She had been tortured by a sense of time slipping by and an unshakable fear that, if Muhammad al-Masri was not stopped, she would never see her children again. She had found a coffee machine and poured as much caffeine into her system as she dared. Then, a large mug next to her and a coffee pot not far away, she had sat down at Georgina's computer and gone hunting. When they got back, she joined them in the living room and told them what she had found.

'The conference is under the nominal chairmanship of President Mubarak, who plans to attend all the sessions. However, since he's a key player in the peace negotiations, he won't actually chair any of the sessions in person. They've brought in a handful of Nobel Peace Prize winners to do that. There's no way we can get to Mubarak himself. Not in the time we have available, probably not at all.

'The person we have to reach is the Minister of Foreign Affairs, Megdi Yusuf. Yusuf is the real power behind the conference. He set the whole thing up with his Israeli counterpart, Avraham Edri, he contacted all the heads of state personally, and he retains overall control of the proceedings. His neck is on the line if anything goes wrong.'

'Such as an atomic bomb going off during the opening ceremony,' quipped Georgina.

Jack smiled. If there had ever been a time for ghoulish humour, this was it, he thought.

'The problem,' said Samiha, 'is that Yusuf is

everywhere and nowhere at the moment. He's meeting heads of state alongside the President most of today, and every time he gets a break he's off checking every last detail. His schedule is online at the Ministry, and it's horrendous. He even looks after the catering. Obviously, he can't or won't delegate. However...'

She hesitated. After her first excitement, she was starting to have doubts. Would her information be enough? she wondered.

'There's one area he doesn't delegate, though, and that's security. Rather than let the individual countries do their own security and get in each other's hair, he has appointed a private US company to handle it for the conference. Responsibility for individual heads of state remains with their own bodyguard corps, but they have nothing to do with overall security. Yusuf has appointed one of his old friends to oversee the general security. He's called Khaled Selim, and he used to be a big shot in one of the national security agencies.'

'He was my boss in the Mubahath al-Dawla,' said Jamila quietly. 'A bastard to work for, but efficient. He'll see the security operation runs like a train under Mussolini.'

'Did you see much of him?' asked Jack.

She shook her head.

'Once or twice. He was the top guy. Men like him never mix with the lower ranks.'

Samiha continued.

'The US company deals with things like perimeter security, press control, biometric ID checks and so on. But Selim also has a force of ten thousand armed guards recruited from the military and the security services.'

'Where's this leading?' asked Jack.

'I think Selim is easier to get to than the President or the Minister of Foreign Affairs. If he can be persuaded that the conference is in danger, he has enough men to search for the bomb. He may even be able to cancel or postpone the opening ceremony by putting out a top-level security alert.'

Jamila shook her head.

'He won't do that. The President would lose face, and that matters. No one would come to Egypt for an event of this kind again. Mubarak is trying to cancel out the country's reputation for violence. Yusuf has staked everything on this conference going without a hitch. If it's a success, he's in line for a Nobel Peace Prize himself, and that could eventually put him in line for the presidency. He would take a lot of persuading, and we just don't have time for that. In any case, Selim himself won't be exactly easy to reach.'

Samiha had no answer. A few suggestions came from the others, but none held up for more than a minute. They looked at one another blankly. It was already early afternoon. It was then that Georgina raised a hand.

'The embassy keeps secret files on all Egyptian politicians and assorted bigwigs. This fellow Selim will be in there somewhere. In fact, it's probably quite a fat file. Most of the dossiers contain things we can leak to the press if ever the need arises. Usually we don't have to resort to that. It's not really cricket.'

The files were an open secret among some embassy staff. Georgina was one of them. She had arrived with impeccable credentials, most of them social. For all her junior status, she had already become part of an inner circle made up of old public schoolboys, Oxbridge graduates, and relatives of diplomats and military personnel. One of her uncles had been ambassador to Egypt back in the seventies, and a great-uncle in the fifties. She'd never talked about this, of course – it would have been bad form – but everybody knew, and even quite senior people shared confidences with her that they would never have mentioned to the new breed of redbrick-educated social climbers.

It took her fifteen minutes to hack in, find Selim's file and read it.

Back in the living room, she shared her findings.

Selim had a mistress, a French woman who lived in Zamalek, the northern half of the large island in the Nile where Naomi's school was situated. He visited her every Thursday night – Friday evening by the Muslim calendar – always in her large and expensively furnished flat in one of the old British-built apartment blocks on Saray al-Gazira Street. It was not exactly an open secret, but a handful of people knew what went on, his wife included. She had her own paramour, a struggling young Egyptian poet called Misbah, and preferred to say nothing about her husband's philandering.

Selim's French girlfriend was the Egyptian correspondent for *Le Monde*. Twenty-eight years old, she was impossibly pretty, *soignée*, and brunette, as intricate and clever as Houdini, and an adept at certain sexual positions that only a child of French parents and a product of French education could have adopted. Her breasts, it was rumoured, were as pert as a fifteen-year-old's, her lingerie drawer smelt of violets, and her powdered bottom was as firm and provocative as a pair of delicately rounded loaves, floured and just emancipated from the oven's hot embrace. Selim was besotted with her, and the 'French lessons' in her perfumed boudoir once a week were all that kept him sane in his important but highly stressful post.

He always paid his visits to the adorable Adrienne after dark. Sometimes he went home after midnight, sometimes he stayed the night. If professional duties kept him late at the Mubahath, he would turn up at midnight or later. She never visited him, and they never went out in public together.

On these occasions, he would arrive at her flat in a private car a black Lexus, which his driver parked outside Clarendon House, an apartment block dating back to the nineteen-thirties. A second car, a Mercedes, always followed closely behind. It carried two bodyguards, always the same ones, men Selim trusted for their discretion.

'Surely he won't be there tonight,' said Jack. 'This is the most critical time before the conference starts.'

'Maybe he will,' said Jamila. 'There's a gala New Year dinner at the Mena House Hotel this evening. He's bound to be there, taking care of security. The dinner ends about ten, to give all the guests time to unwind and get some sleep before the morning. He may well slip away for a little recreational sex to steady his nerves.'

'We can't know that,' said Georgina.

A phone call to the Cairo office of *Le Monde* elicited the information that Mlle. Dussollier would attend the press conference that was being held before the banquet, but that she would not be making an appearance at anything else that evening. Georgina, who spoke schoolgirl French, made the call. She quipped that Adrienne must be planning to take it easy.

'She's had a lot of engagements this week,' said the secretary. 'We have extra people in from Paris, and she's been on the go for days. I think she wants to get an early night before this thing starts tomorrow. Which paper did you say you were from?'

'*The Times*. Tell her I was asking for her. I might bump into her tomorrow. *Au revoir*.'

'Now,' said Jack. 'What do we do? Does Georgina here invite herself in for drinks in order to have a chinwag with Selim?'

No one answered. They just sat staring at one another. Everyone looked glum. Then Georgina broke the silence.

'Actually, it's blindingly obvious when you think about it. Polite isn't going to work. We have to kidnap him. Just for a few hours. We'll talk to him till he sees sense.'

Jack went to Zamalek half an hour later, accompanied by Jamila and Samiha in veils. His hair and beard had been dyed blond with stuff that came from a bottle in Georgina's bedroom. In this cosmopolitan neighbourhood, he did not stand out as glaringly as he might have done in some other parts of Cairo. They drove to the island, past bunting and flags that were already looking slightly worse for wear, their colours muted by the eternal smog.

They found the apartment building easily enough, but things grew tougher after that. The building had a secure front entrance at which a uniformed doorman stood watch. That meant they'd have to deal with him or his replacement as well as the bodyguards.

'Let's check out the rear,' suggested Jack. 'Wait here. I'll go round.'

The back of the building was a lot less well kept than the front. A narrow alleyway divided the rears of one Street from another. The people who lived in the apartments, with their Armani suits and bulging wallets and weekly pots of Crème de la Mer on their dressing tables, would use the front entrance only and know nothing of the world that existed in the alleys behind.

In the alley, there were shadows everywhere, and among the shadows were people who eked out some sort of existence in this interworld, people who had fallen from grace, crammed close together against an impossible salvation.

They would put someone back here, Jack thought. Somewhere near the back door probably, where they could keep a close watch on anyone coming in or out of the building: cleaners, servants, tradesmen – anyone who would use the rear entrance. It occurred to him that Selim himself might go in and out this way. There was no fire-escape, no other way to enter or exit the building but through the back door. He made a mental note to approach the doorman to find out which entrance was used by the security chief. The *bawwabs* of Cairo, like the concierges of Paris, possessed a minute knowledge of their employers' comings and goings, and were generally bribable.

As he made to leave the alley, Jack looked back at the poor people who had made it their home. He felt pity in a way he'd never known in such great measure before. His own losses and the knowledge of the devastation that was waiting made him see these beggars, so achingly familiar to him from all his years in Cairo, in a different light. He thought of Darsh, and his promise to give the boy a future. And he remembered the kindness that had been shown him by the *zabbalin* in the village to which Jamila had driven him after the wedding party.

On the way to Zamalek they had passed a little family of the rag-pickers making their way slowly down another street; a man, a woman, and their two small children, a family team of rag-pickers.

The thought of the *zabbalin* stirred ideas in Jack. He thought of how the garbage collectors were seen by everyone, yet moved through the city as though unseen, like the beggars. Everyone saw them, but no one noticed them or gave them a second thought.

'Of course...' he said. 'Of course.'

He handed all his loose change and some notes to the beggars, and went back to the street, to where Samiha and Jamila were waiting. He could

370

scarcely tell them apart in their veils, but when he looked more closely he recognised Samiha's eyes. He wondered how he could have mistaken them. The irises were the colour of beaten gold. And she was looking straight at him.

At that moment, the light began to change. The sun's last rays stroked the tips of the city's minarets, then burst into fire across the western horizon, sinking behind the pyramids and the funerary temples, covering the tent city with layers of golden fabric. From every minaret, the voices of muezzins rose, calling to the sunset prayers that marked the start of the New Year.

'Where did we see those *zabbalin?*' Jack asked.

Samiha, for whom they had been a strange sight, remembered and pointed towards the river.

'A few streets over that way,' she said.

A short walk took them there. The family of *zabbalin* were still at work, even on Christmas Day. If Jesus came to earth again, thought Jack, he'd be born in one of their villages and would grow up to lead a donkey through the streets in search of garbage, dressed in rags.

PART FIVE

Chapter Forty-Five

ILL-MET BY LAMPLIGHT

Georgina's flat
One hour later

From Zamalek, they had driven straight back to Georgina's flat. Jack had gone out again soon afterwards, leaving the three women to download and print out all the evidence they'd been able to compile on the Ahl al-Janna and their plans. In the end, however, they knew it would boil down to one thing: whether or not Selim believed Samiha. Knowing his penchant for pretty women, Georgina secretly hoped the security chief would find himself drawn to Samiha's looks. Assuming they could get him anywhere near her, of course.

Samiha kept glancing nervously at the clock, wondering when she should start worrying about Jack. He'd gone out without being able to specify a time for his return.

As they worked, they chatted, sticking to English for Georgina's benefit. She talked casually about boyfriends, only to find that this was something neither of her new friends could understand. Samiha had been married off late at eighteen: before that, she'd known that the price for seeing boys was death, even if all they'd done was hold hands. Jamila had come from a more emancipated family, and twice she had had lovers, but never openly. She was an independent woman like Samiha, but in Egypt it was still all too easy to cross the line between what was tolerated and what was strictly forbidden. Georgina's stories both thrilled and shocked the Arab women, and once she realised that she played to the gallery.

Jack got back by mid-evening. He'd spent an hour buying a rail ticket for Naomi to use later that evening, and another hour visiting her at the hospital. He'd taken more money from the bank and paid one of Dr O'Malley's nurses to take her to Ramses Station at the right time and accompany her to Alexandria. A large donation went to the clinic. In return, the doctor had given him something that would be vital for what Jack planned in Zamalek.

He'd left Naomi sitting up in bed eating a light meal. O'Malley thought she was out of danger, though he wasn't happy at her being sent north, and insisted that she be taken straight to a clinic there.

Now, back in Georgina's small but elegant apartment, he agonised over his decision. Naomi was well supplied with money and phone numbers for the consulate and for her aunt and uncle in Nottingham. But if the bomb exploded, Jack knew there would be chaos throughout the country. The nurse was a nun from one of the orders who helped finance the clinic, a charming woman from Galway called Sister Clare. According to Dr O'Malley, Sister Clare handed out condoms like sweets and pretended they were balloons for the children in order to soothe her conscience. She had seen too many dead babies to preach abstinence, and she'd told Jack so. He'd liked her, and trusted her. But he knew he might never see his daughter again.

They snatched a little sleep, but none of them slept well. It was night, and in the moonless dark shadows of coming death flickered like the shades of dead people.

At nine o'clock, Jack woke everyone. They tried to eat a little, but no one had much appetite. In the end, they pushed their plates away, and Jack got to his feet.

'Time to go,' he said.

Georgina stayed at the flat, still working her way through computer records, in the hope of finding something more substantial. Jamila and Samiha had done as much as they were able on Arabic-language sites, and now Georgina was filling in with material in English.

Jack and his two companions got to Zamalek five minutes later. They drove in a cheap second-hand car he'd bought in Imbaba to serve as the getaway car. It was a 1994 Peugeot 405 that looked like all the other Peugeots throughout Cairo. Once away from Zamalek, it would merge effortlessly with the traffic.

Earlier, he had paid handsomely for the cart and donkey, together with a heap of rags that would disguise them as *zabbalin*. These had been left for them in an alleyway near Saray al-Gazira Street, watched over by one of the older children from the *zabbalin* family. They changed into the rags, which gave off a stench of foul proportions. On such a dark night and with only street lights around the apartment building, they knew they would pass for the real thing.

The child, a boy of about fifteen, drilled them in everything: how to walk (quickly, self-effacingly), how to get rubbish from bins onto the cart (carefully, avoiding spills), how to make the donkey start and stop (by coaxing, slapping, pushing, and sometimes bellowing). They practised up and down the alley. It was the best cover they could have thought of. No one would give them a second glance.

They had left the car parked a few yards down from the front of Adrienne's building. Jack had spoken earlier to the doorkeeper and been told that the man had been given the night off, as he was every Thursday. There would be no one to complain about the battered Peugeot. Leaving the others, Jack went to the car and took out the two handguns, both freshly loaded. One was for himself, the other for Jamila. He didn't want Samiha going anywhere near a gun.

He walked back to the cart, and they started the exhausting and noisome task of collecting garbage from the back alleys. The boy, having trained them in his peculiar trade, made his apologies and set off to find a taxi to take him back to his village.

Just hanging around for hours in one spot would have been foolish. Instead, they decided to imprint their presence on the neighbourhood, walking silently through streets and alleyways. They stayed on the main streets for a while, walking backwards and forwards as though picking up rubbish. They never strayed more than a few streets from the entrance to the flats. Every time a car came past, they stiffened, but each time it drove away again and silence returned.

Jack had come away from Dr O'Malley's clinic with several sprays of Gebauer's ethyl chloride and ready-to-inject syringes of Diprivan propofol. They'd have to use them quickly, without the benefit of anything but the crudest of dress rehearsals at Georgina's place.

It was a clear night, and even seen from the city the sky was packed with stars. On earth, a string of streetlights flickered, shedding a dull yellow glow across the pavements. Music came from an open window, a lively number by Mohammed Raheem. Elsewhere, a couple were arguing over who should take the dog for a walk. An elderly couple walked by, hand in hand, heading down towards the river. Music drifted across the night from cruise ships as they drifted up and down the Nile.

The hours passed. They all knew what it would mean if Selim did not turn up, tonight of all nights. It seemed ludicrous to think that the fate of thousands, perhaps the fate of the world, hung in the balance of one man's desire or the lack of it.

Just before midnight, they took up positions nearer the apartment block. Small wisps of cloud whispered across the stars; the streets were filled with shadows and the dreams of sleepers. A steady hum of traffic filled the night. Here, in one of the wealthiest areas, cars still came and went.

People went in and out of apartments, taxis picked up or deposited passengers, the elderly couple walked past again, still strolling hand in hand. Life went on, thought Jack. But all the time, he imagined the air filled with the dark leathery wings of the Angel of Death.

A car approached slowly, its headlights full on. As they watched, it drew up alongside the building and stopped. In the lamplight, Jack could tell it was a Lexus. A Mercedes followed close behind.

Jack was already at the bottom of the steps, rooting about in a corner among rubbish he had put there himself. He watched, not knowing what order this would be done in. Jamila was in charge of the cart. She brought it slowly round and steered it until it was blocking the Lexus.

The bodyguards got out of the Mercedes and made for the entrance, intending to check the area out before the security chief stepped out of his car. The presence of the *zabbalin* irritated them.

They stepped up to Jack, one on either side.

'What's going on here?' one asked. 'Get the hell out of here. You shouldn't be out here at this time anyway.'

Jack replied with a long string of Egyptian Arabic. Meanwhile, Samiha came round next to the second bodyguard. Each of the bodyguards had an earpiece in his ear, and they weren't really listening to Jack or giving a damn, they just wanted the *zabbalin* family out of there, with the cart in tow. Jack took the spray from his pocket, and Samiha followed him exactly. They lifted the

380

little tubes and sprayed the volatile ethyl chloride onto the mouths and noses of the bodyguards. Both men collapsed in seconds.

Jamila already had the car door open and was spraying the driver. He slumped over and Jack manhandled him onto the pavement.

'Mr Selim,' Jamila said, as soothingly as possible as she slipped behind the steering wheel, 'please remain where you are. You will not be harmed in any way. Please trust me. This is not a kidnap for terrorist or financial purposes. All we want is to talk to you and to show you some things that I hope you will take seriously. Many lives depend on what you choose to do next.'

Jack and Samiha injected the bodyguards with the Diprivan propofol, an anaesthetic that would take effect quickly and keep the men unconscious for much longer than the ethyl chloride. Once they were properly unconscious, Jack dragged them to their car and pushed them onto the rear seats. He removed their weapons and communications equipment, and wrecked the car radio. He closed the doors and knelt down, letting the air out of each tyre in turn.

While he was doing this, Samiha injected Selim's driver and dragged him out onto the road. Jack came over and helped her manhandle him into the front passenger seat of the Lexus.

During all of this, Selim had sat silently and motionless in the rear of his car. He asked no questions and passed no remarks. But he was thinking hard about what to do next, remembering all the things he'd taught an entire generation of Egyptian statesmen. Somehow, none of what he'd been taught seemed to match the present situation.

Jack got up in front while Jamila and Samiha sat on either side of Selim. The donkey had been tied to the railings. The boy would return in the morning to take it back home.

Jack started the car and drove off, knowing they had just crossed a Rubicon.

Chapter Forty-Six

THE PEOPLE OF PARADISE

Georgina's flat
Early morning

The journey back did not take long. From start to end, no one spoke. Selim did not ask his captors who they were, where they were taking him, or what they planned to do with him. They looked like rag-pickers, he thought, yet the two women were strikingly beautiful and the man didn't even look Egyptian. That it had something to do with the conference he did not for a moment doubt. That his own life might now be measured in hours he also did not doubt. He was a proud man, and the extent of his corruption in public life had been his illicit relationship with his mistress, of whom he was inordinately fond. It was almost certain, he thought, that they would seek some way to breach security at the conference. He surprised himself by his immediate resolution not to betray his country when it stood on the verge of a tremendous breakthrough. Even if they tortured him, he thought, he would give them nothing.

They did not torture him. Instead, they introduced themselves by name and assured him they would not harm him in any way.

'All we want,' said the man, 'is to talk to you. To explain something to you in as much detail as possible. Then you may walk out of here if you wish. We won't try to stop you.'

'You say that, Professor?' Selim asked. 'While your name is all over the papers? While half the police in Cairo are hunting for you right this minute? You killed your own wife and daughter, your own parents, two children and six Egyptian men in a church – and I understand those are only a fraction of the murders you've committed. Why should I believe you when you say you won't harm me? Credit me with more intelligence.'

'I didn't bring you here to persuade you of my innocence,' said Jack. 'You're here because something much more important is happening, and you are the only hope we have of preventing it. Let's have some coffee. This is going to be a long night.'

Khaled Selim was not an easy man to convince. He'd spent too much of his life working in Egypt's brutal security services under a succession of presidents, and in that time he'd heard more tall tales and conspiracy theories to fill several volumes if he ever came to write his memoirs. For over an hour, he persisted in his conviction that the whole affair was a ruse to get Goodrich off the hook, to pin the blame for his crimes on a shadowy group of Islamic terrorists.

The yarn about the sword was quite clever, he grudgingly admitted; but artefacts like that simply didn't surface these days. If there was a sword, it was bound to be a fake, of that he felt certain. Though, he admitted, he was no expert in these things. And then his unconscious supplied him with a deeply buried memory: in the course of a busy day, he had seen a report about a sword. It went back – what? – six months? Yes, now it came back. A sheikh at al-Azhar had been asking around about a sword, a relic, something that might have been brought to Cairo by a gang of art smugglers, people who dealt in stolen antiquities. The sword had been mouldering in the basement of the Museum of Antiquities in Baghdad, and had been one of the thousands of objects looted from there after the US invasion in 2003. The report had been written by the police department that dealt with antiquities smuggling, and had been passed to him because the smuggling sometimes had links to terrorism. He had put it out of his mind until now.

He started to listen more carefully to what was being said. Of course, it might have been easier, he reflected, if the three women alone had been handling the matter. Goodrich, whom he still regarded as a cold-blooded murderer, was a fly in the ointment.

He remembered Jamila Loghoud, of course.

He'd only met her a couple of times, but he'd never forgotten her face. More than once, it had crossed his mind to... He smiled inwardly and tried to drive down the old cravings the sight of her had raised. What really nagged him, however, was why a woman like her was involved in a sordid business like this at all. Could she be Goodrich's mistress? he wondered. Was that why the professor had killed his wife?

But that did not explain why a woman from the British consulate was putting her career and possibly her life on the line. And he couldn't make sense of the third woman, the one called Samiha. He recognised her accent as Palestinian, of course, and he could not see what her part in this could be.

Goodrich was talking about the group that had obtained the weapon, about their bunker and the possibility it had been built to withstand the fallout from a nuclear explosion.

'You haven't told me what this group is called,' Selim said. 'I might have heard of them.'

'The Ahl al-Janna,' Jack replied.

'Yes, that rings a bell. Some of our informants have mentioned them. But I'm afraid they're just a bunch of Johnny-come-latelies. I certainly don't think they would be remotely capable of setting up an attack like this. Let alone claiming the caliphate and taking over from Osama bin Laden. That reminds me, you haven't told me what their leader is called.'

Samiha answered, and something in her voice made it clear that she spoke from personal experience.

'He's called Muhammad,' she said. 'Muhammad al-Masri. He has a brother called Rashid who does all the dirty work for him. Rashid led the attack on the church in Shubra al-Khayma. Rashid killed Jack's wife and kidnapped his daughter.'

She stopped speaking. Selim had turned pale.

'You should have told me his name earlier,' he said. He had never forgotten the gunfight in Shubra a few months earlier. His department had lost good men in the fight, and he'd been reprimanded by the Minister when it turned out that the al-Masri brothers had escaped.

'Tell me more about the mini-nuke,' he said.

As Samiha went over the background to the weapon that had gone missing in Kazakhstan, he started to feel on home ground. He'd long been aware of similar cases involving al-Qaeda, and the story Samiha had told about the weapon stolen in Chechnya and flown from Afghanistan via Germany had the ring of truth about it. Most people had never even heard of these things, and the details the Palestinian woman gave him could not have been picked up in a newspaper or over the Internet.

It was the nature of the Iranian materials that finally convinced him. It was another detail that the average person could not have made up. Samiha said they had not been building a bomb from scratch, but planned to use one that had originated with Chechen rebels. He knew that Chechen Muslim terrorists had sold several nuclear weapons to Bin Laden several years earlier, and that these had been acquired from the 12th Main Directorate of Russia's Ministry of Defence, the Glavnoye Upravleniye Ministerstvo Oborony, the organisation in charge of all Russian nuclear weapons.

There was a peculiar character to Russian bombs of this size: they needed regular maintenance. Without it, the yield they could produce would dwindle and dwindle until it reached zero. Regular maintenance meant something like every six months. Which involved replacement of the tritium each time. According to Samiha, the planes from Isfahan had been carrying tritium.

Not many conspiracy theories added up like this. And it was hard to see how Jack Goodrich could benefit by spinning a tale that would be proved false in a few hours' time if it really was just fiction.

It was the middle of the morning before Selim nodded and told them to stop.

'You've said all I need to hear,' he said. 'You've convinced me. I have to run fresh security checks this morning, before the conference starts. Now I have something concrete to tell my people to look for. If this does turn out to be a hoax, then it will fall on your own heads. You'll come with me to Giza, and you'll stay in the compound until we either find this bomb or it goes off. If there is no explosion and no bomb, I will personally see to it that you are all handed over to the police and arrested on charges of kidnapping a state official. The penalty for that is death. And I think Jamila knows what can happen to three attractive female prisoners before they are hanged. As for you, Professor, I will ensure that you are not extradited to the UK, but dealt with under Egyptian law and put to death on as many counts of murder as I can make stick. Of course, even one will be more than enough. Let's just hope you're all telling the truth.'

He smiled, but nobody smiled with him.

'Can we trust you not to have us slapped in irons the moment we set foot in Giza anyway?' asked Georgina, who wasn't too sure about how diplomatic immunity worked in a case like this.

Selim looked at her.

'You can't. None of us can trust the others. Not entirely. But I think you have made a good case, and I think the danger justifies the action you chose to take. You'll be frisked going on to the plateau. I can't let you in with weapons. But if you aren't carrying explosives, you can join in the search. I intend to close the perimeter and bring in reinforcements.'

'Would you be willing to cancel the opening ceremony and evacuate the heads of state if we don't find anything?' Jack asked.

Selim shook his head slowly. He'd been thinking the same thing.

'Only the President could give that order. I could go to him, but by the time I'd convinced him, we'd all be dead. It's due to start at nine o'clock. Let's not waste any more time. The sooner we start searching, the better.'

Chapter Forty-Seven

SON ET LUMIÈRE

Giza

Dawn was still some hours away when they reached the site. Here, on the edge of the city, the sky was blacker and the stars brighter than before. Tomorrow night, thought Jack, the galaxies would be blotted out by a pall of smoke and ash, smoke and ash in which the atoms of over a thousand human beings would be mingled, fragments of princes and presidents mixed with those of Cairo's poor and downtrodden in equal measure.

Selim saw them through the security perimeter that stretched all round the circumference of the plateau. He sent for his second-in-command, and the second-in-command sent for his deputies. The security firm manager who was on duty that morning was fetched from the main security control office, and his boss was telephoned at his room in the Mena House Hotel. They all met, along with Jack and the others, in a temporary cabin that had been put up a year earlier to house a team of archaeologists who had carried out excavations in the necropolis just west of the Great Pyramid.

The security chief introduced Jack simply as 'the Professor', and the women as his assistants.

He proceeded to tell everyone what they were looking for, but did not mention the word 'nuclear' once. He reckoned that, if word leaked out that there might be a nuclear device on the site, panic would set in and every guard on the plateau would be in a car driving as far from Cairo as he could get.

'Look for something in a rucksack or something similar. Something big enough to weigh between thirty and sixty kilos. Report back here every half hour. Scour the place, but for God's sake don't let this look like anything but a final security check, and don't say a word to any of the presidential bodyguards.'

There were questions from everyone, but he just stood and said they could have details later. Their priority was to find the bag of explosives. No one was to touch it: the bomb disposal squad would deal with it. When his subordinates had gone, he rang the bomb disposal unit at the military barracks in the Citadel.

An American woman who worked for the security firm made a thorough search of Jamila, Samiha and Georgina. She took them to her own quarters and made them strip. Georgina tried to lighten things by making a joke about what was happening, only to receive a frown and a stern rebuke. Jack was searched by one of Selim's men.

Selim was waiting for them when they came out.

'One thing troubles me,' he said. 'When could al-Masri have put the bomb here? This place has been sealed off for weeks. The pyramids have been closed. Security has been tight. If we knew when the bomb might have been brought in, it might give us a clue to where it is.'

He ordered the floodlights used for son et lumière performances to be switched on. The Sphinx and the three main pyramids were brightly illuminated. By contrast, the rest of the plateau seemed darker than ever. Torches were handed out, but there simply weren't enough to go round everybody. The search started, concentrating on the sector where the dignitaries would be seated during the ceremony.

Guards fanned out across the plateau floor. This was the one task they had all feared. Looking for a single bomb in Giza was like seeking the proverbial needle in the proverbial haystack.

Jack and the others broke up. Jamila went off with Georgina, and without Jack's asking Samiha went with him. He knew the area fairly well, having come here on numerous occasions with friends visiting from the UK or newly arrived members of staff or students. He was able to orient Samiha and give her a picture of where everything stood in relation to the rest.

'It's enormous,' she said. 'We don't stand a hope in hell of finding the bomb.'

'This is one of the oldest cemeteries in the world,' he said. 'Perhaps it's fitting if it ends this way. Fitting and very sad. But you're right, it would take weeks to do a proper search, and it would take a cast of thousands to do it. There are tombs, mastabas, temples, the three large pyramids and seven small ones. There are holes in the ground all over, underground chambers, hidden chambers in the pyramids. But we have no choice.'

She had long ago lost her faith in God, years ago become an apostate in her heart and mind. Her culture permitted no such digressions from the straight road, encouraged no deviant or original thought, punished every stripe of unbelief. Outwardly, she had remained a good Muslim, there had been no choice. Inwardly, she had sought something else.

Without consciously meaning to, she did the most shocking thing a woman in her position could – she reached for his hand and put her hand on it and did not take it away. Where she came from, a woman could be killed for such intimacy with a stranger. He smiled and let her hand lie there, and said nothing more.

'I'm frightened,' she said.

'Frightened of dying?'

'No,' she said. He could not see her face. 'Frightened of dying here alone. This place doesn't feel real, it's like nowhere I've ever known. I was snatched from everything I ever knew, and I've been like someone dead for all these months. Perhaps I am dead, perhaps this is just a nightmare I'll live through for the rest of eternity.'

'I'll stay with you,' he said. The sense of closeness he'd started to feel when with her had grown stronger. Now, in the darkness, her hand seemed the only thing anchoring him to earth.

They explored everything that fell in their path. Every crack, every crevice, the back of every wall. Jack shone the torch they shared between them into every dark space. Nothing. Perhaps the bomb had been placed in a deep opening and covered up, perhaps they had already passed it without knowing. He felt tired, and he could sense Samiha's exhaustion as they walked together, still hand in hand. He thought of Emilia and Naomi, thought above all of Naomi in Alexandria by now, thought of her alone somewhere for as long as she lived. People would always remember that her father was a mass murderer, that he had slain his wife and parents.

Dawn rose out of the desert sands, turning them blood red, then gold, as though sheets of molten metal had been poured across them. It was seven o'clock. Jack looked at Samiha. He decided then that, when the search ended and it was time to stand and wait for the explosion that would end everything, he would take her in his arms and hold her. It was all he had left.

During the hours they scoured the site, they talked. She told him her story in detail, and he reciprocated. He told her haltingly of the day he'd found Emilia dead. Not every detail, not every nuance of emotion, but enough, more than enough. She listened, his every word pulling at her heart. She wanted him to be happy, to take the emptiness in his heart and fill it with what little substance of feeling and understanding she had left. She thought them star-crossed. Their pain meeting here in a place of tombs, for no purpose. Death would take all the pain away and give them nothing in return. She had long since ceased to believe in a paradise. This strange man was all she had now, for the little time that was left before darkness took them both.

He looked at her, felt her hand in his, a small hand the weight of dust, and he thought he was still dreaming. The nightmare was starting to fade.

They met Jamila and Georgina at a spot next to Queen Khentkawes's Funerary Monument, across the causeway from the Sphinx. Their search had been as futile. So far, no one had come up with anything.

Jack and Samiha set off again. He wondered if Selim had brought in metal detectors, then thought of how many it would take. He guessed that the bomb would be timed to go off at the moment the entire audience was seated and the ceremony began. Time was passing rapidly now. For a while, he'd been glancing at his watch every five minutes, unable to stop checking. Now, he forced himself to stop. The next time he looked, it was almost half past eight. Over at the area across which the seating had been laid out, functionaries were straightening chairs and rolling carpets across the uneven ground. Some guests had started to arrive. Television crews were making the final touches to their equipment, presenters were mugging at cameras and straightening their hair.

The lights had been switched off now, and only sunlight lit the pyramids. He looked at them, at the vastness of the Great Pyramid. That was when several thoughts came to him at once.

There was every chance that preparations for the ceremony would stretch past nine o'clock. Heads of state did not like to be hurried. The main dignitaries – the Egyptian president, his counterparts from the US, the UK, and France, the King of Saudi Arabia – would be the last to take their seats, and Jack was sure that would not be till well after nine.

He found Selim in the control room, shouting orders to all and sundry.

'Selim, this will take just a moment. I need to ask something.'

'Go ahead. Not that it will do any good. Your bomb could go off at any moment. If there is a bomb.'

'You said the plateau had been closed to tourists for several weeks. Before that, apart from tourists, was anyone else here? Archaeologists, for example.'

Selim thought, shouted at an assistant, and thought again.

'There are always archaeologists here,' he said. 'They come from everywhere. There was one group digging over at the Western Necropolis. Americans, I think. I checked them all out. I think there was a Japanese team at one of the mastabas outside the Great Pyramid. Oh, yes, there was a small party from a German university. They were working with robot explorers inside the three main pyramids.'

'What university?' Jack asked. He felt physically sick.

'You've got me there,' said Selim. 'Look, I need to get on. If your bomb doesn't go off, I have a ceremony to keep secure.'

Jack turned to go. Perhaps he'd been wasting his time. But as he got to the door, Selim turned.

'I remember. They had to spell it for me. The University of Wildeshausen. Heard of them?'

'Oh, yes. Many times,' Jack replied before hurrying out.

There was no university of Wildeshausen. But there was an airfield.

The phone inside had been constantly in use. Jack took out his mobile phone and found the number he'd been given for Sister Clare. He rang, hoping her phone was switched on. It rang several times. Samiha, standing next to him, watched anxiously.

The nun answered. Jack asked if he could speak to Naomi.

'Well, she's a wee bit tired after the journey and the fever and everything. I said she could sleep in, poor mite.'

'Get her now,' Jack said. 'This is urgent. More urgent than you can imagine.'

Naomi was wakened and put on.

'Darling,' said Jack, 'I have no time to talk now. I need to ask you something. When you were in the hospital, you said a lot of things that weren't clear. You said something about that man, the man who cut off your finger, you said he'd told you he'd put something in the sanctuary.'

Naomi, disturbed by Jack's tone, could not get her thoughts straight at first.

'Sweetheart,' he said. 'It's very important that you remember.'

'Oh, yes,' she said. 'He said he'd put something in the *haram*.'

'Now, think carefully. You were speaking in English. If you'd been speaking in Arabic, what would you have said?'

She said it again, this time in Arabic, and he knew he was right. There are two words *haram* in Arabic. The first, with a harsh letter 'h' means sanctuary, and Jack had thought al-Masri had planned to leave the sword in Mecca, one of the two sanctuaries of Islam. But the other, with an ordinary 'h' has a different meaning. It means 'pyramid'.

'Did he say which one?' he asked.

'Which one? Yes, Daddy. The big one. The *haram kabir.*'

The Great Pyramid.

'Darling, I will ring you later and if all goes well, I'll see you later. Remember that I love you very much. Whatever happens.'

He clicked the phone off.

'Samiha, if Selim asks, I've gone to the Great Pyramid.'

She nodded.

'It's in there?'

'Yes,' he said. 'Stay here. Pray to all the gods that I can get there in time.'

'Will you be able to disarm it?'

'I can try. If Selim finds somebody from the bomb disposal team, tell him to send them after me.'

He hesitated, then took her in his arms and kissed her on the forehead.

'Do that, then wait for me here.'

He began to run, knowing the lives of everyone in a radius of over a mile depended on how soon he could find the bomb, and whether he could dismantle it.

Samiha watched him go, knowing she would never see him again, that she would die alone after all. She went into the control centre, all hope severed.

397

Chapter Forty-Eight

IN THE CHAMBER OF THE KING

8.45 a.m.

He'd once been fitter than a gazelle. Long hikes in the SAS had tuned the muscles of his legs, giving him endurance and speed when he needed it. He was out of condition now, but urgency and fear gave him wings. It was hard country, and he had to get to the north side of the Great Pyramid.

He'd been there several times. Now, his problem was to out-guess al-Masri. There are several chambers and numerous corridors through the body of the Great Pyramid: the two main chambers, the King's Chamber and the Queen's Chamber, and deep below them, dug into the bedrock, an unfinished room commonly called the Pit of Chaos. In addition, there was an ascending passage, a descending passage, a shaft between them called Greave's Shaft, and the long vaulted passage known as the Grand Gallery.

As he ran, Jack tried to imagine the pyramid as he'd seen it on his last visit. There was no time to explore more than one chamber, and if that was the wrong one, he knew he'd never see the sun again.

The most likely place was the King's Chamber, a large bare room that stood off-centre about half-way up the pyramid. The passages that led to it were long and steep, and his legs were already faltering, but he knew he could not afford to let up. Above him, the massive bulk of the pyramid reared up, blocking the sky.

Rounding the north-east corner of the pyramid, he hurried to a spot on the north side where in the ninth century the Caliph Mamun had sent workmen to dig through the stone in an attempt to find whatever treasure might be buried inside. The claustrophobic tunnel they had carved out had become the way in to the interior of the pyramid.

Switching on his torch, Jack went in. The tunnel went downwards for about one hundred feet. His heart pounding with exertion and terror, Jack crawled down it until he reached the ascending passage that climbed through the heart of the great structure. He realised that he had not said where he was headed, and that if the bomb disposal unit turned up, they would just have to guess where he'd gone. He wished he'd paid more attention in the short course he'd attended on bomb disarming.

His thighs were screaming at him to slow down, his breath was coming and going as his lungs fought for air in the stifling narrow passageway, his heart was pounding hard against his chest. He was out of condition, and his muscles would not respond the way they had done years ago. The darkness almost numbed him, making him think how simple it would be to lie down and wait, to go from this, the most perfect darkness in the world, into that other darkness. He gritted his teeth. Two thoughts kept him going. One was Naomi and the other, to his astonishment, was Samiha. If he ever did come out alive, he knew he'd have some thinking to do.

He came to the Grand Gallery. To his surprise, the lights that had been put there for tour parties had already been switched on, ready, no doubt, for the grand tour planned for the more intrepid dignitaries after the ceremony. There was a wooden handrail on either side, and under his feet duckboards ran the entire length of the Gallery.

However many times he'd been here, he had never ceased to marvel at this passage. It ran, straight as a die, for one hundred and fifty-seven feet, and its corbelled roof rose twenty-eight feet from the floor. It looked exactly as it must have looked when King Khufu's mummified remains were carried down it four and a half thousand years earlier. Stone lay upon stone, great blocks of masonry so heavy a giant might have laid them in their courses, so tightly aligned that not even a sheet of paper or the head of a pin could be fitted between them.

As always, Jack felt dwarfed by the stones, his spirit crushed and silenced by the impossible grandeur of the place.

At the far end of the Gallery, Jack stepped up into a short antechamber. Beyond this lay the King's Chamber, the room where the empty sarcophagus of the Pharaoh Khufu had been found all those centuries ago by Mamun's workmen. Now, Jack thought, another Caliph was about to blow the whole thing to pieces.

A light was coming from the chamber.

Seeing it, Jack finally understood what was about to happen. He had already observed that there was no way of knowing exactly when the ceremony outside would begin. And he remembered that it was going to be broadcast to television audiences round the world. He knew that al-Masri would not be able to resist the temptation to make the explosion coincide with the moment, minutes into the broadcast, when the ceremony was properly underway. Viewers in every land would see their screens go black, then to sit stunned and horrified when, half an hour later, the first reports of a nuclear explosion in Cairo would come through.

The bomb would not be detonated by a timer. Someone would be waiting in the King's Chamber to press a button or depress a switch the moment he was notified – by radio, probably – that President Mubarak had stepped onto the podium to welcome his assembled guests. The ultimate suicide bomber. The martyr of martyrs. The man of the End Times.

Jack made his way down the antechamber silently, then stepped through the entrance into the King's Chamber. Rashid al-Masri was seated on the floor in prayer, a rosary of amber beads shimmering through his fingers. He was dressed in the uniform of a security policeman. Next to him on the floor was a walkie talkie, the sort used by tour guides. And on the other side sat the bomb in its shiny metal casing – the 'robot' brought inside the pyramid by his German friends. It was not big, perhaps three feet long and two feet wide. It was hard to believe it could do so much damage.

For a moment, Rashid thought that Jack, with his blond hair and beard, was one of his German assistants. Then he took a second look, and a smile passed over his lips as he recognised his foe.

'How strange to see you here, Professor,' he said. 'I feel like the Angel of Death who, seeing a man in Samarqand, felt surprise because he had been told to meet that same man that evening in Baghdad. Perhaps you've been looking for me. Perhaps God sent you to witness my brother's sacrifice, my sacrifice, my children's sacrifice.

'When this is done, and you and I are less than dust, when I am in heaven with virgins, and you are in Jahannam burning with your whore of a wife, my brother will announce a new age for Islam, a new age for mankind. He will be acclaimed Caliph from one end of the earth to the next. There's nothing you can do to prevent that from happening. There will be a new world order under the laws of God.

'Tell me, did your daughter find you in the end? Did that slut Samiha get her to you? Did Samiha tell you she is a whore and an adulteress? Or is your precious daughter dead now and with her mother in the deepest pit of hell?'

Jack was about to rise to the bait when everything changed. In that great tomb, in the greatest of all tombs mankind has ever built, in that chamber of death where a pharaoh's body had been laid to rest, a walkie talkie chirruped once and a second time.

Rashid picked it up, listened to a crackling

voice, and put it down again.

'It's time,' he said. 'If you have any last words, perhaps a prayer to your false gods, say them now.'

He started to get to his feet. His love and his pain were evident in his shining, God-obsessed eyes. He feared nothing, wanted nothing. Nothing but a martyr's death and an eternity with his virgins in paradise.

He was half-way to his feet when Jack launched himself on him. Years as a blindside flanker in rugby matches at school and university had created him for this moment. He had never in his life before moved with such momentum, tackled a man with such driving force. Rashid's legs went out from under him, and he fell hard against the floor, hitting his head hard on the solid rock.

Neither man moved for half a minute. They were both winded and in pain.

Rashid was the first to move. As he struggled to his feet, his hand went inside his robes and came out holding the long knife he'd used to kill Marie and Hannah Yaqoub.

He came for Jack, moving slowly, but sure of his mastery of the situation. His body ached from the fall, his head was splitting, but he knew he would kill Jack with a single lunge.

'Well done, Professor. That was brave of you. But foolish. There is plenty of time for me to kill you. It need not be quick. If you have any sense, you'll crawl back out of this room and let me get on with what I came here to do. A sacred act is about to be carried out. The presence of an unbeliever would only pollute it. You should have

403

stuck to your books, Professor. Grammar and syntax is more your *métier* than attacking an armed man.'

It was then that Jack realised Rashid's mistake. The Egyptian had taken him for a scholar and only a scholar. Of Jack's military experience, he had not the slightest idea. It was not just a mistake, Jack thought. It was a fatal mistake.

Jack lay a moment longer, gathering his strength for the final move. Rashid, thinking him too hurt to move, bent down to lunge at him with the knife. As he did so, Jack rose effortlessly and twisted sideways. Rashid staggered. Jack grabbed him by the forearm, swung back, and broke the arm at the shoulder. Rashid screamed in pain, and the knife clattered to the ground. Jack took Rashid by the left arm and broke it with a single snap at the elbow. Rashid screamed a second time, then started to whimper. Jack bent down and picked up the knife.

He took Rashid by the front of his robes and dragged him to the red sarcophagus. There, he took his right arm and placed it on the stone.

'This is for what you did to my daughter,' he said.

He put the knife to Rashid's wrist and severed the hand just above the joint. Blood poured everywhere, a darker red against the red of the tomb.

Jack looked at him. All the arrogance, all the grim superiority had gone. But Rashid did not beg for mercy, and Jack did not have it in his heart to grant it. He recited the names of his dead, and he knew that the man in front of him was beyond redemption. He could hand him over to be tried and hanged; but the chamber was filled with the souls of his dead, and he knew they were waiting.

'And this,' he said, 'is for all the innocents you killed. If you died a thousand deaths, it wouldn't be enough. This little death will have to be enough. Your death, and the knowledge that there is no paradise, there are no virgins, and there will be no Caliph.'

He forced Rashid to his knees, then took the blade and pressed it to his throat. The cut was quick and deep. He let the body fall and stepped away. He could almost hear them say their good-byes. Emilia, his mother and father, the Gilfillans, Marie and her sister Hannah, Simon... He sat down and wept.

Samiha found him like that half an hour later, still weeping. Soldiers from the bomb disposal unit came in after her. It was time to go.

She put an arm round his shoulders, and with her free hand took the bloody knife from his fingers. It dropped to the floor with barely a sound.

She led him out through the antechamber and the Grand Gallery, and finally through the narrow passage at whose end daylight lay in wait.

They walked the rest of the way in silence. She never asked him what happened in the King's Chamber. Not then, nor in all the years that followed.

Chapter Forty-Nine

ACROSS AN ANCIENT SEA

Cairo

An area in Shubra was evacuated. One hour later, an Egyptian air force jet passed overhead and dropped a bunker-busting bomb on Muhammad al-Masri's concrete hideaway, reducing it to rubble. The sword that had led to so many deaths was never recovered. Within two days, the first rumours were heard in certain quarters, saying that the Caliph was still alive, but had gone into occultation, awaiting his return at a more auspicious date.

All charges against Jack were dropped. Rashid al-Masri's fingerprints were taken from his corpse and given to the detectives who had come to arrest him. The same prints were found all over the crime scenes at Jack's parents' home and in Scotland. The detectives went home, the cases were closed.

Jack, Jamila, Samiha and Georgina were invited to a private interview with the Egyptian President. At a short ceremony that took place without publicity, he awarded Jack the highest honour Egypt could bestow, the Star of Sinai, normally bestowed for great heroism in battle. Jamila, Samiha and Georgina all received the next order

406

down, the Star of Honour. Later, at President Mubarak's request, Georgina was invited to Buckingham Palace, where the monarch awarded her the Queen's Gallantry Medal.

A few weeks after that, an unusual item appeared on eBay. It was a man's vicuña overcoat, and the advertiser said it had originally cost £17,000. Offers were invited, starting at £500. About that time too, several names disappeared from the staff list of the British Foreign Office. Several adverts were placed in the better papers, saying that the Secret Intelligence Service, MI6, was looking to recruit new members. The British embassy in Cairo was restaffed almost overnight, leaving several other embassies a little short. And in the UK, a senior judge was asked to come out of retirement in order to carry out a discreet service for the Crown.

For Samiha, an altogether better award was to come. On hearing her story, the president made personal contact with his Palestinian counterpart. Samiha's husband granted her a divorce, and she was awarded custody of her children, who were flown to Cairo the same day. They were all there to meet them: Samiha, Jack, Jamila, Georgina, and Naomi, whose finger had started to heal properly following a skin graft.

A memorial service for Marie and Hannah was held at St Sergius. They all attended. Afterwards, in private, Jack told the Yaqoub family what their sacrifice had meant. If they had not given Jamila and him shelter, al-Masri would even now be leading his armies against the Jews and Christians.

Jack went with Samiha to al-Azbakiyya one day, where they found Darsh kicking a football in the usual alleyway with the usual friend. After some banter, Jack asked to meet Darsh's parents. They were both at home, for Darsh's father was out of work again. Jack explained that he had put money into a special bank account so that a sum could be paid monthly for Darsh's education. There'd be enough to help the family live, so Darsh didn't have to start work early.

'I've spoken to someone at Zamalek,' Jack said. 'When you're old enough, you'll get a trial for the junior team. But only on condition you continue with your education. The money will be there, even if you have to go to university, even if you decide to do a PhD like me.'

'Why are you doing this?' Darsh's parents asked.

'Your son did something for me, something very important. He helped me get my daughter back alive. Indirectly, he did something for Egypt that no amount of money can repay. The President knows about him. One day, Darsh may get an invitation to Abdin Palace. I'll visit him when I can.'

Jack had an emotional conversation with his sister Sandra. A few days later, Sandra received a cheque more than sufficient to cover the costs of her IVF treatment. Jack knew now that the huge sum of money he'd been given had been a pay-off, a way of keeping him silent and cooperative. After what he'd been through, he wasn't going to give it back.

One by one, they parted. Georgina had to go to London to meet the Queen, after which she would head for a top job at the Paris embassy.

'It won't be the same as Cairo, of course, and I shall miss all the smells and everything, but, really, you must admit, Paris is so nice at all times of the year, and I won't get fat, because French women never do, whereas lots of Egyptian women – not Jamila, of course – but lots of others do get terribly fat and... Oh, dear.'

She started sobbing and hugged them one at a time.

They watched her through the departure gate, waving goodbye, promising to meet up in a year's time.

Jamila was offered a senior position working under Khaled Selim, but turned it down: Adrienne and her lovely bosom would be heading back to Paris, and Jamila did not want to fill her shoes. Hearing of this, the President offered her a post on his personal staff. She turned this down as well.

'What *do* you want to do?' asked Jack.

'I paid a visit to your Dr O'Malley,' she said. 'He's going to help me set up a clinic for the *zabbalin*. And a community centre. I won't have the slightest problem getting state funding. It's what I want to do, Jack. This business has made me rethink everything.'

'Let me know if I can do anything,' he said, and kissed her gently on the cheek. 'And invite me to the wedding.'

'What wedding?'

'Any wedding. Yours would make a good start.'

'I think I'll wait for yours, first,' she said. 'Take care, Jack. You too, Naomi: I hope we'll meet again soon.'

She embraced Samiha and, as she did so, whispered something in her ear. Both women laughed, then Jamila turned away, wiping her eyes.

Alexandria

Nabil and Adnan had never been to the beach, never seen the sea. Samiha had seen the sea only from the deck of the ferry that had taken her to Cyprus: waves crashing on the shore were new to her. Naomi had told the boys all about it, and there was soon a clamour for a seaside break.

'Why don't we all go to Alexandria?' Jack suggested. 'Samiha, you can have a chaperone. Sister Clare, perhaps.'

Samiha smiled and shook her head.

'No chaperones. I'm fed up being told what to do by women in veils.'

They travelled there by express train the same evening. Jack booked rooms for Samiha, the three children, and himself in the Salamlek Palace Hotel. The Salamlek had been the magnificent hunting lodge of Khedive Abbas Helmi II, where he'd kept his Austro-Hungarian mistress, Countess May-Torok von Szendro. It stood among beautiful gardens, overlooking the white sands of Muntaza Bay.

Samiha had never seen such luxury before. It contradicted everything she'd known of the world. All she'd experienced had been harshness and the rule of violence. Yet she cared nothing for the grandeur of the place, for the liveried servants, the chandeliers, the marble, the inlaid ceilings, and least of all, the casino.

But the beauty of the Muntaza gardens, with their tall palms, their flowering bushes, their heady scents, and the view from the terrace, with a soft breeze sighing across the ancient sea lulled her into a hesitant belief in the goodness of things. She imagined triremes and biremes come out of Greece, dromons and pamphyloi heading from Byzantium, Venetian galleys filled with all the riches of the Orient, the sea golden by day and silver by night, no sound but that of oars dipping and wooden boards creaking.

On the second day, she and Jack took the children down to the long white beach together. For hours, Adnan, Nabil and Naomi played at the sea's edge, running into the waves and back again, screaming with pleasure, Adnan racing across the sand with all his nine-year-old vigour, kicking a plastic ball. Jack taught him how to build a sandcastle, using a bucket and spade he'd bought in the hotel shop.

When Adnan had tired himself and grown hungry, Samiha took out beach blankets and opened the hamper the hotel had prepared for them. There was almost no one else on the beach. Near the hulk of an abandoned rowing boat, a dog barked and was hushed by a soft voice.

A flock of seabirds braced their wings and turned in tight against the wind. Samiha watched them twist and turn, her mouth slightly open, her tongue bitter with the light salt taste. The wind came from the Mediterranean, and had nothing of Egypt in it. The only sound was the falling of waves and the voices of the children coming from further down the beach. A lifeguard from the hotel stood at a discreet distance, keeping a close eye on them.

Jack and Samiha left the children to eat and drink pop. They walked together along the beach, their fingers linked.

'I still have nightmares,' Jack said.

'That's no surprise. Later, maybe you should find someone to talk to.'

'I am talking to you,' he said, and she smiled. No psychologist would ever understand the way she did.

'Then talk.'

He walked further in silence, then spoke again.

'Samiha, have you thought about where you want to go after this?'

'A little. I can't go back to the West Bank, I know that. Israel, perhaps, if they'll have me. Maybe Jordan. Maybe Cairo. I don't know.'

'Samiha, the truth is, I need someone to look after Naomi. I can't do it myself. You... She knows you very well. She says she likes you a great deal. And ... she keeps asking when I'm going to marry you.'

He looked at her and saw her cheeks turn bright red.

'Of course, it's much too early to talk like that,' he said hastily, seeing he had embarrassed her. 'About marriage or...'

'It's all right,' Samiha said. 'We hardly know

one another. Naomi's a born matchmaker, that's all.'

'It's just...'

She stepped towards him then and put a hand against his cheek. He put his hand behind her head and drew her closer. Their lips met. It was the gentlest of kisses, a first kiss, as if they were teenagers, clumsy in their first contact. When, after long minutes, they pulled apart, it seemed that the world had undergone a permanent change, as if the slowly retreating tide had taken their old lives with them, to bury them a thousand fathoms deep.

They kissed again to the sound of waves hissing against the shore. This time, when they stepped back, they looked out to sea, to the blue and green waves where a wonder of the ancient world had stood, across water that appeared to be a cloth of gold, to the horizon, where sea and sky met and parted again.

'I think,' Jack said, his voice awkward with emotion, 'we have to stay together. Something will happen in time. I still have to finish grieving for Emilia. Do you understand that? I intend to go to Dublin. I've been offered a post as Curator of the Chester Beatty Library. But I can't reply until I know whether you will be willing to come with me.'

'To look after Naomi?'

'Nabil and Adnan would come with us too, of course. It's a good city to bring up children in. Ireland does a lot of trade with the Middle East. There'd be a demand for someone with your skills who speaks Arabic.'

She took his hand again.

'Jamila told me to look after you. She seems to think you need looking after.'

'Then come with Naomi and me to Dublin.'

'All right,' she said. 'That will be nice.'

'It's a deal, then,' he said. 'I'll book tickets. Should I get one-way or return?'

'One-way, of course,' she said. And she kissed him again, and the salt on his lips tasted like the fruit of paradise.

In the city of Alexander, where Antony and Cleopatra had loved, where the greatest libraries of the ancient world had drawn scholars from Greece and Rome and Byzantium, where the Greek poet Cafavy had written the two hundred poems of his life, where east and west had met since the beginning of time, the soft voices of the muezzins rose over the traffic and the murmur of the sea alike. For a time, the world was safe again. It was time for the noon prayer. There was no god but God and Muhammad was still His prophet.

This Large Print Book for the partially sighted, who cannot read normal print, is published under the auspices of

THE ULVERSCROFT FOUNDATION